The Treasures

The Treasures

The Sevenstones Trilogy: Book One

HARRIET EVANS

**PENGUIN
VIKING**

VIKING

UK | USA | Canada | Ireland | Australia
India | New Zealand | South Africa

Viking is part of the Penguin Random House group of companies
whose addresses can be found at global.penguinrandomhouse.com

Penguin Random House UK,
One Embassy Gardens, 8 Viaduct Gardens, London SW11 7BW

penguin.co.uk

First published 2025
002

Set in 13.5/16pt Garamond MT Std
Typeset by Jouve (UK), Milton Keynes

Printed and bound in Great Britain by Clays Ltd, Elcograf S.p.A.

The authorised representative in the EEA is Penguin Random House Ireland,
Morrison Chambers, 32 Nassau Street, Dublin D02 YH68

A CIP catalogue record for this book is available from the British Library

HARDBACK ISBN: 978-0-241-74137-5
TRADE PAPERBACK ISBN: 978-0-241-74138-2

Penguin Random House is committed to a sustainable future
for our business, our readers and our planet. This book is made from
Forest Stewardship Council® certified paper.

For darling Susie
in a crowded field, my favourite American

To every thing there is a season, and a time to
every purpose under the heaven;
A time to be born, and a time to die . . .
A time to weep, and a time to laugh; a time to mourn,
and a time to dance . . .
A time to love, and a time to hate; a time
of war, and a time of peace.

– Ecclesiastes 3

I have decided to stick with love. Hate is
too great a burden to bear.

– Dr Martin Luther King Jr

Contents

SEVENSTONES

Tallboys, Wiltshire

5 bed/3 bath

Price on application

A unique and outstanding opportunity. Sevenstones
is one of the most exciting properties in this area to
come to market in years. A 15th/16th century cottage
combined with a sympathetic modern extension, in an
idyllic location with a superb south-westerly aspect, set
in approximately 2 acres of parkland, within which is a
separate studio building.

Stunning location steeped in remarkable history

A beloved family home for more than five decades,
Sevenstones has a fascinating history. Recent
excavations have revealed the house sits within an
ancient stone circle comprised of seven upright
sarsens. It was named Sevenstones as early as Tudor
times, when it is mentioned as forming part of the
Seymour Estate. The excavations have also unearthed
antler picks, broken plates and coins.

'A safe place'

In addition, Sevenstones played a special role for
hundreds of military personnel during the Second
World War. The house was a safe place where
WAAFS, pilots, agents, attachés and others could

stay before deployment and where they returned after successful missions. It featured in the Channel 5 documentary *Keep the Home Fires Burning* in 2019.

Fabric of history

Sevenstones is perhaps most well known as the birthplace of the late Alice Delaney, founder of the eponymous beloved global lifestyle brand, which famously started life at the kitchen table of the house. Alice drew her inspiration for all her designs from the surrounding countryside.

The property combines the beautiful period features of the original cottage with an elegant modern addition designed by the present owner, a distinguished architect. Both parts have views via full-length windows and doors that open towards the garden, and the studio.

Original oak beams span the older part of the house; walls in this area are two feet thick. The modern extension benefits from insulation and excellent storage space.

Now looking for a new owner to make more history in this unique house, Sevenstones might be called the original 'Forever Home'. Early viewing is therefore highly recommended by sole agents Wright & Mitchell, Bath. Please contact Sophie Roberts-Miller to arrange an appointment.

Prologue

Spring 2024

Emma Raven sat by the window, listening for the sound of the cab. Her back ached, as it did when she sat for too long. She hadn't done her stretches that morning. She must speak to the GP about her HRT. (She must try to get an appointment.) She had to mend her headphones before the Teams meeting. She hated Teams. She must remember to buy the birthday present for Ted. Call the locksmith about her own front door lock jamming (she'd been trapped in the house last week, and had had to climb out of the kitchen window). Buy ham. Try probiotics! Go for a run. Book the tickets for that pottery course, and the silent disco, and then there were the summer holidays she'd done nothing about . . . But, before that, sort out the recycling tonight, not tomorrow, as tomorrow she was off early. Book the dog into the groomer's, pay the house-clearance company, call the auction house about the new auction date, upload the missing information to GOV.UK, don't forget car-insurance renewal. Remember to breathe. Take a breathing workshop. Be articulate and well informed about everything that is wrong with the world, but also full of joy.

The old house sat with Emma, quietly waiting. It had been with her as she had boxed up beautiful old Puffin paperbacks, crying as she found old notes behind the ancient fridge – *ples can I have some ise crem* – peeling off old stickers from the windows, standing in shock at the bare, bare rooms in which only the faded outlines remained where family photographs and pictures had hung, the merest suggestion of the story of their years there.

But it knew. It understood it was time for a change. That the seasons had passed – spring, summer, autumn, winter – and now it was time for a new spring. *To every thing there is a season* – isn't that what Dad used to say?

Spring was coming, the scent of narcissi and wet earth and something new wafting towards her as she pushed open the tight casement window, swollen with winter rain; then she shifted impatiently on the old stone windowsill that had served her as a seat all those years, from Sindys and stickers through to different Body Shop bottles and, behind the wooden panel below it that you could pull out, secret packets of cigarettes and her diary. She wondered if they were still there.

Impossible to think back over it all, the arc of time in the house. It was too big. She kept recalling silly things. The hooks Dad had put up by the fireplace for the Christmas stockings, hitting his finger and swearing so loudly about how stupid it was that Emma'd figured out there was no Father Christmas. Funny, because he was such a gentle man, but it had been a terrible year, the worst one. Or the time one of her siblings – she couldn't even remember which now – tumbled into the stream and Uncle Guy toppled in trying to save them, and squashed a toad, and all the children cried about the squashed toad, gave it the first of many animal funerals. The Royal Wedding street party that ended in disaster. The Great Storm, when the others woke up and there were eight, ten fallen trees across the lane, so many that there was no school, and it was like Christmas in October. Driving blindly back from the pub after too many vodka and tonics, sobbing, aged seventeen. Carol singers at the door; the Summer Solstice out in the stones. The long refectory kitchen table covered

4

in pieces of material, Silver Jubilee Wedding mugs, geranium cuttings in jugs, seed packets, hammers, deely-bobber head-bands, feathers, children's drawings, empty cereal bowls. All gone long ago: broken, sent to charity, sold, thrown away.

Emma dropped to her knees, groaning only mildly. There must be an unopened packet in here; there'd been that duty-free one that Aunt D kept hidden for Christmases. She pulled at the wooden board of the windowsill. It came away with barely a grumble – she was always amazed at the ways the house shifted round throughout the year without ever cracking or crumbling – and, too late, she remembered that it was the wrong board, that the secret hiding place was under the other window.

But the board had come away. And there was something there. A small drawstring bag. Emma snatched it out, suddenly afraid, she didn't know why.

Each little piece in the bag had been tightly bound up in cloth; she unwrapped them and laid them out on the floor, a mismatched Noah's Ark. Emma stared at the treasures before her, a strange collection of animals and stones and oddments. A metal wizard, the paint worn off, a quartz elephant, a darling little china deer . . . a raven with a chipped wing. Raven! She held them up in delight. A carved wooden house, the chimneys snapped off. A little blue-and-white china cat. A brooch: a severe-looking woman in profile. And, finally, a small rose-gold necklace with a star-shaped gold pendant set with sapphires, and, on it, a tag: *For Emma, from her father.* Why were they there? Why were they hidden away? What was the point of storing them here?

There came the humming *shrooooom* sound of the electric car pulling into the driveway. Emma wrapped up the pieces and put them back into the bag. She placed them carefully at the top of her knapsack, aware as she did so that they were the key to Sevenstones, the key to the mystery of her parents, her family, and the happiness and sadness that was at the heart of the house. Over a hundred years – and this was the first lie, the biggest of the lot – since her great-grandfather had bought it, a tumbledown stone shack in a field. It was only ever meant to be a retreat, somewhere to paint. The little trinkets clinked very slightly as she slung the bag over her shoulders.

Emma went down the curving slippery staircase where children's feet had thudded and through the long sitting room with the great hearth, cleared of cinders for the first time in decades. So strange to see it bare. It was all . . . very strange, that was all. She felt the bag of treasures shift inside her knapsack again, as if their discovery had awakened them from a deep sleep and she remembered, as if climbing back through time, her mother telling her about them. About why they were there, what they meant. Emma hot and flushed after waking from a nightmare, to find her mother caught on the floor of Emma's bedroom, holding these little things on her lap, tears running down her cheeks. She stopped on the stairs, held by the memories.

What could they tell her now? The gold star necklace or the friendly china cat, the worn, battered wizard, the small piece of stone, the dogs, the raven? She was carrying these tiny treasures away with her, and their secrets too, and she wished she could ask them to tell her everything. She stood looking left, to the old part of the house, then right, to the new part, then slid the key on to the windowsill and walked down the path for the last time. She touched the ancient standing stone, shut the gate and closed the door on their life. It was time for a new family to call Sevenstones home.

But oh . . . the stories left behind! In each echoing, empty room, going back fifty years, even longer, to the beginning of it all. The beginning of their family.

PART ONE

Yesterday

Hudson Valley, New York
June 1965

I

June 1965

On the day her father died, Alice had updated her list of treasures.

- ~ 4 dogs: Poodle, Scottie, Dalmatian, Labrador, all china
- ~ 2 elephants: one blowing trunk, in brass, one in rainbow quartz with a black dot on each side for an eye, trunk down
- ~ 2 cats: blue-and-white-decorated china (smiling)
- ~ 2 cats: wooden, painted black and decorated (holding hands)
- ~ 1 dormouse, eating an ear of corn, china
- ~ 1 black bird, wings spread, painted china (A blackbird? A crow?)
- ~ 1 red-painted wooden figure, a Christmas ornament of an Amsterdam town house, from my father Robert (Bob) Jansen's Dutch grandmother, Christina Jansen (*née* Vanderbilt)
- ~ 1 black jet pin, belonging to my grandmother, Annabel Palmer of Vermont, cameo of my mother, Betsy Palmer Jansen, carved into the jet
- ~ 1 silver pill box with a lock of my father's baby hair
- ~ 1 small polished piece of limestone, from my father's old family farm upstate from Orchard, now long gone and demolished to make way for suburban houses

From her earliest years, Alice was a child who liked ritual. Every year, the day before her birthday, she took the opportunity to look over the wooden shelf above the bookcase her father had made, upon which sat the treasures.

They were all tiny, no bigger than her thumb. The china animals looked like real animals, glossy, glazed, fixed in time. The rest were trinkets acquired by her father in different places – county fairs, antique shops – or relics from her parents' past. Some of the animals were decorated with gold paint; some, like the cats, had painted human faces, curling Betty Boop eyelashes. The elephant, with his smooth, glistening quartz body, or the black bird were her favourites – probably the black bird. He was slightly larger; he had come from England, in the war, and had a chip off his wing, which was how she knew the animals were hollow inside.

Their house, Alice's home, was not theirs. It was owned by another family, and so the treasures were more important because of that. They told the story of her family, of Alice, Betsy and Bob Jansen, where they had come from, and where they were going.

That morning, when Alice woke up, she looked out the tiny window in her little bedroom down at the apple orchards that stretched to the river. Her dad was already walking among the trees, hands on hips, gazing up at the gnarled branches where the small tight apples were scant amid the leaves. He was staring, glassy-eyed, as though not really seeing them. She wanted to shout down at him, a joke, or something, to make him see the beauty of the scene, and to forget the worry of the letters from the bank. But something stopped her; she didn't know what. Afterwards she always wished she had.

It was her birthday tomorrow: she would be sixteen. She wanted a deer for her collection, another bird like the black one, a pair of leather thong sandals, the new Beatles album and some money, because everyone else seemed to have money. After school, she was going for a sundae at Mackie's with her dad, as she always did, and she would be asking him for a birthday favour.

Until it happened, for the rest of the day, in fact, it was a good day.

Mr Fitzgerald, the sweaty, tweed-jacketed, elbow-patched history teacher, had let them off a test on the Civil War. Diane Hendricks, who had been so mean lately, ever since she started ironing her long, already-straight hair, wearing a kaftan and calling herself Sky, had invited her over on the weekend to listen to all the Beatles' back catalogue in preparation for *Help!*, which Diane's dad had heard (because he worked in advertising and had once met Dusty Springfield and was therefore a reliable source) was the name of the new Beatles album.

And, out of the blue, there was a new girl in their class. Attending now would help her to settle in before school went back in the fall, which perhaps explained why she did nothing but gaze out the window, chewing gum. She was called Dolores Delaney. Her parents were divorced, and her mom had moved them back to her hometown of Orchard from Chicago. Diane hadn't invited Dolores to her house, she said, because her mom said Dolores was trashy.

At recess Alice found herself walking out with Dolores. 'Hi,' she said.

'Oh, hi,' said Dolores in a cheerful, Chicagoan accent, still chewing her gum. 'I gotta say, I love your outfit.'

'Really?'

'Sure. It's cool.'

Alice knew she was pretty, or what other people thought of as pretty, because she had long pale gold hair, and green eyes, and was slim, and tall. It alternately amused and annoyed her that she was rewarded for it – she saw it in the way people looked at her, now she was almost sixteen. As if she was worthy of praise for genetics beyond her control.

However, she knew she was not cool. And she wanted to be cool, as much as other girls wanted to be slim, or blonde, because, whatever you were, you weren't enough – all of them had that in common at least.

She looked down at her green shirt-waister dress, which she had painstakingly dyed over the weekend to match the checkered knee-high patterned stocking-socks in brown and green, and her brown loafers. Her mom had had to help her, after the dye got everywhere and Alice had given up in despair.

'Oh, this,' she said, shrugging, feeling a glow of pleasure at this unusual peer-to-peer praise. 'Thanks, that's real nice of you.'

'It's true. Bye, Alice. I gotta go,' said Dolores, pushing past her and waving, stomping off down the hallway. She wore all black: black boots, a curvaceous black dress and a red scarf around her neck. She fell into step with Jack Maynard, and Alice watched them walk away together.

Jack Maynard was the cutest boy in class, in the whole school, in fact. The previous week he had asked her, Alice Jansen, to the senior prom. He was a senior, but had asked her, a sophomore, and she had still not asked her dad if she could go.

The Maynards lived in a big house, Crossings, on the same side of town as Alice, and sometimes she and Jack would meet and walk the trail through the woods by the Hudson into Orchard together. He had long, long eyelashes, clear bright blue eyes, thick dark blond hair that fell in his face. Alice had even seen her mom staring at Jack Maynard; she was amazed everyone didn't stare at him. She was amazed too that, in all the thousands of books she had read in her almost sixteen years on the planet, writers constantly talked about how beautiful this young woman or that was, and didn't write about how beautiful young men were. She knew it was hypocritical to think this about him, when she found other people's appraisal of her based on looks boring, but there was no getting away from it – he was a dreamboat.

He liked books too. He wasn't into that California pop; he loved Bob Dylan, and the Kinks, and talking about stone circles in England. Alice wanted to go to Stonehenge more than anywhere else. Jack did too; he liked *The Once and Future King* and *Lord of the Rings* and he even had a small metal figurine of a wizard he'd got in a playset for Christmas one year. He carried it around with him for good luck. She knew because he'd dropped it a couple months ago coming back from track, and she'd found it, and he'd thanked her, and that's how they'd first gotten talking.

'Hey: please don't tell anyone else about Merlin,' he'd said.
'Merlin?'

'This guy.' He'd opened his palm to show her the figurine. Most of the paint had worn off. 'It's kind of a comfort thing. I know if he's there in my pocket, nothing bad can happen.' And he'd smiled at her, and his golden hair had fallen in his face; she noticed it was getting longer, like a lot of other boys' hair in Orchard that summer. His cheeks were pink, burned by the sun, fading into his tanned face. 'Don't you have anything like that?'

'I do,' she said, laughing, and his face relaxed.

13

'You do?'

'Yeah. I call them the treasures. Different ornaments and special . . . things.' She felt herself going red. 'It sounds lame.'

'It's not.'

'They're like . . . my good-luck charms.'

'That's cool. What's your favourite?'

Alice thought for a moment. 'I like the black bird. He's mean-looking. But he's beautiful too. And he's got a bit missing where someone dropped him. He's from England,' she added.

'Where do you keep them?'

'On a shelf my dad built for them. My dad gives me a new one every year for my birthday. I never know what it's going to be. He takes me to Mackie's for a sundae, then gives me a clue and I have to find it.'

'So you don't carry them around?'

'I don't want them to get damaged. Or maybe I don't think anything bad's going to happen.'

He'd laughed. 'I think that all the time.' And he slipped Merlin back into his pocket, and they'd smiled at each other.

The following week he'd caught up with her again and asked her to the dance. 'It's cool if you can't go,' he'd said. 'I thought it might be fun.'

'Yes,' said Alice, nodding furiously, smiling at him. 'I'll ask my mom but I'd love to come with you.'

'No, absolutely not, you're too young, and he's a senior,' her mother had said. Alice, normally easy going, pliant even, had slammed her bedroom door and shouted, once inside, 'You never let me do *anything*!'

This had been six weeks ago. She'd told Jack yes, though, the following week at school. She was definitely going. She thought the best way was to ask her dad when he was around, and the birthday sundae at Mackie's was the perfect opportunity.

Sometimes her dad wasn't well and had to stay in their bedroom, at the top of the tall, thin gatehouse where they lived. Once, he was in bed for a long time, and then he went away for a whole week, and when he came back he was real strange, like something from those zombie movies Mom hated. But soon he was back to being kind, and fun, and making plans. He was always making plans, her father. For the orchards he'd taken over, and where they'd live, and what Alice might want to do with her life, and what pies to bake; he was a good cook, making the apple pies, the apple sauce, the apple butter and cider and juice that had given him the idea to buy back the orchards from the Kynastons that had been in his family in the first place.

Bob Jansen had lived in Orchard all his life. He was one of the Cemetery families, his Dutch ancestors having settled along the Hudson nearly two centuries ago. He knew everyone and their children, the streets, the history. He bought Betsy flowers and sang her Frank Sinatra songs when she was down. He let Alice go for sundaes on Main Street, play in the sprinklers on Carly Gianotti's lawn till after dark, roam around the neighbourhood on her bike, riding to the banks of the vast, silent Hudson River, where the mist rose like ghosts on the water, the pine trees fringing the pebbled edges.

The Hudson was the edge of everything. They said it was so deep in places that no one knew what was down there. Rumour had it there were sharks older than the Declaration of Independence, invisible in the black, ice-cold depths; Diane Hendricks swore they had swum there from the Arctic millions of years ago. She said they were growing larger and more dangerous, waiting till the day when they would glide into Manhattan and rise out of the water, snatching men and women from their cars on the George Washington Bridge, or from the river path, and eating them whole. But, for now, Diane said, they were just lurking. Waiting for the right time. Diane also claimed to have seen a skeleton's hand poking out of a tomb in the cemetery in the churchyard where Cemetery Supper was held every year. She said there were hidden messages in 'A Hard Day's Night' if you played the 45 single at 33. She had heard Mr Tucker, the Orchard High School caretaker, was really a warlock.

Diane and Alice had been friends since they were babies, but this was yet more evidence of how they had grown apart, for, while Alice believed in ghosts, and though she increasingly thought society was bogus and needed to change, she did not believe Mr Tucker was a warlock. She could believe in the creatures lurking in the deepest fathoms of the river, though, just waiting. Alice felt life was like that sometimes: waiting. Waiting for things to start. To begin.

'Dad, you know how you want me to be happy and it's my birthday tomorrow?' she began, once she and her father were seated at the table at Mackie's, and Josie the waitress had taken the order. They always sat at the same table – the booth by the window, where, on one side, was the pink marble counter and the different sundaes on a sign behind it, and, on the other, the great glass view of the corner that looked down Main Street, toward the train station and the river. And they always ordered the same thing, ever since Alice was big enough to sit at a booth without sliding on to the floor. Her dad had a Rita Hayworth – chocolate, almond paste and glacé cherries smothered in chocolate sauce, because he loved Rita Hayworth and glacé cherries – and Alice had a Cemetery Supper

Surprise, brownies chopped up into chocolate ice cream in alternating layers with marshmallows, angel frosting and a red strawberry sauce, and a crumbling stick of chocolate on top. When their order arrived, her dad would always taste her sundae and say he wished he'd ordered it.

Bob Jansen took a sip of water, then pushed the glass back to the right place. He didn't answer.

'Hey!' she nudged him. 'Dad?'

'Yes, Allie?' Her dad pushed his glasses up his nose. 'I'm sorry. Sorry, honey. What did you say?'

Alice cleared her throat. 'Can I go to the dance with Jack Maynard?'

'What did your mother say?'

'She said no.'

Her dad spread out his hands. 'There you go.'

'But I don't think it's fair, Dad. Jack Maynard's a nice boy.'

'Your mother knows best,' Bob said, and he looked at her firmly but with the kind eyes that could never really be brought to anger. 'He's seventeen. You're fifteen.'

'Aw, come on, Dad. I'm sixteen tomorrow. I'm a sophomore.'

'Don't I know that?'

'How should I know you know that? You've barely mentioned my birthday. Neither has Mom.'

'Alice Jansen, shame on you for these untruths,' he said. 'What do you want me to do – have you go across to Valhalla and ask Mr Kynaston if he's giving me the day off? Because of all the plans? The plans, Alice?'

'Mr Kynaston gave you the day off?'

'He sure did. And he wanted me to go up to the town hall to get some permit for the orchards, transferring it to my name for our new business, and I said, "I can't go, sir. It's my Allie's sweet sixteenth tomorrow." And he said' – and her father's face creased into a smile – 'he said – never mind what he said!'

'What did he say?'

Her father put on a big, dramatic voice. '"You and that daughter – I'll be revenged as I may!"'

'Very good.'

'Do you know what play that's from, Allie?'

'*Much Ado about Nothing*, Dad.'

'Well done, Allie. We'll go to Stratford-upon-Avon some day and we'll see it.'

'Promise?'

He put his hand on Alice's. '*I am all the daughters of my father's house, and all the brothers too, and yet I know not.*'

'Dad, stop,' said Alice, sufficiently embarrassed by her father quoting Shakespeare to interject, though she was as gentle as he was, and hated doing it.

'You want me to sing, instead? Loudly? You know there's not a verse of "Sixteen Going on Seventeen" I don't know, Allie –'

Her dad had had a bad time the previous year, what with missing the first payment on his loan from the bank to buy the orchards. It had made him ill. So he'd had to go away that time, and when he came back to them he had acquired the LP of *The Sound of Music*. It just cheered him up, he said, Julie Andrews and her voice and those mountains and those kids. Alice knew he was in a bad way when *The Sound of Music* went on the record player.

Wilder Kynaston, routinely touted as America's greatest living novelist, lived at Valhalla, a notable country house on the banks of the Hudson, a fairytale miniature castle with a tower, stepped gables, red roof tiles over creamy rendered walls and a finial-studded wooden porch that faced on to the Hudson. Wilder was her father's boss, and erstwhile schoolmate, since both had attended Parnell, the exclusive boys' school upstate.

When Bob was a boy, the Jansens had lost their money in the Great Depression and sold their orchards to the Kynastons; their family farm was demolished, houses built over it. Bob Jansen became a scholarship boy, taunted by his peers for his too-short blazer and the eagerness with which he studied, for he had to succeed now, to make some money for his defenestrated family. The Kynastons had been on the banks of the Hudson for even longer than the Jansens, before the Civil War, around the time of the last of the Munsee tribe. Most of the Munsee were long gone, of course, having died of fever or been slaughtered or moved on West. Always West.

Wilder's first novel, *Where Munsee Lived*, was described as a quixotic masterpiece about one man travelling across America through different times and places. His second, *Garson Quayle*, featured a quixotic hero trying to find his place in the world. Alice had tried to read both, but couldn't get past Chapter 4 of either. On the basis of these two books was Wilder Kynaston hailed as the next great American novelist, but, though he wrote short stories that appeared in places like the *New Yorker*, it had been almost ten years since he had published a novel. Some people said he wouldn't ever publish again.

One afternoon, after Alice's father had left school and qualified as an accountant (there was no money for him to go to Yale, as Jansen men before him had done), Bob had bumped into Wilder in a bookshop in Manhattan and though he, Wilder, was several years older than Bob, and though he,

Bob, did not have money and Wilder did, Wilder remembered his old schoolmate and neighbour. They'd fallen to talking about literature, which led to the great event of 1958, when Bob Jansen saved Wilder Kynaston from some trouble with the IRS.

What this trouble was Alice was never quite sure, but it must have been significant, because after the crisis had been resolved Bob and Betsy were offered the Valhalla gatehouse and moved in when Alice was eight. In exchange for living there rent-free, Bob gave up his job at the accountancy firm and looked after the orchards, as well as Wilder's business affairs – his tax, his finances, his deals with foreign publishers, the administration of family matters, and so on. While it meant he was always around for Alice and her mother, it also obscured the fact that Bob was not at all suited to this role of meeting someone else's whims and needs, firefighting, managing many diffuse, boring, unpredictable tasks. The matter with the IRS had been extremely simple, easy for someone like him to solve. He didn't care about bookkeeping or accounts. He wanted something of his own.

Fifteen months earlier, Bob had borrowed the money to buy back the orchards, hoping to revive them and his family's name, which had once been synonymous with apples and apple trees in that part of the world. He would make apple sauce, juice, pies; have a stand at county fairs and Halloween and homecoming parades every fall. 'Allie,' he'd told her excitedly, 'good times are coming our way.'

Alice had never known how to describe what her dad did. Mr Hendricks was a lawyer for an advertising firm. Jan and Tag's dad, Mr Martin, was a pastor. Mr Logan worked in accounts. Carly's dad was in jail for killing someone (accidentally: he ran a red and hit them with his truck, but still) but even he had run a bakery when he was around. But she knew, because her mother was always telling her, that this was nothing to be ashamed of, that she should be proud to be one of the Jansens of Orchard, and that her mother, being a Palmer and from Massachusetts, was also a person of importance.

Mr Kynaston was often away, so Alice was in the habit of wandering up close to Valhalla just to stare at the Hudson and the wooded hills on the other side and the Canada geese, flying in a V, silently, up the river. But she rarely went inside. Sometimes she'd look out for Mr Kynaston's younger sister, Teddy, for on the first floor of the grand house, with its small interconnecting rooms like a series of tombs in a pyramid, there were photographs of her everywhere: a bob-haired, long-legged, darkly furious young woman.

Teddy Kynaston cast a long shadow, in the house and in the town, where stories of her exploits were legendary. The time the governess ran sobbing down the driveway past the gatehouse; the time she threw fireworks into the graveyard during Cemetery Supper, shouting, 'They're all dead anyway!'; the time she jumped out of the car rather than listen to her proselytizing father; the time she argued so hard with her brother she slapped him, giving him a bloodshot eye that lasted for weeks.

But more usually Alice would encounter Mavis the housekeeper, and sometimes Wilder Kynaston, snoring in a deckchair, or shouting poetry into the mist, whiskey in hand, or, once, throwing graham crackers into his mouth dressed only in a Hawaiian shirt and underpants. Alice knew he did not live up to his reputation of a great man of literature, but did not say this to her father, who was loyal to a fault. 'He's working on something now. When it does come, it'll be the

Great American Novel, wait and see,' her father would say, while Mavis would silently move through the grounds, picking up the broken cracker pieces, the peanut shells, the empty glasses rolling on the lawn.

'So what have you got me? A deer? Is it a deer?'

'I'm not saying.'

'A tennis racquet.'

'I can't see that fitting on the shelf, can you?'

'Okay. Is it . . .' Alice racked her brains. 'I can't think. Hey, Josie. Do you know what animal Dad's gotten me for my birthday?'

Josie set down the sundaes, took the check out from her pad and slapped it on the table with a smile. 'I'd be risking my life to tell you,' she said, smiling at Alice. 'But you're gonna love it, honey. Thanks, Bob. And, hey, in case I don't see you tomorrow, have a great day!'

Alice smiled at her. 'Thank you so much.' She looked down at the table, at the glistening red strawberry sauce, the brownies, the jelly, encased like geological layers in the curved sundae glass. 'I'm so happy right now, Dad.'

Her dad blinked. 'I'm glad, honey.'

'So . . . what's my present?'

'Okay,' he said. 'But you can't tell your mom, okay?'

'Okay.'

'I mean it, Allie – she doesn't know about it.'

'*Okay.*'

'It's hidden at Valhalla this time. And you have to find it.'

'What is it?'

'I'll give you two clues.'

Alice picked up her spoon and drove it into the sundae, which was starting to melt. She touched the glass, the condensation slowly bleeding into the paper tablecloth in the late-afternoon heat.

'What are the clues?'

'The clues are . . . Well, Teddy's the first clue.'

'I don't know Teddy. I don't talk to Teddy.'

'No,' he said gently. 'But perhaps you should. She's probably lonely. You'd like her.'

'She's – weird.'

'She's not. She's wonderful. Go find out.' He was still blinking. 'The second clue, it's . . . "Sevenstones". That's the second clue.'

'What kind of word is Sevenstones, Dad?'

'You'll see.'

'What does that even mean?'

'It means I haven't finished the clues yet!' He rubbed his face again, chuckling at her fury.

'Dad.' Alice rolled her eyes. 'Just tell me where the present is.'

'I won't. You have to find it yourself. Don't go digging for it. It's not buried.'

'Why do you make everything into a story? Just tell me.'

'The shelf will be full after this,' he said, shaking his head and smiling a little, and she saw something in his eyes, an expression she would wonder about for the rest of her life.

Her father leaned across and dipped his long spoon into her sundae. 'That's darn delicious, Allie. I should have gotten one of those myself.'

And Alice laughed without meaning to, because she was still a little peeved. She reached out and stroked his coat sleeve, the smooth brushed cotton. The arm underneath, the feel of it, flesh and bone, his warm, comforting, steady form. 'You always say that.'

'I know I do,' he said imperturbably, taking another spoonful of her sundae. 'And you always say, "You always say that."'

Afterwards, they walked down Main Street, the June heat shimmering in the early-evening light. They were making their way home, winding past the Victorian-era storefronts and white clapboard houses that lined the street and those off it, which she knew as well as anywhere. Mackie's, the diner. Denny's, the deli and the grocery store. The hardware store – Burt's, though Burt had been dead for twenty years. The beauty parlour, where the mom of that new girl Dolores worked now, and where her mother went to get her hair blown out and swept up. The tiny town hall and tiny fire station, both barely needed for a town that took care of its own.

She looked up as a train thundered down the tracks at the edge of the river. Saw the gleaming grey bullet speeding past, watched it skirt the cemetery until it was out of sight.

She saw her dad looking at the cemetery.

'Cemetery Supper'll be here before you know it,' he said. 'Gosh, every year it rolls around quicker. I'd better talk to Wilder.'

'Oh, Dad. It's so old-fashioned. Do we have to go this year?'

He turned to her in surprise. 'Don't you like it?'

Alice, who noticed and disliked so much of the class system she saw around her in play, felt a thrilling secret shame at her fascination with the Maynards, the Kennedys, the British Royal Family and especially the Cemetery Supper. The oldest Orchard families assembled, dressed in black, faces grave, though Alice always wondered if they weren't secretly thrilled. The dark, autumnal ritual ceremony of it, the dying of the season, the growth of night that meant you were moving toward the shortest day of the year. For the rest of her life she would love any festival that was pagan. She did not see it as anything to do with God. (She did not believe in God, but she had not told anyone at all that.) 'I guess so.'

'You always used to love it. Sitting on Mayor Cooper's knee. Handing round the apple pie. Don't you remember?'

'I was a little kid, Dad. It's just . . .' She scratched her nose, trying to put into words how she felt. 'Going into the cemetery, having dinner with them? They're dead and gone, Dad. Doesn't it seem kind of . . . *pointless*?'

Her dad didn't answer. He just carried on walking.

'Allie,' he said after a few moments, ignoring the question, 'tell me quickly. Are you really mad I won't let you go to the dance?'

'I'm not – mad.' Alice didn't know how to articulate it, how she wanted everything to change and yet to stay the same. 'I just want you and Mom to trust me.'

'Of course we trust you,' he said, a frown puckering his forehead. 'But we want you to keep safe. There's all kinds of nonsense out there. Folks acting crazy. The world is acting crazy.'

'But you – Dad, you always say things have to change. How unequal some stuff is. That's why I don't like the Cemetery Supper so much any more, I guess. It seems so outdated.'

'Okay, honey.' He held her hand for a moment. 'You're right, of course.' He squeezed her fingers. 'You're always right, my Allie.'

And they carried on walking.

Did she say anything else? Was there something more that she didn't remember afterwards, something that explained what happened? They were almost at the railroad line. The bugs were soaring above them in the golden summer light, pricking the rays of sun.

'Did you want to see *The Sound of Music* again on the weekend?' her dad said.

'Dad! That would make it, what – the fifth time? What is it with that movie?'

'It makes me feel happy,' he said. 'As though there's something to hope for.'

Was that what he'd said? She was never sure.

But she remembered she said, 'I'm not sure I want to see it again, Dad. I'm sorry. Maybe, maybe another weekend?'

Her dad was rubbing his eyes and blinking again, and she turned and felt her stomach drop, her heart ache. 'Dad – are you crying? You're not crying, are you?' she said, putting disbelief and almost mockery into her tone to force him to say no, I'm fine, everything's fine, because it was terrifying all of a sudden, and she didn't know why.

'I'm happy, honey. I'm happy.' She remembered him saying that, and it couldn't have been true, but she was sure he said it. 'Let's just enjoy the walk,' he said, blinking, and jangling his change in his pocket, the way he always did as he was walking toward their house, so she could hear him coming. 'Hold my arm, Allie. Let me just enjoy the last moments of you being fifteen. You're going to change the world. Make sure you hurry up and do it.'

'If you let me go to the dance with Jack Maynard, then sure, I'll change the world,' she said, and they both laughed, and he sang softly:

'I . . . have . . . confidence . . .'

And she joined in, holding his hand, and he jumped in the air kicking his heels to the side, like Julie Andrews, and they collapsed together, laughing, holding hands again.

'Ah, happy birthday, honey,' her dad said, and he kissed her cheek.

The heat was oppressive. Her dad was moving more slowly. She could hear the *thock* of someone's tennis game in the park behind Main Street and the sound of clinking glasses, laughter rising into the air – Orchard residents enjoying the relative cool of the summer evening.

In the distance, something, or someone, stirred on the green and golden track that wound away from the town.

'A train's coming,' said her father, but Alice's eye had been caught by a shape disappearing into the green tunnel of foliage down the track. A deer, frozen in the afternoon light, turning to assess the threat, ears pricked, pale caramel hide flecked with white, delicate hooves barely seeming to touch the ground.

Its eyes met Alice's briefly. Then it was off, leaping toward the railroad tracks.

'The deer –' Alice called, and her voice was elongated, low, as if it had been pulled apart and played back in slow motion. In years to come she would try to recall what happened, those last few minutes, and never quite could.

She saw the deer turn, its eyes bright.

'Look, honey,' her father said, as the train approached like thunder, ripping through the peaceful uplands. 'There they are. All your animals, your treasures.' And he gripped her arm suddenly, so hard that she gave a small yelp of pain. 'Honey, I had to go. You understand, don't you?'

Alice turned at the sound of a bird in the trees, calling, then saw the deer darting off the tracks and into the woods.

And someone watching on the street below screamed:

'Bob. BOB!'

There was a loud screech, a smell of brakes and burning

rubber, a whiff of smoke that afterwards she still smelled everywhere on the breeze, especially on hot summer nights in cities.

Her dad was gone. He had vanished and she never saw him again, and that was that – the world was the same, the clinking glasses in the background, the tennis, the calling bird, but forever now horrifically torn in two: before, and after.

2

Dear Dad,

I've been looking for that treasure like you said and I still can't find it. It's been twelve weeks and three days. I guess I need another clue.

I sat on the porch at Valhalla with Teddy again today. I like it there. The seats, they smell of old warmth, you know? Woodsmoke and polish and fresh air. And you can see down to the river, clear across to the other side. Mavis says Teddy waits for me.

What do Teddy and I talk about? She's my age, when we talk.

Look who's back, my partner in crime, Miss Alice Jansen.
'How are you today, Teddy? I cut the last two classes. Math and History. I like History. It's Mrs Finkelstein. I think you know her, don't you? But I didn't feel like staying. So I thought I'd come to see you instead. I like your skirt, Teddy.'
Alice picked up a piece of candy from the bench. It was root-beer-flavoured hard candy, covered with sherbet sugar. She had bought it for Teddy on the way back from school, but she intended to eat it, of course. Exhilaration at her rebellion suffused her.
Teddy lay back on the porch seat, propping up the throw pillows behind her. She folded one leg underneath herself. Her hair, short and shining brown, gleamed like

metal against the mustard-coloured pillows. *I die slowly of ennui, Alice, that's how I am. You're lucky, having school. One time, there was a meningitis outbreak at school and we were sent home for the rest of the semester. I taught myself Russian while we were back home. It came in rather useful, during the war. I'd give anything to be at school again. Anything. Wilder hated school, thought it was a waste of his time. I adored it. That photograph of me in the den, that's me on my first day at Farmington, Miss Porter's, you know. Aren't I a dear little thing? You must go to school, Alice. It's the only way out.*

'I don't care. I hate school.'

When I'm with her, Teddy is clever, sparkling, darned ornery sometimes about being a Kynaston and life here in Orchard. I can ask her anything, Dad, and she tells me. Mavis is really kind to her. She's on her own a lot with her because Mr K is away so much. I heard her on the phone to her sister. Mavis doesn't like being there. She doesn't like the house, all tucked away in the woods, and now that you're gone too they hardly have visitors. She told me you were her friend, hers and Teddy's. I like Mavis. She talks to me about you. Because no one else does, Dad. It's as though you never existed.

Alice, when did Orchard become so provincial? I declare, it's getting worse and worse. Billboards on Main Street . . . more and more stores closing . . . those ghastly housewives in their station wagons with their small narrow minds and their small, awful kids . . . When Wilder and I were little it was a community, you know, of interesting people, the crème de la crème of New York, the writers and artists and everyone in between. I wish the summer were over. I adore New York in fall. You should go sometime, Alice.

*

Everyone was angry with Alice, all because her dad had died, it seemed. Although Alice wasn't close to Diane Hendricks any more, she was still taken aback when, over the summer, Diane had dropped her, as though Alice had done something terribly wrong by having a dead father. Diane had told everyone Jack Maynard was going to ask her to the prom because Alice couldn't go – but he'd asked Dolores Delaney, the new girl, instead. And Diane was more furious than ever with Alice as a result.

Other people crossed roads to avoid her and her mom: they swerved away in hallways, ignored Betsy Jansen in parking lots when she waved cheerily at someone who'd been a friend for twenty years. There had been one day a couple of weeks ago, right before Labor Day, when her mother had started wailing in Denny's Golden Delicious, the grocery. Just wailing, like a banshee baby, a *crazy* high wavering noise like the time a goat got stuck in a tree in the orchards:

'*Booooooobbbb, BOBBBBBBB, Bobbbb, ohhhh, Bbbbbooobbbb.*'

No one had taken any notice. Not one person. The cashier had simply smiled when they got to the checkout.

'Good morning, Mrs Jansen, it's Timmy today packing for us, may I have him pack up your shopping for you? Thank you so much!'

Her mother, wet-faced, pasty, deflated by grief as if all the air had been let out of her heart-shaped face, had simply nodded.

At the back of the store, the Byrds were playing on the radio. *To everything turn, turn, turn, there is a season . . .*

There were lots of things her father had told her when he was alive – not enough, as it turned out, because she kept wanting to ask him questions twenty, thirty times a day. Where was the good hammer with the wooden handle her grandfather had made? What do you do with apple peelings, and was Mr Ford at the bottling place up toward Hudson cheating them with his prices for the apple sauce and the cider? Where were the last two treasures? (Teddy and Seven-stones. What kind of clues were those?) And why was Teddy the way she was? Her dad had told her, but she wasn't sure she remembered it right. She wasn't sure she remembered anything right now. Finally, how could she help her mom, because she didn't want her mother to be locked up? That was the only way things could be worse.

Alice had said, 'Mom, people are staring –'

'Oh, Bob,' her mother said with a small exhalation, and Alice, beside her, felt her heart hurting, and wished she could just vanish, completely disappear. But then her mom had patted her own face, as if someone had pulled a string in her back. 'Thank you so much, Timmy!'

'Have a nice day!' the cashier had told them, nodding as if to dismiss them as they exited, and her mother instantly started crying again on the lonely, silent walk back along the busy road toward the gatehouse. Alice and her mom had passed other people – Carly Gianotti and her mom, Jane, Mrs Cooper, the mayor's wife, the Logan twins, giggling on their bikes – as they walked past, eyes down, heads bowed, straggling along the road, her mother still openly crying, but no one said anything to them and Alice knew then no one was there for them.

To Alice, what was strangest of all was that they didn't know what to say to her about her dad, about the one and only Bob Jansen, who always walked with his fists sunk into his jacket pockets so it looked like he was carrying toffee apples; who, in fact, made the best toffee apples; who served the best punch in town at the town hall meetings, who knew all the words to every musical, especially *My Fair Lady* and *Oklahoma!* and of course *The Sound of Music*, who had a photo of him and Oscar Hammerstein shaking hands on the mantel above the range in their kitchen, who knew *everyone*, from Dolores's mom, Mrs Delaney, when she was Lana O'Reilly, to Griff Cooper, the mayor, to the Maynards and the Olsens and . . . *everyone*. So the idea of Jane Gianotti, Jane Hicks as had been, who had known Bob Jansen all his life and had held Alice as a baby, pretending she didn't know them, it was, well, it was very strange.

They had been the Jansens, but they weren't now: it was the two of them, Betsy and Alice. And it never sounded right. Because it wasn't right. None of it was right.

The sultry, soupy air.

A deer, blinking at them in the clear evening light.

A scream, which, she'd heard afterwards, had come from Mrs Olsen, walking back home, spotting him and realizing what was about to happen. How had she known when Alice hadn't? Alice never did find out, because, once again, no one said anything. But Mrs Olsen had screamed. She had screamed his name, wanting to help. *Bob!*

Then these dark, muddy images about what had happened next would start to creep into the edges of Alice's clear, circular pool of thoughts, and when that started she had to block them out.

> The apples are nearly in. We have to pick the last of them tonight. You did a good job, Dad. I wish you were here to see it. I wish I could ask you about the Beatles' new album, about what college I should apply to, about what to say to Mom in the evenings. I don't have anything to say to her. I've got Teddy to talk to, I guess, even though the

treasures still haven't turned up, and she doesn't seem to know anything about them. When I was talking to Teddy today, she mentioned college. She said Mr Kynaston could help me. I wondered if he would. Teddy went to Vassar, but that was before the war. She thinks I'd like Barnard. She says Berkeley is too full of commies, but that I might like that too. I don't think Mom would approve, though!

Mom doesn't approve of so many things now, but that was different before you left us, Dad. I remember her being barefoot a lot when we first moved here, don't you? I remember her dancing through the orchards with bare feet the day we moved in. Mom, in bare feet, outside! She was laughing. Her hair was longer. Didn't you two used to get all dressed up and go into the city to dance? Is that right? I can't remember, and I can't ask her, and I can't ask you.

'You knew my dad growing up, Teddy, didn't you?'

Long ago, Alice, your father and I used to play together as children, though he's a couple years younger than me. I watched him for his mother, your grandmother. And we used to play hide-and-seek. We hid little treasures all over the estate, and in the orchards, back when they belonged to his family. We'd find them and keep them ourselves. Little treasures. Stones and china ornaments and, once, a gold tooth, though we threw that into the river.

'Hey, Miss Alice.'

Alice stood up, taken aback. 'Hey, Mavis.'

'Miss Teddy's pretty tired. I'm going to take her upstairs for her nap before dinner. That okay?'

'Sure,' said Alice, pressing her hands to her burning cheeks. 'Sorry.'

Young women apologize too much, Alice. Don't be one of them!

'It's fine. She likes the company. Don't you, Teddy?'

But the spell was broken and the real Teddy remained, staring at Alice, talking softly – '*Ravenoose! Ravenoose!*' – moving her hands up and down her knees, rocking very slightly. Her barrette glinted in the late sun, and she smiled sweetly at Alice as she was led away. Mavis paused in the doorway.

'Bye, Miss Alice.' She opened the door and the noise from the radio in the kitchen came floating out. 'Oh, that song again,' said Mavis, wearily.

Alice smiled, nodded. Everyone, everywhere, was playing 'Yesterday'. Her friends had stood in line to buy it as a single. They sang it, hugging themselves and rolling around, tears in their eyes. She heard it floating out open windows, from car radios, even in the auditorium at school, as the principal, Mr Williams, said it was such a good song people should understand the lyrics. And he'd put it on and played it.

Yesterday . . .

Right there in the middle of the auditorium with the whole school, Alice's face had burned; her head had felt fuzzy and there was a ringing in her ears as she tried not to think about the Rita Hayworth sundae, the sound of tennis, the sight of the deer and the sound of the train, again. And, most of all, she tried not to think about losing control.

She had blinked and realized somehow she was in the hallway outside. She must have left the auditorium, with no idea she was doing so.

She had felt a hand on her arm and saw Dolores Delaney, staring at her.

'Hey. You okay, Alice? You're swaying. You need to get some water? Step out and get some fresh air?'

'Thank you,' Alice said. 'I'm fine. It's a little stuffy in there, that's all.'

'I know how hard it is.' Dolores's hand on her arm was cool, and soft. 'I lost my dad too. Take a minute.'

They were standing in the hallway by the principal's office. Alice could smell bleach, air freshener, Dolores's spicy perfume. She was cold; lately she was always cold. Goosebumps formed on her skin.

'You're real skinny, Alice,' said Dolores, and she made as if to put her arm around her, then stopped. 'Are you eating okay?'

'I'm fine,' Alice said again, and she had pushed past Dolores, gone back into the auditorium.

Alice knew she had lost weight, and that there were dark circles under her eyes. She didn't like the way her hip bones jutted out; her skin felt stretched across her body. She didn't know what was happening to her. First, she had worried it was her mom who was going crazy, but now she worried it was her, and that, if they found out, they'd have her taken away. It was the sound of trains, and 'Yesterday' she had to avoid. So, she reasoned, she had to make sure, constantly, carefully, that she wasn't any place where they might play 'Yesterday' or where she might hear the train without realizing it. If she was crossing the bridge on the way back from school that was okay: she sang the Beatles as loudly as she could, a different song every time from *Help!* Just not 'Yesterday'. She had learned how to act just enough, so they didn't see how crazy she was going. And if they said something more, if they seemed to be really trying to see how she was, she'd learned to smile and say she had to dash, she was late for her mom, that they had to get the last of the apples in, which they did, alone this time.

*

36

Bob Jansen had loved the Hudson Valley, the myths and stories there. When he took over the old orchards again, many of the ancient trees had been either dead or tangled with brambles, the leaves spotted black with blight. He had spent a long time getting the orchards up to scratch the past couple of years and he had loved harvest time, climbing the trees like a monkey, albeit a balding monkey in glasses, plaid shirt and jeans – what he proudly called his 'outdoor gear', as though he was one of the first pioneers – calling out to her mother and Alice, 'Save me some supper, I won't be too long!' Though he always was.

Alice's mother was up a ladder, collecting apples, when Alice arrived home from Valhalla. Through the trees, Alice could make out her mother's white ruffled shirt, and her hair tied up in a patterned red scarf. Betsy did not own any plaid or denim. When Bob had said, earlier that spring, as the latest bill had come in for the wood for the new apple stores, and been added to the demands from the bank for the loan repayments he'd not yet made, that maybe they should try making their own clothes, she had told him firmly, 'Robert, you can say all you want about that damn Julie Andrews and her curtains, but I'm a Doris Day kinda girl, not damn Julie Andrews, and Doris Day doesn't make clothes.' And Alice's father had leaned back in his chair and laughed so hard the chair had rocked back and would have fallen over, were it not for the dresser.

'Hi, Mom.'

'Hi, honey. You're late.'

'Sorry.'

Betsy pushed a tendril of hair that had escaped her scarf out of the way. The ladder shook slightly. 'Just these and then I think we'll call it quits.'

Alice set her schoolbag down on the grass. 'What do you want me to do?'

'I'll hand 'em to you.' Betsy rocked a little back again. 'Oh, gosh, how I hate being up ladders,' she said with a bright cheerfulness. 'Don't see how I'll ever get used to it! Thank you, Allie.'

'Let me go up, Mom.'

'No, no. I'm doing fine and it's for me to get it in, not you. Imagine how bad I'd feel if you fell off and broke your neck.'

As this was unanswerable, Alice stood waiting to carefully receive the apples and put them gently in each piece of tissue paper.

A bruised apple would go rotten, sooner or later, and infect the other apples. 'A bruised apple is no good.' She could hear him saying it now, holding one up, staring admiringly at it. Delicious, tart, crisp, the Bourton Pippin, a little-known variety which her father had painstakingly grafted from rootstock acquired from the farm of an old Jansen family friend. Each apple, at the exact moment it was ready to be pried from the branch, must be wrapped and laid in a wooden crate not touching its neighbour; the crates stacked in layers in the apple store; and then sold at market, taken to the apple press up the river to be made into apple juice or made into produce that would also be sold. The crinkling sound of the paper, and the smells of the lichen and apple and faint wet grass – it was apple time, and this made her curiously happy.

'Were you with your friends today, honey?' It was worse when her mother was trying to be perky, like Debbie Reynolds.

'I went to Valhalla.'

'Oh, Allie –' Betsy paused. 'Why do you keep going to see Teddy Kynaston?'

'She's my friend.'

'She's older than your father. I don't see what you have to talk about.'

'I lie out on the porch and we talk. About Dad. About stuff.'

This silenced her mother, but after a few moments of straining to grab a just-out-of-reach apple, she said, 'Mr Kynaston's coming back tomorrow. Did I tell you that?'

'No.'

'He's been away for so long. I guess you won't be able to go up there so much then.'

'I don't see why not,' said Alice, not caring how rude she sounded.

'Allie!' Her mother practically screeched. She handed her the apple. 'The Kynastons aren't our friends.'

'He was Dad's friend. So was Teddy.'

'Mr Kynaston's a gentleman. But your dad, honey –' Betsy sighed. 'The Kynastons, they're our bosses. They're different from us. I don't think your dad understood that.'

'Mom – they were friends!'

'Oh biscuits they were. Listen to me,' said her mother, wiping her forehead and carefully climbing down the ladder, the last of the Burton Pippins clenched in her hand. 'When Teddy had her eighteenth-birthday dance, they hired Louis Armstrong to come play for them. *Louis Armstrong*, Allie.'

'I know. Dad was there.'

'Only because he was a neighbour. Not because they – oh, never mind.'

Alice stared at her mother, fury soaking into her like black ink. 'Don't say things like that.'

'Okay, honey. I'm sorry.' Betsy pushed her hair away from her face with such force that the scarf came untied and she

39

stared at it as it slid off her open palm on to the grass. 'Stupid darned –'

Alice bent down and picked up the scarf. 'We've done enough today, Mom. Let's go in.'

Her mother nodded. 'I didn't mean any of that, Allie. I'm tired, and I'm trying to work out what we'll live on if we can't sell these apples; and, even if we can sell them, how on earth we'll survive. Your father left us a sliver of Jansen money, enough for two years, if we live like we're the Ingalls family and' – she gulped – 'grind our own flour and don't buy any new clothes.' She handed Alice the last apple to wrap, then brushed her hands together with an exaggerated briskness. 'Don't mind me, honey. After all, what did my mom used to say, about problems?'

'"To turn, turn will be our delight, / Till by turning, turning we come 'round right,"' Alice replied.

'That's it,' Betsy said, gracefully brushing a spider's web from her shoulder. Her shining brown hair caught the light, gleaming like toffee, and she gave a great sigh. 'I guess the Lord's plan for us is that we keep on turning, turning, till we come 'round right again, though I sure as heck don't know when that will be, and what Meemaw would make of it all I couldn't tell you.'

Betsy had been carefully raised, then gone through what she thought of as a rebellious phase when she moved to Manhattan aged twenty-two to work in a clothes store (the right kind of clothes store, approved by her mother). As she told it, she had gone wild, going to jazz clubs, and, once, she told Alice seriously, having an egg cream in Central Park with a cousin of the Roosevelts. She referred to this period often, sometimes with a world-weary shrug of the shoulders, as if she had lived a life and understood the gamut of human experience as a result. But Alice knew, because her dad had told her, that Betsy had been as miserable as anything while she was a big city girl. She wanted a home like the one she'd had as a girl, which sounded like something out of *Meet Me in St Louis*: – ice-skating and picnics and dances. So Alice knew that when her mother mentioned Meemaw, her rigidly correct mother, who had died before Alice was old enough to remember her, she really was upset.

Alice pulled the apple cart carefully along to the store. First they unloaded the produce in silence, the sweet smell of apples and hay and heat making her even more drowsy than usual, then they made their way to the gatehouse.

The gatehouse had been built for a family of four, and Alice often wondered if they'd been animals from a children's book, a family of dormice, perhaps squirrels at a pinch. It had three floors, and, while one wall was flat against the perimeter wall of the Kynaston Estate, the rest were gently rounded. In essence it was a tower, Rapunzel-style, and, when eight-year-old Alice first moved in, she had delighted in the novelty, as had her friends. But the gatehouse was not something out of a picture book. It was dark, surrounded by trees, cold in winter, hot in summer. There were one and a half rooms on each floor, the winding, wide staircase taking up much of the space. The apartment in town where they'd lived before had one big room with two tiny bedrooms off it. Alice's first memories were of toddling from one side to the other, its vastness like the plains. Here, everything was slightly too small. Though she had never admitted it, one of the reasons why Alice enjoyed visiting Teddy was Valhalla's sense of space – she could flop out and stretch on the porch, enjoy the sky and trees overhead, the horizons.

On the kitchen table was a wicker basket filled with

apples, and next to it a basket with peelings, ready to go on the vegetable patch. There were four chairs, a grey range and some tired ochre curtains coated in a light film of greasy dust. Every few months over the past eight years Alice's mother or father would say something like 'Let's put up a picture!' or 'Let's buy that delightful wooden coat rack' or 'Let's buy those new coffee cups!' and every time they would think of the dark, strangely cavernous kitchen, a kind of black hole, that was not really theirs, and somehow the items never made it into the house. They were not allowed to hammer into the walls or change the layout, and, while Betsy sometimes wistfully said they should put up some new drapes, they never did. It did not really feel like home; home was always going to be where they ended up next, when the apple business succeeded, when their luck changed.

Their entrance woke a wasp, which started buzzing angrily around them. The sound in the echoing kitchen was too loud, like a drill. Alice hit the insect with a fly-swatter and to her surprise it fell to the ground. She crushed its sides between her fingers, as her father used to, avoiding the sting. It felt good.

Her mother stood watching, not saying anything. It is as if we are both in a daze, Alice thought, drugged by something. She thought often of *Little House in the Big Woods*, of how Jack the brindle bulldog one night barked and barked so much they nearly shot him, but it turned out he was barking to save them from a bear. Alice often found herself thinking: no one alerted us to the bear, to the deer, to the train, not till it was too late.

'Alice –' Her mother was calling her.

'Hey, Mom,' she said gently.

Her mother was facing away from her. 'Alice, I'm falling. I can't seem to stop.'

'I know,' Alice said, trying to keep despair from her voice.

She was so tired of it all: of dragging this misery around with her, of the shame and anger and heaviness that came with it, of how weak she felt. *I can't help you, Mom. No one can help us.*

'Tell me one of your stories.' Her mother had bowed her head so low it was almost in her lap.

'What story do you want?'

'One of the treasures.' When she was little, she and her father used to make up stories about the treasures. Where the elephant had come from, and the cats which were Chinese princesses under a spell, and the dogs which had roamed the streets of Baltimore as a pack.

Alice sucked in her breath. 'I rearranged the elephants the other day. They're so friendly, you know?'

'Remind me what they look like.' Her mother's breathing was rapid, her voice faint.

'One's that rainbow-stone colour, and he's my favourite.'

'That's onyx, honey. Rainbow onyx. Your dad bought it for me on our third date.'

'Where was your third date, Mom?'

'We went to Times Square. We saw *It's a Wonderful Life.*' She paused. 'We had mulligatawny soup afterwards, at a little diner off Broadway. A most elegant place, despite the location. He gave it to me then. He said elephants never forget. And I remember, Allie' – her breathing was steadying, her voice calmer – 'he had a book in his jacket pocket. I was always so impressed with that. How bohemian it seemed to be.'

'What was the book?'

43

'It was *Wuthering Heights*, or something like that. You know he always wanted to go to England –' She broke off. 'Tell me where the elephant is now, Allie.'

'Okay. He's on the bottom shelf. I just moved him, and the brass one too. They seem like they should be the first ones you see.'

'Tell me about the others.'

'Sure. There're the two blue china cats – you remember, you got them from the lady in the apartment below you –'

' 'Course I do. Laurey and Curly. Curly's smiling at Laurey.'

'That's it,' Alice said, nodding.

'And there's one black bird with a chipped wing. And the dormouse – he's on a piece of corn. An ear of corn.' Her mother cleared her throat. She seemed to be regaining her equilibrium. 'I love that blackbird, you know. Your father was given it. Someone knew he was collecting treasures for you. When you were born.'

'They did?'

'Sure they did,' said her mother, and her smile was so sad. 'Your dad was the proudest dad there ever was. Mayor Cooper said he'd never known a father more convinced everything their daughter did was right. He even believed you when you said you'd seen that ghost.'

'Mom! I did see a ghost.'

Little Alice – a determined, blonde-haired girl who said, 'Oh biscuits!' when she was annoyed about something; who could read by the time she was four and who liked following her dad around everywhere – had once told stories, just like he had. Famously, walking back from the Cemetery Supper one evening aged eight, she had seen a man in uniform on a horse; he had ridden up to her and said hello. Riding with him was a young girl about her age, who had offered her a bunch

44

of flowers that dissolved into dust when Alice reached up and took hold of them. She had written about it at school. Miss Harman, her second-grade teacher, had sent her home with a gold star and a note. *Alice wrote a terrific story. She is always truthful even when she's making it up.*

As Alice chattered, her mother relaxed. Alice kept on talking, glancing around the kitchen to see what they might cook for supper, or at least suggest to her mother what they might cook, for, if Betsy thought she was being 'handled', her reaction was much worse.

Her mother looked at the clock. 'Heavens. You must want feeding, honey: I'll put supper on. Corn, ham, apple sauce – does that sound good?'

But a light, pleasant voice called behind them.

'That sounds *marvellous*, Betsy.'

They both jumped. For a split-second Alice thought – and she knew her mother thought the same – *it was a dream. He's back.*

In the open window, smiling through at them, was Wilder Kynaston.

He was city smart, in a three-piece linen suit and a cream panama hat on his head, removing the latter as he spoke. He leaned on the windowsill, glancing from Alice to Betsy, and said:

'Well, hello, Miss Alice – haven't you grown since I last saw you? I hardly recognized you.' He turned to her mother. 'Why Betsy, are you all right?'

'You startled me. We'd heard you were coming up tomorrow, Mr Kynaston,' Betsy said, polite enough but in a cool tone.

'It's far too hot in Manhattan still, and I missed this place too much. This is my favourite time of year. I had to come back. I'm terribly sorry for giving you a fright, Betsy, my dear.'

Her mother walked toward the open window. 'It doesn't matter,' she said, obviously seeing he really looked contrite. 'Please, won't you come in?'

'I'd be delighted to, but only if you're not too busy.' He took her hand and patted it, holding it for a moment afterwards. 'Betsy – I do apologize, you know.'

Alice's mother smiled, her cheeks flushing. She smoothed down her hair. She liked any kind of visitor but especially the right kind, and the kitchen was tidy.

'We're delighted to see you, Mr Kynaston. Come in, come in,' she said.

'Wilder, please. I insist. Dear Bob was like a brother to me. We're practically family.'

'Wilder, please come in.' Mr Kynaston disappeared, then entered through the little front door into the kitchen, as Betsy hurriedly moved the apple peelings into a bucket under the sink and tidied, her birdlike gaze darting around to see what was out of place.

'I hope I haven't interrupted anything,' he said.

'You've come at the perfect time. We've been collecting the apples, that's all.'

'Of course.' He clapped his hands. 'You must be exhausted. How 'bout I fix you some supper instead and you sit down?'

'No, no, I wouldn't dream of it,' said her mother, but Wilder was taking off his jacket and laying it across the back of a dining chair. 'It's the least I can do. I've meant so many times to come and make sure you're both all right. I was walking past from the train and I thought I'd look in, and here you both are. He'd be so proud of you, seeing you two like this.' He looked around rather helplessly, as if not sure where to start, so Betsy took out a couple of pans and started to peel potatoes. Alice thought that he had such friendly eyes, Mr Kynaston, kind and understanding, as if he saw through you – not in a bad way but to the part of you that was good, and special. 'Now, Betsy, put down that peeler. I'm going to make supper and I won't take no for an answer,' he went on hurriedly, wrapping a white frilled apron that she handed him around his waist. 'Every now and then I'm sure it's pleasant to have someone else cook for you, isn't that right, Alice? Will you help me, while your mom sits still and has a little glass of brandy?' He finished tying the apron around his waist and fished a hipflask from his pocket. He fetched a tiny glass from the dresser, poured some amber liquid into it and handed it to Alice's mother, all of it done in a matter of seconds. 'There. Drink that.'

Wilder Kynaston was, like his little sister, excellent company, and Alice hadn't realized how much she and her mother needed another person in the house, a break from each other and their respective griefs. He did not, in the end, do much of the cooking, but he quickly fried the pork loin in butter and the rest of the brandy from his hipflask, and it was delicious. He could make a good salad dressing too, explaining everything so clearly that sometimes she forgot this was Wilder Kynaston, winner of the National Book Award for *Where Munsee Lived* and the Pulitzer for his short stories, a hero of modern American literature. Most of all, he took up space, and filled the dark corners with his warm voice, and it was very welcome.

He made her mother laugh, her initial frostiness melting little by little as they set the table, telling the story of how the plates they were using had come from his great-aunt, of the scrapes Teddy had gotten into when she was a little girl in this gatehouse when they had no one living here, of the time he'd climbed every apple tree in the orchard and knocked off so many of the apples that his father had beaten him with a switch.

Coming back down from the bathroom, Alice paused on the stairs, looking down into the kitchen-diner. The lingering scents of butter and wood and apples hung in the air. She could hear the snatches of conversation. It had been a long time, a couple of years now, since she'd stood on the stairs listening to her parents talk, laugh, discuss the day over supper. Her father had usually been outside looking at the trees or working on them or going through papers for Mr Kynaston; or he'd been ill, locked away, out of reach. Settling herself back next to him, Alice gave him a shy smile as he handed a glass of wine to her mother.

'Isn't this pleasant,' her mother said. 'Company again.'

'Pleasant is the word,' Wilder said, raising his glass to Alice, and then to Betsy. 'I hope you don't mind if we drink a toast to Bob. I feel it's appropriate, at this hour, gathering in the apples, the three of us around this table. It's what he would have wanted, I'm sure. We laugh at death, and we run from it, and we embrace it. The contradictions are the jagged edges of our little life. *Come, away!*' he said softly. '*This case of that huge spirit now is cold. / Ah, women, women! Come: we have no friend / But resolution, and the briefest end.*'

He was silent for a moment, staring into the red liquid.

'That huge spirit,' he said quietly.

'That's lovely,' said Betsy politely, sipping at her wine.

The last apples her father had grown had been gathered in. They had gone from blossom to the tight green globes they were in June at the time of his death; now they were in the apple store. After they were sold there would be nothing left behind that he had grown, or made. Alice put down her fork, blinking hard into the distance, the pork a dry lump of meat in her gullet.

Her mother said politely, 'How is the new novel? Dare we ask?'

'Oh,' he said with a weary smile. 'Terrible.'

Alice's mother cleared her throat. 'I remember Bob saying,' she began with a smile, 'that *Garson Quayle* was an awfully *funny* book. He said not enough people concentrated on your humour. I hope you don't mind me saying.'

Wilder laughed and pushed his hair out of his eyes. 'Not at all, Betsy. I trusted Bob's opinion almost more than anyone's, so thank you for that kindness.'

Her mother nodded, and shrugged, raising her glass again. *My God*, Alice thought. *Mom is . . . flirting with Mr Kynaston. She thinks he's flirting with her.* 'The only joke relating to this book so far is that my editor thinks he's getting it by Christmas.'

'What's it about, Mr Kynaston?' said Alice.

'Well, Alice, it's – about a young girl. She reminds me of Teddy, in fact. A Daisy Buchanan type. You'd like her. And she sees the hypocrisy of the changing world. And how screwed we all are. It's . . . how shall I put it . . .' He banged his hand on the table, quite gently. 'It's not coming together. I left here because there were . . . distractions. But those distractions were nothing compared with what's going on in the city.' He dabbed his napkin daintily to his mouth and sat back in the creaking wooden chair. 'This is wonderful. I didn't have one home-cooked meal in New York, you know. The closest I came was drinks with my agent at his apartment. My agent has two daughters. This past summer they both dropped out of school. One of them ran away to Monterey – hitched her way there across the country, like something out of a story – and she never came back. The other just goes to the beach or lies in bed all day. Has a boyfriend who never washes his hair.' He grimaced.

Alice's mother clicked her tongue. 'My, my. The world sure is an interesting place right now. Bob always says change comes too slowly, then it comes too fast.' Her eyes were bright. 'Too fast.'

'I'd agree with that,' said Wilder, mouthing the words himself. 'I don't recognize the city any more. Yes, sir.'

Betsy looked appalled. 'The hippies and the drugs and the draft nonsense there in California – it's not going to come to New York, is it?'

'It already has, my dear. Beatniks. Hippies. Flower power. Dropouts everywhere. Clubs full of marijuana smoke. Poetry, people with guitars, girls handing out flowers on the street. Signs about the draft, using the coarsest language. Peyote, Betsy. And the coloureds, the Negroes – never seen so many of them, you know, they're agitating, all of them, this . . .' He scratched his head. 'I should be making notes while I'm there, but I don't – ha! Someone will write a novel about it, but it won't be me. Here's a funny thing.' He leaned forward. 'It's a revolution, and no one's noticed. The streets are alive. Young people high and driving round in cars listening to all sorts of outlandish music. They're swarming here from all over the country. And no one's noticed.'

'Oh, my word,' said Betsy, shaking her head.

Alice said, 'But, Mom, you and Dad, you marched against McCarthy, the Red Scare, the bomb. Isn't this the same thing?'

Her mother got up and started collecting the plates with a clattering sound. 'Your father believed in all of that. I just want people to get along.' She swallowed, and Alice felt a new, and alarming, contempt for her, a sour taste in the back of her mouth. 'This is about good manners and supporting our troops and respect and, well, I just don't like it. It feels dangerous.'

'Amen,' said Wilder.

Alice said hotly, 'But the boys posted out there, they say –'

'We don't want to talk about it, Allie! Now fetch some coffee for Mr – for Wilder.' Alice got up and put some water on the range for the coffee pot. Betsy busied herself, clearing away, tidying. She smiled awkwardly at Wilder. There was a heavy, dull silence for several moments, then he said:

'And you, Miss Alice, our representative sample of the decline of civilization. May I ask how is school going?'

'It's good, thank you.' Alice folded her napkin and put it on the table. She was not hungry any more.

'What about your SATs? In my day it was all terribly simple, but I've heard they make it devilish tricky now.'

'They're okay.'

'Elizabeth Finkelstein told me you were scoring 1400 in practice tests. What colleges are you thinking about?'

Alice and her mother looked at each other. 'Alice hasn't made up her mind about colleges yet,' said Betsy. 'She had this notion of Berkeley. I've said we'll have to – you know, talk it over. It's so far away now. Too far. And – everything else. Our –'

Finances was what Alice knew she was trying to say, for she had seen her mother, head bent over the ledgers and the cheque books, in tears, trying to work it all out in the weeks since his death, and she knew that, when her mother referred to the sliver of Jansen money, it did not cover college; it did not cover much of anything.

Wilder nodded thoughtfully. 'I can see that.'

'Did Teddy apply to Barnard?' said Alice suddenly.

'Teddy?' Kynaston's eyes opened wide. 'My sister?'

'Yes,' Alice said.

'I think she did, in fact.' He drank some more wine. 'Why do you ask?'

'No reason, sir,' Alice said. She was tired all of a sudden, and didn't want to think about college, or money, or the reality of their situation. She wanted to be away from them both. She thought of the little shelf of treasures, of putting them neatly in place, of lying back in bed, of closing her eyes, of this day being over.

'You've been over to the house a lot, haven't you?' Kynaston said. 'While I've been away. Mavis told me.'

Her mother turned to her in horror. 'Alice!'

'Betsy, it's no trouble.' He smiled and shook his head. 'It's nice for Teddy to have visitors. We're very isolated.'

'She had no business –'

'Dad said I should,' said Alice, her face burning red, and her throat closing up. 'He said I should go talk to Teddy, try to get to know her.'

'Why on earth would he say that?' Betsy said angrily. 'I'm so sorry, Mr Kynaston –'

'Wilder,' Wilder Kynaston said. 'Please call me Wilder, Betsy.' He smiled at her.

Alice thought about the letter she'd write to her father, when she was sitting in bed.

You said the clues to the final treasure were Teddy and Sevenstones. I need more clues, Dad! I need you to tell me all these things you didn't tell me. Is it a place? A name? A book? What about Teddy? I wish you'd told me about Teddy.

'Dear Bob,' Wilder said ruefully. 'He was fond of her, always was. Teddy's wonderful, Alice dear, but it's really a waste of your time to try to talk to her. I'd be careful around her, if she's not used to you.' He stared at the wine. 'Yes, I'd be careful. Hey, Betsy,' he said suddenly. 'While we're on the subject of college, did Bob have savings? Forgive me for mentioning it at a time like this, but is any of it left?'

'Oh.' Betsy put her hands to her cheeks. 'I haven't the vaguest idea – I suppose I could' – she flapped her hands, and her voice rose – 'ask the bank? But, you know, they weren't very pleased with him, because he'd fallen behind with the repayments on the orchards . . .' She turned to Alice, who was pouring out the coffee, but Alice shook her head. *I don't know, Mom.*

Wilder patted his mouth with his napkin and pushed back the chair. 'Sure. I'd hate to press you, or put any pressure on you. And, of course, there's the question of the future. Let me do some thinking.'

'Oh?' said her mother faintly. 'The – of course, Wilder.'

'And I'm sure you'll have made your own plans, especially you, Miss Alice.' He smiled, accepting the little cup of coffee she handed him. It was gold-rimmed, with a matching saucer. Her father's parents had been given the set as a wedding present. 'I've no doubt, you're destined for great things. But tell me, Alice, if you ever need more reading matter, or someone to show you what you should be reading, studying, you come to me, you understand?'

'That's very kind, Wilder,' said Betsy, nodding gratefully. 'Oh – Alice, thank Mr Kynaston, won't you.'

'Thank you,' said Alice. Her cheeks were still red.

'I mean it. I was very fond of Bob. I want to do right by you both.' He drained the coffee and stood up, pushing back his chair. 'I'll wait to hear from you on your future plans. I'm devastated, having to ask at all, but I know Bob was a man of honour and if the bank calls in the loan the orchards will come back to me . . . He and I had discussed it, you understand, and I'd lent him some money to make some payments, but I'm not sure he ever did.' Betsy's mouth was open, her face frozen. 'So there's the little matter of what you'll live on and where.'

'Where?' said Betsy, frowning, as if she really had no idea what was coming. Alice swallowed, hugging herself, her thin frame shivering.

'I'd have asked you to leave this place in a month or so, for I know you'll have realized I'll be getting in new tenants, someone who can pay perhaps or take over from Bob, but it'd be cruel to do it before Christmas.' He smiled down at her, and her mother stared up helplessly at him, the hard glare of the overhead light casting black shadows in the ruffles of her shirt. 'So let's wait till New Year sometime – shall we say you'll be gone by Valentine's Day? Does that sound okay? As I say, I'd feel just awful making you homeless so soon, and that seems long enough.' He shrugged on his jacket, pulling down the sleeves of his shirt so that they protruded perfectly, one exact inch. He smiled at them, and Alice heard a tiny gas-like series of bubbles gurgle in his stomach. 'You'll let me know if you turn up any of the money? He did borrow from me too, dear Bob. But a debt's a debt, isn't it?'

'Yes! Of course,' said Betsy, her tone gay, her eyes wide. 'Of course, Wilder. A debt's a debt.'

3

Alice ran through the orchards till she got to Valhalla, and the scent of pine, of flowers, of sunshine bleaching wood and grass, came into her nostrils. She slowed down, as Teddy was sometimes startled when she heard sudden noises.

She used to come here sometimes with her dad, her little hand tucked into his large one, walking through the orchards to the big house, and she would sit in the small cosy living room and wait while her father went through the business of the day with Mr Kynaston in the study. She would look at the picture books – *The Little House*, *Green Eggs and Ham*, *Ten Thousand Cats*, *The Wizard of Oz* – her legs dangling, not quite reaching the floor.

She could hear the noise, louder than ever. Sometimes she successfully ignored it. Too much to hope for today.

'*Ravenoose! Ravenoose! Ravenoose!*'

'Hey, Miss Teddy,' Mavis was saying. 'There you are! We were wondering if you'd come.'

'I met some people on the way over,' said Alice.

'*Ravenoose! Ravenoose!*'

'That's nice,' said Mavis. She looked approvingly at Alice, and patted her arm. 'Well done, honey.'

It was almost Halloween. Alice had been walking back from school, looking down at the leaves that had flown to the ground and stuck themselves to the wet path: gold, lime, ochre, mustard stars, shining up. She did not hear the car drive past, but then a voice called:

'Hey! Hey, Alice Jansen!'

Alice looked up, saw a mulberry-coloured Ford Mustang and felt herself turn to water. 'Hey, Jack,' she said, instantly aware of her face turning red. 'How are you?'

Jack Maynard hadn't graduated from high school; having failed his major classes, he was being made to repeat his final year. She'd heard there were big fights at Crossings – about this, about him not getting into West Point and about his refusal even to apply to Princeton. His father was threatening to kick him out. Diane had told her all this in a fleeting moment of engagement, her face close to Alice's to watch for her reaction. Since her father's death, Jack himself had not spoken two words to her. Alice was secretly glad, though, that he was repeating the year.

He said something now to his companion, whom Alice couldn't see, then turned to Alice. 'Wanted to check on how you're doing,' he said, and blew smoke out of his mouth in a leisurely fashion.

He seemed to have grown since the last time she saw him. His leonine hair curled longer, more magnificently than ever; his plaid shirt was rolled up above his elbow, the hairs on his arms golden from the summer sun. He had beads round his neck; and a harmonica was tucked into the breast pocket, where formerly there had been a pack of Lucky Strike.

'Oh, thanks,' Alice said, staring into his pale blue eyes. 'How are you, Jack?'

'Me?' He looked utterly surprised anyone should ask, and a faint flush spread over his cheeks. 'Oh. Thanks. I'm fine.' There was another long, agonizing pause.

'So . . .' Alice pointed at his shirt. 'You play harmonica?'

He looked confused. 'What?' He looked down and laughed. 'Maybe.'

She nodded. 'Cool.'

His lips – his lips were full, and pinker and thicker than the rest of his face, like Mick Jagger. She wanted so much to kiss him then.

There was a squeak of leather. A voice said:

'So, Jack. We going back to your place or not?'

Jack looked from Alice to the person beside him, whom she still couldn't see. 'You know Dolores, don't you?'

'Sure,' said Alice. She cleared her throat and leaned forward. 'Hey, Dolores.'

'Hey,' said Dolores Delaney. She was in a seersucker plaid top and denim shorts. Her shiny black hair was bouffant with two tiny pigtails, a thin red ribbon tied around each. 'Good to see you again, Alice. Every time I see you, you look super-cute. Doesn't she, Jack?' Dolores stared down at the long navy tunic Alice was wearing, which she'd made herself with her mother's old sewing machine, and, underneath it, the coral shirt with the sailor collar, trimmed with a slender navy ribbon. 'You're so clever. Did you buy that or make it?'

'I made it. It's easy, I'll show you how. I like your outfit too,' she said to Dolores.

'I think she looks like a farmhand,' said Jack, and he laughed, but Dolores didn't. 'Hey, don't be mad,' he said quickly, almost nervously. 'I was just joking.'

'I'm not mad, honey.' Dolores opened the car door and stepped out, brushing off her shorts.

'You are. Can I help it if you look a little –' He scratched his nose really slowly, and Alice realized how stoned he was, how impatient it seemed to be making him, as though the pot had trapped him like honey and he had to wade through it, each movement laboured. 'A little trashy? You're still cool, Dolores.' He turned to Alice. 'She's mad.'

'I'm not mad. And you're not funny. You are cute, though.' She pinched his face, staring at him.

'I'm not,' said Jack, his face flushing. 'Hey, Dolores. Get back in the car, I'm sorry.' He seemed genuinely anxious. 'C'mon, Dolores.'

'No, thanks. I'll get out here.' She leaned forward so that the plaid top gaped down and her black brassiere was visible. Alice watched Jack watching her breasts. Then Dolores leaned forward and kissed him, full on the lips, cupping his face with one hand, like he was an orange she wanted to squeeze. She broke away, and he tipped forward, then righted himself. 'See you around, Jack. You're a nice guy. Don't worry.'

'I'll call you,' he said, and Alice saw the dazed, hard, yearning look on his face, like a dog following a scent. Dolores shrugged, then shook her head, the little ribbons of her pigtails flickering, her hair flashing blue-black in the sunlight. Jack said nothing more, simply drove off at high speed.

There was a silence, broken only by the sound of the car revving in the far distance. The two girls faced each other.

'Hey,' said Dolores, raising one hand and letting it fall.

'Hey,' said Alice. She dropped her hand too, and her schoolbag slid off her shoulder. 'Oh biscuits,' she said, leaning over to pick it up.

'Oh biscuits,' Dolores said, smiling. 'Adorable.'

Alice folded her arms. 'What was it you wanted?' she said, to hide her mortification.

'My cousin, back in Chicago, she says there's three kinds of guys,' Dolores said, after a pause. 'You wanna know who they are?'

'Who are they?'

Dolores moved her gum from one side of her mouth to the other. Her dark eyes glittered. 'There're men, boys and hairdressers.'

'What about Jack?' Alice said, fascinated. 'Which one is he?'

'He seems kind of lost. He's a nice kid, though, but he' – she jabbed a thumb backwards in the direction of Jack's car – 'I gotta tell you, he's a hairdresser.'

'What does that even mean?'

'It means he has great hair, and new records, and nice manners, but there's nothing to him, nothing at all. And that's about it.'

Alice started to laugh. 'Okay,' she said. 'I knew you went to the senior prom with him, but I didn't think you were his . . .' She stopped in confusion.

Dolores gave a shout of laughter. 'He asked me to the prom, and we hung out. A few times.' She took a joint out of her pocket and started rolling it in her hands. 'But he's looking for something, and it's not me.'

As Alice was turning over this statement, Dolores lit the joint. 'It's weak, but it's just enough. Want some?'

She handed it to her, and Alice took it. They stood by the side of the road, no sidewalk, the autumn light filtering through the trees, moving the joint back and forth between them, like they were taking part in a ceremony.

'I can show you how to use my sewing machine, if you haven't got one,' said Alice after a few minutes.

'Sure. We used to have one back in Chicago. I guess it got left behind. Most of our stuff did. That'd be great, Alice.'

'Call me Allie,' said Alice suddenly.

'Sure, Allie.' Dolores passed her the joint again. Dolores pushed her hair out of her eyes, inhaled and said in her low, amused voice, 'Good to know you, Allie,' and Alice nodded. To Alice it felt like a golden thread, weaving its way around them both, tying them gently together.

'Hey, why don't you come with me to Mackie's on Friday? It's my birthday. My mom wants to treat me.'

'Mackie's,' said Alice.

Dolores looked at her like she was slow. 'Yeah – it's the diner, up on Main Street? Across from the bank? It does sundaes –'

'Yes,' said Alice, speaking fast. 'I know it . . . sure. That'd be great.'

'Okay,' said Dolores, looking at her rather curiously.

'Thanks, Dolores.'

'Call me Dolo. That's what all my friends call me.'

'I never heard anyone call you Dolo,' said Alice.

'I never liked anyone enough to ask them to call me Dolo.' She took out her lipstick and reapplied it. Alice felt a wave of fondness rush over her. 'I have to go,' she said. 'I have to help my mom in the beauty parlour. I'll see you Friday, Allie.'

'Sure, Dolo,' Alice said. She watched her go, with a smile playing about her lips. She looked down at her brown lace-up boots and her long tunic, and remembered where she was going, what she had to do. Feeling rather light-headed, she ran to Valhalla, her boots thudding across the wet lawns, her hair streaming out behind her.

They were waiting for her on the porch. Mavis looked tired. Teddy too. Alice sat down and took Teddy's hand.

'I want to visit with you after if I've time,' she said. 'But I'm going inside first. That okay?'

Darling, I'll be here, staving off ennui, but do hurry: we've masses to discuss. The time I ate a whole chilli rather than go back to school, and the time your father and a couple of friends tried to sail across the Hudson in a boat they made from corrugated iron – they got twenty yards across and capsized.

Alice crossed the porch and went into the house through the den. The in her head buzzing from the pot was so loud she had to pause for a moment, gathering herself, then she swung her hair behind her back and walked across the strange dark hallway, knocking on the study door, opposite the den.

'Come!'

The heavy door opened into a too-warm room, fuggy and dense with smoke. Every inch of wall was taken up by shelving – row after row of crime novels, small white books with French titles, old red-and-gold hardbacks, and every shelf had black-and-white photographs in silver frames of Kynaston ancestors sitting stiffly in studios: corseted ladies with elegantly dressed hair and cameo pins, dashing gentlemen standing by the river holding oars, children in sailor suits standing in front of Valhalla. All the family represented, the black-and-white images stretching around the room.

Wilder Kynaston was scratching his head furiously, humming to himself, a keening, shrill sound, like a bird in distress. 'Hey! Mavis,' he said. 'She's so loud. Tell her to keep it down. Get me a fresh pack of cigarettes, would you?' Alice cleared her throat, and he swivelled around, whip-fast. 'And you can – oh! Alice. What are you doing here?'

'I'm sorry, Mr Kynaston.' She braided her fingers together. 'I wanted . . .' She trailed off.

'You look like you're being led to the gallows,' he said kindly. 'Untangle your fingers, my dear, sit down and tell me what I can do for you.'

She sat down gingerly. A smell of leather came from the chair and the desk; a fug of cigarette smoke hung over the room. Wilder rubbed at his forehead with exasperation, threaded his fingers through his crinkled hair. He stared at her.

'I'm disturbing you.'

'No, believe me. I can't write another word. This book is dead in the water. Dead.' He slammed his hands down on the desk. 'I may not ever write anything again. And, funnily enough, the more hysterical it sounds, the truer it is.' He gave her a grim smile. 'I apologize, my dear. It's just that I think I'm losing my mind.'

'I read somewhere that they say if you think you're losing your mind, you're not. It's the people who think they're perfectly sane that you've got to worry about.'

'Ha! You're a clever thing.' He gave a mordant laugh.

'Is this the book about the American girl, the one who's like Daisy Buchanan?'

'Yes. The inverse, the turning inside out of the American Dream, oh – hell!' He spat out the words and spun around in his chair, eyes following a jay that had broken free from a pine and was gliding out toward the river.

'I'll help you, if you want.' Alice could hear her own voice, high-pitched, soft, young. 'I – I can tell you why the book won't come alive.'

'You'll – help me?' He stubbed out a cigarette, watching her carefully. 'Why? Tell me what you wanted again?'

Since she had nothing to lose, Alice said simply, 'We need more time to find a new place. You can't evict us.'

He laughed. '"Evict" is a strong word.' He ran his hands through his hair again. 'I wouldn't leave you homeless. But, Alice, the house was always intended for the caretaker of the

62

estate, and your dad – he isn't here any more. I need someone to help me with this place. Mavis is leaving.'

'Oh.'

'Yes, she's finally tired of the two Kynaston children and
their troubles. She says I should have married someone suitable. Well, I didn't, so I need a retired couple, someone who
can move in and run the show. The orchards, and – everything
here.'

'But me and my mom – we can do it,' said Alice. 'Dad
had a list. We can start working our way through it, if you'll
help us.'

'Alice, it's more than just picking apples. It's fixing things.
Your dad made a lot of stuff go away. What bills to pay, when
to chase the paperboys, when I needed more bourbon. He
understood who to let in, who was an autograph-hunter. He
knew it all, and he chopped up logs and kept the stream clear
and oiled the wood and did the gardens and moved things
around – and your mom, sweet as she is, can't do that. I need
another Bob.'

Alice dug her nails into her tunic. 'There isn't one.'

'I apologize. Of course.' He looked at her then for a long
time. 'Alice, you're an interesting girl, you know that? Very
like your father. Which I hope you'll see as a good thing
someday.' His clear, pale blue eyes were expressionless, the
clown-like smile marks around his jowls almost gone. 'I know
what you're going through. Everyone says that, don't they?
But it's because they want to make sense of it, even though
they can't.' A soft evening wind rattled the casement window,
and he turned. There was shouting outside: the same commotion played out every night. 'I have lost everyone close to
me. Twice over, in some cases.'

'What does that mean?'

'It means I blame myself for some of the pain I experienced. But grief is different. Tell me something, will you?' She nodded expectantly. 'What does yours feel like?'

'Mine?' She pushed the heel of her palm against her chest. 'Like I can't draw enough breath. Like I'm constantly short of it. Like I'm struggling to breathe, all the time.' Alice inhaled as deeply as she could. She was looking down as she spoke but could still hear the scratching of his pen; she knew he was writing it down, but she didn't care. 'I go to school and listen to Mrs Finkelstein tell me about the New Deal or the Louisiana Purchase and it doesn't make sense. None of it makes sense. My fingers work when I hold the pen and my voice works when I speak, but it still doesn't make sense. Kids ask me questions in the hall and it doesn't make sense. And I come home, and I eat supper with my mother, and she tells me the same old broken stories again: the time she was staying in Wisconsin with her Meemaw and she went to a dance and a horse broke into the ballroom, or the time her cousin was in Georgia in '39 and saw Vivien Leigh at the premiere of *Gone with the Wind* – and none of that makes sense either. There could be war any day, nuclear war, and there are boys a couple years older than me fighting the Vietcong on the other side of the world. I lie in bed and think about the threads of cotton woven under me, the knots of wood in the bed, and the birds nesting in the roof, and I can't make sense of any of it any more. I think sometimes I'll die because I can't breathe. Except coming here to talk to Teddy – that makes sense. My dad, he's all I want to talk about. He's gone, wiped out, and everyone should be crying, still. Teddy, she'll listen and listen.'

'Yes,' Kynaston said very softly. His eyes raked over her

with something like understanding. 'My God. I'd forgotten what it's like to be young, Alice.'

'I'm sixteen. That's not young.'

'Alice,' he said simply. 'It's so young.'

But she didn't want to hear him. 'I want to die too, but then Dad would be so angry with me. He wanted me to live, you see.' She pushed at her chest, as if beating breath into it. 'And that's why your novel about Daisy Buchanan isn't going to work.'

'What?' He sat back, as if she'd slapped him.

'She's not a real person,' said Alice, and, even if she didn't know what she was talking about, she didn't care; keeping him sweet didn't matter. 'She's a creation by – by a man. It's a cliché.' She hurried on, aware she had just told Wilder Kynaston his ideas were clichéd. 'She's a dream. You can't write a book about a dream – well, you can, 'cause people do it all the time. But you can't write a character study based on someone with no character. No one cares about Daisy Buchanan! Apart from Jay Gatsby, that is. In fact,' said Alice, warming to her theme, 'that's another thing about her. She has no sense of humour at all. Even when I'm so sad I'm in pain, I still find things to laugh about. Trust me, she has – why are you laughing?'

'Alice, forgive me. You touched a nerve, that's all. That's it.' He tapped his pen back and forth on the desk. 'Tell me something else. What are you thinking about now?'

'The apple,' Alice said. She suddenly wanted to laugh now too. She pointed to the bowl of apples on the desk. 'I think about the apples all the time. Our Bourton Pippins. They're – you know, my dad made these, really. Made sure they were the best variety for the soil, that they were healthy, that the right branches were chopped; he'd pick them, store them.' He was staring at her, and she went on. 'And they were just starting to grow when he died. The taut skin, the rough flesh . . . These apples, the ones we just picked – they're his. They grew after he died, because he started them off right. And I used to think about them, the pip and the pippin, the sweetness and the tannin . . . it's where he began and I end.' She laughed self-consciously. 'So . . . I only mean that I often think the apple is the world.'

'"*The apple is the world.*"' He started scribbling furiously. She sat in silence waiting for him to finish. After a while he put down his pen. 'Teddy was expelled from two schools. Thrown out of one for unladylike behaviour. For her tenth birthday she asked for mismatched socks. Ten pairs. She'd wear them every day, carefully mismatched. Did you know that?'

'No,' Alice said, delighted.

'It's true. And she was a hell-cat when they tried to get her to do anything else. She bit me once.'

'When?'

'Oh – it's an old story.'

'I like old stories,' she said, and for a second her chest tightened as she remembered the final treasure from her father – was this it? Something about Teddy that would reveal to her where it was? 'Tell me.'

'Not now. But she was real. Too real. Listen, Alice. I have a solution to your problem.'

'Can we stay?'

'In the gatehouse? Yes, until you finish high school.'

'Mr Kynaston. That's – too much. Thank you.' Her palms were sweating; she felt light-headed. 'Thank you so –' He held up his hand, cutting her off.

'I have one condition.' His eyes smiled kindly at her; she

wiped her hands on the leather seat. 'You tell your mother I've agreed you can stay until you finish school. She'll understand that.'

'My mom will be so grateful. She's mentioned a couple of times that you could use her help around the estate. I know you think my dad was the only one who could do it but, you know, she's an excellent housewife. Loves keeping things just so.'

'Are you like her, Alice?'

'Gosh, no. She does it, and now there's no one to keep it for,' said Alice, knowing this was laying it on thick but not caring.

He didn't seem to notice. 'So we're agreed, yes? And what I want in exchange –'

'In exchange?'

'Yes, Alice. My one condition. Yes, it's a good idea,' he said, almost to himself. 'Even the asking of it, it's art in a way. Alice? My dear girl. This is an exchange, you understand?'

'What is it?'

'In exchange for your security, I want to steal your mind. Perhaps that's a little too hackneyed a way of putting it. Will you come to the house every week and talk to me?'

'Talk to you?'

'Yes. Come by and tell me . . . about school. What books you're reading. What music you like – do you like jazz?' Alice shook her head, trying not to smile. 'I'm so out of touch, you see. Tell me about your father. About what you just told me. How you feel, how you think. The world of a young American girl growing into adulthood. You, my dear, are the apple. And I want to take a bite. I need to, to survive, to be honest. Now I know you think I'm a cliché, but does that simplistic fairytale symbolism make sense? What do you say?

Your mind – for your home. It's yours – until you graduate from high school, that is.' He smiled again. 'There are limits.'

Alice knew there was a reaction to this, a right answer, but she wasn't sure what it was. She knew that a great author was asking her for help, that he wanted to use her to help him write his book, that her mother would be proud and her father too – wouldn't he?

She didn't know. There was so much about him she hadn't known, it seemed, and now there was no choice. 'I'll do it,' she said, 'if you do right by us. You always said you'd help my dad. I know you did.'

Wilder Kynaston gazed down at the blotter, eyes fixed on nothing, gently stabbing the soft paper with the sharp point of his pen. He said softly, 'I'll look out for you both. I promise. And I reserve the right to terminate the agreement if I want.'

She shrugged. 'As do I.'

'Of course.'

'Shake on it now,' he said, and spat into his right hand.

She shook his hand, the wet, bubbling saliva between their palms, too dazed to grasp what she had just agreed to.

4

April 1967
Eighteen months later

'I've been thinking about whether long-lasting change can happen without revolution. Have some Turkish Delight,' Wilder had said to her the previous night.

'No, thank you, Mr Wilder.' Alice slid the plump, rosy square back across the desk toward him; it left a line of icing sugar, a sugar-snail trail.

'Go on. My publisher sends them to me. His driver buys them for me in Queens. He knows I love the stuff. Taste it. Cardamom and rose. Sweet as anything.' He took a bite, his eyes rolling. 'Taste it.'

She laughed, enchanted despite herself, as he rolled his tongue around the candy, brushing sugar off his chin. 'You see?' he said. 'Delicious.' As Wilder swivelled back around to face his desk, she snatched up a piece and took a small bite, swiftly swallowing the toffee-like sweet jelly. She didn't want him to see her taking pleasure in it.

At first, he had offered her candy, little treats, and she had taken them eagerly, for during those initial months she had wanted to please him, to give up good information, to be worth the exchange. But, about a year in, something had changed.

Perhaps it was the general senior year mood; perhaps it was the war; perhaps it was Alice herself. She had quickly grown tired of going to the house every week, tired of lying to her mom about college – she had no idea how they'd pay for it, and she knew she wasn't smart enough, not now. Since Bob's death mud seemed to have silted up her brain, and – though she grew taller and filled out her clothes, and her mom was kind of more cheerful while making no notable plans for the future, and boys asked her out and she even said yes sometimes, sitting in movie houses and Mackie's with other seniors she didn't care for – she was tired of it all. She was truly relaxed only with Dolores.

So coming to Valhalla to talk to Wilder Kynaston – to watch him sometimes gaze into the distance if something bored him, sometimes write intently if what she delivered was good – was a slow, degrading kind of march into soullessness, and still no one, apart from Dolores, knew. The candy stuck in her mouth, the sweetness cloying but delicious.

He glanced up at her again. 'Let's begin. Sit down, if you can fit yourself into the chair – you look like Cinderella in that skirt.'

'Okay. Thanks.' Lately she had moved away a little from the neat pinafore-and-loafers, early Dusty look and taken to wearing long, floral fabrics, skirts that skimmed her ankles that she bought at the thrift store or found at a church sale. She was coming up for eighteen, self-conscious about her height, and somehow long skirts seemed the best way to hide – everything. Her mother hated them – out of all proportion, Alice thought. Betsy dared not say the 'h' word ('hippie'), for to say it might conjure up something demonic, so she settled for 'drifter'. (That morning at breakfast: 'You're dressed like a drifter. A – a folk singer with a guitar.')

'What's new today?' Wilder said. 'Oh, by the way, I saw Elizabeth Finkelstein; she's my cousin, you know. She said there were four seniors now who've dropped out.'

'Five, if you count Tag Martin. He didn't exactly drop out, though.'

'What happened to Tag Martin?'

Alice spread out her skirts, trying to decide what to tell him and what to leave out. 'He ran away.'

'Reverend Martin's boy, that right?'

'Yep. He's in Vietnam.' Alice took another piece of Turkish Delight. 'Tag's a real nice kid but he's – he was real lost.'

That was what Dolores had said a couple years ago about Jack, actually. It was true of Tag too, and all of them maybe.

'What happened to him? I forget.'

She hated him then, sitting there with his pen, ready to scribble down what she said.

'Oh, it started with what happened the end of the last school year. Back in May. Jack Maynard and Tag Martin were given detention, because of disrespect in English class. But really they were tripping.'

Alice had stopped by the classroom, seeing Jack in there. She knew Tag of old too.

'The Maynard boy – he's older than you, yes?'

'Two years. He repeated his senior year last year.'

'Did you used to talk to them? What did you talk about that day?'

'We talked about poetry. They were both flunking English. They couldn't graduate without it.' And Jack hadn't graduated, even though he'd repeated the year. 'I guess that was the last time I saw Tag. Yeah. I helped them with the poem.'

Wilder looked at her over his glasses. 'What poem?'

71

'"To His Coy Mistress".'

'Of course,' he said.

She hated his verbal smirks. The way he hinted that he knew her better than she knew herself. '*Had we but world enough and time*,' he said softly, '*this coyness, lady, were no crime.*'

Alice was silent, remembering the scene in the classroom, though it was months ago. How she had drunk in Jack's appearance, his kind, careful smile for her, even as they both sat quite helpless, watching Tag sway from side to side, licking his lips like they were dry, staring intently at his out-stretched hand.

'So, like, this is some guy trying to persuade his girlfriend to put out,' Jack had said eventually, looking back at the textbook.

'It is,' she'd said. 'It's beautiful, really. I always think he'll show her a good time.'

She'd answered so frankly, her mind elsewhere, that he'd met her eyes, then rubbed the back of his neck awkwardly. 'Okay, thank you, Alice.'

'Hey,' she'd said, smiling back at him, refusing to be embarrassed. She didn't care any more, not about some things. 'It means what it means. I like it.'

'Alice Jansen,' he had said admiringly. 'Where'd you go learning poems like that?'

'*But at my back I always hear / Time's wingèd chariot hurrying near*,' Alice said. She'd slung her bag over her shoulder again and left, nodding at him with a secret little smile in the doorway.

'What are you smiling about?' Wilder said to her now.

'Nothing. Anyway, to finish my story about Tag. The headmaster realized he was high and kicked him out of school. He dropped out the week after that. Ran away to the Village.'

'The Village?'

'The East Village,' said Alice. 'That's where it's all going
down –'

'Jesus, Alice. I know about the East Village.'

'Okay. His family found out and his dad went down there.
They shipped him off to the army. They made him enlist. He's
been in Vietnam since September. He writes these letters to
Jack saying how they smoke weed all day and shoot Vietcong
when they feel like it. They go into villages, choose someone
and pick them off. Tag is, like, only two years older than me.
He's nineteen. He's a kid.'

She was acting cool but in reality found it hard to think of
Tag Martin, whom she'd known all her life, who loved *The
Addams Family* and Joan Baez like she did, and Bob Dylan
more than anything, but who most of all wanted to be free.
The idea of him in Vietnam, in uniform, was crazy. It was
frightening, that a gentle boy from a normal family could be
forced into a war on the other side of the world. 'He'll die
out there,' she said softly, but Wilder wasn't listening – he
was writing. Eventually he stopped and said, 'That's good.
What else?'

'So today, our first class was History –' she went on, recalling herself to the present.

'History. Is that with Elizabeth Finkelstein?'

'Yes,' she said.

Wilder put his hands flat on his chest: 'My apologies:
Please continue.'

Please continue. As if it was normal, sitting here on this
spring evening when she could be with Dolores, or paddling
at the edge of the river, or lying on her bed listening to music.

'Right. We learned about Elizabeth the First and Drake
today. Because later we're doing the Pilgrim Fathers.'

'Yes. Tell me more.'

'And I got to thinking about the people who left England and sailed to the New World. You know the *Mayflower* couldn't dock for weeks because of the weather. What was that like? To sail in a wooden ship for months and months across the vast ocean, without any radio signal or any mail, not knowing a thing about what was on the other side.' She paused and closed her eyes. 'I can't imagine it, can you? And then they did the same, to all the people they stole from Africa. Did exactly the same to them.'

'Not them, exactly, Alice.'

'It's a general point.'

At first, she'd been shy, so shy the sessions had not gone well. Gradually, she had understood that it would be over more quickly if she gave him what he wanted, despising herself at first for doing so. Lately, though, she had realized something else: she liked it.

She liked to tell him stories.

She liked someone finding her important, worth listening to. At school, the jocks ruled everything – their whims, their fitness, their choice of girl, or lunch, or car, all picked over. The cheerleaders had clout too, but not as much. And, once Alice had started to see that, she realized how fake the system was, loaded against others. Girls, mostly.

She'd said this to him early on and he had laughed. When she made him laugh, he rocked backward and forward, his hands on his knees, giving in to it, his eyes locking with hers, then throwing back his head – and she liked it, liked the feeling. Normally, boys didn't laugh at girls, unless you counted the time some sophomore, on a bet, pulled Carly Gianotti's T-shirt over her head during lunch break and everyone saw her bra.

'That's interesting,' Wilder said, when he'd stopped writing. He wrote down everything she said in his own version of shorthand. 'We are a nation founded on those who travelled across the sea. Who braved great hardships to get here. How does that change your outlook, I wonder.'

'There were already people here, though. The Indians.'

'Sure. But they didn't found the nation, did they? It's not relevant.'

'They didn't think they had to.' She cleared her throat. 'Look at the founding fathers, and what they were about.' She shrugged.

'How so?'

'Portraits of them, the ones in the school hall. There's one of Benjamin Franklin and I think he could just be someone I knew. A guy at school.'

'What do you mean?'

'They weren't grand old men. They threw everything out the window. Like now.'

He gave a short, scoffing, chuntering laugh. 'How's it like now?'

'Don't you see? They were young, they were hardscrabble, they fought. There're no rules. Everyone's in a fight for what you want, to change society, build it from the bottom up. That was what *they* were doing. That's what people today are trying to do too.'

'But what about those left behind?' he said, his eyes boring into her, his cheeks reddening. 'The normal hard-working American? Who doesn't want the wholescale chaos and disruption these hippies and so forth threaten to bring with them? Huh? What about them?'

'That's interesting.'

'How?'

'Because two minutes ago you told me the Indians were in the same position and that they weren't relevant to that period of history,' said Alice.

'Ah!' He sat back in his chair, fingertips pressed together, watching her. 'Yes. Very good.'

A bird called outside on the water. Inside, the room was warm, and light, and very still, no fresh air at all, as if everything else was sealed off.

'You mean a re-examination of the way we've sanctified the American Story.' He was writing it down. 'I think you're right. Yes, Alice. Very good. Have another Turkish Delight.'

She shook her head. From outside, she could hear the shouts that were always in the background, pricking her bubble. '*Ravenoose! Ravenoose! Ravenoose!*'

'You were asking about kids dropping out. Another girl left school this week. Her name is Mary-Jane McCarthy, and she went to New York. Her mom and dad went after her, to try to get her to come back, but she's joined the Hare Krishnas, I guess, and she says she's going on to California and never coming back.'

Sometimes she got the distinct feeling that what she told Wilder did not so much inspire and educate him as alarm him. 'Good lord. "Times are bad. Children no longer obey their parents, and everyone is writing a book." Do you know who said that?'

'No,' said Alice, annoyed that she wanted to know.

'Cicero. Two thousand years ago.' He carried on writing, furiously. She watched him, coolly. He was like a spider, hunched and scuttling and secretive.

'Right,' she said, picking up a pencil and starting to doodle on a blank sheet of paper: the stars and stripes of the flag, with little snails, ants and coiled snakes instead of stars. After a few moments, Wilder Kynaston rose from his chair and took the sheet from her. 'Thank you,' he said, his hand resting on hers for a moment.

'It's getting late; I have to get back. My mother and I are going to the city tomorrow morning. Can I go now, Mr Kynaston?'

But she didn't want to get back to her mother; she never wanted to go home. She wanted to check in on Teddy.

'Yes,' he said, looking down at his notes. 'I have enough for today. Goodbye. Enjoy your time in the city, Alice.'

On the way out she paused, looking for Teddy, but there was no sign of her. Sometimes Alice was too late, and she had gone upstairs. Today was one of those days.

It was the first time Alice had been in New York City for years. Her dad used to take her to Yankee Stadium. They'd get a corn dog and sit in the bleachers, he drinking beer and reading the paper in between yelling out for Mickey Mantle while Alice read her book, in between yelling out for Mickey Mantle.

What struck her after several years away was the scale of the place, the Chrysler and the Empire State buildings glinting like blades in the afternoon sun as the train glided over the roofs through the city. The majesty of Grand Central Station, the cream-white stone halls and the gold zodiac drawings high up on the turquoise-green ceiling, which she had entirely forgotten about. Like the roof of heaven.

They came out into Midtown and her mother looked around briefly. 'This way, honey. Come now, Alice, keep up.'

The streets smelled of cigarettes, of sweet burned nuts, of metallic warmth. The sun between buildings flashed and disappeared again, like beams from a lighthouse. Alice trotted after her mother, running a little when the lights flashed WALK. The avenues were so wide it seemed they'd never cross in time and would be mown down by the endless yellow taxis, honking at them. Adrenaline surged within her; it was like opening the window and breathing fresh air.

Yet the city was crowded, something crackling in the atmosphere. Outside a building on Fifth Avenue a group of young people in plaid shirts and rolled-up jeans and sneakers were holding placards and walking in circles, intoning monotonously: *Stop the war. Stop the war. Stop the war.* There were homeless people under awnings being moved on by cops with truncheons; more young people just drifting around, seemingly with no place to go; and, peppered among them all, office workers walking briskly past from lunch, in another world.

'Come on, Alice.' Her mother was someone different in the city, smart and collected. She wore her navy bouclé dress, court heels and a new neat little jacket she'd suddenly bought earlier in the year, slightly to Alice's surprise, though she had never mentioned it. She walked faster, her eyes darting around, a muscle ticking in the side of her mouth. Sirens seemed to follow them wherever they went, the wails slicing into Alice each time, but her mother didn't appear to notice. She nodded at the pretzel guy by the subway entrance, shook her finger in censorious fashion at a jaywalker as they were crossing Fifth Avenue and stopped a guy to ask for directions two blocks from Macy's – this was her mother, who refused to walk into Orchard to get a quart of milk these days.

'How long did you live here, Mom?'

'Three years? Look at that jacket, Alice, isn't it darling? Yes, three years, right up until the day I got married. Over there, you see? That street, leading off the square? That's

Broadway, and it takes you up to Times Square and the park and I lived on the Upper West Side, oh, it was fun.' Her mother looked up and clasped her hands together. 'Four girls; one apartment; our neighbour was an actor on Broadway; our other neighbour, he was a dear man, an antiques dealer who lived with his friend, such a nice man too. This was after the war, and I was at Brooks Brothers, and that's when I met your father.'

'Tell me the story again.'

'Oh, Alice – mind that manhole, honey. You've heard it so often before. He came in to buy a shirt; he tried to buy one with sleeves that were far too long, and I had him try on the right size, and he came out of the changing room and adjusted the cuffs and then he said –'

And they chorused together, '*I'll wear this shirt when I take you dancing.*'

'And I said, "When will that be?" and he said –'

'*On our third date.*'

'And he did,' she finished, and then there was an empty silence even in the roar of the city, and Alice looked down, down at the steam rising from the subway, from the depths of the earth. Something made her look up – perhaps the light falling differently on the ground – and she saw a vast hole in the grid of the block.

'Wait, Mom.'

'Alice, we have to get to Macy's –'

'Look, though, Mom. It's the old Penn Station,' Alice said. 'It was Dad's favourite building. Mom? Don't you remember?'

Her father had taken her to see the great Beaux-Arts Pennsylvania Station before they began the laborious, hateful work of tearing it down. It had been an entire block between Seventh Avenue and Eighth; a Classical temple

79

with colonnades of columns wrapped around it, wide gran-
ite portico entrances that made the passenger feel as though
they were participating in a great human project, that they
were worthy of the place. Huge, graceful caryatids, gods and
eagles, built for eternity, not to be torn down less than a century later, stood atop the roofs; she remembered walking
through the cool beautiful interior, bigger than any palace,
one of the final days it was open.

'Look, Allie. Look at it. This is the last of old New York,'
he'd said, and she'd stood up and stared at the vast exterior
leading to the concourse, far more opulent than Grand Central, the station *she* had thought the most beautiful place in
the world till that moment.

'They thought we were worth all this, you see,' he'd said.
She remembered it so well. Her small hand in his large one,
as the trucks rolled by, wafting the city heat in her face. Her
father had bought her a doughnut from a vendor by the
subway station – the smell of it, dough and sugar, the grease
on her fingers.

Betsy Jansen had put her foot down when Alice told her,
or rather half mumbled to her, that she was going to the
prom – which, of course, Betsy was delighted about – with
Frank Logan, a deeply serious young man from a good family,
which Betsy was even more delighted about. Frank Logan
said things like 'Yes, ma'am' and 'Golly gosh' and wore a
jacket with leather elbow patches. He had stopped Alice at
school a couple of weeks earlier and asked her to make sure
she was 'dressed like a lady'.

'So many girls these days don't keep themselves looking
fresh and pretty,' he'd said, wiping his hands with a pressed
cotton square from his blazer pocket, looking darkly at

Dolores, standing like a guard dog next to Alice, glowering at him, chewing her gum.

Dolores was not going to the prom. She said the whole thing was lame. She'd rather watch *Bewitched* on TV and smoke sitting in her bedroom window, listening to Marvin and Tammi, and drink some of her mom's Jack Daniel's that she secretly mixed into Coke. Though Alice still clung to a faded dream of what the prom would be like, she couldn't help thinking that Dolores's evening sounded much better.

But Betsy was so excited that her daughter was going to the prom. And, a week before this outing, she'd asked Alice what she was going to wear, and, when Alice said she was planning on making a long halter-neck dress out of some old curtain material she'd found at the Goodwill, Betsy had turned pale and, hesitantly, opened her metal money box to reveal fifty dollars.

'Honey, you're eighteen in June. I want to get you something real special,' she'd said solemnly. 'I want to buy you a dress, for the prom.'

'Mom –' Alice had begun, but then she'd happened to glance up and saw Betsy's pink, heart-shaped face, and all she could think of was how her mom made such a fuss every Halloween, baking cookies for all the kids; and how she made the garlands at Christmas, string threaded with nuts and silver paper cut-out stars, to hang up for the visitors they rarely had; and how, once, when Alice had measles, she had come down in the night, hot and confused, to find her father asleep on the couch and her mother scrubbing the range, knuckles white, on her knees, humming to herself, and how she'd picked up Alice and put her back in bed and then brought her some warm milk with nutmeg in it; and how strong she was, and how she didn't look it.

'Where did you get fifty dollars, Mom?'

'Here and there, you know,' her mother had said. 'My mom left me some money, and Mr Kynaston found he owed us a few dollars too. And there's some of your dad's money left – only a little – but . . .' She had trailed off. 'Please let me buy it for you,' Betsy had said quietly. 'I'd really like to.'

'Sure,' Alice had said, not knowing what else to say. 'I'd like that.'

After almost ninety minutes in Macy's they emerged, Alice holding a fabric shopping bag, inside of which was a gun-metal-grey silk dress with cap sleeves and a stiff skirt to the floor. Though it had a gathered waist, it was still curiously reminiscent of a sack, and Alice knew she would never wear it again, but it was the compromise that both could live with.

They went to a restaurant near Fifth Avenue, opposite Rockefeller Plaza, where her mother said Alice could have what she wanted. Alice was exhausted, but also delighted, feeling like a kid again. She ordered meatballs, a Coke and three scoops of ice cream. A lady at the next table was eating alone, reading the newspaper and smoking; when the waiter brought her meal, he said, 'A Waldorf salad, ma'am,' and set down a silver plate of green salad topped with shavings of Parmesan and chicken; and Alice realized she should have ordered something sophisticated, that, for all her thoughts of at last being grown up now she was almost eighteen, she was still, disappointingly, a child who ordered meatballs and ice cream.

The waitress withdrew and left them smiling politely at each other awkwardly, as always when some new iteration of their changed family occurred. Alice swallowed, tasting bile in her throat. Now was the time.

'Mom,' said Alice. 'Can we talk about what's happening next year?'

Betsy busied herself pouring some water. 'When you go off to college? I will miss you. But you must come back and visit.'

'That's partly it, Mom. College. But, also, I wanted to ask you where you're going to go?'

'Me? Go?' Her mother looked confused. 'Why would I go anywhere?'

'But you know what Mr Kynaston said. We have to be out, and the time agreed is when I graduate from high school.'

'Oh, I know what he *said*,' her mother said. 'But there's nothing we can do about it for now, is there? Wilder won't evict us, I'm sure of it.'

Alice changed tack. 'There's no money for college either.'

'We'll find money for it, if that's what you want.'

'Mom, from where?'

'You'll get a scholarship,' her mother said. She seemed remarkably unflustered. 'Your dad always said you were the brightest kid in the year, honey.' She smiled at Alice.

Alice wanted to scream. 'Mom, that was when he was alive. Everything's changed. There're other kids whose SATs are better, who've done the applications, been to the colleges.' Now it was here, she had to say it. 'I – I haven't even applied for financial aid or for scholarships. I haven't done a thing about it. It's April, Mom – that dance is over. I don't know what you think's going to happen, but I'm not going to Berkeley in the fall.' She tensed, waiting for the inevitable questions, the hammering blows of disappointment, but her mother didn't say anything. 'Aren't you mad?'

'I'm not mad,' her mom said. 'I wondered why you stopped mentioning it, but I'm not mad.'

'So –'

'Look, Allie, there's more to life than college. Maybe you'll have to get a job, honey. When your dad's little pot of money finally goes, we have to have something to live on, after all.'

Alice peered at her mother, but Betsey was drinking water, and her expression was unreadable. 'Mom, I stopped mentioning it because I knew you were worrying about money. I kinda . . . didn't know what to do.'

She hadn't known what to do, and now it was April, and it turned out almost everyone else had their offers in and they were going to Notre Dame or Stanford or North Carolina or other places, catering college, teachers' colleges. They were talking about long drives and sororities, majors and campuses. They were all leaving.

And Alice, for the past two years, had got up every day and gone to school, praying someone else would tell her what to do. But slowly, inexorably, change had happened, leaving her behind, and every day she'd known it, and every day she'd hated herself a little more because of it. She had wanted to show her dad what she could do, and she had let him down. She knew there was no money, and she knew her mother couldn't help her, and that her brain didn't work as well as her dad had thought it did. There was no point telling anyone else because they'd say she was crazy.

'Allie.' Her mother patted the dress next to her and stared at her daughter, eyes full of concern. 'You shouldn't worry about money. We'd have found it. Somehow.'

'Mom,' Alice said, using every last ounce of her patience. 'There's no money.'

'I'm certain there *is*, if we just look for it.'

Alice couldn't understand why she was being so upbeat. 'Do you mean the orchards?' she said. They never looked

at the rows of apple trees any more, standing unkempt, surrounded by tiny saplings of pine and sycamore that grew
taller and edged closer every day. 'Did you get something for
them, in the end?'

Her mother gave a short, barking laugh.

'Honey, Wilder owns them. He bought them back off the
bank after they wrote off the debt. He got a good deal.'

The waitress brought their drinks, and Alice took a long
sip of Coke, enabling her to gather her thoughts.

'So Mr Kynaston made money on them?' she said. 'If Dad
bought them from him in the first place, and he bought them
back at a knock-down price, isn't that –'

'Oh, hooey. Who knows.' Now Betsy's eyes were bright
with sudden anxiety. 'You know I hate all that financial business, Allie. And those orchards, they're no good. Might as
well tear them out and put houses on them. That's what I
told Wilder anyway.'

Alice let the wave rush over her again. She took a deep
breath. 'I'm not sure Dad would have wanted that.'

'Oh, Allie. I don't think he would have, no. But it happened.'
Her mother tore at a little flap of skin by her thumbnail with
her teeth, leaving a tiny red ribbon behind. 'Now listen. I
know college was important to you and your dad. But . . .'

'Yes?' Alice prompted her.

Her mother looked down at the pinhead of blood on her
thumb almost in surprise. 'I wish I could have advised you
better, honey.' She took a deep breath. 'I didn't know what to
do, these past two years, I know I got it wrong.'

'No, Mom –'

Her mother waved her hand away. 'So maybe college isn't
happening – it's gone.' She said it as though they'd just decided
to throw away some meatloaf. 'But there's other things you

could do. You could help me around the house and with the Kynastons. We could be what your father was, and Mavis too. Then maybe we wouldn't have to leave! Because Mr Kynaston sure needs that help. So does Teddy. Look how hard it is for them this past year or so since Mavis went, and your dad –'

The waitress arrived with the food and started to set it down on the table.

'Mom, I don't want to help with the Kynastons.'

'Teddy's your friend, isn't she? I thought you liked spending time with her.'

'She's not –'

She thought of the last time she'd been to see Teddy, just for Teddy, to tell her about the prom, because Teddy liked facts, loved hearing stories. But, as ever, her brother had appeared in the doorway, and it was impossible to have the kind of conversations they used to have, impossible to explain how particular, sweet and strange their friendship was – nothing that Alice could explain to anyone else.

You're using me, dearest girl, as a repository for your secrets, but I'm using you, as a conduit for a life I'd love to live. Don't fret – we are using each other.

'I want to ask about the treasures, Teddy – I know it's a couple of years now, but are you sure you can't remember? Did my dad give you anything to give to me? Before he died?'

But Teddy was always silent, never answered those questions, pursed her lips and turned her head away.

Curiosity killed the cat, my dear Alice. Killed it dead.

'I want us to have our own life,' Alice said to her mother. 'Can't you see? I want you to have a place of your own, for

86

us to be secure. Put up our photos of Dad. You could have a cat, Mom! You've always wanted a cat!'

But her mother wasn't listening, she knew. Alice cleared her throat. Her head was pounding, and it was so hard to say these things, to reprimand her like this, to tell the truth about how lazy she'd been, how she'd let her parents down, their dreams for her gone. 'The Kynastons aren't – they're not our family. Dad landed us there but –' and for the first time in a long while she felt a white-hot, searing poker of anger, jabbing at her, toward her father. 'I'm tired of helping them out already. I'm tired of going there, of you giving them free labour, cleaning, doing his little tasks for him, me giving him my spare time . . . It's not my home. Or yours. It's theirs. I want my own stories. My own place in the world. Don't you see that?'

'It's a nice idea, Allie,' said her mother absently, soberly. 'But, for the while, I think things have to stay the same.' She looked up at the waitress, laden with their food on bright plastic plates. 'Thank you so much! Isn't this fun.'

'Mom,' said Alice. 'Thank you for the dress, and the lunch.'

'Oh,' said Betsy turning, her face lighting up. 'I'm having the best time, honey.' She put her hand on Alice's arm. 'I don't think we settled the question of what job you'll do next year. I'll start asking around. And Allie –' Her face took on that distant look. 'I think, perhaps, college isn't for you. It is for some people, just not you, honey. There, I'm so glad we've agreed. Now eat up, Allie. Enjoy it!'

As they were leaving, there were shouts and banging noises from out on the street and a motley group of young people rushed past. Then they heard screaming.

'What's that?' Alice's mother said, clutching the prom dress bag as close to her as she could.

'Protests,' said the waitress, tearing the check off the stub and giving it to them. 'They're every day at the moment.'

People had gathered on the corner by Fifth Avenue. Alice looked at the scene: the contrast of an elderly matron in a powder-blue suit and large diamond brooch entering Bergdorf, a doorman holding the door open with a reverent salute, and young people below, one of whom, a girl Alice's age, was screaming as a policeman dragged her away. She had on a floral skirt, dirty and torn, and a checked shirt tied at the waist. She was clutching something in her hand, which, in a few moments, Alice could see was a bunch of dirty dead flowers and leaves. *I wish I had a camera*, she thought.

'Is she okay?' Alice said, but the girl suddenly stood up and pushed over the cop and, before he could get his bearings, she too had vanished into the crowd, quicker than a whirling dervish.

'Come, Alice, don't get distracted,' said her mother, tugging at her elbow. 'Let's go.'

'Mom,' said Alice. 'One moment –' She broke away and walked toward the knot of young people, ignoring her mother's cries.

'Tag?' she said to a young man thrusting a placard into the air with considerable force and shouting louder than the others. 'Hey! Tag Martin? That you?'

The young man turned around. He was in military fatigues, torn and utilized into a sleeveless jacket, shorts, and a T-shirt. He had on army boots. A livid scar, still white and red, puckered the side of his face and ran into his hair and, with a shock that made her feel like she'd fallen through the floor, Alice saw that where his ear should be was a smooth, white stretch of skin, with a gaping hole and a little polyp sticking out, like a tiny piece of cream-white corn.

'Hey, Alice! How are you?'

'Tag! I thought you were in –' She blushed and looked down. 'Silly question.'

'Wounded,' he said with a twisted smile. 'Came back last month.'

'But we –' She stopped. We prayed for you in school, she wanted to say, and girls cried, and guys said, 'That Tag! He's a helluva guy!' but it sounded so childish. 'Tag, where are you living? Aren't you at your folks'?'

'I'm not going back there just yet, Alice,' he said, nodding. 'Just spending some time in the city. I'm helping some souls down in Chelsea – they're building, making some art. I go and help them. You know.' He wiped his nose on the back of his hand.

Alice didn't know what to say to him, what to give him. 'Here,' she said. She fumbled in her bag for the roll she had saved from the diner for the train. 'Are you hungry?'

'Aw, Alice,' Tag said, smiling at her, but he took the roll quickly. 'Don't worry about me. You all good?' His unfocused eyes moved across to Alice's mother, who had appeared beside Alice. 'Hello, Mrs Jansen. Good to see you, ma'am.'

'Tag,' said her mother, nodding curtly at him. 'Alice, honey –'

'I wrote to Jack,' said Tag, his eyes ranging past Alice and up between the skyscrapers, to the blue, blue sky. 'I wrote him a couple times. Told him to come down here. Check out the scene. You know?' He sniffed. 'It's cool, man. It's all a really cool scene. The fighting, that wasn't for me, not so much –'

They had played all their lives together, running through

sprinklers and throwing sand in sandboxes and sitting together at birthday parties, and this was more than she'd heard Tag say in years. Alice nodded. 'Tag, you should come back. Your folks'll be worried.'

'Don't they know you're here?' said Alice's mother.

'Oh, they know!' Tag said, too loudly. 'They know for sure! But for some reason they ain't so keen on me coming back now I'm not doing exactly what they say!' He wiped his nose with his arm again, snickering, half furious, half hysterical.

'I shall see,' said Mrs Jansen, 'about asking a member of the NYPD for assistance,' and she stepped away from them for a moment. 'Stay there, Alice.'

'You were always nice, Alice,' Tag said, when her mother left. 'You'd like the scene. Down in the Village. Come to St Mark's Place. Come to the Bowery. Check out the scene.'

'Okay. But, Tag, you have to stop saying scene,' said Alice, wanting to inject levity.

'No, don't be like that,' he said, shhing her. 'It's good, Alice. Everyone's kind. Everyone's a lost soul, come from somewhere. We're given freedom to work. To dream. We can build a world that's honest and pure.' He patted the pocket of his filthy, torn fatigues, out of which poked a sheaf of paper. 'I been drawing a lot. Cartoons, mostly, about what I saw.'

'That's great,' said Alice. 'I'd love to see them.'

'They're mostly of decapitated Vietcong and a dog I saw, which they'd cut to shreds . . . They chopped its tail off and they made it into a tailfeather to wear.' His eyes were blank, even though his pupils were enormous. 'It helps me. Drawing. No one making me do what I don't want to do. I'm free. And you can be too. You're talented, Alice. You'd like it there. You could do anything . . . Design posters, chairs, tables . . . heheheh. That's a good beginning to a song.' He hummed gently to himself. 'There's a chick, outside the church, she's always there, she gave away her shoes, and she's waiting to see if she gets a pair back, then she's walking to Monterey, you know? She has a guitar, and she writes songs, and it's – it's beautiful.' Tears were in his eyes. 'I love being here. I love them all, Alice. You'd be welcome.'

Alice looked down at his sign. It said PEACE. The other side said LOVE. And she had seen those words written down on placards before, heard them joked about, but, in the lop-sided, uncertain lettering held in Tag's quavering hands, she found them moving for the first time.

'There, officer,' she heard her mother's voice say. 'He's a runaway. I know his parents –'

Tag gripped her arm, his strength surprising, and she looked down and saw the tattoos, blue-blooded on his biceps, and how the sight of them roused something inside her unexpectedly, her attraction even more surprising than Tag's strength. 'I have to go,' he said, and he nudged her hair aside with his nose and whispered in her ear. 'No. 5, St Mark's Place. The East Village, Alice, that's where we all head. It's a safe place. I'll give you LSD. I'll show you how . . . You'll love that. And making it with a guy. I'll do it to you if you want. You'll love that too. I . . . hey, just come see me. You were the one girl who'd get it, the one girl whose mind would have been open to it . . . Hey, tell Jack! Tell him!'

'Alice, don't let him go, dear! I want this officer to –'

Alice walked away, watching Tag melt into the crowd, swimming back into the blobbed mass of protesters, all curiously alike in their individuality.

5

'So Alice, what was the prom like?'

'It was good. It was fun. I can't stay long tonight, Mr Kynaston.'

Wilder nodded. 'Of course. Have another sip of rye.'

'No, thank you.'

'What's up, Alice? You don't seem yourself.'

She met his gaze. '*I have of late – but wherefore I know not – lost all my mirth, forgone all custom of exercises; and, indeed, it goes so heavily with my disposition that this goodly frame, the earth, seems to me a sterile promontory.*'

Wilder swallowed the rest of his drink, watching her. He was silent for a moment, before lightly tapping the rim of the tumbler with his fingers, then, moving his fingers to his pad, he scrabbled for his pen. His eyes did not leave her face. 'Very good. I see. Did you drink alcohol at the prom?'

She hesitated. 'Yes.'

'Ah.' The pen scribbled across the pad; his eyes briefly breaking contact with hers. 'I won't say a word. Who gave it to you?'

'Not my date.'

'I forget who your date was – the Maynard kid?'

'No, he –' Alice looked down, batting away an idea of Jack Maynard in his tux, his wild, floppy blond hair, his dark velvet eyes, his unhappiness. 'No, he's not at school now, remember? I went with Frank Logan.'

'Some extra unsolicited information; excellent. The Logans, the very definition of upstanding citizens. Did anything interesting happen at the prom? By which I mean, did anyone disgrace themselves, was the band good, did a student misbehave, and so forth?'

'Carly Gianotti kissed the Math teacher,' said Alice. She shrugged. 'She's wanted to forever. They don't know, at the school. So don't tell anyone.'

'I will not betray Carly Gianotti's secrets,' he said, in a tone she found patronizing. 'What's he called, this teacher?'

Alice shrugged.

'Okay. And Jack Maynard . . . you know you always pause when you mention his name. Have you noticed that? I presume not.'

'I don't think that's relevant.'

Wilder poured himself another whiskey. He chewed his lip again, and leaned forward. 'But it is, Alice. Under the terms of our agreement it is. May I ask, since we're talking frankly, why you're restricting your replies to me?'

Alice let her hands drop to her lap. 'I suppose I wonder when the deal is up. When you have enough information.'

'I didn't realize you were so keen for it to end.'

'You think it's my choice to be here? I think *you're* forgetting the terms of our deal. You wouldn't kick my mom and me out of the gatehouse, if I let you suck my brain dry.'

'Your father always said you minded about fairness.' He worked his teeth over the flesh inside his bottom lip, watching her, his jaw moving back and forth. 'Okay. I see. It's fair enough. You're finished. I understand.'

'I didn't mean it like that. I just want to know how much longer.'

'Don't you like coming here?'

'I used to.' She looked out the window, on to the porch.

'You don't ever lie, do you? It'll get you into trouble, Alice. Listen, I'm not sure how useful it is for me to talk to you much longer anyway. You're clever, as you must know, but lately there's a lack of – of *freshness* about you. Perhaps I need some girl from the Midwest who's never even seen a city. I'm very grateful to you – but let's wind it down, shall we?'

She hated him all of a sudden. The hours she'd spent in that room, wasted hours, giving him her stories, when she could have been reading or bicycling into town to see Dolores or studying . . . studying for college. She had given herself away, the best part of herself, and for what?

She shrugged. 'I'll give you the answers you want. Carly Gianotti kissed Mr Fernandez. In the janitor's closet. She has the key. Frank Logan was my date, and he's an ass. Mr Collins from *Pride and Prejudice*, only without the charm. He drank too much whiskey – he had a hipflask with him – and tried to kiss me. The prom itself wasn't much fun. I couldn't . . .' Her voice was thick, for she knew he would get it, would understand, and she hated him for that too. 'I couldn't seem to enjoy myself. It all seemed so fake. So *silly*, when there's kids dying in Vietnam and we're all hurtling toward war and death is all around us. These girls getting hysterical about their boutonnières and what guy . . . Why do they have some idea of the perfect guy? What's the point?' She could hear her voice getting louder. 'With broad shoulders and a lock of hair that falls in his face and – and a nice house and . . . I don't know, kind eyes and a soft voice. Who likes the same books you do, *Lord of the Rings*, and – and so – so forth.' She trailed off. 'All this is – it's crap, that's what it is!'

Wilder lowered his drink, and for the first time ever eyed her with sympathy. 'Oh, kid,' he said. 'You've got it bad, haven't you? Forget about him.'

'I –' she began.

'I mean it. Think about the future. What comes next. College! I heard – is it true? I heard you hadn't applied to college this year.'

'Nope.'

'Why not, may I ask?'

'I should have. But I didn't. So I'm staying home with Mom. Just Mom and me. I'll get a job; we'll move out; you'll be free of us.'

'Is that what you want?'

Alice shrugged again.

'Is that what your mom wants? I don't think so, judging from what she says.'

'When have you spoken to my mother about it?'

'We're friends,' Mr Kynaston said. 'Betsy is worried about you. She wants you to be happy. You should be going to drive-ins. Dancing with boys in the moonlight and accepting roses and having poems written about you . . . You should think about college, Alice – isn't there someone you can ask for help?'

'No one,' she said.

'I bet that's not true. But, then again –' He was staring at her. 'Perhaps you'd be happier staying here. Perhaps college isn't right for you. Hmm?'

The rank hypocrisy of what he was saying was so obvious she didn't know how to point it out without being rude. So Alice stood up. She remembered how it felt to walk away from the prom, walk into the night and leave it behind. How it was allowed to shake Frank's hand, to say, 'Thank you for

95

a pleasant evening, I'll walk home,' to insist on that, how it was allowed. How you didn't actually have to do what people wanted sometimes.

'But how will you get home?' Frank had said, eyes wide with disgruntled irritation.

She'd nodded at a dark, lounging figure waiting in the driveway, alone among the couples walking down the drive, arms around each other, the guys nodding at one another, the girls calling out shrill farewells to their friends.

'Dolores has come to pick me up.' She'd raised her hand at Dolores, who jangled the keys to her mother's pick-up truck, and called out to her.

'Allie! You ready to go?'

And now Alice could hear her voice again, calling. She shrugged on her jacket.

'Hey – Mr Kynaston. I think you have enough material from me. I have to go now. I think that, yep, it's best this is the last time. Thank you for the whiskey and thank you for everything.'

She caught a fleeting glimpse of his face, the surprise on it and then the understanding smile.

'You're making a dramatic exit,' he called. 'I get it, I know. You want me to say that the book won't be finished without you.'

'It's nothing to do with you,' she said. 'Thank you very much.' She leaned over toward his chair and held out her hand. He took it, stroking her palm with his middle finger, and she jumped.

'Goodbye, Mr Kynaston,' she called, and she closed the door gently behind her. And that, she told herself, was that.

Teddy was sitting on the porch, and when Alice walked past she saw her and sat with her a while. She didn't say much, just sat with her. Once, Teddy leaned over and patted her hand. '*Ravenoose*,' she said quietly.

I think you've made a mistake, Alice my dear.

'I know I have,' Alice said. 'I just can't see what it is. But I've screwed up. I can see that.'

I adored college. It got me away from here. Important, I think, to get away from here. While you can.

Teddy made a noise of distress. She tugged at Alice's hand. Alice pulled away. 'Sorry,' she said. 'I think it's too late for that.'

6

It was July when everything started to fall apart.

The Maynard family owned Crossings, the grand old house up from Valhalla. The Maynard money was in railroads, and they must have seen the way things were going, because they had built Crossings on half an acre of land high up on the bank, encircling it with trees, and, before the railroad came through, a bridge and a small stone man-made beach jutting out on to the river. A jetty was there, and a pontoon, and a beach house. It was where they had Fourth of July and swimming parties. Alice had been before, when she was a little girl, but it was more the kind of place the Hickses and the Kynastons had gone to, and the Rockefellers and the Vanderbilts, and all the grand families who built their mansions nestled in the cool woods along the Hudson.

That summer of 1967, Alice was in the gang that hung out at Crossings. Jack Maynard's mom was in Europe visiting family (rumour had it the 'family' was a well-known drying-out clinic in Switzerland); his father was in the city finalizing a deal (waiting for his mistress's baby to arrive); and Jack's big sister, Ellen, was at college (she was actually at college). Jack's meals were made for him by Lola, the maid, and he drove himself to town and into the city. He wasn't doing anything a year after flunking out of school. He went into the city to see Tag, to hang out. His hair was longer. He spoke less than ever. Sometimes, Dolores went driving with him, upstate, across the Tappan Zee Bridge, or up to Rhinebeck.

She said he wanted company, and, besides, she liked the way he chewed gum.

Alice had never told Dolores how much she liked Jack. She wasn't sure if Dolores knew or not, and it was pathetic of her to mind, when Dolores had gone out with him first. She felt, unreasonably, that she should be more mature than other kids her age, given what she'd been through. So she couldn't explain how the sight of them driving off together made her want to stamp her feet, scream out loud and fall to her knees crying at how unfair it was.

'Alice? Where you off to, honey?'

'I'm going up to the Maynards' again, Mom. Do you need me?' Silence. 'Mom?'

But her mother didn't answer.

Up in her room Alice brushed her hair, tying it into a long ponytail, and stared at herself in the tiny round mirror. She found herself gazing at her face, utterly bored by it, by the sameness of everything, and her eye fell on the view over her shoulder of the shelf of little treasures. It had been months since she'd paid them any attention, not even dusting them. The truth was she didn't like to any more; every time she did she was reminded of her dad, and his last day, and the way it ended. But today, with the summer light playing in her small, bare bedroom, she did, picking up each of them in turn. The first thing she took off the cluttered shelf was the silver oval pill box, which contained a lock of her father's hair as a child.

How strange, holding something that had been part of him, from long before she was born. When had it been cut from his head? Where had he been, what room in his family's house? Who had cut it? And what would happen to it, to the shelf? What would happen to her? What would happen if she died, and there was no one to remember him, to carry on his name? Oh, not like Jack's dad, with his obsessions over Princeton and West Point, but rather a line of connection to Dad, with his shining kind eyes and his flat feet that could kick up in the air, his baritone crooning of 'I Have Confidence' and 'Put on Your Sunday Clothes', his smile as he tackled a Rita Hayworth, the sound of him, change jangling in his pockets . . . Who was there? Alice's hands shook; her palms were sweaty. She brushed a tear from her cheek; she hadn't even noticed she was crying. How stupid. Breathing heavily, as though she'd been sprinting, Alice picked up the rest of the treasures, one by one.

The blue-and-white cats, holding hands, their strangely human faces, the delicate brushwork that she had spent hours some nights staring at. The hopeful expression of the tiny grey-and-white Scottie dog. The dormouse, clinging like a monkey to the ear of corn, the thick varnish that made it glossy. And her old friend the black bird. She remembered something – a fleeting thought, gone in an instant.

But – ravens. The black bird wasn't a blackbird at all. It had a thick beak, dark eyes. It was a raven. She'd been wrong, all these years –

'*Allie! Come here, honey!*'

Her mother's voice, sharp and sudden on the stairs, made her jump and Alice's hands, sweaty from the heat, slipped as she was placing the little bird back on the shelf. It fell to the ground, knocking off the Scottie dog, the Labrador and the dormouse with it. They shattered, cracking into small, neat clumps of half-shiny, half-dull china. Only the raven survived intact, one wing neatly chipped.

Alice gazed at the raven's head, smaller than the nail of her forefinger.

'Allie! Can you hear me? Come down to the kitchen, would you, before you go?'

'Sure, Mom.' Alice picked up the broken pieces of the other animals and put them in an envelope, one of the Labrador's foolish bright black eyes smiling at her as she sealed it shut, then wrapped it in newspaper. She did not cry.

'Mr Kynaston came by yesterday,' her mother said, as she entered the kitchen.

'Why?'

'It's his house, Allie. He can come by when he wants.' Alice, in the doorway, saw the tips of her mother's ears were very slightly pink. 'He's organizing the Cemetery Supper. He wants me to help. And, since you've graduated and you have no plans, I thought it'd be nice if you helped out too.'

'Oh,' Alice said. She could not see, yet, the moves Wilder Kynaston had played, but she saw with a blinding realization that she was in the game, and was three or so moves behind him. 'Of course he wants you to help. You're his new Mavis, only he doesn't have to pay you.'

Betsy dabbed at her cheeks and forehead. 'This heat! Now, Allie, don't be so unkind. Mr Kynaston's a good man. He had his literary agent with him. John' – her mother screwed up her eyes, trying to remember, like a schoolgirl reciting times tables – 'yes, John Matheson. A real nice gentleman. They're making plans for the new book, and he was taking him on a walk and wanted to come by and visit. Allie, Mr Kynaston asked if you'd drop by the house. He has something he wants to ask you.'

'No.' Alice picked up her bag. 'I'm not going up there again, tell him.'

'He might be able to help you with late applications to college –' Alice turned away, unable to face it. 'He says he wants to help you –'

'He can whistle for it.'

'Alice Jansen, how rude, when he's been so kind.'

'Oh biscuits,' said Alice furiously. 'I'm not being rude. He's using you, Mom. And me. You told me not to bother about college and now you're saying I should start over with applications all because Wilder Kynaston thinks it's a good idea?' Alice opened the trash can and dropped in the wrapped-up newspaper. It landed with an echoing thud. She tried not to think about her treasures, shattered and broken, lying all in bits at the bottom of the trash. 'There's no money. I have to go. Dolores is waiting for me.'

Alice and Dolores walked up to Crossings past Valhalla, along the shaded path. She avoided looking at the house, in case Wilder Kynaston was looking out for her, though, even as she thought this, she told herself she was being ridiculous, behaving as though he was the Big Bad Wolf. But she was sure then that she heard Teddy talking and yelling as she often did, her flat voice floating out through the trees to her.

'*Ravenoose! Ravenoose!*'

'You're quiet, Allie.'

'Sorry.' Alice was trying not to think of the smashed treasures, the empty spaces, bare circles on the dusty shelves.

'You don't need to apologize.'

Dolores switched her bag over to her other arm. She scratched her cheek, like she was trying to think of what to say. 'Alice, I saw Mrs Finkelstein yesterday. She was at the beauty parlour.'

'Mrs Finkelstein was?' Alice tried to hide her surprise. Their history teacher was brisk and minimalist in appearance, not someone who would have enjoyed having a round mirror held up to her hair and told, 'My dear! You look *divine.*'

'She was there for a haircut. I was helping Mom washing hair, and she asked me if we were friends.'

'She did?'

'She said to tell you something.'

Why did people bother her, when she wanted to be left alone? She knew she wasn't going to like it, whatever it was. 'What?'

'She said . . . Mr Williams had said you – you were the only kid not going to college. Of the ones who could, you know. And she said it was wrong, and that you were to call her – she's in the phone book – 'cause she knows a way she can help you. With scholarships, financial aid and all that.' Dolores stopped. 'I'm sorry, I know you don't like talking about it.'

'I'm getting a job in the fall, Dolores. I'm just taking the summer. I don't care about college.'

'Well, Mrs Finkelstein said you should be going to college.'

'I wanted to. But I'm not, so you don't need to keep on about it.'

Alice didn't want to discuss it. The mood between them was sour, the weather too hot.

'Okay,' Dolores said, nodding. 'But, Allie – will you talk

to her, to Mrs Finkelstein? Oh, go on, Allie. She was really nice about you. She wants to see you. Here's her phone number.'

'Maybe.' Alice stuffed the number in her pocket and, suddenly hugely grateful for Dolores in her life, linked arms with her. 'You know what my dad used to say?'

'What?'

'"You didn't come this far just to come this far."'

'I like that,' said Dolores. 'I wish I'd really known him, Allie.'

'He'd have liked you.' She squeezed her friend's hand. 'Thanks, Dolo.' Then she stopped. Something was shining in the still muddy gap between the hedge where the path forked, the left tine going over the railroad and toward the river, the right a continuation of the path. Alice bent down and picked it out of the mud. 'Huh,' she said.

'What the hell is that?'

Alice thought Dolores might recognize the small metal figurine but no. She held her palm up, flat. 'It's Merlin. Hey, Merlin.'

Dolores looked at her like she was crazy. 'It's filthy, Alice, don't put it in your pocket. What's that noise coming from the river?'

'They're playing games, I guess,' said Alice dully. She could hear one of Jack's friends, Andy Flaherty, a jock who prided himself both on his status as star linebacker and his friendship with Jack. 'They're –' And then they heard a cry of shock, and raised voices, people talking all at once. Alice slid Merlin into her shorts pocket and they hurried toward the river, toward the central golden bowl of light, feet slapping on the soft ground.

*

Jack had skipped out. Gone West, to San Francisco.

He had been planning to join Tag in the city for weeks apparently, Andy Flaherty said. He and Tag were talking all the time. Jack had wanted to get out of here forever. Alice knew that. He and Tag had planned a road trip to California, before returning to New York and setting up a refuge, a commune for other young people.

But Tag was not coming with him. For Tag was dead, murdered in an apartment in the East Village with a seventeen-year-old runaway from Connecticut called Emily. Both their throats slashed. The cops had said it was a drugs deal gone wrong. Jack knew. He had been told by Tag Martin's sister the day before.

Andy Flaherty said, 'Jack said he wasn't living this life any more. He said he had to get away.' He gazed out across the river, shaking with the shock. 'He didn't say anything to me about when he'd be going. Nothing at all.' He shivered. 'He didn't say anything. Why'd he do it?'

All Alice could hear was Tag's laugh, high-pitched, nervous, and see his kind face, his beautiful drawings; she remembered how he and Jack used to laugh together, how Jack looked more relaxed with Tag than he did with other people. She put her hands over her eyes. She would not think about it. She just wouldn't think about any of it.

Dolores pressed her hands to her face. She was white with shock. 'Poor Tag,' she whispered, and her hand, stealing toward Alice's, clutched Alice's fingers, and they stood together, clinging to each other.

They stood in a circle, frozen in that time and place for a split-second under a golden-white July sun, the guys and the girls, and Alice was reminded of a circular version of grandmother's footsteps, the game they used to play at school.

Who would take a step out of the circle next? Who would run toward the centre, drop out?

'Screw them.' Andy turned and jumped into the river. One by one, they dove into the cool, velvet water, free from the heat of the day, as the sun continued to rise up over them, relentless, and still.

7

They buried Tag in the cemetery come September, the Monday after Labor Day. Most of the town showed up, and the men wore uniform and saluted his coffin as he was borne past. Some people stayed away. They felt Tag had brought shame on the town, dropping out and all.

Two more kids vanished between Tag's death and Jack's departure and the funeral: Timmy Seighart, who went to the city, and Tammy van Houten, who went off in a campervan to travel across Europe into Afghanistan. They were kids from Alice's school, and she knew them, but she told herself it didn't mean a thing.

Things fall apart. Alice added the little Merlin figurine to her shelf of treasures. Often she wondered what Jack was up to. Whether he had made it to California, whether it was still warm there; she had heard San Francisco was cold. No one spoke about him now; it was as if he was dead. When people saw Joan Maynard at church or at the train station coming back from the city and asked her how her son was doing, she didn't lower her sunglasses. She'd smile and say:

'Jack's doing great, thank you so much,' and then move on.

'Alice! Come, sit down. I'm so glad you could make it.'

'Thank you, Mrs Finkelstein.'

Alice edged into the classroom as though it might be booby-trapped. She'd graduated from Orchard High assuming she was never going back, and she wasn't sure how she felt about being here again in August. It was most strange, out of season, to be in a classroom in an empty school. The light through the heavy green trees was wrong; the desks covered in a thin film of chalk dust were all wrong, as was the silence magnifying her steps as she trotted through the halls.

'Now, my dear.' Mrs Finkelstein stacked a pile of papers efficiently and laid them to one side. She took out a tin of mints, offered one to Alice, then popped one in her own mouth. 'Do you know why I've asked you here?'

Alice nodded. She said politely: 'Dolores told me you were interested in helping me.'

Mrs Finkelstein stuck her chin out, pursing her lips. 'That's true. I'm helping myself too, I guess.'

'How?'

Mrs Finkelstein closed the mint tin, sucked on a mint and pulled out a yellow lined pad. 'There's no real charity, that's what you'll understand. It always comes with an ego being massaged somewhere.'

'I believe you.'

'We're off to a good start.' She put the mint in one corner of her cheek where it bulged out. 'Now, Alice. I'm a busybody. I was brought up to be a busybody, to do what I can where I can, even if it does massage my ego along the way. How can I persuade you to apply to college? More specifically to Barnard?'

Alice shifted in her seat. She opened her mouth, and then closed it.

'I can understand it's a little awkward,' said Mrs Finkelstein. 'Tell me, dear.'

Alice thought for a moment. 'Thank you,' she said. 'I'd love to go to Barnard.'

'Wonderful news.' Mrs Finkelstein smiled. 'That's all to the good. Your SAT scores are excellent. Can you tell me why you didn't apply last year?'

'Well –' Alice felt buffeted, like a beach ball on the tide of a rocky shore. 'I don't know. I want to learn. My father wanted me to go to college. He –' She stopped and looked down.

'So you and your mother never got around to it, that's what you're saying?'

'It's not my mom's fault. It was me.'

'Why didn't the school step in?'

'I – I don't know. I guess I told them my mom and I had hopes of a job.'

'Where?'

'I don't know. Helping out with Mr Kynaston, I guess.'

This was what she'd told the guidance counsellor, Mrs Palaccio, and what she'd told anyone else who'd asked. Mrs Palaccio, one year off retirement, had exhibited so little interest in her educational career that when Alice realized over half her friends were leaving Orchard – to go to Wellesley or Penn State or NYU – and she was stuck here, not doing anything, not going anywhere – she started to wonder if this outcome would have been the same had her father been alive.

She'd have ignored Mrs Finkelstein's message via Dolores and nearly did but for one thing: she wanted to study more than anything. She wanted to get on. She wanted to travel: go to Stratford-upon-Avon and stand in Shakespeare's house, and walk round the stones at Stonehenge. And then she wanted to see Rome and Jaipur, the Pink City. She wanted to help to make the world fairer and better. Sometimes, at night, the fury and impotence she felt and her rage at everything – her dad, her mom pretty much an unpaid servant to the Kynastons, Tag being killed, Jack disappearing, the war, the politicians who caused the war – overwhelmed her. It made her heart race, her head spin, and she'd tell herself it was because she was young and didn't know any better. It didn't occur to her, until she was in Mrs Finkelstein's neat class-room, with the last of the summer sun streaming in through the gaps in the ivy that ran across the window, that she could change, that something needed to change for her and she was the person to change it.

'You, Alice, were one of my most gifted students. I have an obligation to the Barnard admissions board, my dear, to make you known to them.'

Alice said quietly, 'Isn't it too late?'

'I spoke to them about you, Alice. My views are welcome as far as the admissions board is concerned, you see.' She tapped the side of her nose.

'So they'd let me interview? And I might have a place?'

'Undoubtedly. If you interview well – and they have their own separate exam which I know you'd pass with flying colours, provided we do some practice – I think a place would be found for you. Next fall, not this fall, you understand.'

'I do. But there's still the problem of money.'

Mrs Finkelstein waved at her. 'Ah, my dear, we'll worry about that another time. The exact details are not your con-cern. As I say, my family has made certain endowments, and two of my protégés have dropped out this summer. I'm anxious to send someone to Barnard on my recommenda-tion who deserves it. And who, I should note, is from a *good* family.'

'Ah,' said Alice. 'Mrs Finkelstein . . . did you speak to my mom? Or Wilder, Wilder Kynaston? Isn't he some relation of yours?'

'Wilder? Goodness, he's my cousin. Do you know him?'

Mrs Finkelstein wrote something down. 'Of course, you're Bob's daughter, I'd forgotten.'

'We live at the Kynaston gatehouse.'

'Yes . . .' Mrs Finkelstein seemed to hesitate. 'Yes, I know all about you. I know your mom too. Yes, Bob's daughter. I'm happy to help. Very happy to.'

Later that evening, thinking back over the whole meeting, the school deathly quiet and strange in August, the older woman offering her candy like in a fairytale, Alice realized how odd it had all felt, as though Mrs Finkelstein was a witch. Perhaps she *was* a witch and this was leading to some sacrifice situation. Three kids had been murdered upstate in the summer, their bodies arranged in a pentagon shape. People said it was witches. But then Mrs Finkelstein didn't *seem* like a witch. Even though it was August, the summer break, and she was in the same turquoise bouclé suit and black court shoes she always wore.

'Are you sure?' Alice said.

'What do you mean, am I sure, dear?'

Alice said, 'Is it some plan? Some plot? I don't understand what –'

Mrs Finkelstein looked surprised. 'What kind of a plot?'

Alice realized she sounded crazy. 'I'm sorry. Thank you so much for your help.'

'That's no problem, dear. Wait to hear, won't you?'

Alice stood up. 'Thank you, Mrs Finkelstein.'

'How are you keeping yourself busy in the meantime?' said Mrs Finkelstein, staring at the form and chewing a pen.

'I'm not, really. I'll be helping my mother with the apple harvest,' said Alice, 'and with housework, and making things nice for Mr Kynaston.'

'I heard. Wilder likes to have things nice, doesn't he?' said

Mrs Finkelstein, scribbling on her pad. 'I guess I'll see you in November, at Cemetery Supper. In the meantime, leave it with me.'

'You sure?'

The teacher looked at her over her glasses. 'I am. When it comes to you, Alice, I'm very sure.'

8

'Allie? You've packed your bag?'

Alice appeared at the top of the stairs and looked down into the hallway, where her mother was adjusting the mirror and staring at herself at the same time.

'I've packed my bag, Mom.'

'I don't see it.'

'I put it on the porch.'

Her mother looked up at her as if she'd just said she'd thrown it down the chimney.

'What a place to leave it! What if something gets to it?'

Her father used to leave things on the porch, and it made her mother angry. Once, they'd seen a mama bear making off with some biscuits and gravy her dad had left out there, wrapped up. He'd been in bed for weeks then, not leaving, the windows and drapes tightly shut; and she hadn't seen him for days, because he wouldn't see her when he was like that. Betsy had baked the biscuits to celebrate him getting out of bed. He'd eaten them with greens and chicken and apple sauce and kept some back to take to an old friend's mother in Orchard, but they'd been eaten. It hadn't mattered, of course, but it had mattered. Things mattered to him most dreadfully.

'Okay. I'll bring it in.' Outside, it was still light, but Cemetery Supper, November the First, was the day one noticed not only that summer was over but that fall was far advanced: most usually because after Halloween the sun did not rise above the trees that covered the land from the town to the bank of the river, leaving the house in gloom for much of the day.

'Bring it inside and check one more time you've got everything. There won't be time tonight. We'll be back so late and we may have to go to Valhalla after the supper.'

Alice ventured down the first two steps and sat down. 'You've spent the last week doing nothing but helping him get ready, Mom. Surely you can leave some of the clearing-up till tomorrow.'

A cold wind whistled around the gatehouse, and suddenly the front door blew open with a bang. Alice saw the world flung open to her, the grey skies, the orange-and-black trees, and the leaves whirling past in swift drifts of flame. She heard a tinkling sound upstairs – something clattering to the ground. The smell of fresh air, of outside, was intoxicating.

Her mother slammed the door shut, then leaned against it. 'Damned door keeps doing that,' she said. 'I don't know how to fix it.'

'That's okay,' said Alice automatically.

'It is okay,' said Betsy. 'It will be okay. Oh, honey – I'm so proud of you. I feel like –' She gazed up at Alice, but her eyes glazed over and she turned back toward the kitchen. 'Go finish getting ready. Wilder's picking us up in ten minutes.'

Alice ran upstairs. She looked around her room: on the floor one of the blue-and-white cats lay broken into three pieces where the wind had pulled it off the shelf. Alice heard the car coming along the drive, heard her mother call. Once again, she held the sharp little pieces in her hands, staring down at the funny smiling face, then tipped them on to a sheet of paper and rolled it up.

Without knowing why, she carefully moved the rest of the treasures off the shelf into a headscarf she had on the dressing table. She tied it tightly, wrapping another scarf around it, and, once she was downstairs, placed the bundle carefully into her overnight bag, and dropped the broken cat in the trash.

Cemetery Supper was held at 4 p.m. on the First of November every year, so that it fell midway between All Saints' and All Souls' days. The point was not to have immaculate cuisine, nor silver plates, fine bone-handled silverware, the best crystal. Rather, the day was one of trestle tables, folded and stored in the crypt of St Luke's every year and unfolded only for this evening. It was baked ham with a maple glaze and the last of the corn and the apples, and the best of the cider and the potatoes. And it was eight families only. There was no room for the Delaneys, the Martins, and so forth. Carly Gianotti's mom, Jane, had gone when she was a Hicks, for the Hickses were one of the oldest families along the Hudson, but, when Vincent Gianotti, Carly's dad, went to prison and Jane's father died in the same year, Jane became a double-outcast – no living Hicks relative, and the wife of a felon.

The trestle tables were covered with simple checked cloths. They were set up in the same place every year – the flat spot just outside one of the Maynard mausoleums, midway up the cemetery. The old church was at the top, the lane and the river at the bottom. The gravestones in that area were Maynard graves, and all identical in shape: long, thin and slightly rounded, and they stuck up around the tables like teeth in a mouth. Nearby were the Jansens: Alice's great-great-grandfather, grandfather and her dad.

'Betsy!' Mrs Cooper, the mayor's wife, was removing Saran wrap from a container, her husband lifting cold chicken out of an ice box. 'Come help us, will you?'

'Of course,' said Alice's mother, and she pressed Alice's arm with her gloved hand and said quietly, 'You unpack our food, okay? Be polite.'

Alice set out the hams, the potatoes, the plastic plates and the paper napkins. One by one their fellow diners arrived, wrapped up in the chill, bringing with them the excitement of the festivity, even as a cold wind sliced through the grave-yard. She poured them cider, her arms straining under the weight of the brown stoneware jugs.

Her mother lit a fire in the old metal brazier. The woodsmoke curled up around the graves. The attendees walked slowly through the stones, reading inscriptions, as Alice and then her mother finished laying everything out.

'She's a good worker, your Alice,' Wilder Kynaston told Betsy, tearing off a hunk of bread and chewing it, then choking slightly. He banged on his chest, coughing a little. 'Look at you, Alice. You're like your dad, here there and every-where. Good girl. You're a young woman now, aren't you! Thank you.' He patted her shoulder but she ducked away, and he stared at her in surprise. *He really doesn't know I hate him*, she thought, and she wondered what it must be like to be so oblivious. She waved at Mrs Finkelstein, who was watching her, and thought of the packed bag in the hallway, the train she must take, the ceiling of Grand Central Station, aqua green and gold.

'Wilder,' said her mother, who was opposite him. 'I think we're about ready. Do you want to –'

'Great idea,' he said smoothly. 'Betsy, will you – ah, thank you.'

Her mother struck her fork against her glass. The sound carried through the graveyard, as if it was calling out the dead, bouncing off the graves of Hickses and Jansens, Maynards and Kynastons past.

But everyone kept on talking. 'Louder,' murmured Wilder. Her mother struck the glass again, and nothing happened.

'Hey!' Alice's mother called, hands round her mouth. 'Wilder has something to say!'

Her voice, amplified in the shocked silence, rang around the cemetery. The families turned around, surprise mingling with disapproval on their faces. Alice saw her mom shrink away from them, as if she'd been slapped.

'Thank you, Betsy, my dear,' Wilder said, obviously amused. 'Welcome! Why don't we all sit down. We – ah.' He paused, as if he wasn't quite sure what he was going to say for a second. Pushed his glasses up his nose. 'Yes. Welcome. Here we are, the descendants of those who founded this little town. Another year gone. Here's to us,' Wilder said, raising his glass. 'And those who made us.' He lifted his glass toward the white and grey headstones listing among the nodding gold grasses. 'To those who gave everything so we could live in this blessed spot in peace and prosperity. Long may it continue.'

'Well said, Wilder!' someone called, and Alice looked up. It was Wilder's agent, John Matheson. He was smoking a cigarette and leaning against a mausoleum. Alice had seen him around a few times over the past couple of weeks.

'John! Aren't you supposed to be with Teddy, my good man?'

'She's asleep,' he said, scanning the assembled throng. 'I wanted to come by. My, my, this is all very Shirley Jackson, isn't it?'

'Ha!' Wilder gave a small chuckle. 'Touché.'

'They'll love it. Here, Kynaston,' Mr Matheson said, waving a hand over the assembled group. 'Read these good people your new poem, why don't you?'

'Poetry, Wilder?' said a voice, and Alice looked up to see Mrs Finkelstein, smiling, opposite her. 'Something of a departure, isn't it?'

The guests had shuffled toward the tables and were sitting down.

'Read the poem,' said Alice's mother, nodding at Wilder, and something in the way her eyes met his made Alice's stomach lurch. 'Go on, Wilder.'

Wilder cleared his throat. Alice, squished between older people, looked at him and realized he was nervous. 'Oh, thank you. This is – *huh* – this is a poem from my new work, which will be published next year by Holt, Rinehart and Winston.' A hushed whisper of excitement ran like wind through grass. Wilder had a new work coming.

'It's a departure for me. It is a series of poems, a memoir, a novel, all intended to convey a story, the story of our country and what is happening, and my story too, I dare say. *Huh.*' He cleared his throat again and swallowed. 'It's – it's called "The Apple is the World". Here goes nothing.'

The Apple is the World

The Apple is the World
It is the pip and the pippin,
It is the cock crow and the cox
It is the globe.
It is the peel and the peeling
The sweet and the tannin

The taut skin and the rough flesh
The apple is the world.
It is where I begin and you end
It is you, it is me
It is the orchard, it is the earth
The seeds of life
My seed
In you.

There was a brief pause and then muted clapping led by Mr Matheson, standing next to the tomb. 'Yes, Kynaston! Bravo!' he called.

Elizabeth Finkelstein, along from Alice, leaned forward. 'Wonderful,' she said, her voice deep. 'Kynaston, this is your finest hour. A series of poems is to come?'

'Yes, linking a fiction running throughout,' he said, sitting down, suddenly the expansive host, ladling out potatoes to himself, Betsy, Mrs Finkelstein, Mr Maynard, smiling and clinking his glass with Mrs Finkelstein's as though they were at some medieval banquet. 'I think you'll like them, Elizabeth. The first is called "No One Cares about Daisy Buchanan".'

There was an astonished murmur, and a pause, and then Mrs Finkelstein said, 'Wonderful! Of course! Wonderful, dear cousin Wilder.'

Alice did not clap along with the others.

She must have it wrong. Wilder Kynaston would not steal lines from her, a schoolgirl; she was arrogant for even thinking it. She looked up to see him looking at her.

'You like it, Alice?' he said, and he took an exaggerated, wolf-like chomp of his ham and potatoes.

'Yes, I liked it all along,' she said. She didn't know how else to say it.

'Couldn't have done it without you, my dear,' he said, waving a glass of cider at her.

'I'm pleased to hear Alice has taken an interest in your writing,' said Mrs Finkelstein. She looked carefully at her cousin, and then back to Alice. 'She's a clever young woman.'

'A mind like a fox. Betsy, you and Bob raised a terrific kid,' Wilder said and pressed Alice's mother's hand.

'Aw, isn't this fun,' said June Cooper, who had been talking to Mr Maynard on her other side and now turned to their group. She smiled at Alice, comfortable in her furs and smart blue raw-silk dress. 'I look forward to it every year. Honest, American food.' She helped herself to an ear of corn. It was old and had brown squares dotted across it, like missing teeth. Alice's head rang with noise. She passed Mrs Cooper the butter. There was silence.

'There's smoke somewhere,' Mrs Finkelstein remarked. 'Where's it coming from?'

'There were riots in the city again last night,' Mrs Cooper said, attacking her corn cob with relish. She shrugged, wiping butter from her mouth. 'The Puerto Ricans, cutting up rough again, crying wolf.' She swallowed furiously. 'The city's in flames. It's the coloureds, and the Puerto Ricans, and the Kennedys, you know.'

'It's that Bobby Kennedy sucking up to them,' said a small drab man further along the table.

'It'll all end in a war, I'm sure of it.' Mrs Cooper pushed the plate of potatoes toward Alice. 'Have some, will you? It's good stuff. This apple sauce is delicious. You're a clever girl, Alice, I hear. Elizabeth told me she's been helping you out, that Wilder's suggested you for Barnard – is that true?'

Alice felt cold. She looked from left to right, unsure how to answer. 'Not quite yet,' she said, aware Wilder was listening. 'I have to go there for an interview and a test tomorrow.'

'Well, that's exciting.'

Along from Wilder was Jack's mother, Joan, smooth corn-coloured locks gathered in a twisted chignon the exact same shade as Jack's hair. When Alice looked at her she very slowly turned her head away.

'I hope so,' said Alice.

'If you've got the Kynastons on your side,' said Mrs Cooper gaily, 'you'll get anything you want, my dear! I'm so glad it's turning out all right for you, and your mom.'

The sun had begun to slip over the gravestones. The chill in the air was palpable. Alice suddenly knew she couldn't stay. She stood up, pushing her chair backwards. It fell against Constance Guthrie, d. 1790, An Upright Woman.

'Alice dear!' said her mother. 'Could you see if there's any more mashed potato over by the brazier? For Wilder?'

'I can't, sorry.' Alice pushed her chair in. 'I have to go.'

'Alice! Sit down,' said her mother, laughing in a steely tone.

'I really do have to go,' Alice said. She didn't know what else to say.

'You will not!' her mother hissed across the table. 'I don't know what's gotten into you this supper but you're sitting there like someone just doused you in water. Sit back down. And smile!'

Alice looked at her mother. She put her hand on her heart, and smiled at her. 'I'm sorry, Mom.' She shook her head, hastening away as fast as she could down the steps that led on to the sidewalk, which was a couple of yards below the level of the cemetery, the road sunk down in between the graves.

When Wilder came to find her, she was leaning against the wall, panting.

'You all right, Alice?' he said.

She looked up at him. 'I'm not sure. I can't breathe.'

'Come and sit down.' He put his hand on her shoulder, but she shook it off.

'Leave me be,' she said.

'What's up?'

'What's up?' She laughed. 'You fixed it for me to get a place at Barnard. You want me out of the way, now your book is getting published. Because you stole my poem.'

He laughed and rubbed his face. 'Oh dear, that again. Alice, it's not your poem.'

'You know it is. You know I gave you those lines, those ideas.' She wiped her wet face clumsily with her palms. 'How could you?'

They were down in the hollowed-out lane, the cemetery raised high above them. The lane was the one that carts and people and carriages had trundled up and down for almost two centuries. The sounds from the dinner above them floated over to her. Wilder leaned over and licked a tear from her cheekbone, his teeth grazing her skin. She was so startled she couldn't react, not immediately. He gave a snuffling, grunting sound, and his lips moved down her cheek. She could smell cider and rye whiskey on him. Sweat, something else. Then he stopped.

'We're not so different, are we?' he said, smiling at her, and continued trailing feathery kisses toward her mouth. As his wet, warm, large tongue licked her face, she gave a small gasp and pushed her hand against his chest. He did not move.

'It's your tears. I'm tasting your tears, Alice, tasting them away, honey.'

He moved his tongue into her mouth and she stiffened, and cried out, and he pressed against her, so that his mouth covered hers and she could not make a sound. His teeth clashed against hers. He was stronger than her. Much stronger.

'Stop!' she tried to call out, but it was like being trapped. His right hand roamed over her body, then under her skirt, over her panties – he cupped her, squeezed her thighs hard, like she was a steer and it was market day. But his mouth stayed on hers, his tongue moving, pushing into her.

'We're the same, you and I,' he said, breaking off for a second, spittle drenching her face. 'I hoped you'd – I hoped you'd like it, Alice.' He was panting. He had a glassy, far-off look in his eye.

'What the hell,' Alice tried to shout, but his mouth was on hers. She could not breathe.

When she remembered what to do, it was with a start. She heard Dolores's voice, cool in her ear, in her bedroom, when they'd been talking about a guy who'd put his hand up Dolores's skirt one time in the city. 'Twist their balls. Grab and twist, the harder the better, then just break away, Allie, break away.'

So Alice grabbed, as ferociously as she could, and his head jerked in shock, banging against hers so that her skull hit the stone wall of the cemetery. She twisted the handful she was holding as hard as possible, rage flooding her.

He yelped and swore. 'You little bitch.' He stepped back, bending over and breathing hard, his hair falling in his face.

'Don't touch me again,' she said, sounding calm. 'Don't –'

Footsteps came from the ground above them; Alice felt a flood of relief that now it would be over, that she was safe. She looked up and saw her mother's face, leaning down into the cutaway lane.

Her mother stared at her.

'It's all fine here, Betsy darling,' Wilder said. He patted Alice's shoulder, seemingly uncaring that her skirt was hoicked up around her waist, his shirt untucked. 'Go back to the table.'

Betsy nodded. 'Yes. Of course. If it's all fine, that is.'

And she walked away.

'You ought to be quiet now, my dear, and stop making such a fuss,' Wilder said, turning to Alice, and he smiled, gathering himself together. He wiped his mouth with the back of his forearm then with a pressed pocket square he pulled from his jacket, as if her wetness, her tears, were repulsive. He grabbed his crotch area again, wincing. 'Do you understand?'

'You're disgusting,' she said, backing away from him. 'Get away from me.'

'I can't,' he said, with a laugh. 'You silly girl, you talk about free love and understanding, so what's a kiss? It's nothing. What's a few borrowed phrases here and there? They're nothing. Elizabeth Finkelstein tells me she's fixed the place at Barnard, and that's all to the good –'

'You bought me a place there,' she said. 'So my mom is even more grateful to you. And you're in control.'

'I didn't buy you a place. Elizabeth mentioned you to me after the meeting and I said I'd write them a recommendation – my name carries some sway –'

He tainted everything. His mark was on everything.

'They want me because of you. And her, telling them to take me.'

'Don't be ridiculous. It doesn't work like that. However, you can make sure certain conversations . . . happen. Elizabeth is my cousin and we have another cousin who happens to be dean of admissions. So you might say we have some sway. The Kynastons endowed a chair when Barnard was founded. We support women's right to education. You're a clever girl; you have a soul and a brain, but it needs training. We're almost family. And we're the same. I'm an artist —'

'You're a con artist!' Alice shouted. 'And I don't care about college, or your cousin fixing me up with a place!' She was almost laughing, her body shaking with anger. 'Stay out of my life, you — you pervert!'

His face was a mixture of bafflement and petulance, as if he didn't understand what the problem was. 'I can't stay out of your life. Your mother —'

'Leave my mother out of this!'

'I can't, though — Allie —'

'You treat her like a servant. You act like a lord. And you're — you're *nothing*! You're a washed-up second-rate writer who has to steal from other people.'

'Shut your mouth. Shut up.' His nostrils flared and his hand suddenly clamped around her windpipe, so she couldn't breathe. 'I don't like young girls who make an exhibition of themselves. Your stupid mad father was cracked in the head, you understand? He died owing me the ten thousand bucks he'd begged me to lend him. And he damn well ruined those orchards. He let everything go to hell. Oh, you didn't know that, did you, pretty Alice?' He moved closer. 'I'm never gonna get that money back so why shouldn't I take what's mine another way? Your dear, obedient mom will do any-thing for me. I said anything; it's quite remarkable, my dear. I need a maid again, someone to care for Teddy. I can't do it by myself. And, since you're the one Bob was building the business for — apples, dammit, the fellow must have been crazy, whoever made a fortune from *apples*? So tell me: he owes me, so why shouldn't I take you? Why shouldn't I take you too, before you're out of my hair?' He stared at her blank face. 'Your dad's the one who caused all this, sweetheart. The guy who jumped in front of a train on a whim 'cause he couldn't count properly. It's a kiss, Allie. You have to learn how to kiss; it's neither here nor there.' He pressed his mouth to hers again, then released her, and his tongue slid back and forth in and out of his lips. 'You're so sweet – *hey*!'

With a final push Alice shoved him out of the way, so hard he staggered and fell against the wall. She ran across the road and down the winding lane that led to the gatehouse and Valhalla.

Her heart was thudding, blood pounding in her ears. At the entrance to the Valhalla Estate, she looked in at the gatehouse, seeing her own home as if she was a visitor. She kept on running. She had to try to see Teddy one last time. To tell her she was so, so sorry.

The Victrola was playing some old jazz song. 'Teddy!' she called out. '*Teddy!*'

As she got closer, she could hear the telephone ringing. Teddy hated telephones: they made her anxious, and she would cry and shuffle about upstairs, whimpering. Alice knew she had to stop the noise of it. She flung open the front door and paused for a minute in the narrow wood-panelled hallway, catching her breath. The ringing grew louder, and louder, but underneath it she could hear a sound of sobbing, of someone crying out.

'Teddy!' Alice called up to the second floor. 'It's fine, Teddy, I'm here!'

She went into the den, lined with books and photographs, warm and still in the afternoon sun. A fly, caught in a spider's web, buzzed in the gaps between the ringing telephone. Alice bent over the telephone, panting, pausing for breath, then lifted the receiver.

'Hello?'

There was a distant, roaring crackling sound, and a whooshing rush, as if she were travelling through time. And, then, a quiet, male voice. 'Oh, hello,' it said. 'Can you hear me?'

Alice's mouth was so dry she could hardly speak. She swallowed, and sat down on the window seat that ran around the room, where she'd sat and read books as a little girl while her father conducted his business with Mr Kynaston. 'Who is this, please?'

'Hello? Is that – is that Teddy Kynaston?'

Alice laughed, wildly. 'Teddy's not here.' And then – suddenly – waves of static, the line so bad she could barely hear them.

'I'm sorry to hear that,' said the voice quietly. 'It's quite important I speak to her. I'm – from – land –'

'I can't hear you. England, did you say?'

'Yes! I'm afraid the line's terrible. I am sorry, but do you mind my asking if you know where she is?'

Alice paused, struggling for breath. 'Why would you want to know that?'

'I have a friend who wants to find out. Very much.'

The Victrola had stopped playing. Alice was certain Teddy, upstairs, could hear her. She said, 'It's hard to explain but she's here all the time.'

'Forgive me.' He sounded beaten down. 'Something's getting lost in translation, or maybe it's the line. Is she there?'

'Oh, she's here,' said Alice.

'Who's with her?'

'She lives with her brother,' said Alice. 'Listen, what do you want with her?'

'I can't say. Not over the telephone. I think it could change everything but – I say – her brother? Is he – cruel to her?'

She hesitated. 'Teddy's worth ten of him.' A noise outside made her jump. 'Oh biscuits. I'm sorry but I have to –'

'Oh! Don't,' said the voice. 'Are you all right?'

It was almost a relief to say, 'I'm not all right, no.'

'No, you don't sound it, even taking into account your accent.'

'I don't have an accent,' she said, and she laughed, properly laughed despite everything. 'You do. Who are you? Why are you trying to get hold of Teddy?'

'A friend from England said I should find her. And that I'd learn the truth if I did. And help her too.' The voice gave a short sigh.

'Who's the friend? How does she know Teddy?'

'It's rather a long story, I'm afraid.'

'I haven't got time for a long story. Or a short story,' she said. 'I have to go. Listen, don't come looking for Teddy. You won't find anything here. Good luck –'

'What's your name?' said the voice, clearer now, and urgent. 'Please, just tell me your name.'

'My name's Alice. Alice Jansen,' she said.

'Where are you going, Alice Jansen?' he asked, and there was something in his voice that meant she wanted to tell him everything, wanted to offload it on to him, lean against him. She wondered what he looked like, where he was, why there was so much sadness in his voice.

'I'm going to St Mark's Place,' she said with a certainty she did not feel. 'In the city.' As she said it, she remembered Tag's ruined face, his missing ear, his tired, kind eyes. She could hear his voice. 'No. 5, St Mark's Place. The East Village . . . It's safe there.'

'In New York City?' he said. Alice gave an involuntary laugh of delight: his voice was Stewart Granger and David Niven, rolled into one.

'I really like your accent, sorry,' she said, by way of explanation, to hide how attractive she thought he sounded, because it was crazy to find someone's voice attractive, wasn't it? Then, embarrassed, she added, 'Yes, that's right. New York City.'

'And do you know anyone, in St Mark's Place?' the stranger said.

'I have a friend from home living there. He's run away too. I have to get away from –' She trailed off. Her throat was dry. 'I don't know.'

His faint voice was deep, with a humorous note of despair, that was what it was like. 'The mess the older generation made? Something rather like that?'

'Yes, that's exactly it,' she said, and she found she was smiling into the phone. 'I have to get away from them. I need to be someplace other than here and the world's on fire, and it's all happening in New York. I want to figure out what to do next, you know?'

'I do know.'

'Listen, what's your name? How old are you?'

'I'm Tom,' he said. 'I'm Tom Raven, and I'm twenty-one and I feel like the world's on fire. I had my head in the sand before. Alice – it's weird, I feel as though I know you.'

His voice sounded so close then, and not as though he was on the other side of an ocean. Alice looked round the den, through the open door to Wilder's study.

'You won't believe me, but I was thinking the same about you,' she said, and she twisted the phone line around her fingers, pressing the receiver as close to her ear as she could, the better to hear his voice. 'Hey, I'm not at home, I'm in someone else's house, and I might have to hang up. Tell me something about yourself in the meantime.'

'I grew up in a two-room cottage in the Scottish hills. I love Calypso music, all music, really, and I love drawing, and I have a tiny wooden house my father carved for me that's my dearest possession in the world.'

'Okay,' she said, blinking, because she wanted him to understand she had been listening, that he was heard. 'Let's see if I have this straight. Scotland. Calypso, that's groovy. Wooden house. So I lost my dad two and a half years ago. And I have a collection too. Of treasures. Animals, and figurines, and keepsakes. But I keep breaking them by accident.'

'There are no accidents.'

'Sometimes there are,' she said. 'Sometimes.' She bit her lip, looking around the Kynaston den, at the photographs on the shelves, the fake images of a happy all-American family. 'Tell me something else. Have you been in love?'

'Yes,' he said. His voice was quieter than ever. 'How about you?'

'Yes,' she said, but at the same time she wondered if she was. She opened her mouth to ask him what had happened, and then she saw them out the den window. Her mother and Wilder Kynaston, coming down the drive together, hand in hand.

They stopped by the door. Wilder had his hand on her mother's back. He moved it down to her rear and squeezed it, and with the other hand took her fingers and kissed them, then her neck, and her face.

Alice could not tear her eyes away from them. Bile rose in her throat and she wondered if she might be sick, vomit up the rich heavy meal that sat like fat and stones in her stomach.

She heard the stranger on the other end of the line clear his throat. 'Alice,' he said. 'Alice?'

'Yes?'

'I have to find her,' he said. 'Teddy, I mean.'

She crouched down, twisting the phone cord around her fingers, watching as Wilder and her mother kissed, he holding her face in his hands, his mouth pressed hard over hers, just as it had been over Alice's ten minutes earlier. She saw him stroke her mother's face, saw the way she adjusted his collar, took his hand again, gazing up at him, as if she couldn't believe he was real.

'There's no point,' Alice said. She swallowed again, trying to control herself. 'Don't come here looking for her. I wish you could, but Teddy doesn't like visitors. I'm sorry. You understand?'

'I understand,' he said. 'Alice? Good luck. I hope everything turns out okay for you. And the treasures.'

'Thank you,' she said. 'And you, Tom Raven.'

They had started walking again toward the front door. Alice spoke as softly as she could. 'They're back. I have to go, Tom Raven. I'm sorry. Goodbye –'

She pushed her finger down on the switch hook. The line went dead.

As the front door opened, she heard Kynaston say:

'I promise you, when she sees how happy you make me, she'll be fine with it. She's a teenager! They need treating rough sometimes.'

'Oh. Wilder.' Her mother said the name as she'd been saying it lately, like it was a rush of wind, a delicious new language on her tongue. 'Do I, really? Make you happy?' Betsy's voice was breathless, like a long-drawn-out sigh of happiness.

'You do. And you will. And Alice is a silly girl if she can't see that.'

'It's awfully unlike her, though. To run off like that. She's a little cut up still about everything, but –' Her mother stopped.

'Listen, Betsy. I think she had a little crush on me. That's what it was about. Why she was so upset. And that's why we should go slow. Break her in gently.'

'Oh,' her mother said. 'I'm sure you're – yes, that must be it.'

'Honey, she's a teenage girl . . .'

Alice held her breath. She could hear her own fingers drumming on the wooden shelf in the den, and her heart in jangling syncopation, thumping so hard she was sure it could be heard too. Eventually her mother breathed out. 'Oh, lordy. Why didn't I see it? It all makes sense now. Wilder, you're just about the smartest –'

'And you, my dear, are a sweet little housewife come to blow the cobwebs away, you and your lovely daughter, and I know everyone will be pleased as anything when they have the chance to get used to the news.'

'I hope so, honey –'

'Betsy?'

'Yes, darling?'

'Mmm? Don't call me darling, is that all right? It's so sappy. Always thought so. Call me Kynaston. It's just a little thing. Would you run and get me a plate of food from the supper? Some of that corn, and the ham? Only get the good corn; some of it was spoiled. Tell the others I had to make some calls. Matheson will understand. I can't face them again. No, don't look sad like that. Don't. Come here . . .'

He kissed her mother and Alice watched, until she realized she was watching and shook herself. She stood up and crept up the stairs and opened the door into the room at the front overlooking the river and the mist that she had never been into, not in all those years.

'Goodbye, Teddy,' she said as loudly as she could, so the figure on the bed would hear her. 'Thank you for being my friend. I'm going now.'

But Teddy did not answer.

Creeping back down the stairs, she heard Wilder in the study, pouring a drink. The front door was open, and she froze – too late.

'Alice,' said her mother, standing with one hand on the study door, staring at her daughter.

'Why didn't you tell me?' Alice said as quietly as she could.

The two of them looked at each other: the daughter crouched on the stairs, ready to spring, the mother brushing down her skirt, a curious expression on her face.

'I'm doing this for the best,' said Betsy, speaking almost silently, mouthing the words. 'I know you can't see it, but it is. I promise.'

'Mom –' said Alice. She was terrified. She did not want to see Wilder Kynaston again. She didn't want to be trapped in the house, not able to escape. She knew then she did not feel safe with her mother, and seeing that so clearly was like a hollowing-out, as though she was empty. *Will she make me go back in there, to see him? To do what he wants?*

She stood up and began to walk down the stairs as quietly as she could. Her mother watched her.

133

'Don't worry, dearest,' she said loudly, and Alice froze. 'It's just Teddy, fussing a little.'

'Tell her to pipe down. That I'll come see her in a bit,' came Wilder's voice.

'Sure. Hey! Teddy!' Alice's mother said, speaking directly to Alice. As she was talking, she reached into her pocket and took out her wallet. Silently, she opened it and flipped out four fifty-dollar bills. Alice knew it was the money she'd have been given by Wilder for the supper. She handed the bills to Alice. 'Listen to me, Alice. It's time for a change around here, and that means I live here now. I get that you have a crush on him. Perhaps you'd better understand that. And if you have to go, then go.'

Her blue eyes held her daughter's gaze steadily, without emotion. Not a tremor.

'Don't be foolish, Betsy. Teddy can't go,' called Wilder. 'Where would she go?'

'She's got the world,' said Betsy, and she whispered this under her breath, her voice cracking. 'The whole world to see. She doesn't need us now.'

'You're drunk, or tired. Come back in here, you silly thing.'

'Hey, Alice? You don't need to worry about me,' her mom said, so softly under her breath it was like a whisper. She reached out, touched her daughter's arm. It was like electricity, warm and charged, and Alice felt a jolt. Betsy Jansen backed away into the study again, never taking her eyes from Alice's face; and then, as the noise from Teddy's room grew in volume, Betsy leaned forward and before closing the door hissed, '*Go. Just go, Allie.*'

Alice ran back to the gatehouse and let herself in, scooping up her bag. The treasures clinked together very slightly, so she unzipped the bag and packed them tightly into the middle of her possessions, so they were safe, secure. She took one last look round the kitchen. How far we've fallen without you, Dad, she thought. She wondered, again, where his last present was, where he was, if ghosts exist, if the people we love stay with us wherever we go.

She left the house and hurried through the woods into Orchard, down Main Street, till she reached the railroad bridge where, with a couple of minutes to spare, she paused to catch her breath. A train, going in the other direction, screamed past.

Then it happened. The sound of his body, cracked and crunched into nothing, the sight of the parts of him that had been whole flung across the street. She had found a piece of him, fleshy and wet like a strawberry gone bad, on her sleeve. There were bloodstains on the asphalt that had not faded, even after all this time. One was shaped like a junebug, one like half a heart. His dear body that had been so whole, so full of love for her – Alice saw it all again and could not stop it. As the train whistled further up the track, she closed her eyes.

For the first time in over two years, she relived it again. Every horrific moment.

Now her train was drawing into the station. She willed herself across the footbridge, toward the platform. She was getting on that train.

The doors of the railroad car were flung open; someone gently touched her elbow as she paused, blinking hard before she took the next step. She thought of Tom Raven's voice, curious, encouraging, on the phone. *Good luck*, he'd said, as if he meant it, like he wasn't trying to tell her what to do, how she'd be so much better if she was just a little more like *this*, or like *that*. How he'd just listened. *I hope everything turns out okay for you. And the treasures.*

It was a short ride. In under an hour later, she was in Manhattan. There was still warmth in the streets, leaves scudding down Fifth Avenue from Central Park. Alice ordered an egg cream at a candy store, then wandered aimlessly, drinking it and eating a bag of pretzels. Her bag was heavy, laden with all the things she had needed from the gatehouse. But it was okay.

Just past the New York Public Library someone was playing 'The Look of Love' out a window. It was a perfect fall day. She walked, and walked, shedding her old skin.

Sometimes it's only possible to see whether a decision was right many years after the event. Not in this case. Alice had left her old life behind. And not once, no matter what happened afterwards, and in the subsequent years to come, did she ever, ever regret running away.

PART TWO

London is the Place for Me

Galloway, Scotland

1955

9

There is an old road, the Corse of Slakes, which winds through the hills to Creetown from Gatehouse of Fleet. When Tom Raven had been a wee boy of around five, not grown up and about to turn nine as he was in 1955, he had thought where the Corse ended was where the world ended. It cuts away, up from the gently wooded rivers and copses clinging to the edge of Solway Firth, through the rolling countryside of south-west Scotland, and at times it is like Cornwall, or even, on a clear day when the blue sea and sky merge, the Italian Riviera. But if you take this old road north then, quite suddenly, the skies dramatically open up and you can see a vast plain sprinkled with pine woods and, further on, the hills of southern Galloway, bathed in a golden, diffused light, giving rise to the idea that beyond them is nothing, the end of the world, presumably, and then perhaps heaven.

It was this road Jenny Caldicott took when she came to remove her nephew, Tom Raven.

You could not see the little white building from the old road, which from November to February was impassable in places because of mud and snow. In that dreadful winter of 1955, which lasted well into spring, Tom and his father could not walk to Gatehouse so some days went quite hungry, eking out tins of Spam and soup, until, thankfully, they found a sheep frozen in the snow, which Tom's father skinned and boiled.

'Deep freeze, dear boy,' Edward Raven had said. 'What luck – we can celebrate Christmas in January.' The sheep, which they named Vera, after Vera Lynn, because Edward said she had shapely legs, hung in the outhouse next to their one-storey cottage. Vera lasted them for weeks and the mutton broth was warm, with carrots and the last of the turnips. But by April, oh, they were both sick of the sight and smell of lamb, though Tom would never have admitted it. For the rest of his life, he could not touch lamb. It reminded him too much of that last spring in Scotland.

His father was sometimes cross – about the wind whistling through the cottage, or the leaks, or the way the range smoked, but he was not a shouter like some of the men in Gatehouse Tom knew who yelled at their sons and hit them. Tom's father would go for walks up into the hills, and that meant he could not do his work, which was carpentry – everything from kitchen tables for farmhouses and dressers and shelves to more delicate items like bird cages and house signs, and a new lectern for the kirk in Wigtown. Every year Tom would choose what he wanted and his father would make it for his birthday. Sometimes it was a trolley. Sometimes a box with his name carved into the lid:

TOM * RAVEN

One year, a small raven, itself on a polished oak stand. Its thick beak and hooded eyes terrified Tom and he had to hide it, though he would never have told his father that either.

Tom had another secret which he also did not tell his father: he really wanted a Matchbox toy car. One like Ian Forsyth's. Ian's Matchbox car was mulberry-maroon, a poor colour for a car in Tom's opinion. It should be red. Tom would have been happy with a Matchbox car, of course, but what he wanted more than anything was a crane, which he had seen an advert for in the *Radio Times* in the newsagent's in Kirkcudbright. Oh! It was a fine thing, the Matchbox Yellow No. 11 Jumbo Crane, with a hook on the end. The hook was made of metal, and it actually dangled on a string off the crane of its own free will.

The Matchbox factory was in London, Shacklewell Lane, London E8. Tom memorized this in case he ever went to London. 'Can we go to Shacklewell Lane, London E8, please,' he'd practised saying to an imaginary cab driver. He watched a lot of films, sneaking in at the back of the picture house in Kirkcudbright and he liked the kind of films where there was a car chase, and a taxi driver had to drive fast, and complained. These always made Tom laugh. So he knew how to talk to a taxi driver, when the time came to go to the Matchbox factory in Shacklewell Lane, London E8.

Tom was eight, about to turn nine, in that everlasting winter, and because he was inside so much during that time he started to have questions: how they had ended up there, what had happened to them. So in the late-winter evenings Tom would ask for stories about the time before he was born, his father's early life, how he had met Tom's mother. And his father would tell him: tales of the time he had fallen out of his Hawker Fury when the door wasn't properly fastened, or the pub that his commanding officer had found them all in when war was finally declared, opening the door and calling, 'Back to base, you bleedin' useless lot! Fight's on!' Or, when Tom begged for a story about his mother: the iron bedstead and how it had been the bed of Tom's mother, Irene, as a child in London, and how, after she died and they moved far away, Edward had dismantled it, strapped it to the top of the car and driven it to Scotland using most of his petrol ration, only to find one of the legs had rolled off somewhere in the Pennines, where it to this day presumably continues to bewilder the sheep and stray walkers, who wonder how one leg of an intricately carved iron bedstead came to be in one of the remotest places in the country. Edward had the missing leg replaced by the ironmonger in Anwoth.

All these stories were grand, but they never really answered any of Tom's questions.

The snow took forever to melt, and when it had finally gone the tumbling, chattering Skyeburn was full almost to bursting with the water it carried from the hills down to Fleet Bay, and in those March mornings the light came earlier, pearly and speckled with silver. Yet there was a frost most nights, and Tom had given up hoping for spring until one white-cold morning before his ninth birthday, when he saw a hare outside, squatting on the road, giant, gimlet-eyed, calm, and knew winter must, thankfully, be over.

The hare stared at him without expression, utterly still, as though it had come with a message, then shivered and loped away, and Tom, not knowing why he did so, saluted it.

His actual birthday was a week later. During preparation of a slightly meagre birthday lunch of baked beans and potato cakes, when, in response to a question about how his mother died, his father had embarked on yet another yarn about something funny that had happened in the officers' mess, Tom found himself standing up, walking the seven steps to the front door and flinging it open.

'Sorry, Dad,' he said, his legs shaking as he stood on the threshold, letting in the cool fresh sweet air. He looked down the gravel path, out towards the hills and the sea.

'Spring is here. It's almost like I heard it knocking at the window.' He knew it sounded fanciful. But his father always understood.

'Finally boring you, am I, old boy?' his father said, standing up stiffly with a smile. He flipped the potato cakes over on the griddle and eyed the kettle. 'We'll have lunch soon. Lay the table, would you, Tom my boy? I say! We can play a game later – what do you think?'

Tom was still staring out of the door but he turned back. 'I'd rather go out after, Dad, if that's all right. Muck about a bit.'

''Course. Set the table first, old thing.'

In the corner was the table, under the window for light, an old oak settle just big enough for two. Against the back wall was the armchair, where Tom's father sat in the evenings and whittled – pegs and chess pieces and wooden dowels and chequers and all sorts; some things to sell, some to keep. The range was at the back, along with the door and the sink; and then came the second room (third if you counted the lavatory in the outhouse with the wood store), a tiny bedroom. Tom wished his father would sleep on the cot, so he was nearer the warmth of the range, but his father refused.

When Edward Raven went into the bedroom to fetch the water jug, Tom opened the door again, very quietly, and darted outside. There was still plenty of snow on Cairnharrow. He plucked four or five tiny late daffodils from a clump near the door, and glanced up.

Something, someone, a black dot, was on the horizon to the south, on the Corse of Slakes. He stood for a second watching it.

It was moving very slowly. It was a person.

Hurriedly, Tom went back inside and shut the door,

dropping the lemon-curd-yellow flowers into a tiny cut-glass vase that glinted in the spring sun. His father emerged not with the jug but with a bottle of sloe gin and two tiny crystal glasses. He poured a thimbleful of deep ruby-purple liquid into each and raised the first, clinking his glass to his son's.

'Happy birthday, Tom darling,' said his father. 'Well! Nine years old. Nine. We got there.' He raised his glass, looking up, and downed the liquid with a gulp; Tom followed suit, feeling extremely grown up.

They did not celebrate birthdays much, partly because they did not have the means to do so, but also partly because Tom's birth must have happened with the help of Tom's mother, and she was never mentioned.

As Tom was blinking hard, the sloe gin having burned his throat, Edward put a small package down on the table. 'Here you go,' he said.

Something clattered on the glass: a small twig, caught for a moment in the window frame, then pulled away, as if on a string. Tom stared down at the parcel, wrapped in newspaper, feeling his ears, his mouth, start to tingle.

It was a car. He knew from its curved top and edges it must be a Matchbox car, red and sleek and so beautifully designed, and he would race it around under the range and the cot and the length of the cottage. It might even be a Jumbo Crane. Murdo and Ian at the Anwoth school would stare in silent awe, then clap him on the back and beg to be his friends. He would no longer be a silent weakling in the same knitted cast-offs from Mrs Fairly, the farmer's wife down near Cardoness, day in, day out. He would be: Tom Raven – Matchbox No. 11 Jumbo Crane owner.

Gingerly, Tom pinched the soft wrapping, feeling something poking up through the layers. He did not think it was the metal beam of the crane with the hook at the end. Oh well. Perhaps he hadn't got the crane this time.

'Hurry up, then,' said his father, blinking rapidly. 'Open it, old boy!'

Tom pulled at the string and yanked open the parcel, feeling for the cool metal. But it was not cool metal; it was wood. A small square piece of wood.

'What's this?' said Tom.

It was a carved wooden house. With windows, and a door, and the detailing – from the shape of the tiles to the curved chimney pots to the open casements to the cat sitting in one of the windowsills – was exquisite. It was the size of his palm.

His father folded his fingers over it. His voice was quiet. 'I made it for – for your mother, Tom. It was a promise. A symbol.' His father was still standing there watching Tom, and there was a pleading note to his voice that Tom hated, as if he knew it was a terrible present. 'But I was too late . . . too late to give it to her.' He rubbed at the back of his neck and stared out of the window, and Tom thought how grey his skin looked, how sad he was, and how he hadn't always been like that. 'I promised her a home. I whittled it for her so she'd know I meant it. But she was gone before we could get there.'

'Gone where?'

His father shrugged, his generous mouth twisted into a painful hook. 'My dear boy. She died, I mean.' He stroked his cheek, with a sharp inhalation as his fingers closed on Tom's skin. 'She died.'

One day about a year ago after school, as he was crossing the bridge over the Fleet and had stopped to look for kingfishers, Ian Forsyth had shoved him to the ground and said, 'Your ma's a mad whoor and they locked her up and threw away the key and she died, me ma said so,' and knocked him on to the metal bridge, punching him in the stomach and winding him. When he could breathe, Tom had turned and said, 'Where did you hear that?'

'Yon da was half-cut at the pub, he was sayin' all sorts, all sorts o' nonsense, about stones, and ghosts and how your ma was mad,' said Ian confidently.

'Well, your ma stinks,' said Tom, instantly regretting this, as Ian's mother did smell, very badly, of the farmyard. Ian had turned bright red, raspberry staining his cheeks, and had kicked him again before walking away.

Tom had picked himself up and dusted himself down very carefully – his father was punctilious about appearance – and walked the two miles back along the Old Military Road; and, when he reached home and his father was in the work-shop making a bookshelf for the vicar and he called out as he always did, 'How was school, my boy?', Tom merely said, 'Great, Dad, thanks,' and fetched himself an apple, settling down by the range to reread a *Rupert Annual* that the vicar's wife – along with the farmer's wife, the source of most of the hand-me-downs and the mothering Tom received – had given him. And so, while he wanted to know more about his mother, he was also afraid to know. What he knew was: she was called Irene, and she was from London, and her father was a painter, and she had met Tom's father in the war.

But now, he felt, his father was asking him to ask.

'She was flying with her colonel up to York. Your mother was very high up in the WRAF. The Women's Royal Air Force, you know.' Tom didn't know. He nodded. 'There was still lots to do after the war – she was awfully busy, busier than old dogs like me. The plane – it was a Lancaster – took off near Lincoln but the wing had a fault. It crashed into a tree. Four people died.'

Tom was silent.

'I never liked the Lancasters,' his father said, and he drove a finger into his pipe, tamping down the tobacco. 'In Irene's family, they celebrated the ninth birthday. Her father, he used to say the ninth birthday was when you stopped being a really little child and started becoming an adult. They had a party for every child at that age. Rather a nice idea.'

Tom was silent, turning over the tiny house in his hand. This was the kind of story he wanted to hear. There was a small panel drawing on the wall in the bedroom by Julian Caldicott, and Tom knew he was his grandfather, and a famous artist. Once, he had gone to a gallery in Glasgow with his father on the train, and his father had shown him one of Julian Caldicott's paintings: a portrait of a red-haired girl called *Laughing Cruelty*. But he knew no more than that.

Edward slid the potato cakes on to a plate, and handed them to Tom. 'When I was growing up, we didn't call our-selves the Ravens, you know. No call for it. I was Bessie and Ed's lad and that was it and if you stepped out of line there were plenty of people who'd give you a thick ear for it. We weren't . . .' He searched for the right expression. 'They were good people.'

Tom knew all about the little Cumbrian town by Ulls-water, the little flat above the ironmonger's that was Edward's father's business, Tom's long-dead grandparents. His father happily told stories about that, about diving into ice-cold lakes, fishing, scrambling up steep hills.

'You caught a trout when you were five and the mayor said

you were a right good 'un,' Tom said on cue, helping himself to baked beans.

'That's it! Your mother's family, they were very smart. And London was – oh, it's a grand place, London. The grandest place I ever was. Not that your mother ever behaved like she was too good for anyone. In fact, she wanted to get away. We were going to – to get away . . .' He pointed at the wooden house with his pipe. 'I made her this, you know. To show – everything would be all right. And I never got the chance to give it to her. Well, it's your ninth birthday and I thought that –'

But his father stopped speaking and slowly stood up. He looked out of the window. 'What's that?'

'What?'

'Someone coming up the road.'

'I saw them a few minutes ago. A black speck.'

'Why didn't you say something?' His father's voice was sharp and Tom, for the second time, was taken aback by it. 'Why didn't you say, Tom?'

'I didn't – we were talking –' Tom said, his eyes wide. 'Sorry, Dad – I –'

They didn't have visitors, unless they were walkers lost on the hills, or riders wanting water for the ponies.

Tom's father was moving around the small room, pushing their scant possessions – a shelf of books, photographs, his whittling kit, the bottle of whisky they never talked about – into a wooden box. 'Quick –' he said. 'She's coming. Tom, quickly –'

There was a knock on the door. Three sharp blows. Tom looked at his father, astonished; he did not understand what was happening. Silence, and then the knock came again.

Rat. Tat-tat.

A firm English voice said, 'Edward. Let me in. Please.'

His father remained in the middle of the room, not moving. Then swiftly he took two steps to Tom, grabbed his shoulders.

'You are nine today. I should have said it might happen. I should have said. I love you, Tom. There.' His pale face was twisted, his eyes filled with tears. 'My dear, dear boy. Let her in. Yes. I have to let her in.'

The last moments, the last seconds, of the two of them, and Tom knew everything was about to change.

10

His father cleared his throat, squared his shoulders and opened the door.

'Good morning, Jenny,' he said pleasantly. 'What a surprise.'

'Edward,' said the woman. She peered around the door and Tom saw her large hazel eyes, her calm, quizzical expression. 'There he is,' she said, and there was a catch in her throat. 'Hello, Thomas. I'm your aunt. Jenny Caldicott.'

His father put his arm around Tom. 'So what brings you here, Jenny?' he said, and he did not move to show her in or widen the door.

'You know what, Edward.' Jenny Caldicott was still looking at Tom. She had a rather breathy voice, and a round face, like a moon, framed with gently wavy dark blonde hair. 'Didn't you get my letter?'

'We've had no letters for months,' Edward said. 'And I've not been to the post office. We've been snowed in.'

Jenny looked at Tom. 'It doesn't matter.' She smiled at him. 'I understand it's your birthday today, Tom. In our family, nine is a very important birthday.'

'Dad always said it was.' Tom was anxious to prove his father had done his job well.

'Marvellous!' She smiled at Edward again. 'That means it's time for you to learn to be a well-brought-up little boy. Don't you want to learn to be a well-brought-up little boy?'

'Oh,' said Tom, with relief. 'That's very kind of you, but I don't, thank you ever so much.'

'You haven't told him, have you?' said Jenny Caldicott to his father. She made her way into the cottage and leaned her umbrella against the table.

But Tom's father said nothing. He had turned his face to the wall, and, as Tom's aunt Jenny took off her hat, carefully, calmly removing the pins, one by one, still he said nothing.

At first Tom thought he was going away for a holiday. It took two days for it to all be settled, during which time he was sent outside to play while this woman, his aunt Jenny, and his father talked, sometimes loudly, and occasionally, if he happened to look into the cottage, he'd see his father standing up, pointing at her, and once he heard his aunt shouting something, something about parties. Tom had only been to a handful of parties, but he liked them and the idea there might be some birthday cake at some point was fine by him. He packed if not with total glee – for it was rather overwhelming, getting on a train, going all the way to London to stay with family he knew nothing about – then with some excitement. There were umpteen cinemas in London, as well as Lord's, and he was sure there must be a Matchbox car in it for him somewhere along the line.

His meagre wardrobe of clothes was kept in a small chest of drawers in the corner of the bedroom. He was struggling into last year's jumper from Mrs Fairly as his father came in.

'She says she'll buy you new things.' Edward struck a match and held it to his pipe, puffing gently. 'Now, my boy, make sure you have what you want, as well as what you need.'

'I think I've got everything, Dad.'

His father crouched down in front of him, slowly, and gripped his upper arms.

'Tom darling. Jenny is a good woman. She has come to

take you away because your grandfather and your mother left money for you to go to a good school when you're old enough, and you need to prepare for it. You'll live with her in London. In a place called Notting Hill.'

'Is Notting Hill near Shacklewell Lane?'

'What?' his father said.

'In E8,' said Tom. 'It's the Matchbox factory, remember, Dad.'

'Oh. No. Not really, old thing. It's a lovely part of town. Smart. Listen, Tom,' he said, and the grip on Tom's arms tightened, and he shook him slightly. 'You were born there. It's where your mother grew up. And – it might seem very far away from this place when you arrive but I – I have been in that house. I've walked round it. You'll know, when you're there, that it's a place I've been to.'

'Why don't you come to London with us, Dad?' said Tom brightly. He pulled the suitcase out from under the bed.

'I'm afraid not, my boy,' his father said. 'I said I'd have the pieces of the new chess set ready for Cally Hall by Easter. I can't possibly leave.' He squeezed Tom's shoulder with one hand. 'It's a wonderful adventure you're going to have.'

Tom did not know how to say that he was having second thoughts and would rather stay here. 'Of course. And . . . what if I don't want to go to London on my own, Dad?'

'Jenny will take you, old thing.'

'That's not what I –'

His father clicked his tongue. 'Come on, old boy. You'll like it there. As I say, it's near the park, and the Tube – you'll love the Tube! And the museums. Their house is frightfully grand: it has white stucco and black railings and everyone wears top hats – they did even in the war, you know!'

'Yes, Dad.'

'And the school they want for you – it's a wonderful school, called Westminster, one of the best in the country. Your uncle went there, and your grandfather, and I can't, I can't give you that, old thing! Now,' his father said, changing the subject. 'Have you packed your drawing pad, and those pastels? And *Just William*?'

He was going to school there. Tom didn't know what to say. 'Yes.'

'Have you got everything? Ready to go?'

Tom looked up at him, searching his father's face for some answers. 'I think so, Dad.'

His father reached into his pocket. 'Not quite. You forgot this. The house.' He handed him the little carved house.

Tom held the wooden building in his hand. 'Thanks, Dad.' He stared at it again. 'I don't know what it's supposed to be of. It's not our house, is it?'

'No, it's a house we used to visit, long ago. I made it for your mother. It'll remind you of me. Of us.'

'I'll be back before too long,' said Tom, putting the house in his pocket. 'Thank you, Dad. I'll take huge care of it.'

His father turned and went back into the main room, where Aunt Jenny was sitting waiting, gloved hands clutching her umbrella.

Suddenly, slowly, the importance of this moment seemed to upend itself over Tom like a cold bucket of water. He saw – he knew – that he was in the dying seconds of an old life, something to which, when he had gone, he could never return.

'I'm afraid we have to go if we're to make the train. I arranged at the station the other day for a taxi to come to meet us. Where's your case, Tom dear?' Jenny was patting her cheeks, her breastbone, the back of her hair, suddenly flustered. She stood up. 'I'm sure you'll miss your father, but you'll see him –' She glanced at Edward. 'We'll have to arrange a time for you to come to see Tom, won't we?' She held out her hand to shake Edward's hand, but he just nodded and folded his arms.

'Take care of him,' he said in a quiet voice.

For the rest of his life Tom would remember the crooked half-smile his father gave him as he crouched down and put the bag in his hand. Tom stared up into his eyes, drinking him in – his scratchy jacket, his soft worn trews, his large hands with the careful, long, sensitive fingers. Tom reached into his pocket, showed him the carved miniature house, nestling there in the darkness of the felted, moth-eaten fabric. 'I won't ever lose it,' he said. 'Anyway I'll see you soon, Dad. Won't I?'

His father folded his hand around Tom's, encasing the tiny wooden house. Perhaps, even now, he would say: no, you're not going, you're to stay.

But 'Goodbye, old boy,' was what his father said, and that was that.

11

The car was driven by Linda Moffat's uncle Bob, who had left the Moffat dairy farm and now ran the Co-op in Gatehouse and sometimes, when business was slow, drove people about. He was a terrible gossip, like his niece Linda, and his eyes bulged all through the drive to Gatehouse Station, which was two miles outside the little town, at the edge of the desolate pine forests.

'Goodbye, wee Tom Raven,' he said, flicking Tom's case out on to the ground and shaking his hand. 'You'll be off on the train now, for London, is it?'

Tom nodded solemnly, not wanting a fuss, but at the same time wanting this adult who was outside the situation to intervene, to say, This seems odd: shouldn't he stay here? Can't everything carry on as normal?

The branch line ran through Gatehouse from Stranraer to Dumfries. At Dumfries they changed on to the London train. As they pulled away from Dumfries, moving slowly through the dark red stone buildings and across the churning River Nith, so different to the tumbling burns of the Fleet and soft slate and stone of Gatehouse, a little girl, sitting on a wall by the river eating an apple, waved her hat at the train. Tom felt a lump form in his throat – he didn't know why. He watched her in agony, his stomach hurting, as she waved again, her uneven stubby plaits shaking with the effort, her shining face beaming at them.

Aunt Jenny stood up and shut the window firmly. 'Come,

Tom, sit back, and let's have some lunch. I expect breakfast seems a long time ago now. Sandwiches first, then the rest.'

She gave him two packets of sandwiches, which she had arranged with Mr Moffat – one ham, one mutton – but the smell of the mutton reminded Tom of the frozen sheep and made him feel sick. He stared at the food, trying to will himself into wanting some; it was a tragedy not to be hungry when presented with a spread like this. There was a bottle of pop, an apple and a bar of Fry's Turkish Delight peeking out of his aunt's satchel. He thought perhaps he could manage some chocolate, absolutely, and looked hopefully at his aunt, but she did not seem to notice. She smiled at him cautiously, as if he were a giraffe or a circus performer, something she had paid to see but wasn't quite sure about.

'Eat up, dear,' she said. 'Please,' she added almost imploringly.

They had the compartment to themselves at first, and sat either side of the window, Tom glued to the view, watching the last of Galloway race past – the hills flecked with early purple heather, the sky, the vastness of the bay, the dark fringing of pine trees.

'So, Thomas –' said Aunt Jenny, nibbling delicately but furiously at her sandwich, like a little mouse. 'Tell me what you've been learning at school!'

Tom stared at her. 'School?' He had been off for two weeks at Easter and could not have told you a single thing he had been learning prior to that. He glanced at his sandwich. The waxy greaseproof paper had margarine smeared over it. Nausea rose in his stomach again at the smell of the roast lamb.

'Do you study French? How is your handwriting?'

The old teacher, Miss Nye, had hit Tom with a ruler across

the hand every time he tried to write with his left hand. It had got so bad his father had gone down to the schoolhouse and had a word with Miss Nye, but all that had happened was that an inspector came over from Dumfries and said Miss Nye was quite right, that he must learn to write with his right hand. All this talk of 'right' and 'write' was so confusing to Tom that he had not understood, and so when Miss Nye tied his left hand to his chair to 'help' him he had thrown the chair across the room, only of course his hand was attached to it and the leg of the chair had caught both himself and Jean Davidson across the head, then Mr Davidson had gone to Dad and caused all sorts of trouble, and Jean and Linda called him an English madman, and after that no one would play with him and the name-calling began. Lord Snooty, Scarecrow Boy, Tinker Tailor.

It was not the tying of his arm to the chair; it was the unfairness of it. Surely it didn't matter what blasted hand he wrote with. Tom hated unfairness, from the big boys in the playground who pushed the smaller ones out of the way, to the housewives who pushed to the front of the butcher's queue, to the old, old man who'd fought in the Great War who lived in a shack in the woods by Borgue because he'd had his cottage sold out from under him and survived by selling kindling.

He was about to try to say this when Jenny leaned forwards and took his hands. 'Come on, my dear! I know you're a bright boy. Can you name the English kings and queens?'

'We didn't go in for English monarchs much,' Tom told her helpfully. 'More Robert the Bruce. And we acted out the Rough Wooing.'

'You did what?'

Miss Nye had left not long after the chair incident, and in

place of Miss Nye came Miss Gillespie, who knew the names of all the birds and the poisonous mushrooms and what the different constellations were and set moth traps with a large gas lamp and had a grand passion for Lord Darnley, and life at the little schoolhouse changed, was full of wonder and excitement every day. Miss Gillespie liked to link what they learned to their lives, to make it relevant. But there was not much learning about fractions, it had to be said.

Edward Raven often walked the two miles to the schoolhouse to collect his son. When Tom thought of his father afterwards, it was often like that: waiting outside the low small schoolhouse, set against the old graveyard whose listing stones were studded with skulls and bones, sometimes the only parent there (for all the other children lived in the village or near enough and walked back home themselves), his face lighting up when he saw Tom coming out. There was one day when they'd been playing Spitfires at lunchtime, after Miss Gillespie had told them all about the Battle of Britain.

Ack, ack, ack!!! He ran towards his father. 'Ack, ack! Dad, I've been playing Spitfires!'

'That's not the sound the Spitfire makes, Tom. It's like this.' And he'd opened his mouth and from it this cavernous, howling, thrumming sound of power and speed had issued forth and he'd chased Tom and Ian Forsyth into the graveyard, the boys screaming with delight. One of the girls had said later, sneering:

'Why's your dad pretending he knows what sound a Spitfire makes?'

''Cos he flew one,' Tom said, not looking up from his blackboard. 'In the Battle of Britain. But actually the plane he flew most was the Hawker Hurricane. He's got a DFC, Distinguished Flying Cross –' and then he looked up, just in case his father might be outside, might be listening, because he was so private about the war, never talked about it, ever.

'Your dad got himself a DFC?' Ian Forsyth was standing with his hands on his hips. 'Nah.'

Tom had shrugged. He wasn't that interested; it was long ago. But when this was verified by Farmer Moffat, who was the only person who knew Edward Raven at all, the children treated Tom with more respect. So, if anything, he despised them all the more somehow. That they should like him and his father because of something from fifteen years ago, and not because of the people they were now, seemed so dishonest.

Through the edge of the Lakes and the barren, wild York-shire Dales they went, down into the heart of England, till the landscape grew less distinctive, the towns and villages at first spaced out, then more frequent, until, it seemed, they were all grouped together, like a folded concertina, and they were passing endless rows of houses and suburbs. And suddenly it was dark, and even in the dark Tom could see a thick heavy fog draped across roads lit with weak street lights. Finally, they were drawing into a vast concourse.

'Welcome to King's Cross,' the announcer said.

Tom looked around. 'King's Cross? But – where's that?'

Jenny lifted his suitcase off the rack. 'Come on, dear. We're in London.'

Tom stared about him, at the people bustling past, the porters, the taxis, everyone rushing, dashing, so smart, so unfriendly. A split-second, flashing thought of everything that had occurred since he had held the tiny wooden house in his hand on his birthday morning zigzagged through his mind. Flinging the door open to the sweet, wild smell of spring, luring him out into the hedgerows, up on to the hills, the *toc-toc* of his father's pipe, the plan they had for the picnic on Carrick Bay on May Day.

Tom breathed in the new, wet, coal-smoke smell of London. He told himself not to think about home.

'We'll take a taxi,' said Jenny, hurrying him towards a row of juddering black London cabs. 'Since it's so late.'

'Evening. Smog's bad tonight, madam.'

'It is. Montpelier Crescent, please.'

It was that first journey through London that he would always remember – the buildings covered in soot and darkness, the lamps and lights gold in between, the sheer number of people on the streets. After a while the rocking, sprung motion of the cab relaxed him, and his eyes grew heavy. His head lolled against his aunt's arm, and suddenly he was asleep, so deeply that he did not recall being lifted out of the cab by unknown arms, carried through an open door, up the stairs and into a strange bed where he awoke the next day, still quite unable to believe that he had left everything he knew behind in just one day.

1 2

The first thing Tom noticed when he opened his eyes was the naked woman on the wall.

He raised his head and regarded her curiously. She held her arms above her; her large round breasts seemed to stick out like creamy globes, and she was smiling happily, as if she loved having no clothes on. In her hands was a garland of yellow flowers. Tom blinked, and rubbed his eyes. It was a painting, he knew that, but it was very large, and the room was very small, so it was alarmingly close. There were other women, also naked, holding the garland, all smooth and laughing, and in the background was a grand park with Classical temples. The women were painted with rough brushstrokes and – Tom didn't know how else to say it – you could see the paint.

Somewhere, he heard a clock inside the house strike the hour. He counted: 8 a.m. It occurred to him that Ian Forsyth and Bobby Galbraith would be walking to school along the Old Military Road now, hitting each other with switches of bright green hazel newly sprung on the hedgerows. He felt dizzy, as if a hole had opened up underneath him, and he clutched at the iron bedstead. He stared at the painting, willing it to disappear, shutting his mind to the ugly whorls of paint. After a few moments, he sat up, wrapping the scratchy blanket round him for warmth. I wonder where I am, he thought idly, not particularly bothered because he could smell bacon cooking and in his experience the smell of bacon was usually a good sign: his father cooked thick sizzling slices of it on the range when he'd had some money through.

Tom peered out of the window. It was very high up, so he had to stand on the swaying, rickety bed to see out. He blinked again, unsure if what he was seeing was real, for what greeted him was another world.

Greying stucco houses stretched out in front of him in lines and wedges and crescents, with green spaces stuffed in between, new spring growth everywhere. The effect was rather like a toy town, but the other strange thing was that lots of the houses were cracked, and dull, sometimes with plants growing out of the fissures. And in the street and the street beyond and as far as he could see there were gaps, like missing teeth. Normal-normal-normal, then a blank, a missing house. Beyond that, more roofs, and smoke from chimneys, and a silvery sky. He could smell the smoke; coal, not wood, it was. In the far distance he could hear a train rattling past, and the sound of tradesmen on the street. A nurse was pushing a pram along the pavement far along the other side of the road – the window was too high up for him to be able to look directly down – and she was singing to the baby as she walked along. Two young boys, about Tom's age, ran past, one tugging at the other's torn, dirty shirt, the other ruffling his hair and pushing him away. 'Get off!' he was shouting, though they were laughing, then they fell to the ground, rolling over each other, half pummelling each other, half hugging. Tom watched them hungrily. So there were children in London, he thought.

Without warning, the small, cold room felt overwhelming again. Tom shuddered, and closed his eyes. *Don't think of him.* He sniffed, clambered off the bed, and with fumbling, cold little fingers pulled on his socks, shorts, his shirt and jumper and opened the door to go downstairs, to find where the smell of bacon was coming from.

'Honestly, Jen,' a voice was saying as Tom emerged into the hallway at the bottom of the stairs, four floors down. 'It's all rot anyway. Sell them the painting and be done with it. No one will know.'

'We'll know, Hen.'

'It doesn't matter, then, does it? It's only us. I say! Who's this fine fellow!'

Tom had taken the final flight down into the basement and found himself in a warm, gloomy kitchen. A tall man leaped up, jamming a piece of toast in his mouth. 'Hello, old thing,' he said, spluttering crumbs over Tom as he pumped his hand up and down. 'I suppose I'm your uncle Henry. Good to meet you at last. Dear me,' he said, stepping back, his blue eyes blinking brightly. 'I see what you mean, Jen. Spitting image.' He swallowed.

Tom put his hands behind his back, clenching them to hide the fact his uncle had gripped his fingers far too hard. 'How – how do you do,' he said.

'Tom darling.' Jenny came over to him, and put her arm around his shoulders. 'Forgive me, you must have been dreadfully confused when you woke up. But you were sound asleep last night, and I didn't have the heart to disturb you.'

'Bacon did the trick, what!' said Henry, winking at Tom. 'Sit down, have some breakfast.'

Tom said nothing, but leaned shyly against the large pine dresser.

'It's fine,' said his uncle, kicking out a chair with one foot. 'Sit down, young 'un. You'll soon forget home – ah, well,' he added, awkwardly. 'So, Tom. Jenny's told you about your new school, I suppose! A fine place. I had no end of fun there. Like school, do you?'

Immediately, Tom knew with a sense of alarm and also with a quiet thrill that, much like his sister, this person was someone not used to talking to children: you did not *ever* ask a child about school in the school holidays. He shrugged, and edged on to the chair. 'Yes . . . sir,' he said.

'Here,' said Jenny, manoeuvring eggs and bacon, with difficulty for they had stuck to the pan, on to a small chipped plate, upon which danced gold-and-blue patterns of an intricate, if sadly worn, design. 'Mushrooms?' she said, brushing her hair out of her eyes with her oven glove and leaving a smear on her face. 'Do you usually have mushrooms, Tom?'

'Oh! No, thank you,' said Tom. He swallowed. 'Please may I – have some –' He trailed off, and bowed his head.

'Poor feller,' said Henry, looking at him with kindly concern, as if he were an exhibit in the zoo. 'Can barely understand a word he says – the accent, you know.' He raised his voice slightly. 'What's that, old thing? You want some coffee?'

'Henry, don't be ridiculous,' said Jenny, and she rushed to the worktop and poured some milk. 'Here, dear one.' She passed him a cup – also chipped, and with a large crack running down it, so that beads of milk blobbed through it. 'Drink this.'

He stared at her, at her kind, flushed face, holding out the cracked mug, at her smudged cheek, her hand shaking slightly, and he saw she was nervous too. That she did not know what she was doing either. He took the milk and drank it – it was thin, and blue coloured, and without any cream, and he thought briefly of the milk from the Belted Galloways dotted around the gentle rolling pasture leading down to Kirkcudbright. It was some of the richest milk you could get, that's what they said, pure cream, and every year Tom's father made a set of chairs or a table or something new for a farmer over in Twynholm in exchange for all the milk he wanted for a year, and when he delivered the new piece of furniture in Twynholm he was always given a pie, a proper pie with gravy and potatoes, by the farmer's wife. This was usually in winter, and they would celebrate with extra wood on the fire so it crackled all night and eat the pie and his father would raise a glass of beer to Tom: 'Have you ever been so cosy, Tom, my dear boy? Have you?'

No.

'Now, Tom,' said Jenny, when he'd finished his breakfast. 'You'll start school on Monday, and we must be ready. I've ordered your uniform –' She coughed, and Henry sat up. 'It needs to be collected this morning from Arlington and Frobisher, which I shall do presently, so that we can try it on and they can make any alterations before you begin at Knoll Hall. While I'm gone, Henry will – yes, dear?'

'Excuse me,' said Tom. 'What's Knoll Hall?'

'Knoll Hall, dear, it's a very good preparatory school on Holland Park Avenue.' His aunt rolled her *r*'s, giving the syllables in 'preparatory', a word Tom had never heard before anyway, distinct and separate emphasis.

'I thought I was going to Westminster,' said Tom, confused.

'Silly! Not until you're thirteen, and you're only nine, aren't you!' she said, as if he were the one exhibiting a deplorable lack of clarity. 'Knoll Hall is jolly nice, Tom. You can walk there – Henry did – and there are lots of nice young boys there and in the area roundabouts – you'll make some nice friends –'

'I saw some boys playing on the street,' said Tom hopefully. 'I was wondering if I could go out and find them in a bit.'

'Oh, no, Tom,' said Jenny, flushing with alarm. 'You mustn't play out in the street. There are some very rough boys who play on the bomb site.'

'A bomb site?' Tom said eagerly.

'Twenty people died, Tom, it was dreadful. And some of those children were caught up in it. There are some roads that aren't' – she hesitated, then fell back on a favourite word again – 'at all *nice* round here, not at all. Start as you mean to go on.'

'Area's gone downhill,' Uncle Henry said. 'Like everything.'

'Isn't this a . . . nice street, then?' said Tom, not sure what this meant.

Henry took another sip of coffee. 'Was once, Tommy old boy. But the war, you see. And the repairs, the bomb damage . . . no money.'

'No money?'

'No money to fix things, no money to buy things. Can't sell the paintings either. No market for Father's stuff – bottom's fallen out of it, you see.' He drained his cup.

Tom felt as though he kept saying things and they kept hearing something completely different. 'What bottom?'

'Yes, well,' Jenny interrupted sharply, 'in any case, Father didn't want us to sell, and that's that.'

Henry said shortly, 'We may have to, now you've decided it's time to play happy families.'

Jenny pushed the fluffy hair that fell in her face out of the way, raised her head and stared at him, and Tom saw the steel in her eyes. 'We agreed. Always, there was an agreement we would take him. For Irene.'

166

'For Irene my foot,' said Henry, and his tone was not kind.

There was a short, charged silence. Uncle Henry stood up and pulled a moth-eaten deerstalker off the hatstand. 'I say, young Tom – what do you say to a walk round your new neighbourhood?'

'Rather,' said Tom, leaping up. 'May I go, please, Aunt Jenny?' He carried his chipped cup and plate to the side and started washing them up. His aunt and uncle watched.

'Good grief,' said Uncle Henry. 'A Caldicott. Doing the washing-up.'

'Oh,' said Tom, standing back from the sink. He felt his cheeks burning red; he had made a mistake yet again. 'I'm sorry, should I –'

'No!' said Jenny. 'No, dear. You see, when we were children we had maids to do all this –' Her hand swept round the dingy basement, at the bare floor, the dusty corners, the acres of neglected space. 'We weren't ever in the kitchen.'

Tom didn't know how to point out without being rude that they were, at this exact moment in time, in the kitchen. Instead he said, 'You don't know how to wash up?'

'Of course we do,' said Henry indignantly. 'If you'd seen me in the war, at Sevenstones washing up – twenty plates a minute, I did once!'

'Sevenstones?'

'Rubbish,' scoffed his sister. 'Both the claim and the standard of your washing-up. You never did the washing-up at Sevenstones. Irene, now, she made the place sparkle within ten minutes, top to bottom, then she'd be out in time to report to the air base after no sleep.' She turned to Tom. 'Irene was one of those people who was good at everything,' she said.

'My mother,' said Tom proudly.

'Yes,' she said, her blue eyes shining.

'What was Sevenstones?'

'Sevenstones was my father's little bolthole,' said Jenny, glaring at her brother. 'He gave it to us in the war, so our friends had a place to go. It's where your parents met. Run along now – go and get your coat on. It's chilly outside.'

Tom wanted to laugh; if she thought this was chilly she should try March in Galloway, but he did not say this. He fingered the wooden house in his pocket. Sevenstones. Now it had a name.

13

As they emerged on to the street in daylight, Tom saw his new home for the first time. What struck him was how strange it was to have white houses – white showed the dirt, most dreadfully, and these houses were most dreadfully dirty. Something about the white stucco with the black railings, like skeletons, terrified him. Uncle Henry tapped at the railings with his walking stick.

'What happened to the missing houses?' said Tom, trying to be polite about the state of the street as they walked along its curved outer pavement, towards a larger road.

'Air raids, old thing.' Henry swung his stick out again, clattering it along the railings. Tom stared up and down at the blackened houses with boarded-up windows, the blown-out houses with no windows at all – No. 32, the Caldicott house, it seemed, was a rarity, in being relatively unscathed. He wondered why his father had thought it such a fine place to live. Tom thought he probably hadn't been here for a while.

He peered at his uncle as they walked along together. He wasn't used to having relatives. This new uncle was, Tom thought, rather magnificent, from his battered deerstalker and his worn dove-grey soft wool jumper to his wide tweed trousers. He was tall, and slender as a reed, lifting his hat to passing matrons on the other side, raising his eyebrows at a fluffy grey-and-white cat winding its way along the railings as though they and it were magnetic. Walking beside him, Tom felt proud.

'Were you here in the war, Uncle Henry? What was it like?' Tom mimed with a gun. 'Pop! Pop! Ha!'

'Ah! parts of it.'

'When did you meet my father?'

Uncle Henry ran his stick lightly along the railings. 'Used to come to Sevenstones, the place in Wiltshire. Fine fellow, your pa, bravest of the brave. We all fell for him, Irene most of all, of course. I remember the first time he walked in. Bam. Right in the middle of the hairiest fighting in the skies, 1940 this was, felt it was all over at times and in steps a chap straight off 87 Squadron, fresh from shooting down five Huns in one night. That was the night that started to turn the tide – I remember it well – and he was in the thick of it, your pa.' Henry gave a shout of laughter at the memory. 'He breezed in, you know, carrying a bottle of champagne he'd begged off a barmaid in a pub. Had his uniform on, so they knew where he'd been. I should think they'd have given him the whole damned pub if he'd asked,' said Uncle Henry ruminatively. 'That's your father. Sell water to fish. Life and soul of the party. You know.'

'Not really,' said Tom cheerfully, skipping alongside him, hands in pockets, having forgotten all about his vow not to think about his father. Hearing about him from other people wasn't painful, it was marvellous. 'We don't have any friends. And we never had a party.'

'Never had a party? What rot. Don't believe it.'

'There's no room, honest. And Dad didn't like visitors. If they knocked, he wouldn't let them in. So they stopped knocking.'

'How extraordinary. Didn't you mind?'

'Oh.' It hadn't occurred to Tom to care one way or the other. He was happy with his father, and that was that. 'No, not at all.' And then he felt the dizziness that had struck him earlier in his room creeping across him, the sense that if he didn't block everything out he might start to feel how much he missed him. He gritted his teeth, then said, 'Uncle Henry, what's Sevenstones like?'

'Old tumble-down cottage, size of a shoebox. Father bought it to paint. He went through an ancient history phase, very into Constable's *Stonehenge* and true England, druids and all that rot. Some chap he met on a train sold it to him. Supposed to be on the site of some burial chamber, not that we ever found any gold crowns or any such thing, but there are seven stones circling the place, rather jolly. Still, on Midsummer he'd waft round the garden and we got into the habit of it too, quite fun, thirty people watching the sunrise together, it rises just so – between the hills –' He held his hands about a foot apart. 'Then we'd all go orf, to get shot.' He blinked rapidly. 'Last one out had to clean up and leave a bottle of champagne on the mantelpiece for the next lot. Gate locked, key under the stone.'

'But . . . could anyone go there?'

'Yes, he gave it to us to use in the war. We painted it, Jenny, Irene and I, great fun. Dragged some furniture up from town and had a phone put in; I think someone even got the Yanks to pay for it, Special Ops, you know. That was it. Then it was open house, you see, it means anyone and everyone,' said Henry. 'Anyone . . . glamorous fighter pilots like your pa and his RAF pals, GIs and WAACs, girls serving in Fighter Command, those American drivers, Leila and Katty and Teddy . . . anyone who could get to the place by car – anyone and everyone was welcome, especially if you had a pash on someone, a trip to Sevenstones usually helped things along, what? Now here –'

They had turned into a narrow road lined with shops, in front of which were stalls selling fruit and vegetables, immaculately stacked together as though at a slight touch the potatoes and cabbages would become dislodged from their display and roll down the road. 'This is Portobello Road. Antiques here; fruit and veg there. Listen to me, young Tom. This is your patch. Don't go further north than Blenheim Crescent, you understand? Up there. And behind you' – he jabbed the stick back behind them towards the crescent – 'don't go west of Portland Road. Just stay here, the streets around here, and you'll be fine.'

'Why?' said Tom, who was used to roaming where he liked, when he liked, for hours at a time.

'Unsavoury lot over there, and up there,' said Uncle Henry. 'Times are changing. Not our kind of people. Didn't used to be like this. Before the war . . .' He trailed off. 'You don't want to go mixing with them, the poor' – he jabbed his thumb in the opposite direction – 'or the Blacks. Understand? Stick to our patch.'

Tom didn't understand, simply because in his life so far he had not really encountered either class or race, at least so far as he was aware. He knew that Donald Murray, who had been at Gatehouse School until last year, was to be a sir one day, but Donald Murray was a fool who didn't know how to play catapult games and ran to his father when he was called names. But so much of what Henry or Jenny said didn't seem to make sense, so yet again he nodded.

'Understand,' he said, and held his uncle's hand as they crossed over the road. 'What about Mr Smithers – is he poor or Black?'

'He's trade; it's different,' said Uncle Henry. He waved his hand airily and took a slim flask out of his pocket, one which

Tom recognized from the breakfast table, and took a large gulp. 'And, as for the business about Sevenstones and the parties, the Americans and whatnot – look, see, don't mention any of that to Jenny, I beg of you. Fearfully sensitive about some things, my Jen, not up to questioning.' He pushed gingerly at the peeling grey door of the antiques shop. 'Anyone about?' he called.

'I say,' said a quiet voice, a woman's. 'Henry dear, how could you possibly have known I was alone?'

'Ha!' said Henry hastily. He turned to his nephew, who stood on the threshold, and gently nudged him back outside. 'Why don't you push off, what? Have a wander round, find your bearings.' He took five shillings from his wallet and handed it to him.

'But I don't know how to –' said Tom, but his uncle's expression had rearranged itself. Henry stared at him quite blankly, making a shooing motion, as the door of the shop shut with a slam and a frenzied jangling of a bell and Tom found himself, for the first time, alone in London.

He had never had five bob. He so rarely saw money, his father being paid in favours or food, that he wasn't really sure what to do with it. He felt like that Midas fellow they'd learned about in school. Five whole bob! He tucked it carefully into his pocket and headed north up Portobello Road; and, when he reached Blenheim Crescent, continued on past it, ignoring his uncle's instructions. A large grey scruffy dog trotted by, barging past Tom and growling, and Tom jumped out of the way: he didn't like dogs.

The rain was coming down harder now, and the carts were shutting up. On the corner back towards Ladbroke Grove, a blank expanse caught his eye. A square hole in the ground, a few yards below street level and filled with the most extraordinary collection of bricks, dust, iron; small hills and cathedrals lay within it, arched windows with no glass; and, holding it all together, dusty rubble like snow, only it was rust-coloured snow, brown and black. Some children were there, climbing in and out of the half-walls, the alcoves and pitted basements; from the last, strange roots with the beginnings of leaves sprang forth. It was the bomb site Jenny had mentioned.

The children were calling to each other, laughing and chatting. One of them, a boy about Tom's age, threw something to the other; it missed him and he swore loudly, then disappeared, as if vanishing back into the one part of the wall still standing. Then, a second or two later, he reappeared and opened a front door. They carried on laughing. One of them pretended to shoot the other, who pretended to fall down dead.

Their accents were so strong that Tom couldn't understand them. He edged a little closer. 'Your mum bought it here!' one of them shouted at one of the older boys, who stood at a distance, arms folded, face red. 'She's right under here, ain't she? You listening to me?'

It took Tom a while to take in what he'd heard. Someone's mother was lying under all that rubble, years after the bombing. Overwhelmed by everything, and very tired, Tom stopped still in the street. A sudden, irrational panic gripped him. Everything here was black and white: the white buildings, the black railings, the rubble, the front door that had belonged to someone once. No green, no blue, no yellow-silver skies, no amber. Black and white. He ran, his legs like jelly, and the five-bob note fell out of his hand but he carried on running. He banged into someone, winding them; then he fell backwards. It was a Black man in a brown suit.

He gripped Tom's wrists and said, 'Hey! What're you doing, going so fast?'

Tom pushed him out of the way, gasping for breath. He ran, and ran, not listening, a tide of panic washing over him. He hated it here. He didn't want to be here. It was too different, and they didn't feel right, they weren't his family, these two odd people. He didn't care about school or being a Caldicott. And in his mind, he could only hear his dad agreeing to let him go, and a voice saying, *He didn't want you any more.*

Someone was calling him, running after him. Tom carried on running, his strong legs bearing him back home, although it wasn't home. Home was hundreds, thousands of miles away – he didn't even *know* how far away. And the voice was still calling out to him. *Tom, Tom!*

Eventually he had to stop – he didn't know where he was – and, as he did so, someone clapped a hand on his shoulder, squeezing it tightly. He turned round, his face crumpled. It was the Black man again, and he was peering down at Tom.

'Hey, you. Sorry to chase you. But I think I know you. Are you Tom? Tom Raven?'

Tom nodded, too exhausted to speak, his shoulders heaving.

'You're so small,' said the man. 'But you run like a cheetah.' He smiled at him. 'Listen, I'm Gordon! Listen!' he said again, because Tom was sobbing so loudly now he could hardly be heard. 'Hey! Shush.' Gordon rubbed his back gently, then patted it, then rubbed it, then patted it, and the motion was hypnotic, warming, and Tom stopped crying and stood, shoulders still rising and falling, gulping for air until his breath slowed.

'How do you know my name?' said Tom, staring at

Gordon, because he had never in his small, remote life seen someone with skin a different colour to his own.

'I'm a friend of Jenny,' Gordon said. 'I saw you on Portobello, with Henry.'

'Oh,' said Tom. 'Do you live in her road too?'

'Not me. I knew her in the war. Jenny helped me; she's helped a lot of people. She's –' He stopped. 'She's glad to have fetched you back; she's glad to have you here, Tom.'

'I don't like it. I want to go back, I want to –' Tom tried to run off again, but Gordon caught up with him, held on to his arm.

'I knew your dad, Tom, in the war. And your mum. Jenny, she's giving up everything for you, you understand?'

Tom rubbed his eyes. It was so new, all of it. 'I want to go home,' he said. 'Do you know the way back to Montpelier Crescent, by any chance?'

'Of course I do,' said Gordon. He bent down. 'Hey, Tom. Hey. You think you're alone, and I promise you, you're not.' And he put his hand on the back of Tom's head, cupping it gently, and Tom felt the warmth of his skin against his scalp, and the touch of another person was so comforting in that moment, but then he pushed it down, and they walked together to Montpelier Crescent, side by side.

Gordon showed him where Jenny kept the spare key: under a plant pot with some waterlogged spindly plant that had long since died, then left him with a wave.

'I'll see you, Tom.'

'When?' said Tom, not wanting him to go, the first truly friendly person he'd met in London.

'Soon,' Gordon said.

'Thank you,' said Tom. He had recovered a little by then.

'Sorry about earlier.' He looked at Gordon curiously. 'Where are you from?'

'I'm from Trinidad, my boy,' said Gordon. 'The most beautiful place in the world.' He nodded. 'Plant a stick in the ground, the stick flowers.'

'Really?'

'Oh, yes,' said Gordon solemnly. He adjusted the cuffs of his neat suit and cleared his throat rather formally. 'But I'm here now. Came back after the war.' Gordon crouched down, so he was eye level with Tom. 'You feel like an outsider, don't you? So did I, even though I was fighting for England. And Jenny and Henry and Irene, they made me feel like Seven-stones was home.'

'Home,' Tom said the word blankly.

'Yes, home.' Gordon was brisk. 'This is your home now. Make the most of it. This is who you are now!'

He sounded a little like a teacher, which Tom was to discover was one of the many jobs Gordon could have done well. 'Thank you very much,' said Tom, shaking his hand. 'I'm fine now.' He held the key. 'Good morning.'

'You're polite, aren't you? Goodbye, little man.' And he lifted his hat to Tom and walked away. Tom let himself in and shut the door. The dank cool of the house overwhelmed him for a moment. He stood in the hallway, shivering.

'Is that you, Tom?' Jenny's voice echoed up from the kitchen. 'I've been to the uniform shop. When you've a moment, come down and wash your hands please!'

Tom walked slowly upstairs, carefully examining the house as he went, for he felt it was like a detective film, something new to notice every time. A couple of spindles were missing on the banisters. There were marks on the striped silk wallpaper where pictures had once hung. One of the windows on the landing was boarded up. He stopped and looked at it, as his aunt emerged from the basement and followed him upstairs to the first-floor landing. She looked pale, and unformed, her white lace shirt loose, her hair astray, quite different from the smart woman who had arrived to take him away.

'It was blown out in 1940 and we never got round to replacing it,' she said, pointing at the window. One hand gripped the newel post, and she brushed a lock of hair out of her eyes with the other.

'Was it bad here, the bombing?' Tom said.

'Yes,' she said. 'Dreadful. The war changed everything.' Her eyes were large and unfocused. She moved towards him and brushed something away from his face. 'You're her son,' she whispered, her soft voice cracking, and she leaned forwards and kissed him, then stepped back, as if he'd given her an electric shock. 'Her son, and you're here, finally – you're here –' Tom thought about what Henry had said, not mentioning Sevenstones. 'Come on, then, let's measure you for these clothes.'

Tom washed his hands and obediently followed her into the pale yellow drawing room, where she shut the heavy wooden shutters. 'Take your clothes off, Tom.'

The feeling that everything was wrong, too large, too black and white, no green, no wilderness, overwhelmed him again, and his eyes hurt. Digging his hands into his pockets, he drew something out of his shorts. It was the wooden house. The tip of the chimney stack had snapped off. Sevenstones. Tom laid it quietly on the side, as his aunt ran a tape measure round his chest, staring at him with those wide, empty eyes.

14

Dearest Tom

All is well here. Summer has arrived, the skylarks wake
me up most mornings and the swifts are in full fettle –
the streams are full, Tom, and I've eaten like a king on
trout, perch, and so forth. I saw Miss Gillespie last week
in Gatehouse, she asked to be remembered to you and
says to work hard and mind your P's and Q's.

I'm not a great one for letters as you know, dear boy. Please
write to me, I long to hear from you about your new life
and the exciting things you are doing and the great lessons
you are learning, Tom. I shall not think about the past; we
were happy, weren't we, old thing, but instead shall set my
course to a time when you are a grown man and can look
back and see why I did what I did. You will remember your
old father I hope and understand that, though at times he
made a catastrophic mess of it all, he was earnestly trying
to do right by his son.

Cheerio, old thing, and do not look back with sadness but
forward with a smile

Dad

I would love a short note from you to let me know how
you are getting on.

That first year in Montpelier Crescent Tom grew used to feeling sad, or, if not sad, then in a state of perpetual shock. He was being told, after all, he was someone completely different from wee Tom Raven who walked back from school swinging his satchel over his head and who knew the fieldfares and the thrushes by their individual song, who knew where the otters played and the best, plumpest blackberries grew.

32 Montpellier cresent
London W.
16 July 1955

Dear Dad

Thank you for your letter.

Please past my best on to Miss Gillespie.

I've just broken up for the holidays after one term at Knoll Hall – that's my new school. We go on longer here in London but I still have some time off for sumer holidays. Dad, can I come and see you?

I have a posh uniform: it is a blaser and a cap with a wee eagel sown on but most of the boys dont know what an eagel looks like, even though they jaw on about the comic. Most of them are soft, Dad, they cry when they fall down. I dont cry. School lunchs are grand, dad, there's boiled beef and marro peas all you can eat and last week treacl pudding. I eat all the time.

I like Maths and History and I hate the rest of it. I hate spelling I like my books but hate spelling and rugga because I'm a weed compared to the rest of them they

LONDON IS THE PLACE FOR ME

say. But I don't cry lots of them cry for their mas when something doesn't go their way.

There's a bomb site round the corner from the hous and I know two of the boys who play there, they live a few strets over and they are called Tony Powl and Johnny Hilman. Tony is meen and says wild things. Johnny's brother is a teddy boy you heard of them, Dad? He has slicked hair and he carries a knife, dad. He's called Robert, I dont like him. I have a friend, called Gordon, he is from Trinna dad, he has dark skin. He sais Robert holds the knife up to people like him and whispas bad things at them. But Johnny's ma is kind and works at the pie and mash shop on a road off an impotant road called Portobello Road. I think there was a battle or a river or somthing there they do like to talk about it.

Aunt Jenny works at a Church of spirichual inlight ment and I don't know what that is. She goes and prays there and hands out soup. It's digusting soup, I had to help her one time.

Uncle Henry goes off on important busness most of the day I dont know what. He's funny, but I don't think he likes children.

Aunt Jenny has taken me to the library and I've got my card. I go in there all the tim when there is no one at home when I get back from school. Sometimes I go for a cup of tea with Gordon and he gives me tost. Gordon says he knowse you dad, and that he knew my mother. He says my mother was remakkable. Gordon works on the buses, and people ask him for help. He is kind even if he is a bit strict about sitting up strait and the Ps and Qs like Miss Nye.

One more thing I am drawing with the pastils you got me for my birthday. I am drawing our hous and the hills and evrything so I never forget it. I can't tell you where it is a secret and I'll get in trouble.

Well Dad Id better go.

Your loving son Tom xxxxx

I'm to post this letter now. <u>Please dad write to Jenny about when I can come and see you.</u>

Tom's world was smaller geographically – less than half a square mile all told – but within that world were infinite possibilities and events and stories, from the bomb site to the school to the streets off Portobello, the garden squares, the houses jammed with new arrivals, the noise of building everywhere. Sometimes it was overwhelming. As the days stretched into months and life in London assumed some kind of shape, Tom spent most of his spare time with Gordon, or with Tony and Johnny on the bomb site, and then, when they cleared it of rubble, at the library. His other refuge was his room. He had his pastels from his father and a couple of pencils he'd snaffled from school and he'd embarked on a project.

He didn't allow himself to think of home but for some reason he found it easy to draw it instead. Drawing was assembling a world, building it just as the men were building blocks of flats and houses around here, brick by brick. It was a record, accurate and true, of his own place. When he felt so lonely that his thoughts ran around his head like rats, he quietly unhooked *Helen Caught Bathing*, rested it carefully against the chest of drawers and began to draw on the wall, an intricate world that would become so vast that he was running out of space. He had the endless skies and the swathes of cloud hanging over Solway Firth towards the Isle of Man. In one corner, behind the bed, he had drawn the full Milk moon, hanging low over the firth in May, not milky so much as amber-gold, the sea liquid metal and still. That was the only piece of colour he wanted for the wall, he thought. A tiny touch of gold, for the moon, plump like a snowberry, waiting to be plucked. He had seen Smithers, Uncle Henry's friend, repairing an old mirror with gold leaf so he could sell it on to someone as a Renaissance masterpiece or some such, and Tom had watched fascinated at the fluttering, blinking feather-light gold, like an insect wing held between tweezers. Yes. He would paint the whole wall and then beg or steal a scrap of gold leaf.

The painting stretched from behind globular, beaming Helen, snaked along to the bed and then round the headboard, which Tom got used to pulling out very quietly in case he was disturbed. But neither Jenny nor Henry ever came up to ask what he was doing.

He had swiftly put away the dream of a Matchbox crane, much less a visit to the factory in Shacklewell Lane, E8. There were ten streets on either side of him, then another ten, and they were all still in W11. E8, East London, was another world away.

The carved wooden cottage lived on the windowsill, which Tom placed there because he had a compass that faced north, back towards Scotland. He did not dare take the cottage to school again: on his fifth day some older boys had held him upside down to shake out his pockets because they said all Scots hid money. He had managed to scrabble to pick it up and hide it, and that evening he had put it on the windowsill behind the curtains, and touched it every morning and night. One day he would go back.

Tom told himself he was fine and didn't miss his father, which was good. His father didn't write back. Tom kept writing, though he couldn't tell him what life here was really like. Partly because he didn't want him to worry, but partly because Tom didn't understand it, any of it.

15

Dear Tom

Autumn is being chased away by winter now; there's a sharp sting in the mornings and mist lying lower than ever and it's hard to believe a month ago I was swimming at Brighouse. It was a good long summer, Tom, plenty of rabbits to catch and trout to be had and I managed to bag a pheasant or two a few weeks ago – don't tell young Murray – and I'm awfully burned on the neck and arms from the sun working outside. I've taken a job painting and odd jobs on the estate, just to get me out of the house, and it turns out I'm rather good at it. You know I love the sun and suffer in winter, whereas you're perhaps like your mother, who loved the freezing cold, the ice and the chill. The last of autumn lingers up in the hills, where the heather is the deepest purple, turning to copper, and the water seems a little darker now, not so turquoise as it was in summer. We have had such fine days till now I'm thankful.

When we first came here, you and I, it was January, seven months after we were left alone. I never really talked to you about it, how we came to live here. Lately I have thought how little you know and how it's best that way sometimes but there are some facts I should like you to know now

185

that you are so far from me and the opportunity to pass them on might not arise when we meet, which will be one day I know.

I had joined the RAF when war broke out and because my dear dad, whom you never knew, was Scottish, I was posted to Glasgow with 602 Squadron, where we trained, before I joined 87 Squadron. One of the fellows I was training with, Sandy McCullough, came from a wee place near Kirkcudbright, Twynholm, and he drove me down to Fleet Bay one weekend in spring.

I grew up in Cumbria and you know I hold the Lakes to be the most beautiful place in the world but that day I realized I'd been trounced. Go north, between the Pennines and the Lakes and turn left into Galloway . . . the place where there's the sea and the pine trees and the hills – the bay that's a whole other land when the tide's out. I'd rarely seen beaches, you understand. One-day trip here and there.

Coming out of fighter-pilot training . . . leaving Glasgow and the factories and the sense of impending doom and them men and women with faces tightly knitted together, and pitching up in this corner of paradise. Anemones like jewels in the rocks, whelks everywhere, coves and beaches and little islands and those hills, always in the background. Sandy had brought sandwiches, I'd brought beer, and we sat on the shore and shared our pack-up and talked about what we'd do after the war. It seemed so distant, war, then, that was before all of it. Sandy died in the Battle of Britain, shot down off the coast of Kent a few months later. Most of my friends were gone the following year, Tom.

So I remembered the day well. It was the last really pure day, in a way.

Later. This letter is longer than I realized it would be.

What would have happened if your mother hadn't got in that plane? If she'd said to the colonel, no, I can't come today, I have to go for a picnic with my husband and son. I have to go and walk in the woods. I have to lie on a rug and hold my baby up in the air. It would have been unthinkable to do such a thing, and yet if she had – !

I wonder what we would all be like. If we would simply be very happy all the time. If I would be in a job in London, working hard and barely seeing you, and she would be at home, organizing – the house, her siblings, her surroundings. She was an organizer, Irene Caldicott. She organized me into marrying her and thank God I did. She organized you into arriving when I wasn't sure about it, not at all. And on that last day, in her last moments, she must have been so terrified. She must have cried out for you, and me – oh dear, Tom, sometimes the thought of it overwhelms me. Darling boy, she loved you so much.

She believed in service, getting things done. She had an infinite capacity for understanding and forgiveness, as I know all too well. She had limitless patience with you when you cried and would not settle, and I was always, always in awe of her, darling girl. When your mother died you were a year old. I didn't know what to do for a while. I hadn't considered the possibility of losing her. What a simpleton: now I see disaster everywhere, only now it's too late, of course.

We were living at a flat in Kensington. An old friend of mine from 87 Squadron, who'd been posted elsewhere, lent it to me. I was looking after you very badly. London was not the place for me, quite the opposite of what Kitch sang about. It was a tired city, we were all tired, there was nothing there, no hope, and I didn't care for it enough to overlook its scars and wounds. I realized I had to get away and bring you up somewhere new, somewhere where there were no memories of her.

They were not happy with this decision, but Jenny was not well – we were all not well, after the war. The plan had been that we would stay in Montpelier Crescent and you would grow up a London boy. I can't explain why but I had to get away. I will try, one day. And then one morning I saw an advertisement in *The Times* for a woodsman job at the Murray Estate accommodation included – I had some money from my parents, and, as my eyes fell on the advert, I remembered that day at the beach with poor Sandy. I knew we would go. I made a pact with Jenny, you see, that was the only way to go. I promised you would have an English public school education, the envy of the world, something I could never give you. And I packed us up, our meagre possessions and very few mementoes of Irene – she was not a sentimental woman. We were in Scotland the following week. We drove up – the petrol nearly finished me off, and that's when the leg of the bed was lost. You sat in your carrycot beside me in the front of the van fastened in with a seat belt and sometimes you grabbed my finger.

We walked to the beach at Skyreburn Bay and I set you down on the sand and you started crawling, then and there, on the muddy estuary, in the middle of winter! You had never crawled before. I watched you, like a crab scuttling towards the sea. I thought to myself, this boy wants to go places, he wants to roam, he wants to see the world.

I had you for nine years. All to myself. So when I miss you terribly, so much my stomach hurts and my eyes cloud over with black smog, I tell myself it's for the best, for in those nine years we were two halves of a whole, and it had to end, dear Tom. Perhaps here life was too small for you, for all its vastness.

All my love, Tom
Dad

November 1956

Dearest Tom

Another letter from your old man. It's been almost a year and a half since you wrote now, old thing. Can you scribble me just a line or so? I'd love to hear from you.

I wonder if you open them or simply throw them away. No matter, I write anyway in case. Making amends? We had Guy Fawkes, a big bonfire up at the Murray Arms last week, it's a new thing, a lot of fun. All of the village and the other surrounding villages. I miss you most days all day but especially when I see the children who were your schoolmates and see how they've grown. I miss your hair, which grows in thick thatches that go in random directions and at different rates. All manner of things.

It is very odd, when one thinks of what your mother and I hoped for the future, when we were married and starting out, and now it is just me, on my own, having bid farewell to the best people in my life.

I was so intimately involved in your life: what you did, where you slept, when your toenails needed cutting. It really was just us, wasn't it? And I know nothing of you now. How is school? Your letter said you weren't enjoying English – I know you will one day, just give it time. Spelling doesn't matter, Tom, it's not what makes character. Spelling comes out just right in the end.

I know you don't want to write back but know that, at the other end of the country, your old man does miss you most dreadfully. Forgive the self-pity. Another letter soon, with tales of more cheerful deeds!

Dad xx

March 1957

Dear Tom

I'm sending you, a little early, a five bob note for your birthday. Are you all right, old man? It's utterly wonderful to think of you as an eleven-year-old. But I do wish I could hear from you, whether you've finished the secret picture you alluded to, though that was well over a year ago. Two. Two years since you left.

I didn't want to break off communications, my boy, that's not ever what I wanted. Do please write back – if you want. The money is from a recent commission at the Cally

Palace; they are pleased with my work and I find myself with some money to spare for once!

All my love to you, Tom dear boy,

I miss you most fearfully – try and drop me a postcard, even if just to show me what your handwriting is like now.

Dad xx

September 1957

Dear Edward,

I am returning your letters to Tom enclosed herewith. Please don't carry on writing to him. He does not open them; he finds any mention of you too distressing. He is happy now, and has entirely stopped missing Scotland. He has a full and busy life, is excelling at school, and making suitable young friends. His teachers say his progress is remarkable. We said we would take care of him now and that we will do. There is no need to write again.

When I saw you, you asked if I could ever forgive you. The answer is no, Edward.

Yours,
Jenny

16

Spring 1958

Tom and Gordon Baxter were friends now. They went walking together through London. Gordon worked for London Underground, and had made it his mission to get to know the city above ground.

Jenny knew Gordon; Tom had proof of this now. One day in spring, three years after he'd arrived, he was walking past the building site where the bomb had fallen. He had just turned twelve. The previous week Tony Powell had found a nest of rats and had boasted to everyone he was wondering what to do with them: whether to barbecue them, or release them into posh nobs' houses, or put them down the dresses of girls at school.

Tom had waited around a bit, wanting to make sure Tony didn't do anything stupid. He felt anxious, stupidly concerned, but, more than anything else, he hated unfairness, and bullying. It was March, but it was freezing cold, smog filling the wide pavements and avenues. It hung over the bomb site like a ghost house. Tom turned to go, on the way out bumping into Johnny Hillman on the pavement.

'You off?'

Tom nodded. 'Seems stupid if you ask me.'

'La di dah,' Johnny muttered. 'Piss off, then.'

'I will, thanks. Don't know why you bother with Tony.'

Johnny had shoved him. 'I said, piss off.'

Tom was surprised, but Johnny was like that sometimes,

usually nice but then angry out of nowhere, whereas Tony was angry all the time, and Johnny's brother Robert was even worse. He'd been in trouble with the police and all sorts.

The smog chilled him to his bones. Scotland was cold but the smog was worse: it made you cough, made you feel like melted coal was seeping into your throat. He stopped on the corner of his road to cough, and that's where he saw Gordon.

He was standing outside their house, and Jenny was on the front doorstep. Tom walked towards them, as quietly as he could, then hid behind a car for a few seconds. He didn't know why he didn't just make his presence known.

'There're no more letters, Jenny. I told you.'

'But it's been two months, Gordon. Two months. It's never been that long before.'

'Her friend, that fella, whatever his name is. He's ill sometimes. Sometimes that delays it. You got to be patient. He'll write.'

'Are you sure you haven't missed something?'

Tom could just see round the corner of the car. Jenny was gripping Gordon's hands. 'Are you sure no one's interfering with the post, Gordon?'

'It's not me,' Gordon said, shaking his head. He pulled his hands away, held them up to the skies. 'That's all the news I've got, Jenny –'

'You're lying to me –'

'Me? You're lying to everyone.' Gordon raised his voice. 'You want me to say it out loud, in front of all these nice neighbours? "Hey! This kid, she stole him off his dad!" When you going to tell Edward, hey? When you going to tell that boy?'

Jenny's voice was a hiss. 'Shut up. Go away.'

He heard Gordon sighing. 'I said I'd help you. For Irene, and Edward. You gotta help yourself, my dear. I can't do any more.'

A van drove past, and Tom took the opportunity to return to the pavement He approached Jenny and Gordon, smiling, as if everything were normal, and watched as they sprang apart.

'Gordon was just passing and he thought he'd say hello, which is lovely, because I haven't seen him for aeons,' Jenny said. 'Especially now he's such a great friend of yours.'

'Will you come in for a cup of tea, Gordon?' Tom asked politely.

'Nah, boy. But I'll see you for one of our walks, yes?' Gordon's hand squeezed his shoulder and he stared at Jenny for a moment, then walked away.

Tom was a pragmatic child. After three years in London, he understood uncertainty and disengagement with reality was just how Jenny and Henry were. They didn't know their neighbours; they never walked north of Blenheim Crescent; they bemoaned the changes that meant people didn't queue properly and never said please and thank you; and they were visibly repulsed by the cracked, broken city still recovering from war. Tom had learned about Dante Gabriel Rossetti from his aunt and how he grew tired of his models when they got old; he thought Jenny and Henry were rather like that about their city: they loved it only if it looked nice, with no interest in what was underneath.

The old houses towards Kensington and the park were still lived in by families like theirs – his. These were people who remembered Julian Caldicott and a world of servants,

Oxford and Cambridge boat race parties, cabinet ministers and Royal Academicians as neighbours.

The one activity Tom undertook with his aunt and uncle was a walk every few weeks, on a Sunday. They walked to St James's Park via Kensington Gardens and the Peter Pan statue, the boating lake in Hyde Park, the still-wild patches through which he liked to imagine Henry VIII had gone hunting, down to Harrods, then across to the Ritz, where Uncle Henry and Aunt Jenny had both drunk White Ladies and gone dancing during the Blitz.

The route always varied: sometimes through Mayfair, and the little lanes of Shepherd Market, or the grandness of backstreet Mayfair, where countesses were helped out of ancient Daimlers purring on St James's Square, and old boys in top hats nodded as doormen swept open the vast porticoes of the private clubs on Pall Mall, where the country was really run, and then to the Mall, where Jenny had stood on VE Day, tossing her peaked grey-blue WAAF cap in the air and cheering for the king and queen.

On these walks Jenny was not a half-figure of shadow, sitting at the kitchen table looking blankly at sums or writing letter after letter about her father's work to dealers who never wrote back; and Henry was not absent – whenever Tom thought of his uncle in later life, he remembered him as constantly shuffling away down a corridor, out of sight, on the way to the pub. For a short time they were brother and sister, full of gaiety and high spirits, with a constant supply of good stories and jokes: the time Henry had tried to rescue a cat in the park and got stuck up a tree; the day they drove from the Ritz down to Sevenstones, and during the journey Jenny and an American WAAC friend had produced a cat they'd adopted; the evening Irene had got into an argument with an American serviceman and then slapped him across the face, leading to a night in a Mayfair police station. Tom loved hearing them talk about their family, their lives, for in these stories Jenny and Henry and all their friends were people with purpose, who believed in something – freedom – and were willing to fight the enemy – the Nazis – for that freedom, for the common good of all, and so they put up with bombing and friends dying and indignities and terror, and when the situation called for it they had rolled up their sleeves and dug deep – people out of holes, in some cases.

It was this London that Tom loved exploring, the private and the public, and it was this London that he loved showing Gordon, with whom he would re-create the walks a week later.

Gordon brought food, wrapped in waxed paper in small tin containers – curried lamb, rice and peas, patties stuffed with meat and spices, peeled pink grapefruit and oranges – and cordials that tasted of velvet and musky sweet fruit, and bottles of beer. Tom did not remind him he was only ten and shouldn't be having beer; he just drank it. Occasionally they joined the early market traders off for the day in a pub on the Edgware Road, and once Tom drank with such gusto that he elbowed one of them and caused him to double over in pain, and Gordon had to pull Tom away before there was a fight.

Sometimes there was more food than at other times, depending on whether Gordon had been to a 'shebeen', which is what he called the parties and gatherings of his friends, Jamaican and Trinidadian, where they ate food and danced and talked, usually in someone's house, because where else could they go? But, even if there wasn't much food, Gordon always brought apples. There were no apples in Trinidad, he said; there was breadfruit and papaya and something called cocorite, which had a hard shell and firm, sweet juicy flesh inside around a large black stone and was the most delicious fruit in the world. But no apples. One of the things he missed most about England when he went back to Trinidad after the war was apples. When he'd first come here, in 1942, he'd had an apple straight off the boat, given to him by a man in a pub in Southampton, and it had been so friendly, such a kind gesture. His favourite apple was the Cox, sharp and sweet at the same time, he said. So he always brought apples, from September to January onwards.

As they walked, Gordon often recognized bus conductors, or musicians, or electricians fixing the street lights, or men working on the roads. He would stop to talk to them, and he always introduced Tom. These men would smile politely and shake Tom's hand and they'd slap each other on the back and talk about a party, or a gathering, or a new house that was being let with an understanding landlord if Gordon knew anyone in need and Gordon would always nod and make a mental note, repeating it to himself, then carry on walking. Sometimes someone on a bus, hanging on to the back, called out to him. 'Gordon! You go and see Yvonne! She needs some help. You hear me?' And Gordon would repeat what they'd said, nod to show he'd taken it in and then carry on walking.

In Hyde Park he always, always stopped before each statue, no matter how obscure the military figure, and took off his hat to pay his respects. Tom would stand nearby, feeling awkward, because Gordon was punctilious about everything to a degree that Tom sometimes found embarrassing – he suspected if they'd been schoolmates he would have pointed at Gordon and yelled, 'Swot!' But at the same time he realized he was proud of his friend, who was so sincere in his emotions. His father was too; most people weren't.

'Do you like London?' Tom asked him, about a month after he'd seen Gordon and Jenny talking.

They were walking through Green Park. Gordon threw some patty crumbs to a pigeon. 'Why do you ask me that?'

'I don't know. I want to know what you think. I'm not sure if I like it.'

'How?'

Tom stopped and looked at the gently undulating park, the trees edged with new green growth, the rows of striped deckchairs, the flag fluttering from Buckingham Palace in the distance. 'I feel I'm in a film all the time. And it's not a film about me. It's not who I am.'

Gordon bent over to pick up a tennis ball and hurled it towards two young players with a smile. 'So who are you, then?'

Tom shrugged. 'Dunno.'

Gordon nodded at a woman passing by. She had messy blonde hair, rolled-up jeans, flat velvet shoes, a tailored jacket with a velvet collar and an orange scarf knotted round her neck. She was smoking a cigarette. She smiled at Gordon. Gordon smiled at her.

Tom cleared his throat. 'Is it hard to meet girls? Can you tell me how to, when the time comes?'

Gordon let out a shout of laughter. 'Oh, my word. Yes, I can do that. When the time comes.'

'Is it hard, though?'

'No, it's not hard. You don't need to worry about that yet, okay?'

Tom sunk his hands into his pockets; there was a chill in the air. 'Okay,' he said, trying not to think about Joy, the girl

at the fold-up fruit-and-veg stall on Portobello who sometimes helped out her dad and who had pink plump lips and
a shape to her that made him feel embarrassed. 'I want to,
though.'

'Oh! Child, there's time for that. But I tell you, when I first
came here, in the war – oh, boy.' He trailed off, as if lost in
reminiscence. 'Oh, boy,' he said softly to himself.

'Was that when you met Jenny?' said Tom curiously.

'It was. She was beautiful back then, you know? And your
mum too. We were all together, you know that. I was arriving
to stay at Sevenstones – you still not been there, have you?'

'They don't go any more. Jenny said she wished she had
a reason. But she doesn't. The place is just standing there
empty.'

'Shame.'

'Tell me about it. Tell me about my mum and dad.'

'Ah.' Gordon smiled. 'The first time, your mother and
father were just leaving when I met them. That was the
rule, see? You gave way to the next party at Sevenstones.
Anyone who needed it, no questions asked, no regrets the
following day.'

'Who did you come with?'

'I came with an American girl, Teddy.' He nodded, speaking fast. 'I knew her, and she knew Jenny. She made me drive
her to Sevenstones. That's where I met your mother. In a
field, waist high with those large daisies, you know? She was
sitting on a swing, with your dad, and she was whittling in
wood.' He screwed up his eyes. 'Some spoons, if I remember
rightly.'

'My mother whittled?'

'Oh, sure. Did you know that?'

Tom wasn't sentimental about his mother. He wasn't old

enough to see the loss that had shaped so much of his life. 'I don't know many real things about my mother,' he said. 'Thanks. And about her and my dad.'

Gordon said gently, 'Ah, Tom. She used to just . . . light up when he came in the room. Your father had something magic about him.'

'Who was Teddy, then?' said Tom, sifting through the information as an afterthought. 'I've heard that name before.'

Gordon threw the apple core in the air. He caught it, whistled and took an extra bite out of it. 'A friend of mine. That's how I met your aunt.'

'Was she – from Trinidad?'

'No, boy. American.' He chewed and swallowed.

'How did you know her?'

'I was working on tanks for the Americans, down in Dorset before Exercise Smash. She knew Jenny; they'd driven some bigwigs around together down to Dorset, I think. Jenny told her to bring me. That's how I first came, like I say. And Tom,' he said, shaking his head, 'Sevenstones was the kind of place where anything goes. I was myself, in the war. I knew that was where I was supposed to be. We all did, at Sevenstones. Music on, dancing till we were half dead, laughing with all that champagne, acting like fools, boy, and we were all . . . *ourselves*. That's it. Not what other people wanted us to be. It was that kind of place. I hope you go there sometime. I got back to Trinidad, you know, after the war, and I couldn't stand to be there no more. I'd changed.'

'So you wanted to come back,' said Tom.

'When I sailed back in '48 I came straight here and found a flat – only everything was different. Not the same in peacetime, London.' And he took out the paper bag in which the patties had been wrapped, plucking out a few last morsels of spiced meat. 'Not the same at all, Tom.'

Every time they were out together something would happen. At first Tom thought Gordon didn't see well, as he didn't appear to notice the ex-serviceman in his beret with his gabardine belted tightly around him spitting at Gordon as he walked past him, or the gaggle of schoolboys who called Gordon horrible names, threatening him even though they were half Tom's height, or the young woman with a pram who hissed at him, almost desperately, 'Just go back home all of you, why don't you?'

'To answer your question, I do like London. I can see myself here for the rest of my life,' said Gordon, and the simple, easy way he said it made Tom jealous. 'What makes you feel it's not for you?'

Tom shrugged. 'I feel as if I'm waiting.'

'For what?'

'For something to happen.'

'To you, you mean?'

'Yes,' said Tom. 'I can't explain it. I feel something's on its way. Something that will change everything. Something I don't know about yet.'

17

Summer 1958

You knew when trouble was coming because the weather was too hot. It had happened before: days of sultry,
oppressive heat, people shut up in tenement flats. The
smog, stench, flies and dirt were scarcely bearable some of
the year but, when the sun shone for too long, they sent
everyone slightly mad.

'There are no riots in November,' Uncle Henry remarked,
as he and Tom walked up to the market one August day to
find Aunt Jenny some cherries. She was not well.

The first summer here three years ago Tom had thought
people were joking about the heat. How could it ever be too
hot? But he had never experienced southern English heat,
much less city heat. Aunt Jenny couldn't cope and took
to her bed, staying indoors for days on end. Uncle Henry
started the day in crisp linen – however indifferent he was as
a guardian, his clothes were always beautifully pressed, Tom
never knew by whom, but they were – but, by 4 p.m. he had
always wilted, his bald pate and long face glistening. He had
many spotted handkerchiefs he would press to his face as he
muttered oaths, cursing the heat.

The stall-holders had packed up and gone for the most
part and so Henry and Tom continued up past the Electric
Cinema and towards the Golborne Road end of the Portobello Road.

'There's a chap up here who stays open later,' said Henry,

mopping his brow. 'Gets deliveries from Cornwall, but they're not here till tea time.'

At the coffee bar on the corner of Portobello Road and Golborne Road, four Teddy Boys were huddled together in a knot; leaning against the windows and smoking, they were talking so intently that their quiffs bobbed in the still breeze; they turned when they heard footsteps, then resumed their closed conversation.

'Damned hot,' muttered Uncle Henry, glancing at them uneasily. 'Ah, here we are, young Tom. Harold's is still open. Didn't I tell you it would be? Hurrah. Jenny shall have her cherries.'

Harold's was Perlman's Grocers, but the owner, shaking his head at Henry, said regretfully that he was closing up early. He slammed the shutters and dropped the iron bar across them, then went inside. 'I'd clear out of here if I was you, Mr Caldicott,' he said. 'There'll be trouble later on.' And he nodded at the group of lounging boys.

'Pish,' said Uncle Henry, following him inside. 'Young indolent fools, Perlman.'

'They've got bars. Sawn them off railings of houses, they have. And I seen them making Molotov cocktails.'

But Henry ignored this. 'I merely require some cherries for my poor sister, Perlman.'

'The old trouble?' said Mr Perlman sympathetically, bagging up large handfuls of smooth, shining cherries. 'The nerves again, is it?'

'Something like it, I expect. Women,' Henry muttered, handing Mr Perlman some change. 'Tom, let's go. Poor Jenny was right,' he said, tucking the bag under his arm as they left. 'It's a wasteland up here these days. Dreadful.' He said this loudly enough for Mr Perlman to hear. Mr Perlman shrugged, went in and shut the door.

'Bloody nosy fool,' said Henry furiously. 'Who's he to be prying into Jenny's life, our life? Good God, it makes me angry –'

'Let's take these back to her,' said Tom, because he was worried about the look in his uncle's eyes. 'Aunt Jenny will be so pleased. She seemed better today, I thought, didn't you? Stronger. Sitting up, anyway –'

'Oh, her trouble's all in the mind,' said his uncle almost without thinking. 'She's – it all gets to her now and then, as you know.' He mopped his brow again with a handkerchief. 'Cheek of the fellow.'

They were walking back along the Portobello Road. 'What gets to her?' said Tom curiously.

His uncle began to say something, then stopped. 'All sorts. You, mainly, young Tom. Ha! Just a joke. Onwards.'

The road leading away from Perlman's was lined with town houses blackened with grime and decay, flakes of paint almost peeling off before one's eyes. Every other window was boarded up with rusting, corrugated iron, railings bent or sawn off. Children played in the street, while mothers sat on the steps, talking to each other. The children were dressed neatly, but their clothes were filthy, too small or too big. A few didn't have shoes.

'Hey!' a voice behind them said, friendly, unguarded. Tom looked up to see Gordon on the pavement on the other side of the road, smiling at them. He was wearing a smart grey suit with sharp creases at the front, a matching trilby, and a thin orange, red and green striped tie. 'What are you two doing up this way?'

'Hi, Gordon,' said Tom.

Henry tugged at Tom's arm, like a child. 'I say, Tom, let's be off.'

'You remember Gordon,' said Tom.

'Oh, of course,' said Henry smoothly. 'Hello, old boy, how are we?'

Gordon smiled, and stood to attention. 'Major Caldicott.'

'Yes, of course,' said Henry, entirely uneasy.

'How's Jenny?' said Gordon.

'Oh – well,' said Henry, giving Gordon a quick, charming smile. 'You know. Thank you so much. She'll be awfully touched you were asking after her, old thing –' He made to move off and seemed surprised when Gordon stood in his way.

'You act like you don't remember me, Henry,' he said politely. 'Like we weren't all in it together during the war, and what happened after. But I remember, you know. I remember it all.'

'I remember too, old thing. Awfully grateful to you. Awfully.' Henry's face was sweaty, and red patches, like raspberries, bloomed angrily on his pale, flank-like cheeks.

'That's good, then. Glad to hear it,' said Gordon, and he stood back, as if collecting himself, and touched his hat to his head. 'Off you go now –'

'Wee Tommy Raven!' Turning, Tom saw Robert Hillman and Tony Powell in the middle of a gang that were throwing home-made fire-crackers on the ground. They didn't usually go up this way; this was not their patch. It was Robert, Johnny's brother, who had called his name. Tom stared at him.

'I don't like you, Mr Raven,' Robert said, smiling. His eyes were slightly glazed over and Tom thought he'd been taking purple hearts. The Teddy Boys loved purple hearts; Johnny had told him about them and Tom had seen them throwing the tablets down their throats outside the Tube like they were shots of whisky in a Western. 'You're always in the way, you little bastard.'

'Hey, Robert,' Tony said. 'Leave him.'

'Piss off, Tone. I said, I don't like him. Prick.' Robert started to walk towards Tom, but was distracted by a little girl, a toddler with curling red hair in front of him who had lost her mother. She had tripped and was crying, blocking his path. Robert stopped, lifting her up by one arm and dumping her out of his way on the pavement like she was a sack of rubbish. She cried even louder. A woman nearby picked her up and put her on her hip, giving Robert Hillman a dirty look.

'Let's go,' said Tom, and he put his hand on Gordon's sleeve. 'Gordon – come on.'

'I'll stay,' said Gordon, shaking his head, his eyes huge with a rage Tom had never seen in him before. 'You run now, Tom, okay?'

'But it's not safe. Come on, Gordon. This isn't anything to do with you and me. Come on.'

Gordon was looking around on the ground. He picked up a small stone. 'They'll find a way to make it our fault. Wait and see. The most depressing fact about growing up, you want to know it?' He was nodding. 'It's easier when you preserve the status quo, my friend. It's less terrifying.' He pushed Tom, hard. 'Go!'

'Hey, you! Little shit!' Tom turned, and Robert's face was twisted, ablaze with hatred, almost insane. 'What you doing with that n—'

Tom turned away, pulling Gordon with him, but as they turned it happened. Something landed on the road in front of them, shattering into pieces, and there was a blinding light. The little girl was still screaming, someone else was screaming, and there was the sound of yelling, and of bicycle chains rattling, and sticks and iron bars clattering against railings – when you heard one up and down the crescent, it was loud, but this was ten, twenty, like drums. Gordon shouted something, but Tom couldn't hear him, the sound of the explosion echoing in his ears. He saw some boys further up the road. One of them was holding a green bottle, something on fire inside it.

'Molotov cocktails!' Gordon was shouting, and Tom heard him this time. 'Get up, Tom, and run! Get out of here!'

Tom was dizzy, so dizzy it took him a while to realize he was on the ground and could not get up. He could not see.

'Get him!'

'Get them!'

He blinked, but still he couldn't see anything. Something was flowing – water, blood, what was it? And Gordon's voice was in his ear, shouting at him to keep moving, and there were men's voices everywhere, cursing, and the banging of metal on metal, and then he could smell more than the usual tar and smog and sewage smell that you got in some slums – something was burning. He kept blinking, then he rubbed his eyes, and it was like fire burning into them. I can't see, he said in a quiet voice. Uncle Henry, I can't see? Uncle Henry? But there was no answer. He scrambled to his feet again, just as someone, a tall boy with a bobbing quiff like a cockerel's coxcomb and a face distorted with hate, opened his mouth and screamed something before throwing a bottle towards them.

The force of it blew him back: a wall of heat. Something, or someone else, landed on him. There was screaming, and thuds. Everything was on the ground, and then everything was black.

18

When Tom woke up, it was like swimming to the surface of a deep lake, pushing up through the weeds into the light. He was breathing fast, and someone's hand was on him. He cried out when he realized he still couldn't see, although in fact he could make out figures, the wall of his room; and then he shouted, because he could tell *Helen Caught Bathing* had been moved and his drawings were exposed. But no sound came out, and the hand that stroked his hair was cool, the palms callused.

'Jenny! Where's Gordon? They were after Gordon!' he tried to say, but his throat was so dry it came out in a rasping whisper.

'Darling boy,' said the voice, and Tom blinked again. 'Well, well. What on earth have you been up to?'

Tom shielded his eyes from the light, which was too bright, and saw the outline of a figure standing before him. He closed his eyes again. He was so tired. 'You're not real,' he said.

'Oh, that's a shame,' said the voice he knew so well, and a warm hand enclosed itself around his smaller one. 'I brought you a present, old boy, and I was hoping very much to give it to you. But perhaps you're right, in which case I should vanish.'

'Dad!' Tom cried, struggling slowly up in bed, flinging his arms around his father, who, stiff with astonishment at first, hugged him back after a while, so fiercely that Tom scarcely had any breath left and simply clung to him, too weak to do more. 'Dad! You're really here.' He felt dizzy, like he'd fallen over, even though he was lying in bed.

His father laughed, his kind, gentle laugh, as if it had been five minutes, not more than three years, and then, as he realized Tom was crying, said, 'Shh. Here – I say – I'm here, Tom. I'm here! Shh. It's all right, old thing. Yes, it's all right.'

'What happened?' Tom asked his father a little later. 'I don't remember. Anything.'

His father told him what he knew: Tom had been knocked to the ground when the Teddy Boys started chasing the Black men and the white woman who was married to one of them. There had been running battles with white boys on the streets, people attacked, shops looted. The force of the second petrol bomb had knocked Tom backwards, and he had hit his head. They couldn't wake him up.

No one could find Henry, so Gordon and his friends had carried him back to the house on a makeshift stretcher: a door a friend of Gordon had taken from a ransacked shop on Blenheim Crescent. They bore him back down Ladbroke Grove, stepping over the glass from smashed milk bottles and broken windows, looted fruit and veg; rubbish and sheets of discarded newspaper flew into their faces in the hot, tundra-like summer wind.

Jenny had been in bed, still ill with this flu that had laid her low for so much of the summer, but she had struggled downstairs, fainting when she saw Tom, carried in Gordon's arms, and so they'd had to bring her round too. When she came to, she joked that she'd just wanted to be carried upstairs as well. She'd made Gordon and his friends tea while they waited for the doctor. When he arrived, Tom was still unconscious, and the doctor had said his father should be contacted, just in case. So Jenny had done so, sending a telegram, then making a telephone call, placed to Mrs Fairly, the farmer's wife down the way, and the next day Tom's father had arrived, having caught the first train down. But Tom was asleep, Jenny was back in bed, and Edward had to near-enough bang down the door before Henry let him in.

At first Tom didn't remember any of it, but then he started to piece it all together, extraordinary events popping up in his brain like road signs as he tried to speak, to see properly.

In his little room, a festive atmosphere developed. Tom apologized for scribbling over the walls. Jenny said that was fine, and started to cry, then laugh rather manically. Edward opened a bottle of cherryade; Jenny produced some more Fry's Turkish Delight; Henry suddenly appeared – apparently someone had tried to steal his wallet and he'd had to give chase, which is why he'd ended up far away from Tom – and Edward told a funny story about his journey down, Henry chiming in afterwards with a story about having his pocket picked after D-Day, on leave in Leicester Square. Tom, sitting in bed and smiling along, could not quite believe it; they were all there, in this little room, for the first time, together. A sort of family.

So he did not tell them his head ached dreadfully now; when he sat up black spots danced in front of his eyes, growing larger, obliterating more of his vision, and he couldn't seem to blink them away.

'I hoped I'd see you again, my darling boy,' his father said when it was just the two of them again. 'But I didn't expect it would be this dramatic. You could have just dropped me a note!' He gave a rather forced hearty laugh.

Tom closed his eyes. He felt less dizzy and sick that way. 'I didn't see the point.'

'I rather got that impression,' said his father, which Tom, through waves of confusion, found rather a strange thing to say. 'Well, I'm here now.'

'You won't go, will you?' said Tom. 'Not ... right away, I mean,' he added, trying to sound brave. 'But stay, just a little bit.'

''Course I will, Tom!' his father said. 'I'm not going any-where.' His voice sounded thick, and strange. He looked older too. His thick dark hair was streaked with silver, and his five o'clock shadow, always prominent, was noticeably less so now. Tom clutched his father's worn, callused, dear hand.

'I wish you'd written,' he said eventually.

'I did, old boy. Every week. And I was rather sad when you told Jenny you didn't want to hear from me.'

Tom kept blinking, unsure as to whether he'd heard right. 'Dad – that's not true.'

'It is, my boy. She wrote me an extremely firm letter.'

Tom struggled to sit up straight. 'No, Dad. Jenny told me – she said you didn't want to hear from me. She said you'd said it was easier not to write. That I should write you one letter and then a clean break was best.'

'She – no, I didn't do that, Tom. I wouldn't ever have done that.' His father said something under his breath. 'All this – you – oh, Jenny. I didn't say that. I wrote to you at least once a week, for months.'

'But I didn't get any letters from you. None. I just thought you'd – stopped bothering.'

'God dammit, Tom, no. God, Jenny.' Edward climbed out of the bed. Tom watched him, trying to quell the rising tide of panic over the black spots that kept arriving and vanish-ing in his vision, like blots on a reel of film.

'Dad –'

'Has she mistreated you, Tom?' He caught his son by the shoulders. 'Beaten you? Has Henry – done – done anything?'

'No, Dad, honest.' said Tom. 'We keep ourselves to ourselves. I do most of the cleaning and the cooking, though, neither of them knows one end of an egg from the other.' He paused, waiting for his father to laugh. 'They're mostly in their rooms, Dad – I've no idea why they wanted me with them. They're really not very interested in children.'

'She promised me –' His father was standing up in the small, cold little room, his fist pressed to his forehead. 'Did she say anything to you? Anything about your mother? And me?'

'No, Dad.' Tom could not see his father's expression clearly enough – he could not see anything at all beyond blurred, expansive shapes, like large woolly monsters. 'No, but she's sad. She cries a lot. She gets letters from Gordon once a month, and they make her cry.'

'What kind of letters?'

'I don't know.' Tom paused. 'I saw one once. She left it on the sideboard. It had an American stamp on it. I don't know why they can't come straight to the house.' His father was very still. Tom said, faltering, 'Once she didn't get any for ages and she went to bed for a whole week.'

His father was quiet for a while. He stared out of the window, across the rooftops, where smoke from fires and police sirens filled the air. 'Ah, Tom. I'm sorry. What a fool. Yet again. Listen to me. Jenny's played a trick. On both of us. She likes being the one at the controls. Only she's very bad at it. But, you have to understand, she was doing it for the best. For the best. God dammit –' He caught his son's hands. 'Never again, you understand?'

'Yes,' Tom said. He wanted to say more, but his vision was

so blurred and dark now he could hardly see, and he sat back, catching his breath.

'Nothing will prevent our being in touch now. Don't worry. You're my son, and I shouldn't have bloody well sat back and accepted it all. Trust me, it'll be different. I've found you again. Don't worry –'

'Dad?'

'Yes, my boy?' His father dropped to his knees beside Tom's bed. 'What is it?'

'Dad – you're vanishing,' Tom said.

The blackness was burning through the drawings of the cottage and the hills, it was burning through the wall and his quilt and his father's strong, tanned hands. Everything, slowly, was vanishing.

'Ah, you poor thing. I shouldn't have – I'll speak to her. Don't worry. You're tired, my boy. Rest up,' his father said.

'No, Dad,' said Tom, his voice small. 'Everything's going black. I – I can't see you any more.'

'What?'

'You're melting away. Like the witch in *The Wizard of Oz*. I can't see you. I can't see you at all, Dad –'

His eyes hurt from blinking; he heard his father swearing under his breath, the scraping of the chair on the splintered wooden floor, the retreating thunder as his father ran downstairs, roaring for Henry and Jenny, his voice thick with anger, with terror.

He was alone in the room again, and now the darkness would not shift. It seemed to have settled over his sight, like night falling.

19

In St Mary's Paddington, they made him lie on his back for two days without moving at all and then for two weeks, barely moving. A nurse fed him food through a straw, mopped up the water streaming from his eyes, wiped his bottom. It was like being a baby again.

He wondered about those women, the nurses, for the rest of his life; he would never recognize them, or the thin, reedy house doctor who cleared his throat repeatedly and, in a monotone, told him he would never regain his sight. He did not know what any of them looked like. But bits of his time in hospital were always with him. On his wedding day, when he put on his shirt and the smell of the starch on the collar made him want to cry, or whenever he caught the edge of the sweet, boiled smell of school food, or when he was dying and could smell disinfectant in the hospital ward and could not remember why it made him want to shield his eyes repeatedly, hold his hands up to his eyes as if to guard them from further damage – throughout his life there were tiny reminders always of what had happened, of how it had been, of the madness of the sensation of being helpless.

His retina had detached: someone should have spotted this, apparently. The reedy-voiced doctor hadn't known what he was talking about, thankfully: Tom's left eye was saved; in time, with plenty of rest, and because those wonderful nurses were so strict about his lying on his back at all times, the retina reattached itself. But the right eye, which had been nearest to where he'd landed when he fell or was pushed over: his sight did not come back in that eye. Sometimes he thought he could make out shapes, or colours, but it was always a delusion.

Tom used to wonder what would have happened if he'd left the scene by Ladbroke Grove with Uncle Henry a minute earlier. But not often. He had told Gordon he was waiting for something to happen.

This, it turned out, was it.

The first night Tom screamed so loudly in his sleep that the following day, when his father arrived, Sister Partridge requested he read aloud until Tom fell asleep. Edward read him books he wouldn't have tried before: *The Go-Between*, *Animal Farm*, *The Day of the Triffids*. He listened to the Proms every night on the wireless: *The Dream of Gerontius*, the premiere of a Shostakovich piano concerto, Stravinsky's *Firebird* suite, Vaughan Williams's *London Symphony*, which made him cry – for what was lost, and for the love he had for the city that was now his home. He cried a lot, in those strange days. His father came in one day to find him sobbing over *Hancock's Half-Hour*. Eventually they gave Edward a cot bed, and he slept next to his son, and when Tom dangled his hand over the side of the bed, his father's hand would shoot up to clasp it.

When he left hospital, he could not see in one eye and barely with the other. But he didn't want to leave, to end this glorious, wonderful expanse of time he had been given with his father, the person he loved more than anyone or anything in the world. The smells, sounds, feel of the ward was like a cocoon, a beautiful holiday from an existence he mostly found bewildering. He couldn't explain it to anyone for a long time, but for the rest of his life Tom would see the day he lost his sight in one eye as a blessing, not a tragedy.

It was a bright September day, fresh as summer. It had rained heavily while he'd been inside all that time. As they descended the steps of the hospital, Tom drank in the wet autumn air, greedily.

'Where are we going now, Dad? Back home?'

'I thought,' said his father, hailing a cab with a whistle, 'we thought it'd be awfully jolly to go somewhere special for a few days. Somewhere where you can recuperate.'

'Where?'

'A place I've always wanted to show you,' said his father. 'I thought we might go to Sevenstones. Hmm?'

Tom was not sure. Though he was furious at Aunt Jenny for not passing on his father's letters, he wanted to go back to Montpelier Crescent, to the safety of his little room with the drawings of Galloway and the hills on the walls. Being outside was already overwhelming – the sounds of the city, the people pushing past them. 'I don't know,' he said, stepping carefully aside as a commuter dashed towards him, late for a train. 'What does Aunt Jenny say about it?'

'Aunt Jenny says she'll meet us there,' his father said, and that was all.

The train was cold: another passenger wanted the window open and there was a sharp breeze. Tom sat on the scratchy seat with his thin knees knocking together. It felt like his first time on a train, when he'd left Scotland. The claustrophobia from his reduced vision worsened with the noise, the smell of coal, the rocking motion, the stares of other passengers.

'We'll be there soon, old boy,' his father said. 'Rest up and catch your breath. Jenny is driving down. She'll meet us at the station. We thought the train would be smoother for you than the car.'

'I don't want to see her.'

'Tom,' said his father sharply. 'She was trying to help, in her own way. I think she believed it'd be easier for you not to hear from me. Go easy on her, old thing.'

'She's cracked, Dad. She should have stayed out of it. Out of the whole business,' Tom said in a low, choking voice. He folded his arms, gritting his teeth. 'She didn't need to come and take me away in the first place. I was jolly happy where I was.'

Tom found it hard to speak. To express quite how angry he was, how unfair it had been to the kid he was, how wrong it felt, still, in ways he couldn't explain. He shook his head. 'All those years, Dad. No letters from you. I thought you'd just forgotten about me.'

'And I thought what I was doing was for the best,' his father said. He took Tom's hand, their knees touching, joined. Tom moved on the scratchy seats, his legs itching. He felt hot, and strange, and tired, and raring to run around, like a wind-up toy. But his father's hand was warm, and calm. 'Tom, Jenny and Henry love you. They loved their sister. They feel it's their duty to look after you, to raise you as Irene's son should be raised.'

'I'm your son, Dad!' Tom said, trying to control his voice. This was the central point, the heart of it all, and yet it didn't seem to matter to anyone else. 'I want to be with you! Not them! Can't you –'

His father gave a small, painful smile. ''Course you are. First and foremost. We're the Ravens. Us two. You listen to me, Tom. You're my boy. But I made promises that I broke.

Jenny wants to do right by you. That means giving you the best chance in life.'

'But I want to be –'

'Tom!' his father said, his voice slightly sharp. 'What's best for you? Growing up in a shack? No money for wood or a square meal at the end of some months? Going to school with farmers' children and the tinker's boy? Or living in London, in a beautiful house surrounded by important paintings, going to a school with the sons of prime ministers and lords and boys who'll run the country one day? Don't you see? You'll have the world at your feet, if you just stick it out.' His grip on Tom's hand tightened. 'I've failed to provide for you at some times, my boy – oh, I know,' he said, seeing Tom about to protest. 'We were happy enough, weren't we? But to say no to this – to say no to what Irene wanted for you too – then I really would have failed you.'

'They don't behave like they're bothered about me,' said Tom.

'That's just who they are,' said his father. 'But trust me. They're bothered. I'd say it's the only thing that matters, to Jenny anyway. They – oh, here we are.'

'What were you going to say?'

'I was going to say about Jenny, and me and your mother. We all make mistakes. That's the thing about Sevenstones: why it was wonderful, you see, was because you were always forgiven. You were just yourself.' Edward stood up straight, his air force bearing still evident, and took down their case, then brushed the seat. All the little, precise details that made his father so special, so thoughtful, so bewildering. 'Wait till you see it, that's all.' He was smiling. 'You'll understand.'

He helped Tom up. 'Gordon said almost the same thing,'

Tom said, holding on to the table by the window, as he looked out at the chalk downs, the golden autumn afternoon.

His father flicked a speck of dirt from Tom's coat. 'Gordon was right.'

They had arrived at a station called Tallboys, and Edward leaned out of the window to unlock the carriage door. His father had said Jenny would meet them, but Tom was still surprised to see her there, in a loose long linen dress, quite unlike her silk London frocks, a straw hat jammed on to her piled-up hair, her cheeks shiny. She held out her hands.

'Dear Tom,' she said, eyes burning. 'I am so glad. So glad. You're here.'

Tom stared at his aunt. Waves of fury roiled inside him. His father got off the train first. 'Here we are,' he said, and he helped Tom down. Tom hated how pathetic he felt, not even able to judge the steps correctly, but he took his father's hand.

'Hello,' he said, barely audible, surly.

Jenny said something very quietly. He stared at her.

'What did you say?'

She scratched her nose. 'I'm sorry. I said I'm sorry. I thought if you weren't close to your father any more, because you believed he had sent you away, that it would be easier for you to adjust,' she said blankly.

It took Tom a moment to realize what she was talking about. 'But –' he said, moving out of the way as another passenger brushed past them. 'But that's . . . that's crackers, Aunt Jenny. That's not how families . . . *work*.'

'I made a promise,' Jenny said. Her jaw was set, and there was a stubborn look in her eye. 'To someone I love. That I would take care of their son. I keep my promises.'

He stared at her, her vague, hazy gestures and her flow-ing loose dress and those eyes, burning with conviction. He thought for the first time that he was seeing the real ver-sion of her, not dressed up, not anxious, not forcing herself into another role for which she was ill-suited. Jenny bent and picked up his suitcase, turning towards the car.

'Are you excited about finally being here, Tom?'

'Hugely,' Tom said, to be polite, though he really didn't mind where they went; he just wanted to go to sleep. 'Can't wait to see it.'

'Yes!' Jenny was still fussing with the car door, her skirt, the gear stick. She said, 'Edward, the ravens are back.'

'No!'

'Oh, yes! In the pine trees behind the house. Vast eyries, awfully high up. In winter, Tom, they loom over you; you can see them flying to and fro with twigs and food for the young – a nest fell out once. The eggs are a beautiful tur-quoise green –' She paused to gather breath, and jammed the car into reverse.

His father said, 'I don't remember that. Perhaps I wasn't there in winter.'

'You know the saying,' said Jenny. 'Raise ravens, and they'll gouge your eyes out.'

'Where did you hear that?'

'Gordon,' she said. 'It's Italian, or Spanish; he heard it from a soldier – don't you remember?'

'What does that mean?' Tom said, peering at them both from the back of the car.

'It means "Reap what you sow,"' Jenny said. 'Doesn't it, Edward?'

'It does,' he said. 'And its meaning is often misunderstood.'

They were both silent in the car; Tom sensed his father

had bested Jenny. After a few moments, Edward said, 'Do you remember the birds nesting in the chimney, though – the time that Easter, when someone lit the fire –'

'Oh, of course. Starlings. Poor things. I've never recovered.' She gave a great, ragged sigh, her shoulders slumping as if bowed down with the weight of memory, and turned the key in the ignition. 'And that parrot, do you remember the parrot someone bought?'

'A Gurkha – what was his name?' His father turned to him, as Jenny drove away. 'It was the place we all went, you see – not too far from Tangmere, or Charmy Down, where I was stationed, from where we launched our raids.'

'And Henry's barracks, and Irene was at Hendon – bit further, wasn't it, but she made it, didn't she?' Jenny said to him.

Tom had not been out of London for such a long time that he stared in wonder, his good eye straining to take everything in. Fields, barns, two young women on bikes cycling slowly up the hill. A normal, lovely September day, like something out of a film, or a Ladybird book in the library on the Countryside.

'Is the gate still there?' his father asked. 'There's a wall, runs along the road, and there's a gate set into it – it was green –' said his father to Tom. 'And it was always open, to anyone, serviceman or woman, who wanted a bed for the night and a hot meal and a dance and a drink before they had to go off to fight, fly, drive, whatever it is we were all busy doing those days. Tom my darling – it's still there, isn't it, Jenny? Once you were through that gate, you jolly well knew you were safe.' His voice broke.

'Yes, Edward.' Jenny put her hand over his. Tom, in the back, saw, through his half-veiled vision, the pain on her face, how she did not turn to look at him.

'I miss her too,' Jenny said. 'Edward, I'm so sorry. For everything. If you understood it all –'

'I don't need to,' Edward said. She gave him a strange look. 'Raise ravens, Edward. Remember?'

'Jenny,' he said. 'Irene is dead. Teddy is gone. The others are all gone. Whatever happened, Tom is here, and you are here, and me and – that's all that matters.'

The blackberries and early sloes were thick on the hedge-rows; freshly minted orange comma butterflies basked in the amber sunshine. Edward helped his son out of the car and they stared together at the decrepit gate set into a high wall. It had peeling green paint and a rusting latch; next to it, half buried in the earth, was a large stone. 'Come on,' said his father, and pushed open the gate. It gave a long, slow creak like a scream.

The path they found themselves on ran alongside the wall. To their left was an orchard, a tangle of ill-kempt trees with the boughs hopelessly overburdened with apples, many of which had already dropped. They passed a tiny pond in which a battered little toy boat was wedged on to a rock; and a row of hollyhocks, raspberry-pink and wine-red, listing drunkenly against the lichen-dappled stone of the old cottage. It reminded Tom instantly of his childhood home, the croft, and he stared at his father, who nodded – he understood. But it was quite different, this place. It was bigger, with a second floor, and a large honey-coloured porch. And it was gentle, and golden, and flecked with colour: self-seeded daisies that crowded out the space along the pathways and flower beds in front of the house; white anemones, nodding; fiery red and burnt-yellow dahlias. The plants thronged with bees.

'On Midsummer morning the sun rises directly into the centre of the house,' Jenny said. 'Through the front door. Whoever built it – it is about five hundred years old, we think – built it to sit within the stone circle. A couple of the stones are missing. They might have been used to build the house. The back of the house is in shadow, so it's as though the house is split in two, day and night, summer and winter. Sunrise, sunset.'

Jenny faced the valley, looking down to the overgrown garden, where Tom could just about make out two large, jagged stones five or so yards apart. Then she said, almost to herself:

'Life is not about the line of time. You understand that when you come here. We see time as linear; we treat it as a progression. It's not. It's the repetition of the seasons. The cycle of the year's route. Time turning over, a repetitive process.'

Beside the door was a huge bell-pull, a foot long or more. Above it, the words SEVENSTONES half carved, half painted on to the yellow-grey lintel. The old arched stone doorway was partially obscured by a rose that had gone to bright orange hips. The window frames, like the gate, like the windfall apples, were on the way to being rotten.

'In winter, at the Midwinter Solstice,' his aunt said, picking off rosehips and tucking the overgrown shoots out of the way as her other hand fumbled in her pocket for the key, 'the sun sets through the little round window there, at the back of the house.' She unlocked the door. 'Sunrise, sunset. Ah, it's been so long. So long, hasn't it? Come in, dear. Edward, you too. Come in.'

'By George, it hasn't changed,' Tom's father said, stepping cautiously over the threshold.

'I know,' said Jenny quietly. 'Most extraordinary.'

Inside it was dark, and small, and very warm, the late summer heat trapped inside, the scent of old, worn wood and faint log fires throughout.

'There's a cold room there,' said Jenny, pointing towards the back. 'Useful for gin, and champagne. There's – oh, look. There's the record player, and the wireless. Goodness, some-one's left a glove behind.' She picked up a navy leather glove. 'Henry's, I expect. And there, look – you'll be upstairs too, Edward.' She scrunched up the glove and threw it on to the windowsill. She was quite different here, like the old Jenny he'd first known: brisk, efficient, eyes darting round the small space, assessing, shrewd, like a bird. 'And that was the sitting room – see, there's even some archaeological remains. Look, Edward, do.'

'My God.' Tom's father followed her gaze. There were two champagne bottles balanced on a narrow shelf that ran round the wall on each side of the fireplace, and two more on the ground, the labels mottled with mildew.

Her eyes, half-moons of merriment, met Edward's. 'Tom, Harrods delivered, and Irene would bring up extra when she drove from Hendon or wherever she was posted. Daddy paid for most of it, bless his heart. He said it was for morale.' Jenny pushed a messy tendril of hair out of her flushed face. 'Edward – oh dear, the records are all gone, I suspect some-one knows where the spare key is and they've been sleeping in here you know.' She peered through into the back room. 'Well, if it's kept someone dry what's the harm.'

His father was moving around, touching things carefully. He picked up an old captain's hat. 'Henry pretty much moved in after Dunkirk, didn't he?'

'He and that Dutch bit he had. Absolutely enormous

bosom. I'm sure she was a spy. Hiding a microphone or something down there.'

'Jen, you absolute devil.'

'You were the one court-martialled over the business of the dance, Squadron Leader.'

Tom leaned against the door. 'Court-martialled, Dad?'

'Your father,' said Jenny, dusting off a worn wooden bench with her scarf and gesturing for Tom to sit down, 'took Irene to a dance in Wales – in *Wales*, no less, in a Hurricane he – ahem – *borrowed* from RAF Charmy Down. Around Midsummer, wasn't it? May I tell this story, Edward? Ah, he's nodding, even as he blushes. Listen, Tom. He arranged to meet her at Bath Station, drove her to Charmy Down, asked her if she liked dancing, and, when she said yes, he flew her to Wales for the dance, then drove them both back to Seven-stones so he could shave and present himself at base in time for orders.' She looked from Tom to Edward, who was bright red, even in the dull of the room. 'That's about it, isn't it, Edward?'

Tom's father acknowledged this with a nod of the head. 'We arrived back having not slept a wink. Rather tired – you know, we'd danced for hours. She was – a tremendous dancer. She never tired, never.' He scratched his chin, smiling at the memory. 'And it was getting light – you know, it does for hours before the sun actually rises. I made Irene some coffee, and we both had a wash and I shaved, and we were sitting inside with the door open – it was rather chilly, you know – watching the morning arrive – and the sun rose, over the hill there. Shot straight into the sitting room, like a ball of flame. Woke up two WAAFs who'd bedded down for the night on the floor.' He shook his head. 'Quite extraordinary. I looked at Irene, and I said: "Did you know this happened?" And she said, "All these years, and, no, I didn't know." We simply sat there, and we felt the sun pouring over us. It was remarkable. As if everything were alive, as if we were part of the cycle of the world and all we needed to do was carry on. Yes.' He stood there, staring at the front door. 'Navy silk.'

'I remember the very dress,' said Jenny. 'Ah –' She looked over then. 'Tom, my dear, you look done in.'

Tom's head was aching with the close warmth of the room and the sense that everything was, once again, utterly different, that the world had shifted. He nodded, and shrugged.

His father said, 'Upstairs, old man. You can sleep as long as you want. There's time for everything after you've rested.' He looked around. 'Jenny, I can't believe we're both here, my dear. Thank you.'

Nodding, Tom allowed himself to be taken upstairs but, while his father was fetching the suitcase from the hall, he picked up the blue glove. It was stiff, dried out, a soft worn label peeping out from the edge like a tongue. He peered at it.

Saks Fifth Avenue.

His eye stumbled over the strange words, which he had never seen together and which didn't make sense. What was Saks Fifth Avenue, he wondered, and dropped back the glove. It wasn't Henry's anyway, whatever Jenny might say. It was too small: a woman's glove.

He loved his room in the eaves upstairs, palest pink, with curtains the colour of iced lemon sherbet. He sat on the edge of the bed, so tired he thought he wouldn't be able to undo his shoes, but soon he saw that, from the window, you could see down the valley, all the way to the horizon many miles distant, where there was a white horse carved into a hillside, dancing, shimmering in the midday sun. He rubbed his eyes gingerly, certain that he was now hallucinating.

But the horse remained, and is still there today, visible from the same window, along with the half-carved, half-painted name over the front door.

20

For two weeks, as September gave way to the beginning of autumn, they sat in the garden, losing each other in the high grass, breaking mildewed deckchairs pulled from the summer barn halfway down the lawn towards the pond, choked with weeds. A rambling custard-yellow rose covered the side of the house, and Jenny deadheaded so many faded blooms and hips that in one or two places the roses began to flower again, small yellow buds that smothered the lean-to. Hollyhocks fell like falling trees. And everywhere the sound of apples dropping on to the ground, whereupon Edward would shout '*Apple!*' and Tom would leap up, scramble in the wilderness and come back holding aloft the apple in question.

Every morning the sun rose above the horizon, shedding golden September light into every nook and cranny; and every evening rays of ochre flooded the back of the house as the ravens called loudly, and flew back to their eyries with food. Sometimes rotten apples, sometimes berries, sometimes wiggling, tiny mammals – Tom, squinting, once saw a mouse, its tail clamped in a raven's vast beak, wiggling in panic before they vanished into the trees.

Tom ate more apples in that fortnight than in his life to date: forever more they were linked for him to that time, when he lost so much but found his father. In the early evening they would walk out to pick blackberries, which they brought back and cooked or ate fresh with cream, and then Edward lit the fire, as the nights were suddenly cold, and

Tom and Jenny played Scrabble, and his father smoked his pipe, and the ravens circled overhead, calling furiously to one another in the tall, dark pine trees behind the house, building their nests, like mythic eyries.

There was a stream at the bottom of the garden where he and his father fished for trout and where they cooked it over a special outside grill, the juices spitting on the coals; and they scattered it with the rosemary that grew in vast throngs along the paths below the green gate.

There was the pheasant that wandered into the garden along the banks of the stream one evening, wild-eyed and waving its luxuriant plumage, and his father killed it with the shotgun, and they had pheasant for supper the following evening and Jenny made bread sauce and Tom remembered things he had forgotten: the winter his father skinned and butchered the frozen sheep; how he drowned rats and broke chickens' necks, and, once, in front of Tom, stamped on a tawny owl with a broken wing. How he was brutal, and tough, to survive, because he had to be, and how far it was from Tom's life now, where he lived on tins mostly, tins of beans and Spam and mulligatawny soup.

The pheasant was delicious, and so was the bread sauce. He would try to make some of the latter when he was back in London. He would try to make everything different. For he knew then that this was a magic time, never to be repeated. These were calm, idyllic days and nights, marred only by one incident, which Tom didn't think much of at the time.

He was stronger than before; he slept well; he was tanned, spending most of his time outside with his father clearing the garden, hacking at brambles and briars and lifting up paving slabs to remake paths. A few days before he and his father were due to leave, they were down at the stream, clearing the irises and heucheras and other plants trying to clog the flow of the water, and removing the rocks and stones, placing them on the bank.

'I wish I could stay,' Tom said suddenly. 'Not go back to London.' His father grunted. 'Don't you think, Dad?'

'We were going to live here, you know,' his father said, wiping his brow on his sleeve. He leaned on his spade. 'Irene was very like her father; she had his spirit. He loved it here: the ancient stones, the history of it, so did she. It was in her bones. She'd have loved to stay.'

'Why didn't we, then?' Tom was filled with a wild certainty that things would have been okay if they'd stayed there. 'Couldn't Mother have asked Jenny and Henry to let us?'

Edward shook his head. 'Not as simple as that, Tom.' He drove the spade into a hard bank of mossy earth. 'I wanted to stay on afterwards too, but the family wouldn't hear of it. Shut the place up. Too many memories.' He thrust viciously at the clod of earth, shovelling it away in a shower of black crumbling soil. 'They couldn't forgive me.'

'For what?'

His father stopped. 'I'd hurt your mother. Very much. It was all in the past, you know. We'd made it up. But Jenny – Jenny and Henry, they wouldn't forgive.'

'Why? What did you do?'

His father raised his eyebrows. 'I was a fool. I made a mistake. But it was just one mistake. I wish –'

'You think that's why?' a sharp, steady voice behind them said. Edward whipped round, Tom too, nearly falling over in the process. His aunt stood in front of them, holding a tray with two teacups and some biscuits. 'It's not why, Edward.'

'Sorry, Jenny,' his father said. 'Didn't mean for you to hear all that.'

'I know,' she said with a tight, cold smile. She put the tray down on a tree stump. 'You can't possibly understand. Yes, you hurt Irene. Yes, you broke your marriage vows. But you don't know it all. You – don't know, Edward, so don't try to understand.' Her knuckles, clutching the tray, were white.

'I'm trying,' said his father slowly. 'Jenny – I am.'

'Raise ravens, and your eyes will be gouged out,' Jenny said, pointing a finger at him, at the trees behind the house, where the ravens called to one another. 'You reap what you sow, Edward.'

A songbird was singing in the thicket across the way, on the other side of the stream, flowing like liquid gold. Tom strained to listen to it. He didn't like this conversation. He turned to his aunt. Her face was very pale. It held the most curious expression: a sort of triumphant anger.

'Jenny,' said his father quietly. 'I'm sorry. It's all in the past.'

'It isn't. It never will be, Edward.'

She turned and walked back up to the house.

That evening, they played Scrabble, which Jenny won, and, when the fire in the large hearth had burned down to soft ash, Tom popped another piece of Fry's Turkish Delight into his mouth and looked around at his aunt and father. There had been a slightly strained atmosphere that evening, and he wasn't sure why.

The last cinder in the hearth gave a small, sharp popping sound. His father was engrossed in a book, chewing at his pipe. But his aunt, who was writing something on a lined pad, sat back slightly with a start at the noise. When she looked up from the letter, Tom caught her eye and saw she was crying, without expression, tears flowing freely down her cheeks. Before he could react, she had raised one finger to her lips, motioning for him to be silent. She brushed the tears away, resting her forearms on her knees, head forwards, staring into the fire again, then carried on writing. His father did not notice any of this.

'You've been writing for a while, Jenny,' Tom said eventually, unable to bear the silence.

She nodded and smiled mechanically. 'Oh, just some instructions. There's a girl next door who's coming in to measure for curtains, and her father's the farmer, and I wanted to mention about the stream flooding.'

She wrote late into the night, the tip of her tongue protruding between her lips as she scribbled, for, when Tom came down at midnight to get a glass of milk because he could not sleep, she was fast asleep by the fire, the letter, several sheets thick, clutched between her fingers.

The next day Tom was going for a walk, and, when he asked if he could give the letter to the farmer for her, his aunt said she had already delivered it.

On the day they left, Jenny locked the door and put the key under the stone beside it. Tom watched her, shocked.

'Jenny. Anyone could get in.'

She turned to him, smiled her sweetest smile. 'That's the point. Anyone who wants to can come here. Anyone who needs it. They might not have anywhere else to go.'

The grass was taller than ever, the apples weighing the boughs so heavily you felt the branches might crack; the sky was gossamer light, silver and gold, such as comes only in September. Two fresh, heart-shaped ochre-coloured butterflies, small wings dusted with black freckles, landed on the wild grasses, then darted away, caught in a sharp, cold breeze. Summer was almost over – they all knew it.

They dropped his father at the station, for he was to journey up to Scotland by train.

Tom sat beside him, trying to quell the anxiety he felt at this new parting, for his father had been distant the past couple of days. Tom thought he knew why. His father did not want to say goodbye again. He understood. But it was different now, and he would make sure he saw that.

'I wish you'd come back for a day, to London, Dad,' said Tom, hugging him tightly, trying to keep down the knot of sadness inside. 'If not now, soon. Christmas! You can come for Christmas – Jenny does this really strange confection of foods; it has to be seen to be believed, Henry starts drinking first thing, as you can imagine . . .' He nodded. 'It'd be quite a relief to have you there, to be honest.'

'Oh! Gosh,' said his father, looking at his watch. 'Sounds about right. Listen! I think that's my train.'

'Yes, but, Dad – when will – I'll see you soon, yes?'

'Soon,' said his father, and he gripped his shoulders. 'Tom. I love you, my boy. More than anything and anyone. But – ah.'

'Ah what?' said Tom, smiling.

'That's good,' said Edward, and he dashed his finger across Tom's cheek. 'Keep that smile in place, darling boy. Look here – Jenny and I agreed yesterday –' He turned to Jenny, waiting in the car, looking straight ahead, not at him, face impassive. 'We had a talk. Probably best if we leave things at least for now, what?'

Tom didn't understand. 'What?'

His father was smiling rigidly, his handsome, kind face inches away from his son's. 'I came because you were in trouble. I will always come if you're in trouble. But, old man, why don't we simply say: all the best, and I'll see you sometime soon?'

'What are you talking about, Dad?' Tom could hear the pleading tone in his voice.

'I won't be back here. I won't come to London. Yes, here's my train, old man, buck up.' He nudged him on the back. 'Don't keep Jenny waiting. It's too hard, that's all. You were all mine, dear boy. And they've taken you and shown me how deficient I was. And so – perhaps it's best that I don't come.' He sounded as if he were just checking a train timetable; Tom stared at him, utterly uncomprehending. 'Jenny knows best, old man. I promise you that.'

'No, Dad,' said Tom. 'What's she said to you? Don't be silly, not again.' He knew then, understood that the letter Jenny had written was to his father. That she had warned him off again, somehow.

'Ah!' Edward turned, as the final screech of the brakes came. 'I must go. Cheerio, dear boy. Do take care.'

And he leaped up and over the bridge, running, literally running like he couldn't wait to get away. The train covered everyone and everything in steam and smoke, and, when it cleared, the platform was empty.

Tom watched the snaking carriages swing round the corner of the track. He squared his shoulders, turned and went back to the waiting car. Jenny was happy. She sang most of the way home.

21

A year later

It took Tom one week at Westminster School (est. four-teenth century, motto from I Corinthians 3:6: *Dat Deus Incrementum* / 'I planted the seed ... but God made it grow') to see that this was another lie they'd backed him into. The worst thing was that they made you work. Work so hard that at first Tom cried every night, wondering how he'd keep up, because here was another lie: he'd been led to believe that they were agog to have him, which it took him about half a Maths lesson to see through.

Westminster taught Tom how to think critically; to exam-ine all sides of an argument and coolly, calmly, break it apart. He was grateful for that. But everything was a code he didn't understand, and the uniform – a navy suit, with house tie – was designed to show the code of the boys whose fathers' tailors had made their clothes. He was not rich like Pewsey Minor, son of Richard Pewsey, scion of Pewsey's Bank, or already a peer of the realm like Leighton, fourteenth earl of Wincanton. He was not intellectual like Dickie Osgood, who would one day run Osgood's, the publishers on Albe-marle Street. He was not even exotic like Ram Ahmed, head of Liddell's House, about whom the boys constantly made jokes, which he was a sport about and took in great humour. Being a good sport was very important. Tom's father was from a village in the Lake District and his mother – well, who cared about Julian Caldicott, these days? The headmaster, hearing he was from Scotland, nodded his head as though he'd said he was from the moon, and then asked him whether he'd seen any good cricket that summer.

'Unfortunately not, sir.'

'What about your father? He enjoy cricket?'

'No, sir,' said Tom, not sure how to tell him that he hadn't seen his father for a year, and that he wasn't sure why. 'He's more of a rugger man,' he lied.

'Very good, Raven,' the headmaster had replied, nodding. 'Very good.'

He'd assumed Knoll Hall, his prep school, must be a little like Westminster, but he soon saw that was like assuming you knew London because you'd been to Tunbridge Wells. There were umpteen phrases and traditions he didn't understand – the Greaze, Up School, 'Remove pupil' – so he learned to keep quiet until he knew them too, and for the rest of his life watched men who looked like him bluff their way through situations where they were out of their depth and get away with it. But there were things about Westminster he enjoyed. He made friends: Guy Mannering, whose father was something very high up in the Civil Service, and Antoine Renaud, who'd been at Knoll with him and whose father was an attaché to the French Embassy.

In the spring of 1960, six months after he'd joined, Guy Mannering invited him to a birthday tea. 'The dear old pater wants to treat me. Asked me to bring a friend. We'll go after school. Sound all right, Raven?'

'I should say so,' said Tom, his mouth watering at the idea, not least because meals at Montpelier Crescent had become more and more erratic and eccentric; the previous week, for example, he'd had anchovies on toast five nights in a row.

The following Tuesday they left school, crossed the road and went into the Houses of Parliament to meet Guy's father.

'Awful bore, hunting for Dad every time,' said Guy, after they'd trailed round for a while, eventually being directed to the right place by a kindly police officer. Guy's father was in a meeting, so they waited for him, kicking their heels outside a minister's office high up on the third floor, smog hanging over the dark grey Thames. 'It's deathly dull here, sorry,' said Guy, yawning and stretching his long legs out on to the dusty green carpet.

Tom did not find it dull. He found it fascinating, from the High Victorian Gothic decorations to the identikit quiet men in pinstriped suits and black horn-rimmed glasses who brushed past them. One of them, Tom realized, was Alec Douglas-Home.

Guy's father, when he appeared, was apologetic, jamming a hat on his head and ushering the boys out and into town in a black cab, begging them to forget his behaviour. But Tom never forgot it. Opposite their school was Parliament, and to Guy and many other students this was quite normal: it was where their fathers spent their days.

Tom came to see that it was rather like the rugby team in Gatehouse. He had always wanted to try rugby, but his father didn't play and Tom didn't know any of the other locals who did. The boys who went to the club grew up feeling confident playing rugby and so, when they were twelve, thirteen, and it came time to select the Under-Sixteen Galloway team, the boys who had been playing rugby every weekend and at school and with their fathers and their pals were good and the boys who hadn't had that weren't, and Tom hadn't had that, and so he wasn't. And it turned out the country was run on similar lines.

But thanks to Mr Carter, who made Maths jolly interesting, and M. Le Maout, who gave him a life-long love both of philosophical arguments and of France, and Miss Aplin, the Art mistress, who'd been an artist's model before the war, as well as an air-raid warden – thanks to these teachers Tom learned to train his brain, to examine what he was told, to build worlds and understand their construction.

His years in Notting Hill – where he knew everyone, more or less, and the best pie shops and record shops and the best garden squares to sneak into and play; the streets where he'd wander for hours with Gordon and trade insults with Johnny – all of that world receded. Westminster was his life now. Afterwards, he would remember this period as speeded up, summers and school terms and interminable evenings at Montpelier Crescent flickering by as though on a screen. For now he was waiting for one thing, which was to leave his school days behind and to get on with life, for that was the only way to escape whatever it was he had with Jenny and Henry, to forge his own path.

He wrote to his father, and his father wrote back. It wasn't like before. But every time Tom said, *Come to Sevenstones this summer, Dad! I miss you!*, Edward, in his reply, never alluded to the invitation.

Jenny did not mention his father again.

Once, Edward actually came by for tea, when he was delivering a set of table and chairs to a client in Sussex. He had a van, and Tom went inside to see the four smooth chairs, gently curving, strapped firmly against the sides. There were a couple of woodchips on the floor, his father's chisel and hammer and plane poking out of his neatly wound-up tool bag. Everything was always neat, with his father.

He stayed only an hour. Jenny was perfectly civil and made

him tea; Henry came out and shook his hand; and he and Tom sat in the kitchen, chatting.

'Are you all right otherwise, old boy?' Tom had nodded. 'Good! Excellent!' His father leaned forwards, patted his knees. 'Well done. Ah, Tom.'

He had bruise-coloured half-moons under his eyes, and pale little dots across his skin. He looked much older, and smoked incessantly. And then he was off, waving goodbye, before Tom could say: *But it's all wrong. And there's something badly wrong, Dad, it's getting worse and I don't know who to tell.*

The problem was Jenny. Something had changed in the last year or so, perhaps since he began at Westminster. She was often ill, staying in bed for days at a time, then leaping up and painting empty rooms in the house strange meat colours or an intense teal, selling or burning furniture without telling Henry, bringing down his fury on her head. There was the time Tom came back and an old man who sold game at Portobello Market was sitting in the kitchen calmly skinning a rabbit, his shoes resting on the range; he claimed Jenny had said he could move in. Then came the day the men from Sotheby's turned up while Jenny and Henry were both out. They said Jenny had asked them to store one of Julian Caldicott's paintings, *Daphnis and Chloe Out Walking*, before the sale, and Tom couldn't stop them. When Henry returned from wherever he'd been and saw the bare wall with only the outline on the faded wallpaper, the only clue that it had been there at all, he gave a great roar and raced upstairs to find his sister, who was in her bedroom, which was below Tom's. They had a huge row and he slapped her, actually slapped her.

'For God's sake, Jenny! What the hell is wrong with you!'

'Leave me alone! Leave me be!' she had screamed at him. 'I have to do what I have to do! It has to go!'

'Jen! You have to stop this! For Father's sake! For Irene's sake! For Teddy's sake, for Christ's sake! And for the boy!' he'd said, his voice hoarse and cracking; and Tom, having hurried to where they were, stood in the doorway, his good eye straining to adjust as it sometimes did with two focal points, and saw a vignette he would never forget: his aunt, clutching her cheek and weeping, her eyes huge over her fingertips, no sense in them at all; and his uncle, fists clenched with sadness, not rage, staring with despair at her, the two of them locked together like in some Greek tragedy or biblical parable – Guy would have had the perfect comparison, but then perhaps not, for Guy came from a normal family, where they remembered birthdays and there were parents and there presumably weren't anchovies on toast for tea five nights in a row.

If Henry was in and not out drinking somewhere, the two read in the first-floor drawing room, the only sound the wireless in the basement and the intermittent thudding of the ancient, temperamental hot-water geyser above the bath. Neither spoke to the other, and so at some point Tom took to slipping out at night and walking up Ladbroke Grove to meet Gordon.

He and Gordon would go to a café, or a dance club, and it was on these visits that Tom fell in love with Calypso, truly fell for it – not like the thin intense white boys he went to Ronnie Scott's with who sat and sneered at anything too experimental. Just as he loved watching the buildings go up around Ladbroke Grove – loved seeing steel girders and concrete breeze blocks, the men in hard hats with large detailed plans on boards – so did he love watching the interplay between the steel drums, the guitar, the percussion, how each musician talked to the other without words, how everything knitted together. Patterns. Beauty. Chaos. Perspective.

He had felt he needed to thank Gordon for the night he lost his sight, but Gordon wouldn't hear it. Keen on accuracy as ever, Gordon said, 'It wasn't me. We shouldn't have been there; we shouldn't have had to come out to defend ourselves. You fell well, my boy. You folded yourself up. You fell real well.'

And, as always, Gordon was interested in everything. Tom wondered when he was ever at home. He was in a chess club that met in a park in Willesden. He played cricket in Kensal Rise. He went to evening classes, in metal work and French, with some friends from the London Underground at the Working Men's College in Camden. And every week he went to listen, and dance, to Calypso in the cafés and clubs around where he lived.

One Saturday, eighteen months or so after he had started at Westminster, Tom was sitting in a café high up Ladbroke Grove with Gordon. He had had goat curry, and some drink he wasn't entirely sure didn't have rum in it; anyway, he had a nice, fuzzy feeling. He could smell spring in the air, and he was happy. The night before he'd been to the eighteenth birthday party of Susan, Guy Mannering's eldest sister, at her family's house in Eaton Square. He had drunk two glasses of champagne and then, partly at Antoine's urging, had asked Susan's friend Barbara to dance.

Barbara had kissed him, outside on the terrace of the house for ages, pushing him against the stone balustrades, putting his hands on her waist for him then sliding them upwards, so that one touched her creamy cool skin, the swell of her left breast, then she gasped and stepped back, dark eyes full of mischief. 'Aren't you naughty,' she'd called over her shoulder as she'd walked away. 'Susan and I had a bet about you. Make sure you tell her, if she comes looking for you. You're delicious, aren't you?'

Tom didn't know what to say to this. 'Umm.' He nodded, hating himself. 'Umm – sometimes?'

'*Sometimes*,' he'd hissed to himself in the silence after she stepped back into the room and he was left alone. 'You bloody idiot. Who says sometimes. For Christ's sakes, Raven, pull yourself *together*.'

Having given himself this pep talk, Tom downed a glass of champagne that he found on a side table and strode back into the room, where he almost careened into a young woman. She had short, dark hair, and was in a fuchsia-coloured tulip-shaped dress. He'd noticed her earlier, couldn't remember where he'd met her before. She had eyes like a doe: black, velvety.

'Oh! Hello,' she'd said, smiling at him, her lips parted. 'It's Tom, isn't it? I see why Susan kept saying we had to invite you,' and Tom had blinked, his vision in his good eye still rather blurred from having someone else's face pressed up against it.

'Hello?' he said cautiously.

She'd raised an eyebrow at him. 'Evening, Tom Raven,' she'd said. 'I'm Celia – Guy's sister. We were charades part-ners when you came to us for New Year.' She mimed racing a chariot, holding the reins. '*Ben Hur*. Remember?' Her eyes raked him up and down.

'Oh,' said Tom, sticking his hands in his pockets in a piti-ful attempt at nonchalance. 'Wotcher, Celia.'

Wotcher. Celia stared at him, eyes widening.

'I – er –' said Tom, wanting to die. 'Sorry. Of course I remember you. Hello, Celia.'

She gave a gurgle of laughter that caught in her throat and he felt something jump in his heart.

'You do look handsome tonight. Don't let Barbara break you in, will you? Guy says you're one of the nice ones.' And she'd smiled at him, her lovely dark brown eyes glinting in the haze of the doorway. Tom had swallowed, feeling himself falling, falling far into a pit of something.

He had told Gordon all this, head down, unable to meet his gaze. Gordon slapped him on the back.

'There you go, boy! What have you done!' he said with great amusement. 'Yes, boy! That poor girl, Tom, you best make it right with that first one, so she don't think you're going to be calling her up taking her to dances and things.'

'Oh, no,' said Tom firmly, thinking of Barbara grabbing one of the band members by the arm and retreating into the little galley kitchen with him. 'I'm pretty sure I don't need to do that.'

'Hmm,' said Gordon, draining his glass and covering it with his palm. He stared at Tom, seriously. 'Listen, when it comes to women, listen to me, boy.'

'What?'

'You are trouble.'

'Eh?'

'Oh, yes, you are, Tom, they like you. Look.' He nudged Tom and glanced along the bar, to where a young woman was waiting by herself, apparently absorbed in a magazine, but in fact looking at Tom over the front cover.

Tom smiled at her, blushing slightly, then turned to Gordon. 'Gordon, can I ask you something?' He lowered his voice a little. 'With . . . with girls, I mean. Do you just – act normal? Or should you act in a different way?'

'Normal, boy! Always act normal. The more relaxed you are, the happier you are. Boy, there've been times I thought I'd be dead the next day. And I'd still act relaxed, because what's the point otherwise? I'd drink some champagne, some gin, whatever. I'd dance. Maybe a dance with a girl. I'd sleep well –' He gave Tom a quick smile. 'Then I'd go and fight.'

'Is this in the war?'

Gordon nodded.

'At Sevenstones? Girls just – around? All the time?'

Gordon nodded, pushing his cigarette out slowly, methodically. 'Yes. But we thought we might die the next day: you got to understand that.' He looked out of the window, as if he were looking into the distance, the past. 'How's she doing, your aunt Jenny?'

Tom stared down at his small glass of rum. 'I don't know.'

Gordon watched him, then poured himself another glass, and drank it. 'I don't see her much these days. When I first came back, I saw her all the time. And, for a while, I was delivering letters to her, from her. But that's all stopped now.'

Tom said, 'She has nightmares, Gordon. She keeps saying someone's name, in her sleep. She shouts it and I can hear it in the room above.' Tom ruffled his hair, mortified to be saying this to someone. It felt like a betrayal. 'Teddy. She keeps calling out for Teddy.'

Gordon was staring at him. 'You serious?'

'Of course. More and more,' said Tom, relieved to be finally telling someone. 'I don't know what to do. It wakes me up. It's awful. I can't help her. I can't ask her.'

The champagne from the previous night, and the lack of sleep, and the dehydration, and whatever Tom was drinking now, were all conspiring to give him a blistering headache, which he often got when he was tired and his good eye was having to work too hard.

Gordon looked round, his eyes moving slowly, and Tom realized that he had drunk too much. 'The way they treated her. Wasn't right, to my mind. Wasn't right at all.'

'My mother?'

'Not your mother, boy. She died and it was tragic. No, your aunt. Jenny and her girl.'

'What do you mean? Jenny had – a girl?'

'You're so green. You don't even understand. Jenny doesn't like boys. She likes girls.'

'Girls?' Tom had heard of this obviously, was aware it was possible, something one laughed about at school – maiden aunts and games mistresses and the like. But he didn't actually *know* anyone like that.

Gordon didn't even seem that interested in that aspect of it. He said, 'One girl especially. It was bad. And that's why your aunt, she can't live any more.'

Tom shivered. 'What girl?' he said.

'Ah, what can it hurt for you to know that bit. She had an American girl, a WAAF. They were drivers together and they fell in love. I guess that's how I first knew Jenny, wildly in love. Her and the WAAF.' He leaned forwards. 'She was crazy, you know? Mad at her family, mad at the world. Used to see her at Sevenstones all the time.'

'Jenny doesn't seem the sort of person to –' Tom began. He didn't know how to finish the sentence.

'You look shocked, my boy. You have to understand, no one cared about that sort of thing in the war, and especially not at Sevenstones. We were there to dance and drink, be free. Anyone was welcome. Used to see them sitting under the apple tree, like the song. Jenny was so happy. But I knew it wouldn't last. I knew . . . Ah, me.'

'How come?'

Gordon sucked in air through his closed mouth with a whistling sign. 'It wasn't reciprocated. Oh, maybe a little. But the other girl, she didn't feel the same way. She wanted passion. And, Jenny, she requires too much. She always has. She doesn't really know what she wants, that's how I see it. She grew up with a domineering father, an invisible mother, a dashing hero for a brother, and a sister who could do no wrong. You see? She's in the middle, although she's the youngest, but she doesn't know who she is. I always felt . . . she wanted to live through another person, to suck someone dry. It was long ago. But she's not over it.'

'What happened?'

'The girl got taken away. And Jenny can't get over it, and she can't forgive.'

'What does that mean, Gordon?' Tom said.

'It means she lost the love of her life. You'll know, when you fall in love, you'll know how it hurts.'

'But you've never been in love,' Tom said.

'If you'd seen what it did to them,' Gordon said, 'you'd understand why I'm not so hasty.' He stood up, drained his drink and patted Tom on the back. 'Goodbye, my boy.'

'I'll see you soon,' said Tom, yet he felt for the first time that something had changed between them.

22

1961

One evening the French ambassador gave a party for an actress who had come to town, and Antoine invited Tom and Guy. The ambassador's residence was on a private road behind Kensington Gardens. The boys, being three fifteen-year-olds, drank slightly too much champagne, then stole one of Antoine's father's cigars and escaped to the front garden, where they sat in the still, warm autumn night, taking it in turns to suck alternately on the cigar and the bottle of brandy Antoine had purloined from the drinks cabinet while pretending to enjoy both.

The road was wide, and quiet, since no traffic was allowed. Inside, the lights of the party and the chandelier in the grand ballroom glittered, the soft chatter of the guests just audible.

'What do you think,' Antoine said into the silence between them, 'is going to change the most? In the next few years?'

Tom, leaning against a magnolia tree, felt light-headed and intensely wise – as though he understood all the problems of the world. 'People,' he said. 'How we see each other. Man's inhumanity to man and all that.'

'Revolution?' Antoine raised an eyebrow. 'The British will never revolt. You are too bourgeois, every last one of you.'

'I say,' murmured Guy.

'I think you're wrong,' said Tom. 'I think a revolution will come. Class, race, everything. We will all be changed at the end of it.'

Antoine laughed. 'Ah, no. You are all too – what is the word? The way you boil your vegetables is the way you attack life. You will over-boil the vegetables of change. You will boil everything so it is tasteless and shapeless.'

'Absolute rot,' said the always amiable Guy, but he didn't move, just handed the cigar to Tom.

A policeman walked slowly past, truncheon over his shoulder, staring at them. 'Good evening, officer,' Antoine called to him, nodding, and the policeman, peering at them, said, 'Ah. Mr Runnow. Goodnight to you, sir.'

'Your police are placid, lazy, they do not fire, they do not shoot. Yes, it is as I say: you boil the life out of everything. Ha.' And, as Antoine moved to lean back against the magnolia tree, he missed the branch behind him and fell backwards on to the ground with a loud, cursing oath. The other two roared with laughter, then helped him up.

'The vegetables of change have deserted you,' said Tom. He found he couldn't stop laughing. 'But, still. I think change will come.'

'You sound like Celia,' said Guy. 'She's always banging on about it. Drives mother up the wall. She says Celia needs to go to finishing school and start wearing gloves and frocks and going for tea with old ladies, like Susan. And there's Celia hopping about the place in black polo necks, trying to break out at night and go to folk clubs, smoking surreptitious cigarettes and talking about fomenting riots.'

'Oh, Celia,' said Antoine appreciatively, lingering over the syllables of her name, and Guy, who was untested when it came to girls and any mention of that sort of thing, looked horrified. 'That's my sister, old chap,' he said, stiffer than ever.

Tom swallowed, and hoped Guy didn't notice how uncomfortable he was, how any mention of Celia made him feel rather funny. He'd seen her several times since her sister's party, but he had thought about her far more.

'Mr Carter asked me, what do I want to be doing in ten years' time?' Guy said, when a little later they'd thanked their host and left, walking up towards Notting Hill. 'One couldn't say, for example, one loathes politics and all that reading gives one a headache and what one would *really* like to be doing is, oh, I don't know, playing cricket or messing around on the trumpet with some other chaps for a living.'

The others listened in sympathetic silence. Guy's place at Trinity and his career in the Civil Service, like his father and his father before him, were clearly mapped out. But jazz was his life, the trumpet his closest companion. Tom had never seen anyone work as hard at anything as Guy did at the trumpet. He practised for hours on end. And Tom loved, on the rare occasions that he saw him play, how Guy's face changed: his diffident, rather world-weary natural expression giving way to someone experiencing almost unconscious ecstasy – utterly unselfconscious, unaware of his surroundings, head flung back, eyes slightly rolling in their sockets. He didn't care how he looked: he was the instrument and the instrument was him.

Antoine, by contrast, was to train to be an *avocat*, had a place at the Sorbonne and was looking forward to returning to Paris. He knew a girl, Sophie, whom his family liked and whom he fully expected to marry. He had lost his virginity, the only boy in the year so far as they knew, the previous summer on the Île de Ré with the older sister of a family friend. Antoine had no reason to lie about this; he did not

court popularity, one of several things he had in common
with Tom and Guy.

'In ten years' time it will be 1971,' said Antoine, blowing
out his lips and taking the cigar from Guy. 'I shall expect
to be on my way to my own practice. I shall have an apartment in Paris, and a house in the South. I shall have travelled
across America –'

'You? But you hate America!' said Tom, astonished.

'Do not be reductive, Raven. It doesn't suit you. I do not
like the striving for a new imperialism of America when
France and Britain struggle to release themselves from theirs.
That is all. It is a philosophical question, not an ideological
position. You understand. Besides, I love hamburgers.'

'Mmm.'

'Absolutely.' Both the others nodded certainly. Tom noticed
with some relief that Guy was walking in a slight zigzag, one
eye partially shut. (He had, famously, fallen asleep the year
before, as they walked back from a coffee bar in Soho.)

'What about you, Raven?' said Antoine. 'In ten years' time,
what do you want to be doing?'

Tom screwed up his nose, concentrating on the view
ahead, which, in the dark and after a few drinks, was trickier
to navigate than it had been on the way there. 'I have no
idea,' he said.

'Typical,' said Guy. 'A man of mystery to the last.'

'I'm jolly well not.'

'Oh, you are, Raven. One doesn't know your people, your
house, your views – you take the long view on everything.'

'You've met my aunt!'

'Barely. To wave to on the street. Look here, it doesn't
matter,' said Guy, smiling. 'Don't look so furious.'

'I'm not furious.'

'Of course.'

Tom hated it when Guy was reasonable. He said, 'You sound like a ruddy civil servant already, Mannering.'

'Come off it. Forget I spoke. Now, tell me what you'll be doing ten years hence: 10 October 1971.'

'I want to be in love.' Tom spoke without thinking. The brandy seemed to make his mouth heavy. 'I want to love someone so much that it's my life's work, that we exist only for each other, that we make the world – the world better because of our love.'

The other two laughed. 'How bourgeois, Raven,' Antoine said.

'I don't think that's bourgeois,' said Guy, and Tom turned to him gratefully. 'But I do think it's so pretentious as to be sickening.'

Tom shrugged, as if he couldn't care less. 'You're entitled to your –' He stopped. 'Oh dear.'

They had reached the top of the street that opened on to Bayswater Road. The night was colder now, the stars visible in the sky above Kensington Gardens. Autumn was coming. A man was leaning against a lamp post, the light pooling down on his bent form as he emptied his stomach contents into the gutter.

Guy, who was a compassionate chap, said, 'Should we perhaps –'

'No,' said Tom, disgusted. 'Leave him.'

'He's a tramp,' said Antoine. 'I often see him. Ignore him.'

'I don't think he's a tramp,' said Guy. 'Oh, I say. He's waving at you.' The man had straightened up and, oblivious to his recent troubles, was waving at them enthusiastically with one hand, cramming a battered old trilby on to his head with the other, all the while smiling at them and running his tongue ruminatively around his teeth. 'He's rather noble-looking, actually. Help! What should one do?'

'Ignore him,' said Tom. He was sure, even from here, he could smell the old man's vomit. And then the man called over:

'Tom! Old thing! I say! You walking this way?'

'I'd better go,' said Tom, striding off. 'I'll see you chaps on Monday. Thanks awfully for a terrific evening –'

'Tom! I say, can you hear me? Tom, old thing!'

The cheerfulness was the worst part about it, how oblivious he was to it all.

'Raven,' said Guy. 'I think he knows you –'

'Yes,' said Tom, and he took a deep breath. 'He's my uncle. I'm coming, Uncle H. Stay there.' He crossed the wide road, dodging a lone cyclist. His friends watched in silence. Tom nodded at his uncle. 'Come on.' He walked on, motioning for him to follow. Henry stank of alcohol, of vomit, of staleness. Tom's cheeks burned but he did not flinch. Raising his arm to his friends, he set off west, followed by Uncle Henry, stumbling quietly in his wake.

'Slow down, young Tom!' Henry muttered, as they passed Notting Hill Gate, then the cinema, with hordes of people coming out of the late showing of *What a Carve Up!* He paused to stare, open-mouthed, at the poster: Shirley Eaton taking her clothes off. 'I said slow down, my boy!'

'We're nearly home, Uncle Henry,' Tom said, stopping to wait for his uncle, and it was then he realized he felt nothing like disgust any more, just vaguely sorry for him. 'And I'm not a boy any more, sir.'

23

Summer 1963

'What *is* this rubbish?' Tom stuck his head around the doorway of the kitchen into the living room.

'Oh, darling,' said Celia, sprawled on her front, hands on her chin, watching the small television (a rare and surprising purchase by Jenny, as Henry wouldn't have one in the house in London) in rapt attention. 'They're sending up the new *Doctor in Distress* film – you know, Dirk Bogarde. Isn't he dreamy?' Her pale, heart-shaped face was flushed. 'Isn't he?'

'I haven't the faintest,' said Tom. 'I don't like Dirk Bogarde. I like you.' He bent down and dropped a kiss on her head; she rolled over and pulled him down.

'Stop being boring,' she said, kissing him, wrapping her arms around his neck. 'Come here for a bit.'

'I can't,' said Tom, in a panic, for he had planned out everything, and the part he had control over was that he was going to cook her an amazing meal first. 'The potatoes are boiling.'

'Boiling potatoes.' Celia gave a yelp of amusement. 'Oh, gosh.' She turned back on to her front, gently pushing him away, and he stood up, trying to hide his discomfort. 'Go back to your potatoes, awful boy. How dreadful if they boiled too long.'

It reminded Tom of that evening with Antoine and Guy a couple of years ago, and he smiled, blinking in disbelief that this was here and now . . . this was Guy's sister, his best friend's sister, and no one had any idea she was here. He swallowed, nerves getting the better of him. 'Just wait. You'll be dreadfully sorry. I'm making a meal of utter subliminini . . .' Tom petered out, but she was watching TV again. He turned back to the kitchen, glad she wasn't paying attention.

Celia Mannering was a year older than Guy. She was about to start at Edinburgh University, but she had agreed to come to Sevenstones for one night. Tom and Jenny had arranged as usual that they would go that summer but that she would leave him there for two days, as she had to go back to London to help the Reverend Bryant at her Spiritualist Church with a laying-on of hands. 'He needs me,' she'd told Tom, delighted, and Tom did not say anything, for he was glad she was happy, but also glad he'd be alone for a while.

Celia and Guy's family holidayed in Cornwall, on the Roseland, every summer. Tom had joined them the previous year at their white Arts and Crafts house overlooking St Mawes, the harbour and the peninsula towards the Helford River. Tom had not enjoyed himself much, since Guy was withdrawn and strange, as he often was with his parents, unable to play his beloved trumpet, and Celia was with her current boyfriend, a family friend named Toby whom Tom considered to be an idiot, but he had enjoyed Celia, especially the sight of her diving off a boat in her two-piece bathing suit. He thought about her all the time, but really he had done since they'd first met.

Tom was seventeen now. He felt as though his life were divided into three separate parts. Life at home with Jenny and Henry which remained the same, year in, year out. Then there was his time at school, and after school, with Guy and Antoine. And there was being with Gordon in London, which was what he actually thought of as London now Gordon, as with everything else, was extremely particular about good places to go versus those not worthy of his attention. They sat in the Warwick Avenue Station staff room having cups of tea, or went to Totobags, a café off Ladbroke Grove, or they wandered through the city, taking in the sights and sounds of Oxford Street, Soho and the fabric stalls of Berwick Street – Gordon's father had been a tailor – and the royal parks. He loved the parks, Gordon did.

Celia fitted into none of these parts. She was posh, like Guy, terrifyingly clever – Roedean – and deliciously liberated, more so than any other girl he knew, not that he knew many girls, but often they seemed awfully silly, giggly or tongue-tied; or, on television, utterly unrealistic. She was older, and had travelled around America on a Greyhound bus the summer before university with three friends, and thus could report first-hand on segregation and seeing Dr King, in person, in Albany, Georgia. They had watched Bob Dylan play in Greenwich Village, tried marijuana, swum in the Pacific Ocean. She'd had an Italian boyfriend, studied in Florence for a bit, was going to study law, then after that go to live in Rome. Tom had never dared to hope it might come to anything, his hopeless passion for Celia, but, when he had telephoned Guy on holiday the following year, something astonishing happened.

Celia had answered, Guy being out, and they had talked. She was having a miserable time with her parents, she said, and Tom jokingly said she should come here for a night. Before Tom knew what was happening, they had fixed up for her to visit, to relieve Tom of his virginity.

'Are you sure you want to come?' he'd said into the phone.

'Gosh, yes. Didn't I say years ago I didn't want anyone else to break you in? Unless someone's got there first, darling, and I will be cross.' She gurgled down the line, a full-throated, caramel chuckle.

'Oh –' Tom said, glad no one was there to see his face turn red. 'Oh. Right, then. I say – thanks.'

'Don't tell Guy, will you, darling? Terrific. Swell. See you tomorrow.'

As he put the phone down and the hand holding the receiver started to shake, as if unable to contain the import of what he had just agreed, Tom leaned against the wall in the warm, dark hallway of Sevenstones. Had he read this right? Was she really coming? And – for that? Tom, indeed, was not entirely sure that was the deal, but she had definitely said she was coming. He looked down at the piece of paper with the train times in his hand. He hadn't dreamed it.

'You're awfully quiet,' Celia said over the pork chop and potatoes a little later, in the warm, sunny kitchen.

Tom took a gulp of the gin he'd found in an old sideboard. It tasted as though it had been there since the war. He cleared his throat. 'I suppose I wonder if you're here for the same reason I want you to be here.'

'To play Mah Jong?' Celia said, turning her dark eyes on him. 'Hope so. Shall we get right down to it after supper?' Tom swallowed. She smiled at him and pushed the pork chop away. 'This is awfully dry.' She licked her lips.

'Sorry,' said Tom. He tried not to stare at her lips, wet where she had licked them. Why were her lips so red? Why were they like that, plump and mobile at the same time, like – like –

'I like you, Tom. You're not like other boys.'

'How so?'

'Not sure. You're interesting.'

She speared another small potato with her fork and ate it, and, as he watched her mouth open and close, he blinked, half flattered, half hypnotized, then remembered his role, that of a grateful but world-weary friend.

'You're kind, and clever, and you haven't made your mind up yet. So many people our age aren't enlightened, Tom. They think they are but it's a kind of cheap version of it. Something they bought on a market stall in Camden. Not you.' She swallowed, put her arms on the table and met his gaze steadily. 'And, of course, you're absolutely divine to look at, but you know that.'

'Well, of course,' Tom said, struggling to maintain his composure. He could not reveal that he had endless dreams about her in the apricot two-piece bathing suit, about rescuing her from the sea, about carrying her to safety, about what her lush, soft naked body would feel like, pressed against his naked body . . .

'But the trouble is you're like all boys: it's the struggle within that counts, and it's remarkably uninteresting for the girl. Rather like sex.' She ate another potato, eyes sparkling. 'I don't want to be tediously attentive to practicalities, but just so we're clear . . . This is your first time, isn't it?'

Tom was so relieved to have it confirmed this was the object of her visit that he nodded too enthusiastically and swallowed a large chunk of potato, nearly choking. It bruised his gullet and he rubbed his throat.

'Good lord,' said Celia, watching him. She passed him a glass of water.

'It's awfully kind of you,' Tom said incoherently.

'What? This trip? Don't worry. It's entirely selfish. One of Daddy's school friends is staying and his son, Edmund, is an absolute creep. So I lied and said an old school friend was staying near Stonehenge. It's true, anyway. You are an old school friend, of Guy –'

'But Guy doesn't know about it, does he?'

'No, do calm down.' Celia stood up and walked over to him. 'When I said it was selfish of me I meant it. I like you. Come on, darling. I'm absolutely not hungry any more.'

He could not tell her that he was hopelessly in love with her, that he had been since her sister's eighteenth birthday party, that he had to go into public conveniences sometimes to fumble with himself if he accidentally thought of her, that he was disgusting, that she drove him mad, that he had written poetry for her but couldn't show it to her, that he had dreamed of falling in love but never thought it would be like this. As Celia undressed and got into the narrow bed in the tiny room with the sloping eaves, Tom hurriedly removed his jumper and his shirt, but turned his back to do so. He could not look at her; he was worried he would get too excited and the whole thing would be even more of a disaster than he was certain it was going to be. The thing was, he *loved* Celia; he wanted to marry her; he had everything planned out; he was going to be a sketch writer for a revue, something jolly witty like *That Was the Week that Was* and he would make pots of money – vulgar but necessary, to be able to tell Sir Hugh Mannering that he was a serious person. They would move to a flat in Pimlico to start with – he wasn't sure he could afford Eaton Square, like her parents, at first – and she could carry on with her career; she'd probably have to give up being a lawyer after they had some children; he'd be an awfully good dad, just like his father, but he'd be a proper family man, white stucco house with a front garden, holidays in Cornwall with the family, cricket with Guy, and lovely, lovely Celia to come home to, Celia in her thin nylon nightdress with her remarkable, sweet, round breasts he could see through the lace trim and the shiny material – oh, God. He would hold her hand in church and she would – oh, God, she was kissing him. With difficulty, Tom pulled off his shorts over his erection, and his Y-fronts. He hopped under the covers, squashing her legs so that she yelped. The sensation of her smooth, bare skin underneath him was overwhelming, and he shuddered.

'Dear lord,' said Celia. 'Tom darling, calm down, won't you.'

'Oh, absolutely.'

He rested himself between her legs and began to kiss her – her milky shoulder bone, her neck, and was encouraged that she moved against him, and then he put one hand on her soft, plump right breast, gently but firmly, and she murmured. Tom breathed in, and then gave a huge sigh, adjusting himself, so aroused he was rather uncomfortable, but unbelievably happy. Sometimes he stopped and asked her if it was right. After a few minutes, Celia said:

'It's all fine. Time to get going, darling.'

She took his jutting, hard penis in her hand. 'Hello,' she said softly and smiled at him, just for him. 'I thought so.'

'Thought what?' he said, breathing carefully.

'Doesn't matter,' she said, and he heard her breathe in sharply, as she slid the rubber johnny he had purchased from the chemist's behind Victoria Station that summer over his penis. Tom held his breath. He followed Antoine's advice, which was to distract himself, and thought of Mr Carter, Mr Tonks, of the shops on Portobello, of the stops on the No. 23 bus. He breathed deeply. He set his knees between her thighs and, holding his penis in one hand, slowly pushed it in. It was incredible. Nothing like doing it himself. She gave a little cry.

'All right?' he whispered, hopelessly unsure as to what to do next. She moved his hand to between her legs. 'I'm not – is this all right, Celia?'

'Yes. I like it. Bit big. I want you to go on, though. Move inside me, darling. Now – touch me here.' She bit her lip, her cheeks flushed, and, guiding his trembling, sweaty hand, she made him stroke her. They moved together.

He was inside her. It was very – very – unexpected. It was tight, and rather terrifying. He wasn't sure if he was hurting her. She didn't seem to mind. One hand was flung out above her head, her neat, curved breasts splayed across her body, the dark nipples pointed and tight. He kissed them, tasting her on his lips, and she moaned, and thanked him, which he found incredibly endearing. Her other hand was on his bottom, pushing him into her. After a moment he stopped and looked at her, and she smiled at him encouragingly, wrapping her legs more tightly round him. It was the kindness, the sense of unity, that he found unbelievably arousing – it was just them, the two of them.

'Bit harder, Tom. Don't stop. Do it like that, yes –'

She shifted, and tightened around him, and her eyes opened in surprise, and then he saw a flush spreading from her clavicle outwards across her breasts, the dark pink nipples hard like little berries – it was all like fruit, all of it – and suddenly, without meaning to, he thrust hard and came, collapsing on to her in a silent roar, head against hers. Sensation exploded across him, turning his body rigid with ecstasy, his hands gripping on to her, wanting to stay inside her, to keep this moment going for as long as possible – life! He was alive! It was blissful! Evening sun poured in through the round window, reminding him of the world outside, how this was usual, how other people knew this feeling, how wonderful everything was. He could scarcely believe it.

'Sorry,' he said after a moment, panting. He could not see; his good eye seemed to have blurred over, his body seemed to radiate heat. He blinked, and grinned. 'Sorry, Celia – I didn't –'

She was staring at him. 'Tom, that was really not bad. I expect great things from you.'

He rolled off her carefully and clumsily pulled the condom off himself, still light-headed, but at the same time astonished at how depressing it was, the slime, the retreat, the mundanity of it. Slowly, joyfully, he scooted back against her and they stared out of the window.

'Look,' she said, kissing his head, half mumbling with sleep. 'On the hills over there. That's a white horse, isn't it?'

He nodded, stroking her thick, soft hair, wondering if, thousands of years ago, people had, in this same spot, in this same way, come together. Sunshine blazed over them, and she turned towards it, like a cat, letting it bathe her face, and he gazed at her, astonished.

Then she fell asleep. Tom dozed too, wondering if everyone felt this happy, wondering how he would tell his two best friends he had done it, wondering how soon he and Celia could do it again, and knowing, without a doubt, that this, finally, was love.

24

Alone in his room, Tom slumped to the floor, pulling his bow tie from his neck and, without realizing it, gave a low, animal moan of pain that grew louder and louder, until his throat hurt, and his neighbour, Richardson, banged on the walls.

'You made an utter idiot of yourself in front of everyone, Raven. You're drunk – go to bed, old chap. Think about what the hell you've done.'

Outside, June's sweet, frothing scenery tapped at the windows, the night scent from the honeysuckle in the gardens drifting over the mullioned casements and into his room. He could hear the shouts of laughter, of drunken merrymaking coming from the quad, the thud of various feet dashing up and down the stairs. Someone was playing the Stones. (Someone was *always* playing the Stones.) It was 5 a.m. and they should absolutely not be, but everything was topsy-turvy.

Tom lay on the floor. He did not think he could move. He swallowed, his throat hurting: he was so thirsty. He'd drunk nothing but champagne for hours. Memory kept assaulting him. His voice echoing around the sweltering marquee. The uncomprehending faces, expressions of stilted embarrassment turning to open contempt as he stuttered on. Try as he

262

might to block them out, images from the evening unfurled across the room as though they were playing on a big screen: Celia, in a black satin minidress, her dark pixie haircut and flushed cheeks, her incredible silver shoes, her slim tanned fingers entwined round his, clutching his arm as they set off from his room towards the sound of the ball. And, as always, the utter pride and joy he felt when she was by his side, a longing to shout to the world: *Look! Look at my wonderful, darling girlfriend! I'm in love!*

It had been four years since their first summer meeting, and while he was in his final year at Westminster and Celia was still at Edinburgh, at her suggestion they had put the thing on a shelf, and Tom reluctantly tried seeing other girls. There was someone nice called Judith who lived around the corner from him and went to St Paul's, but it turned out she would meet him only if her sister came along too. When he tried to put his arm around her during *Goldfinger*, Judith had screamed as though he were trying to abduct her; then, while her sister hit him with her handbag, she had twisted his hand so hard he hadn't been able to hold a pen, or anything else, for several days. Judith was swiftly rechristened the Scream Queen. Then there was the Jazz Girl, someone he met at a gig at the 100 Club with Guy, who, oblivious to his best friend's deep, great love for his sister, blithely kept asking him whether he liked any girls and, if so, which girls and what did it feel like, worrying at him like someone with a hangnail. Jane, or the Jazz Girl, was the other extreme – she was gone, man, she drank too much, she did a little too much pot, she went with anyone and everyone, and word was she had a father who took too much interest in her and it had screwed her up. When she turned up at Montpelier Crescent at 2 a.m. one night, screaming and banging on the door to be let in, Tom didn't know what to do. But Henry, succinct for once, did. 'Tell that little bitch if she comes back here in the middle of the night I'll call the police,' he'd said as the three of them met on the landing, moonlight coating them in silver stripes.

'Oughtn't we to let her in?' Jenny asked anxiously, actually holding a candle, like something from a nursery tale. 'She sounds terribly distressed.'

''Course not. I'm going back to bed. Tom, stay away from girls like her, I'm warning you. Trouble.' Henry had turned, slamming the door to his bedroom behind him, prompting more hammering on the front door.

Then Shirley, a girl he knew from various Calypso scenes with Gordon, who finished with him because she only went with Black men, then Jazz Girl again, more and more unhappily, then Frances, the doe-eyed daughter of an MP who was dull as ditchwater and kept a drawer full of lichen samples in her bedroom. Tom wouldn't have minded that, but she wouldn't show them to him. It spoke to a meanness of spirit that he couldn't abide.

None of them was Celia. None had her body, and her funny droll ways, her quick intelligence, her eyes, her body again, because it really was remarkable, her smile, the way she smiled at him, knew things, held his hand, his heart. Tom was astonished at how unhappy he was, how love consumed him. It was like the time he and his father had been caught in a fog out on the hills, and you couldn't feel it but it surrounded and enveloped you. He was weary of school, of the boys and their smells, their wild enthusiasms for the same three records, their pranks, their ridiculous sporting jokes, their mortifying jingoism and arrogance, their lack of finesse. Celia, in one smooth fingernail – her fingernails were so beautiful, the pale crescent like a delicate moon – had more sensitivity, class, maturity – oh maturity, it meant so many things – than all the people he had known in the last year combined. He wanted her; he pined for her. He felt he was wasting away. He sent her poems, copied out in his tiny, difficult handwriting: 'A Valediction: Forbidding Mourning' and 'They Flee From Me'; and a curated selection of what he solemnly told her he considered the best of Shakespeare's Sonnets. And she would reply, postcards scrawled in her unique hand: *So clichéd, darling, try harder / Did you write this? / You are a poppet. /* And the last, which he kept close by at all times: *See you at Sevenstones?*

The following summer, 1964, they met again and it was different. He had left school and travelled around Spain, and could speak a little Spanish. He had stayed at the foothills of the Alhambra Palace, and camped by the Alcázar, sailed across to Fez, swum off the coast of Africa. Lying with her on the sweat-soaked sheets of the little bedroom with its view looking out to the white horse, he did not tell her he had done all these things to make himself seem more interesting, to show he was nothing like her brother, that he was becoming his own man, someone worthy of her. In the end they were alone for three days; they had sex almost continuously, parting sore and happy and with their stomachs empty but both their hearts full, so full. She had kissed him at the station, panting into his ear as she held his head, furiously, in her hands. 'I thought it was just fun, it's not fun, it's it, isn't it? It's it –'

'Yes,' he'd whispered, unable to believe she felt the same way, but she did.

The following autumn he went up to Pembroke College, Oxford, to read History, and they took the train between

Edinburgh and Oxford when they could, but mostly they wrote and telephoned. Everything was working towards his graduation and hers, when they would move to London together – it was all about that for him. He fell into life at Oxford within days, finding a group of friends akin to Guy and Antoine: clever, amusing, thoughtful, kind young men with a detached, amused approach to life, and he thought – oh, yes, he thought – he was himself.

For his second year at Oxford he and Celia agreed on another period of time apart. She was busy, studying abroad, and working out what she wanted to do after, be a barrister or a solicitor. She was older than him, and she wanted him to experience everything Oxford had to offer. He took her up on this suggestion, telling himself he must not lose her by being too intense, that he must step back and let her think he was fine. So he enjoyed himself, and saw some other girls – but that summer, back at Sevenstones, Celia came over for a week this time, and they realized they were as much in love as ever, and for their final year they tried to see each other as much as possible. Their relationship was always easy. No drama. She did not turn up at midnight, with eyeliner around her eyes, torn tights and broken heels, having had a huge row and stormed off, then changed her mind, like Foley's girlfriend. She did not write him intense letters detailing their future life together or send him a pair of baby's booties she had knitted, like a girl at St Hilda's whom Richardson had gone out with, albeit extremely briefly. She was just enormous fun, enormously sexy – God, he wanted her all the damn time – and she was far, far out of his league. Guy, and Sir Hugh and Lady Mannering, were hugely welcoming, and he grew to love family evenings at Eaton Square, and

Christmases in London with them, and even, once or twice, to understand what Sir Hugh meant when, on a Boxing Day walk in Hyde Park, he suddenly began talking about 'the future' with long pauses and a waggle of his eyebrows.

Even Guy, who at first had coped with the news his best friend was going out with his elder sister by playing the trumpet whenever he saw Tom at home to avoid having to talk to him, had got used to the idea and was happy about it. Everyone was happy about it.

One incident made him uneasy, but he brushed it out of sight, told himself it meant nothing.

Back in London, after his first Michaelmas term, Tom was hurrying to post his father's Christmas present. It was sleeting so thickly he could hardly see a thing, and, as he was passing by the café that had been Totobags – the Caribbean place where he and Gordon used to go and that had been succeeded by Mike's Café, where some chilly-looking hippies stood looking forlornly out into the wintry storm – someone stepped out and he ran straight into them.

'Tom!' The stranger gripped his arm. Tom, staring into his face, gave a shout of joy.

'Gordon! How the devil are you!'

Gordon slapped him on the back, grinning so widely Tom felt moved to tears. He gestured with his thumb to the straggly dressed men and women in the café, and to the Dog Shop, next door, Tom's favourite shop. It sold water beds, jewellery, candles, psychedelic posters, records, dope stuff – chillums and pipes – and was packed to the gills every weekend with young men and women who'd travelled from miles around to visit.

'What on earth is happening to this neighbourhood?' said

Gordon, his eyes shining. 'Talk about bringing the place down!'

They both laughed, and then were silent. Standing on Blenheim Crescent, hands on each other's shoulders. Tom couldn't get over how delighted he was to see him, and couldn't remember now why he hadn't caught up with him for so long.

'Dad – I'm bored,' said a little Cockney voice below them. Tom looked down. Gordon had a little girl with him, and she stood next to her father in glistening yellow wellingtons, her hands in her shiny blue mackintosh coat pockets, staring at Tom curiously.

Gordon had married a white woman called Beryl, and they had moved out towards Acton and had two children, Robert, who was five, and Angela, who was just three. Gordon had brought Angela with him to buy a Christmas present for her mother, but in general he still came here to go to the café up on Ladbroke Grove that he said did proper goat curry, to see his friends, to hear about the plans for the new Carnival, to keep in touch. He continued to work for London Transport, now overseeing the hiring of new bus drivers and training them. He had even been back to Trinidad, and gone to Jamaica too, on a couple of recruitment drives.

It was very cold as they stood there chatting, the wind whistling along the crowded streets. Gordon tucked Tom's large Pembroke scarf back around his neck.

'I'm forty next year, boy!' Gordon had said with great amusement when he noticed Tom glancing at his grizzled grey temples. 'I'm an old man, like all the old men round here. I'll be on the allotment complaining about the weather . . . you'll see. I've got an apple tree,' he said, proudly. 'Full crop this year, two boxes.'

'You always loved apples,' Tom said. 'I'm so glad, Gordon.'

'I love them, my boy. And one day you'll come to Trinidad with me, and you'll try a cocorite.'

'Yes, please.' Tom smiled but suddenly gripped Gordon's wrist tightly. He remembered that first dreadful day, when he'd run away from the bomb site. Gordon had picked him up, hugged him. 'It's good to see you,' he said suddenly.

'You too, boy. Be good to know what you do next,' said Gordon, inclining his head as if he wasn't sure about something.

'Can I write to you?' Tom said suddenly, taking a small pencil and a scrap of paper from his jacket pocket and thrusting them at Gordon.

''Course, Tom.' Gordon wrote down his address. 'Keep in touch, you understand? And – listen to me, Tom. Go well. You're a good boy. A good man, I should say. Look at the size of you. A young oak, aren't you? I bet I was right about you and the ladies.' Tom blushed.

'Dad!' said Angela, tugging at his coat. 'I'm cold. There's sausages for tea. Let's go!'

'Okay, okay, Angie. Just one moment.' Gordon looked down, stroked the pink-and-blue beads in her hair and turned back to Tom. 'How's your aunt? She okay?'

'Not really.'

'I'm sorry to hear that.' Gordon looked round, at the red-and-green lights on the road, the twinkling Christmas decorations in the window of the house next to them. 'You still never heard about it all, I guess. And it's so long ago now.' Angie tugged on her father's arm again and Tom knew time was running out. Someone pushed past them to get into the shop, and Gordon moved closer to Tom. 'But I sure wish they'd tell you, Tom my boy. I wish they'd free themselves from it. For themselves, but for you too, Tom. It's coming for you, and you can't avoid it.'

'What on earth does that mean?' said Tom, trying to sound jolly.

Gordon hesitated. 'We both came to the city looking for something new, right, Tom? I found it. You didn't find it, not yet.'

'Oh, I did!' said Tom happily, but Gordon shook his head.

'None of this, Tom, none of it's the person you are. I know you, remember. I knew you before you were born. I know where you come from. What . . .' He stopped. 'I'm just saying, perhaps this isn't it, not yet.'

'I'm very happy,' Tom said. He had to shoehorn her name in whenever he could. 'I've got a lovely, wonderful girl-friend, Celia. Guy's sister. You'll have to meet her, Gordon. You'll love her.' He smiled at him. 'Honestly, you're wrong. It's all fine.'

'Ah, take no notice of me,' said Gordon suddenly. 'I'm wet and tired and grumpy, that's all.' He handed him his address, folded over. 'Yes, Angela, I hear you, and I'm ready. Say goodbye to Tom. He's a good friend of mine.'

Tom shook Gordon's hand and patted Angela on the arm. She glared at him through her dark eyelashes, turned around and stomped off, her little arms wrapped awkwardly round her small body, then began to splash defiantly in puddles, kicking up the grubby sleet-water.

'Oh, that one. Boy, she gives me trouble,' said Gordon, looking thoroughly delighted about it.

Tom watched them walk away towards the bus stop, on their way back to Acton, where there were sausages for tea and the maps of London, the city Gordon had introduced him to, on the wall no doubt, and the allotment and a family life. He turned and hurried back to Montpelier Crescent, and tried to forget what Gordon had said.

Tom had planned out the whole evening. He was on the events committee, and knew when the band were on because he was introducing them. He had primed two chaps to be on standby with the requisite items. He had the ring in his breast pocket, which he had extracted from Montpelier Crescent by prior agreement.

'Mother's ring!' Henry had said over Easter, when Tom had asked for it. 'Dear God, what on earth do you want that for?'

'Well . . . for Celia.'

'Who?' Jenny had said.

'Celia Mannering. My girlfriend, Aunt Jenny – she came to tea, remember? You've met her. I told you before. I'm going to ask her to marry me.' Tom cleared his throat. He knew he mustn't sound nervous; they were so odd, Henry and Jenny, unaware of anything outside their front door – 'Who *is* Sergeant Pepper? Why does the wireless keep droning on about Sergeant Pepper? Young idiots' – but they had a canny operational ability to pick up on insecurities, cracks in a smooth façade. They were like the bedraggled old herons you found along the canal up by Paddington, standing hunched on the tow path, perfectly still, only their chin feathers swaying like wispy beards, waiting to dive, dive in, snatch, grab.

'You're marrying someone?' Henry looked up from *The Times*, which was spread out on the kitchen table. He had an old pair of reading lorgnettes in his hand, like a maiden aunt in a drawing-room farce. 'Tom, really, dear boy. You're a child!'

'It's very good news,' said Jenny, blinking. 'Hugh Mannering

271

is a super chap – you remember him, Henry dear, a few years below you, in Liddell's. He was at Caius with Donald Urquhart, you know. This is their daughter. We'd love to meet her, Tom.'

'You have met her, Aunt Jenny.'

'Oh. Really? When?'

'Several times.' He had had Celia to stay, in the tiny, ordered bedroom at the top of the house, wilfully disregarding convention, where he had spent all night fucking her, with an intensity more usually shown by her, not him. He had found it intensely, satisfyingly liberating to have this gorgeous, gamine, svelte, curvaceous, smooth, divine beauty on top of him in the room where he had spent so many sad hours missing his father, conjuring up worlds around him. As he climaxed inside Celia yet again on the first night she stayed over, pushing as far inside her as he could, shifting around so she gasped, holding her face between his hands and rasping into her ear, 'I want you so much', he kept thinking of Tom, aged nine, in bed, staring at *Helen Caught Bathing* – how silly a painting it was, how unrealistic the women were, with their globular breasts and their pert, come-hither luridness, nothing like real life, and then, to help him delay coming, he wondered where *Helen Caught Bathing* was now, whose eyes rested on it, in whose house was it on display. And, as Celia arched her back and then collapsed on to him, sweating, smiling, red-faced, glistening with happiness, and he rolled over in the tiny bed, riding out the last waves of pleasure with her, he wondered if his aunt or uncle could hear them. But they didn't seem to.

They didn't even notice when, the following day, she came downstairs to breakfast and drank a cup of black coffee with them. Or, if they did, they didn't say anything.

Since then his aunt and uncle had met her in more formal circumstances: at his twenty-first birthday dinner at Simpsons of Piccadilly, a supremely awkward evening when Henry drank too much and Jenny fussed and started at everything; and at a cocktail party given by their new neighbours on New Year's Eve, where Jenny wore a straw hat, hair escaping wildly around the sides, and talked about mysticism and runes with their bewildered hostess, a Swedish diplomat's wife, then cried and had to be taken home.

'I'm going to ask Celia to marry me at the Commem Ball in June,' Tom said to them now. 'I'm going up on stage in front of everyone. She's always saying I'm not wild enough. I need to make her believe I'm not square.'

'You could never be square, Tom darling!' said Jenny. 'You have the soul of an artist. Being wild is overrated, anyway. It's more of a philosophical attitude, not knocking policemen's hats off or streaking or being fined for all sorts of dreadful things, like those Rolling Stones.'

'I suppose,' he said.

'Oh, yes!' Jenny said, beaming. She stood up, went over to the bureau and handed him a gold-tooled black leather box. Inside was a gold ring twisted at the top into an intricate, beautifully wrought knot, topped with a large diamond and sapphire in a claw setting.

'Jenny,' Tom said, suddenly rather afraid. 'Are you sure?' He had been worried his family ring wouldn't be good enough for Celia Mannering, granddaughter of a duchess, and now, staring at it, the enormity of what he was about to do swept over him, felling him. He felt knocked for six by it.

'It's rather special. Burne-Jones designed it for your great-grandmother, Aurelia. She was Julian's mother, a great beauty, even the prince of Wales thought so.'

His uncle gave a loud, trumpeting laugh and lowered his paper, an incredulous expression on his face. Tom looked over, confused. Jenny glared at her brother, a look of spite and fury.

'Oh!' said Henry. He made a *moue* with his mouth. 'I – awfully sorry. Lovely ring,' he remarked drily. 'Delightful history, and all that.'

'Nevertheless,' said Jenny, dismissing Henry with a sideways glance of irritation. 'You may give it to Celia with our love.' Then she hesitated; taking out the ring, she clutched it between her fingers, gazing intently at it. 'Let me go and polish it up.' She stood up, stumbling towards the pantry, and he saw tears filling her eyes.

Next to her, Henry raised the paper to his face, flicking it out flat with a loud whipcrack that echoed around the kitchen. The light was fading as the sun edged higher into the sky. LEFTIST MPS JEER US VICE-PRESIDENT, the headline said.

'Damn commies,' Uncle Henry muttered, one hand shooting out from behind the paper to swill some more from his glass. 'Got us all by the throat. Out to ruin the whole damn show.' He burped loudly.

Tom sat quietly, waiting for Henry to say something else but he didn't. So he read his paper instead. The war in Vietnam, the protests in Paris, the MPs jeering the vice-president of the US. There were assassinations in Cuba, and a massacre in Aden. He suddenly felt small, rather stupid, sitting there, his concerns so . . . bourgeois. He didn't know where half these places were. Hadn't troubled ever to find out himself.

'Here,' said Jenny, reappearing after a moment. 'There it is.' She laid the ring on the table, where it rolled towards Tom, shining merrily, the diamond glinting.

Tom caught the ring and put it in his pocket. He put his hand on hers. 'Thank you, Jenny,' he said. 'I'm awfully grateful to you.'

'If you have found her,' she said under her breath, catching his hand so tightly it hurt, and he gasped, 'if you have found her, Tom, never let her go.' Her eyes were white-grey pools of emptiness, her bony hand squeezing his. 'Do you understand?'

'Of course,' said Tom, nodding. 'Of course, Jenny. I love her. Honestly. Thank you.' Her skin was papery soft underneath his. He squeezed her hand and then remembered with a flash Gordon's words to him, so long ago. *But I sure wish they'd tell you, Tom my boy. I wish they'd free themselves from it.*

'I don't know when we'll get married, what our plans are – I haven't asked her yet. But I probably won't be here for most of the summer after that. All being well' – Tom coughed, deprecatingly – 'Celia wants to go to America – and Istanbul – I want to go to Turkey. And, if I may, I'd love to take her to Sevenstones this summer. Would that be all right? Oh –' For Jenny's eyes had filled with tears. 'You won't be there?'

'No, no,' she said, shaking her head. 'I'll only be able to go for a week this summer, at the end of June. Reverend Bryant needs me for two months, you see; his charlady has to have her varicose veins done. Henry dear?'

'What?'

'Will you need Sevenstones?'

Her brother grunted no, flicking out the paper again.

'You know where the key is, Tom,' she said. 'It's always there if you need it, remember? Will you – come back here, after you come down?'

'I'll be back now and then after finals. But' – he said it

lightly, to disguise the import of the moment – 'probably best if you don't keep the attic room just for me.'

She nodded, her jowls shaking, her eyes watery. The idea that, after he'd gone, Jenny would have the wherewithal to clean out that room, paint it, buy new curtains, replace the dangerous old geyser, put up a notice in the newsagent's advertising it to lodgers, was laughable. He kissed the top of his aunt's head, patted his uncle's shoulder and left, the ring in his pocket.

And now it was Midsummer's Eve. The wild, beating music; the smell of perfume, of talc and starch, loosened by sweat into the June air; the heat inside the marquee, hotter and hotter as the music grew louder, and Tom and Celia and his friends, Tim and Anthony and Roger and Rick and their girl-friends and dates, all drinking, dancing, whirling round the tent in the grounds of the college. Bottles of champagne upturned on the floor; scarves and shoes and handbags dis-carded; faces red and glowing with joy; and the band played on. It was the end of three years of university – the best three years of Tom's life. In front of him, Celia danced, waving her hands in the air, screaming the words to the songs, jump-ing around without constraint. Sometimes she would pull his hands against her waist and kiss him. 'Yes!!' she'd scream, her beautiful face flushed with exertion, like sex, like pas-sion, like life, and he was in heaven at the sight of her, the evening, what he had done.

When the band finished, waving their guitars, and the drummer slumping down on to his kit, it was as though every-one acknowledged the intensity of the music and the evening. Some people fell to the floor, so exhausted by the whole thing they could not stand. Tom clutched Celia's hand, suddenly nervous.

'Are you off to do your speech?' she said, lifting his fingers to her mouth and kissing them. 'It's a wonderful party, Tom darling. I'll be here, waiting.'

'Th – thank –' he began, as she stood to the side, smiling, clapping, and he ascended the stairs to the stage, like a prisoner walking towards the guillotine.

The rowdy crowd cheered, some booed, one of the microphones crackled with feedback and everyone winced. 'Thank you for a wonderful evening, first and foremost, to The Megalodons!' Tom shouted, gesturing to the band – or rather where the band had played, except they weren't there now; they were halfway back to London – and everyone cheered, and some people laughed.

Tom thanked the caterers, the college, the wardens, the bursar and the events committee. He threw in a few light jokes, and people laughed again; they were enjoying the come-down after the evening's revelry, and he realized they were on his side; he'd watched some chaps pelted or booed off stage at these affairs. He took courage.

'Finally – ah, if you'll permit me –'

At the back of the room a table collapsed, and people looked round. Someone screamed, others laughed, but it threw Tom off, just a little. 'A small indulgence, I wanted to very much, up here, ask someone something.'

'What?' someone said. He saw Roger, one of his friends, shift from one foot to the other. Another, Rick, put his fingers to his mouth.

'Celia –' He pointed at Celia, in the front row. 'That's my girlfriend, Celia.'

'Woohoo!' someone in the crowd yelled. Other people were starting to drift away.

It wasn't going how he wanted it to, and yet he didn't know how to pull back.

'It's the Summer Solstice tomorrow. The longest day. And so I wanted to say something.'

Had his voice always sounded this high? So posh, so . . . *English*?

'Yes, uh. Uh – I want, on Midsummer's Eve, at the point when the Earth stops in its course round the Sun, I want to just stop and celebrate love for a moment.' Someone booed; he held up a finger, blinking, and ploughed on. 'Because we ought to, really, celebrate it more, shouldn't we? Isn't it the most important thing?' He cleared his throat, too loudly, into the microphone. 'Celia darling, I love you. Utterly love you.'

Roger, below him, was holding his head in his hands. Celia was watching him, a bemused expression on her face: not horror, just confusion.

'I wanted to –' He tried to remember the speech he'd written, and saw in a flash that it was so hideously self-indulgent, so precious, that to say any of it out loud would mean social death. But he had come this far, and he had to go through with the main event now. 'So, in the interests of – because we're celebrating love tonight – ah! This morning . . . I wanted to . . . oh, dammit. Celia darling, will you – will you marry me?'

Fumbling in his pocket, he drew out the small black box, his sweaty fingers struggling to open it. Something was in his good eye – an eyelash or something – and it meant he couldn't see it properly. Silence fell over the crowd. Tom bent down, his good eye trying to focus on Celia, who had come urgently to the edge of the stage.

'Tom darling, let's not do this now –'

'Oh!' Tom said, in a camp, Kenneth Williams-style voice into the microphone. 'She's not sure!'

Afterwards, he thought that was probably the lowest point of the whole bit.

'She's not sure!' people started to say, mimicking his high, quavering voice unkindly.

'Celia! What do you say? It can't be any more embarrassing than this . . .'

'Christ,' Roger said, at the front. 'Tom old boy – please don't –'

Tom edged closer to Celia, holding the microphone towards her. Celia smiled at him, shook her head. Quietly, she said:

'Tom. I don't want to marry you, darling, I'm sorry.'

He let the microphone fall and said quietly: 'This was a mistake. I'm insane. Celia, forget this. I'll do it properly –'

She was backing away. The crowd, silent in sympathy, was starting to murmur. Tom waved his arms at them. 'Sorry, everyone. As you – as you were . . .'

He ran after her, outside into the sweet night air. Celia was walking as fast as she could round the great lawn, towards the lodge.

'Celia! Come back!'

'I should go – I can go and stay with Emmy, you know, at St Hilda's –'

'Celia!' Tom caught her hand. 'Please! That was a disaster. Oh, God.' He rubbed his face with his hands. 'I shouldn't have done it. I only – I've been planning to for ages. To ask you to marry me. I love you, Celia. I want to marry you. I want us to be married, darling.'

But she put her hand on his lips, silencing him. Her eyes

were glistening with tears in the moonlight. 'Don't, darling Tom. I don't want to marry you. Please don't say it again.'

'Oh, Christ, what a mess. It was the wrong time, I know.'

'It wasn't the wrong time.' She caught his hands in hers. 'I don't want to marry anyone. I want to travel, I want to work.'

'You can do that –'

'No, Tom.' He saw now that her dark eyes were full of rage. 'You've never listened to me when I've talked about what career I want, what chances there are for me. We've had so much fun. I adore you. But I've always been perfectly clear. I want to do all sorts of things, darling. I know I don't want to be Mummy. I wouldn't ever have said yes, no matter when you asked. I have to be me first, Tom.'

Tom, stock still, realized he hadn't given any thought at all to her constant mentions of working, and living, and seeing the world. He'd always assumed she wanted to get married and have babies and a house – wasn't that what girls wanted? Wasn't it what one *did*? He didn't know; he hadn't had any of that growing up, but he assumed most other people had.

'I have to go, darling.' Celia's face was pale. 'I'll go to stay with Emmy.'

'But I love you!'

'I love you too, but I don't want to get married. To be someone else's.'

'But – don't you care? That I love you?'

And Celia said, with the first sign of irritation, 'You're a boy, Tom, you're lovely, but you're still a boy.'

Tom felt as though he were in a wind tunnel, sound roaring in his ears. He blinked, gritted his teeth. 'I deserve that . . . God dammit, Celia! I'm sorry. Please don't go.'

Her beautiful face was drawn, heavy with sadness. 'Tom, I'm so sorry – I have to. Please, darling. Just let me go.'

And she walked away, into the enveloping night. Tom watched her, and wedged the ring into his breast pocket. He couldn't quite feel it yet. It was too awful to let himself revisit what he'd heard. The flaps of the marquee were lifting and falling in the dawn breeze. It was almost light. He exited and stood in the quad, breathing in the night air.

'Hey,' said a voice behind him, and he felt a touch on his arm. 'Tom – where are you off to?'

It was Anita Knight. Tom knew 'Nita': she was always on the scene, and she'd gone out with a couple of his friends. Nita was cool. She was at Oxford Polytechnic studying fashion; her father, David, was a record producer; her mother, Priya, was Indian, and a model, and they lived in Chelsea. Nita had met Brian Jones, so the story went, and shared a spliff with him. She wore only black and lived on coffee. She had a huge mouth, a big smile and dark, desolate eyes. Despite her tragic, Juliette Gréco-like appearance, she was enormous fun.

'I'm going home,' Tom said. Anita's grip tightened.

'Oh, don't go,' she said. 'Come on, stay. Don't let a dolly bird get to you like that.'

'She's not a dolly bird, Nita,' said Tom. He shivered. 'I was in love with her. God, I've been an idiot.'

'Tom, Tom.' Anita ground her cigarette into the lawn with one white, patent-leathered toe. 'She's one girl. You don't see it, do you?'

'See what?' Misery overwhelmed Tom. The adrenaline that had fuelled him was crashing. He felt as though he'd been hollowed out.

'See what?' Anita mimicked, with a smile. 'Tom, you're blind.'

'Don't remind me.'

She had the grace to blush, colour flushing her cheeks. 'Oh, hell, how tactless.' She let her hand rest, tantalizingly, on his shirt front, playing with the small buttons. 'Some stuffed shirt's daughter used you for a couple of years and then decided to go travelling with some even more stuffed shirt's son who's got more money than you. You got your heart broken. It'll hurt like anything. But, hey, everything's an experience.'

Tom leaned against the marquee frame, his head spinning. 'Nita, what did you say?'

Anita grimaced. 'Listen, I know you feel like you want to die. And I wanted to find you to say: Tom darling, every girl I know wants you. She had you for so long that you don't damn well realize it.' Her hand, still on his arm, tugged the cufflinks, grew more urgent, until she was jerking him gently towards her. 'You have no idea. You'll get over it, baby.'

He stood back, shaking his head. 'Not that. Do you mean Celia was seeing someone else?'

Nita shrugged. 'Sure. It's been agreed for ages. My father knows her father. He's some stockbroker, Tom. Of course he is!' She gave a rasping laugh. 'You're so pretty, and you're so green, Tom darling. That lot, they stick together. They all do.'

Tom looked at her. He was tired, and he wanted her to leave him alone. She ran her forefinger and thumb over the points of his shirt, smiling at him. He pushed her away gently and walked off, but his vision was blurred, and he stumbled up the stairs knowing the pain was about to hit him. When he reached his room, he slammed the door open so hard it banged against the windowsill. That was when he slumped to the ground and could not help but groan, as waves of shame started to wash over him.

25

It wasn't until he'd sat in silence staring at nothing for a long time, that Tom realized he knew what to do. He'd go to Sevenstones.

His exams were over, and he would be packing up soon anyway. Why not now? Why not this very moment? His time at Oxford was over; what was there to stay for?

It was as though a light had gone on and suddenly he could see. Groping under the bed he plucked out his kitbag, his head spinning. He was so tired, not quite sober, could barely see straight, but this was the answer; he knew it, just as he knew that once his father had taken him to Sevenstones when he was at his lowest ebb. The house was waiting for him.

It was Midsummer's Day, the solstice. He could be at the coach station for the Salisbury bus in thirty minutes. He'd be there by lunchtime, halfway through the longest day. *You know where the key is, Tom. It's always there if you need it*, she'd said. In Scotland, he and his father never went to bed on Midsummer's Day. It never seemed to be fully dark, not even at 2 a.m.

Tom was filled with purpose now. He pulled down the cheap prints of favourite paintings – Samuel Palmer's *The Magic Apple Tree*, some Aubrey Beardsley prints, a photograph of his hero Isambard Kingdom Brunel smoking a cigar in front of a wall of heavy black chains, and postcards, stuck to the wall: the Alhambra, and Rajasthan and Marrakech from Celia, from his father in Scotland, from Antoine, and others, all around the world, all the world that he wanted to see, that he would see now. Yes, he would see it. The future was his again. Heartbroken though he was, he was, now, in fact, free to do what he wanted for the first time in his life.

He had been so blinkered – literally and figuratively. Thought he knew everything. Shame rolled off him in waves both at the memory of the evening and as he considered resetting the muscle memory that had formed him for the past few years: how to be Celia's boyfriend, how to win her, what they would do afterwards. He was not going to be a stockbroker and live in Dulwich. Christ, no, he wasn't.

Celia had known. She had understood more than he did – but he could not think of her, could not touch the thought, like a tongue poking around a sore tooth. Celia – no. He listed, instead, the places that he would go, now that it was over.

Tom packed and tidied the room almost methodically – he would ask the porters to send his bags after him to London. Thirty minutes later he was ready to go. He slung his kitbag over his shoulder, slid his father's carved house into his pocket and, pulling the door quietly shut, he left without a backward glance. He crossed the quad, coming out under the oriel window, the nameless Gothic revival gargoyles of men whose deeds he knew nothing about staring down at him. Across the way, the huge bell of Christ Church, Great Tom, tolled loudly. It was morning, on the longest day.

Ox-eyed daisies, that was the name of those large, nodding flowers cramming out every other flower in the hedgerow on the lane leading to Sevenstones. Tom remembered the name. Ox-eyed, he said softly to himself, smiling. He felt ox-eyed, or, at the very least, most peculiar, due, he was sure, to the circumstances, as well as to the fact that he hadn't had any sleep. It was not unpleasant, just a curious feeling, as though he might suddenly float away. His head ached – but these days he had headaches more frequently than he would have liked. Celia had told him he should get glasses. She'd said the good eye was working too hard, and it needed a rest, but he hadn't wanted it to be true. He wanted her to forget he was a bit bashed about.

The greengrocer's on the high street in Tallboys was open, and there he remembered that Jenny loved peonies. Henry had surprised her with some once, in waxed paper, and she had cried. He remembered her shining face as she reached up to take them from her brother, far too grateful. 'Really, Henry? For me?'

Tom plucked out a large bunch of them from a bucket on the ground, recklessly pressing two shillings into the shop-keeper's hand and dashing back out into the sunshine. It occurred to him suddenly he should telephone Jenny after he'd settled in, ask her to come down and stay. He would phone his father too, tell him what had happened, beg him to visit. Surely he'd come if Tom begged. They could have one more glorious Sevenstones summer. Perhaps even with Uncle Henry, too. Tom stood on the high street and lifted his face to the sun, breathing in slowly and listening: the old familiar sounds that told him he was here, in this place that felt like home: a horse's hooves, far away in the distance. A child calling in a house nearby. The sprinkling sounds of birds in the crab-apple trees behind the shop, and the toll of the church bell, ringing for midday.

He set off through the high street, the warmth of the sun on his head and the back of his neck.

*

There was a *Beginner's Italian* at Sevenstones; rather ancient, the book had been bought for Henry when there was a chance he might have to go to Naples in 1944. Tom remembered it as he struggled up the last hill. He'd learn Italian that summer. He'd get Jenny to test him. By the end of August he'd be fluent. He could go to Rome. Then he remembered Celia loved Rome, was fluent and might end up there. No to Rome, to the whole of Italy. Paris, he'd check out the scene in Paris. Or perhaps Marrakech. Or even further. Then, come September, he'd be ready to find a job. Wherever he ended up, he had a plan.

The curving lane was fringed with a high, dense hedgerow, more ox-eyed daisies and foxgloves and dog roses. And he was there, at the corner, and there was the green gate.

To his surprise the gate was open; someone had finally given it a fresh coat of paint.

'Hello?' he called, pushing open the gate and rounding the path. He walked towards the front door.

The front door was open too, as it usually was in summer, before midday, to let in the cold morning air. And there, on the coat rack, was a familiar sight. He stopped, his heart swelling. Jenny's cotton wrap and her battered straw hat. She was here, and he realized suddenly how glad he was.

'Jenny!' he called. 'It's me!' He dumped his kitbag on the wooden floor and stretched, inhaling the old familiar smell of the place. 'Aunt Jenny! It's me, Tom – I've come to surprise you!' And he pushed open the sitting-room door.

Her hair was the first thing he saw, streaming gold across the sandy carpet, like a film he'd seen where someone melted and their hair turned into rivulets of gold.

She was lying on the rug by the hearth at a strange angle,

crumpled, like a dropped coat, one arm flung out in a gro-
tesque gesture of flamboyance.

Tom breathed in. 'Oh, no,' he said very quietly.

Gently, he moved her arm back across her chest. Her
hand, when he lifted it, was cold, soft and heavy, the palms
smooth and unworn.

The signs of her occupancy were scant, but that was Jenny:
she left so little behind. Scarcely anything that was hers; everything in the house had been her father's, he supposed, and the
happiest she had been was when other people were here.

It was only after he had called the police that he found the
half-written note, creased and torn, the fountain pen and its
lid scattered across the room nearby.

For Tom, it said at the top.

For your eyes only.

He opened it, but then, at the sound of a noise from outside, he turned, folding up the letter immediately.

It was a deer in the garden, staring blankly at him. Looking
for somewhere to put the letter, as though on autopilot, Tom
looked down to see what he was wearing, only then remembering he was in a dinner jacket. He blinked. The events of
the previous night were as though from another life, and suddenly they seemed to roll towards him like a wave, and then
the enormity of this, which was even greater, broke across
that and he started shaking. Jenny was dead; she was gone.
He slid the letter, unread, into his breast pocket, where it nestled next to the ring she had given him. Then, barely awake,
hardly knowing what he was doing, he went to wait outside
the open gate for help to arrive, leaving the note unread and
utterly forgotten about, and the front door wide open, to let
the sunshine in, on Midsummer's Day.

26

Henry organized the funeral with remarkable finesse and care, to Tom's surprise. Jenny had left meticulous instructions with her brother, picking the church, her favourite hymns – 'I Vow to Thee My Country', 'All People that on Earth Do Dwell' – and readings: Henry himself read, most beautifully, 'To Every Thing There is a Season' from Ecclesiastes.

She had had heart disease, Henry told Tom, as though Tom should have known. 'The doctor kept saying she should go for a rest cure, should move out of London, but I honestly don't think she listened to a word of what he ever said to her.' He was bright-eyed, feverish. 'That was our Jenny. Didn't hear what she didn't want to hear.' The death of his sister seemed to have woken him up, even if only temporarily, from a long, slow decline. 'Been killing her for years. Doctor said he was amazed she lasted this long.'

'I didn't know.'

'She didn't want you to know, Tom. Wanted to press on with it.' Henry had smiled politely, without any warmth, and gone over to the drinks tray. 'Ah. All out of Johnnie Walker. Might be time to finish some of that sherry Jenny liked. After all, she's not going to want it now, is she?'

The last of the old Notting Hill families came to St John's, the church that had been built at the same time as the curved crescents and white stucco streets around it. Old friends of their parents, people Tom had never met before, connections lost after the war and because of Henry and

Jenny's reticence about – well, everything. Gordon was there, having slipped in at the back. The Reverend Bryant of Jenny's Spiritualist Church stayed away, miffed at not being asked to officiate, and being told by Henry, galvanized by his sister's death, to hop it if he thought there was anything in it for him. Through his grief and pain Tom rather liked this new Uncle Henry.

My dear Tom

I wanted to tell you how sorry I was to hear of Jenny's death. She loved you, Tom, I know she did. You had a grand education, and now you have come down from Oxford, and the world lies ahead of you, and that is because of Jenny, pushing for you, all these years.

I loved her like a sister. I caused her great pain and she tried her best to forgive me. Through you, she found a way to do so.

I will always remember her at Sevenstones, in '42, dancing with a friend on the terrace, her sandy-gold hair shimmering in the light from the sitting room. She was alive then. I think she was in the wrong life. You gave her a chance to change someone else's life. I hope you will remember her for that.

I will come to see you soon, my boy. You are with me always.

Dad

A month after the funeral, Tom had taken a job working as a labourer over at the Westway, building the flyover. It wasn't much, but it was enough to contribute some rent to his uncle, and to pay for the odd pint with Johnny Hillman at the Ladbroke Arms now and again.

'Come and be a postman,' Johnny would say every time. 'Think you're too good for us, with your nobby education, don't you? The Royal Mail's where you want to be, Raven. Good pay, outdoors, and you're all done by twelve.'

Tom could see the attraction of a job where you worked half a day. But he knew that Jenny was watching him, had not got on that train and tramped her way over the hills and up the Old Military Road to his cottage all those years ago to bring him to London so he could be a postman. 'I think my aunt had an idea of my being an architect,' he said.

'She isn't here, though, is she?' said Johnny. 'So what's it matter?'

Tom would shrug. 'Maybe it doesn't.'

'What do you want to do?'

'I like building things, you see. She was right,' Tom said. 'I'd like to build something, one day.'

'Building things,' Johnny had said, nodding. 'I've got a mate who can give you a job if you want. Desperate for men, they are.'

'Wonderful,' said Tom.

'When you said building things, Tom old chum, it really is building things, you understand?'

'Yes, I understand.'

'You think you can do that, what with . . .' He winked, pointing at Tom's bad eye. 'You got to be strong.'

In response, Tom put his hand under the table and raised it up with one hand.

'Yep,' said Tom. 'I think I can. Ask your pal if I can come and speak to them tomorrow.'

'Trying to prove something,' Johnny said into his pint.

'Pathetic.' But he was smiling, nodding at Tom. 'All right, then. Think you got yourself a job.'

Four months after Jenny's death, Tom had to go to Kensington and Chelsea Town Hall to collect her death certificate, and he left work early. On the walk home from Kensington through the white-and-black crescents and squares, he felt autumn, creeping towards him in the silent, sunny streets, the slight chill in the air, and in his head he could hear and see as he did so frequently since her death, his aunt arriving that day in Scotland, how she had buttoned up her jacket and walked over the hill from the train station, two miles in little leather shoes, to fetch him to London. Tom patted the death certificate in his coat pocket, feeling desolation spread over him at the thought of another evening at home with his uncle.

He had not seen Guy since his break-up with Celia; Antoine was still in Paris. Gordon was away for the summer; his Pembroke friends were either scattered to the four winds or too embarrassed to get in touch.

As he stared idly at the front façade of the house, fishing around for his keys, Henry opened the door, unsmiling.

'Sorry,' said Tom. 'I —'

'Doesn't matter. Where's your dinner jacket?' said Henry. 'I can't find mine. There's a party at the Grosvenor I'd rather like to go to.'

Henry would travel into Mayfair on buses in his black tie, gatecrash smart parties, drink all their champagne and eat all their canapés, then catch the bus back. He did this two or three times a week.

Tom stopped, wondering why he felt rather sick. 'Not sure,' he said, but something was pushing up the memory, knocking at the door, begging for it to be opened. 'I think it's in my room,' he said eventually.

With a half-wave, Henry walked slowly into the drawing room. Tom went upstairs. It was not until he was halfway up the stairs, staring at the missing spindles, that he remembered where his dinner jacket was, and that he hadn't worn it since the day he found Jenny, and then the memory started to emerge.

He could feel it, burrowing out from the deepest recesses of his mind, towards the front of his brain, into the space where he could recall it.

The note.

She had written him a note.

He had shoved it into the breast pocket of his dinner jacket the day he found her. Her cold, soft hand. Hair flowing across the floor. The scent of roses. He had been reading it – a sound – a deer in the garden, then the ambulance came and he'd put the note away, had wiped it utterly from his mind.

He knew where the jacket was – in the giant wardrobe in the hallway outside his tiny old bedroom. Tom moved like a fox, slowly, carefully, not wanting to be heard. He crept upstairs, to the top floor.

Tom didn't know why he didn't want Henry to hear him. He didn't know why he was shaking. He reached the wardrobe, gently plucked the letter from the jacket and went into his bedroom, shutting the door behind him and putting a chair under the handle, just to be sure. Then he sat down on the narrow bed, the drawings of his old life closing in on him for the last time in the fading autumn light as he read.

Dear Tom

I thought I'd come here one last time. I know I am dying –
my heart, it is gradually, slowly, giving up on me. Today is
very bad, forgive my handwriting. I am not sure that I will
finish the letter.

I loved someone. She is called Teddy Kynaston. They
are hiding her from me. They took her away and the
letters stopped two years ago. A kind man, her family's
accountant, was writing to me about her. But I had a note
from the housekeeper to say he had died, and I don't hear
anything of her any more.

Valhalla, Orchard, Hudson River, New York. I lied when
I told you it was my family's ring. It was not. It was hers. I
couldn't find a way to tell you. I've told lots of lies.

She gave me that ring you are giving to that beautiful girl
today to make your own family. It was her mother's. She
gave it to me to give to you. Before she left. I promised
one day I would rescue her. The pain is so awful, Tom
darling.

Give Teddy the ring, please, Tom – go and give it back to
her. You can give that dear girl any other ring. But Teddy
needs it back. To complete the circle. You must. And tell
her I loved her.

You must go to find her. Please.

She is your mother, Tom, she is your mother.

27

You have three minutes, the operator said. *After that the pips will go and you'll be cut off. Is that clear?*

'Yes,' said Tom, his fingers winding around the telephone cord. 'Yes – thank you.' He looked around anxiously at the sound of footsteps outside, below the drawing-room window. He prayed Uncle Henry would not suddenly return from wherever he usually spent his days. Overseas calls were fiendishly difficult to make but also fiendishly expensive.

The line crackled, passing through the thousands of miles of copper cable at the bottom of the ocean, a telephone ringing in a house on the other side of the world. *Valhalla, Orchard, Hudson River, New York.* He could hear the ghostly ringing of other telephones, the tinny, reflective sound of other conversations. The telephone rang, and rang. He knew then that his mother would not answer.

And then – suddenly – a voice, more crackling static, so distant he could barely hear them.

'Hello?'

It was a woman. 'Hello?' said Tom. 'Is that – is that Teddy Kynaston?'

She laughed. 'Teddy's not here.'

'I'm sorry to hear that. It's quite important I speak to her. I'm calling from England.'

'I can't hear you. England, did you say?'

Her voice was like waves of sound coming towards him, then retreating. But he could hear her.

And then – suddenly – waves of static.

'Yes! I'm afraid the line's terrible. I am sorry, but do you mind my asking if you know where she is?'

'Why would you want to know that?'

Her voice: it was so near, as though she were in the next house, and then it almost disappeared. But when he could hear her, her voice was husky, like gold, slightly out of breath, as though she'd been running. He cleared his throat.

'I have a friend who wants to find out. Very much.'

'It's hard to explain,' she said, 'but she's here all the time.'

'Forgive me . . . Something's getting lost in translation, or maybe it's the line. Is she there?'

'Oh, she's here,' the girl said, and she gave a gentle sigh. He remembered Aunt Jenny saying time was not linear, it was seasons, and cycles, and he wondered where Teddy was, and whether he wanted to find her at all.

'Who's with her?'

'She lives with her brother,' she said, and her gilded husky voice hardened. As though she'd had enough. 'Listen, what do you want with her?'

'I can't say. Not over the telephone. I think it could change everything but – I say – her brother? Is he – cruel to her?'

'Teddy's worth ten of him. Oh biscuits,' she said. 'I'm sorry but I have to –'

'Oh! Don't.' Tom knew he couldn't let her go. 'Are you all right?'

She gave a great, whooshing sigh and said, 'I'm not all right, no.'

'No, you don't sound it, even taking into account your accent.'

'I don't have an accent,' she said, and she laughed, and he

realized he'd do anything to make her laugh again. 'You do. Who are you? Why are you trying to get hold of Teddy?'

'A friend from England said I should find her. And that I'd learn the truth if I did. And help her too.'

'Who's the friend? How does she know Teddy?'

'It's rather a long story, I'm afraid.'

'I haven't got time for a long story. Or a short story,' she said, and the static between them crackled and he thought she'd gone for a moment but then he heard her say, '. . . don't come looking for Teddy. You won't find anything here. Good luck.'

'What's your name?' said Tom suddenly. 'Please, just tell me your name.'

'My name's Alice. Alice Jansen,' she said.

'Where are you going, Alice Jansen?'

'I'm going to St Mark's Place. In the city. No. 5, St Mark's Place, The East Village. It's safe there.'

'In New York City?' he said, feeling like an idiot. She gave another gentle laugh.

'I really like your accent, sorry,' she said. 'Yes, that's right. New York City.'

'And do you know anyone, in St Mark's Place?'

'I have a friend from home living there. He's run away too. I have to get away from –' She stopped. 'I don't know.'

Tom found himself holding his breath. He knew she understood. 'The mess the older generation made?' he said. 'Something rather like that?'

He was delighted when she gave a small laugh. 'Yes, that's exactly it,' she said. 'I have to get away from them. I need to be someplace other than here and the world's on fire, and it's all happening in New York. I want to figure out what to do next, you know?'

'I do know.'

'Listen, what's your name? How old are you?' she asked him, and he felt this extraordinary certainty that she *wanted* to know, that she cared who he was and how he was, that he could tell her anything, he who hadn't told Celia so much because he was too scared.

'I'm Tom,' he said. 'I'm Tom Raven, and I'm twenty-one and I feel like the world's on fire. I had my head in the sand before. Alice – it's weird, I feel as though I know you.'

'You won't believe me, but I was thinking the same about you,' she said, and he thrilled at her saying this. But then her voice changed, and she said, 'Hey, I'm not at home, I'm in someone else's house, and I might have to hang up. Tell me something about yourself in the meantime.'

'I grew up in a two-room cottage in the Scottish hills. I love Calypso music, all music, really, and I love drawing, and I have a tiny wooden house my father carved for me that's my dearest possession in the world.'

'Okay,' she said. 'Let's see if I have this straight. Scotland. Calypso, that's groovy. Wooden house. So I lost my dad two and a half years ago. And I have a collection too. Of treasures. Animals, and figurines, and keepsakes. But I keep breaking them by accident.'

'There are no accidents.'

'Sometimes there are,' he heard her say, her voice catching a little. 'Sometimes. Tell me something else. Have you been in love?'

'Yes. How about you?'

'Yes,' he heard her say.

'Alice,' he said.

He could hear the line crackling and fading, and she was silent. 'Alice?'

'Yes?' she said faintly.

'I have to find her,' he said. 'Teddy, I mean.'

She was moving around, her voice muffled. 'There's no point. Don't come here looking for her. I wish you could, but Teddy doesn't like visitors. I'm sorry. You understand?'

'I understand,' he said, though he didn't, but he could hear the pain in her voice and he understood that. 'Alice? Good luck. I hope everything turns out okay for you. And the treasures.'

'Thank you. And you, Tom Raven.'

Then she said softly, 'They're back. I have to go, Tom Raven. I'm sorry. Goodbye –'

The line went dead, but the sonorous waves of sound, the chatter of other lines and wires thousands of miles away, continued for a few seconds, and then the pips sounded, and it was over. Tom sat back on his haunches, waiting for a sign. He thought about the girl leaving Valhalla, whoever she was. He thought about Jenny's hair, and Celia's face, and Henry, downstairs. He took up one of the pencils on the desk and started writing on the wall. Eighteen pounds a week wages. Flights were at least three hundred pounds. There was a travel agent he passed on Ladbroke Grove on his way up to the building site. Carefully, scribbling on the wall above his drawings, he calculated how long he'd need to work, how much he had to pay Henry, and when, precisely, he could go to New York, to No. 5, St Mark's Place, to find the girl on the other end of the phone, the one who knew about Teddy, the one who knew what he didn't. Of that much he was certain. Alice. My name is Alice Jansen, she'd said. She collected treasures and her father was dead and she said, 'Oh biscuits!' when she was flustered.

*

Henry died in the summer of 1981, in his filthy, faithful arm-chair, probably watching the Royal Wedding, though no one was sure when exactly as it was several days before his char-lady found him. Other than the removal men who cleared the house when it was sold after Henry's death, another living soul did not enter Tom's room after he flew to America, in March 1968.

The day he left, Tom stood in the doorway, his kitbag already too heavy on his shoulder, and had one last look round. Henry, slumped in the drawing room, raised his hand to him, but Tom went in, knelt down, shook his hand.

'I'll write to you. I'll come and see you when I'm back. Thank you, Henry,' he said, trying not to stare at his uncle's lined, scaly, pale face. Henry looked at him.

'We don't need to pretend any more, Tom. Good luck to you, old thing.'

Then he picked up the paper and disappeared behind it. Tom heard the slosh of whisky as Henry drained his hip-flask. He picked up his kitbag again and went downstairs, shutting the door carefully behind him.

When the house was eventually sold to a family in 1982, the youngest child, Clare, dancing into her new bedroom at the top of the house, flung open the door and gasped, then cried out, causing her mother to run up the stairs, thinking she'd hurt herself.

But, no, she was standing in an empty room, its walls covered two thirds of the way up with drawings of hills and mountains, the sea, the scudding clouds, rays of sunshine shooting across the landscapes, and, at the centre of it all, a tiny square house, and a man outside it.

Then, above it, in clear black writing, $4/2 + 3 + 6/2 -$ sums, and sums, every coin, every last shilling, penny and pound Tom earned in those five months, added to the drawings on the wall, the final pages of the story of Tom's final months of the years in that room, in that house, in that life. What is it? Clare asked her mother, jumping up and down. Can I keep the pictures? What does it mean?

But her mother, tired after the long, dreadful day of moving, worried about the area they had moved to, disgusted by some of the magazines the horrible old man who'd died there had been storing under the floorboards, shushed her and told her of course she couldn't, and the drawings, the record of Tom's strange, vast childhood, were painted over.

Clare, the little girl, was happy in that bedroom. She remembered the drawings only once, when she was older, watching a documentary about cave paintings, and suddenly laughed to herself, as the image of the scribbled walls popped into her head, dredged up – from where? She told herself it was a dream, that her childhood bedroom, now also dated and worn, peach-coloured paint and trimmed with stickers and Blu-Tack stains, had been a blank canvas when she moved in, not the dreamscape of a small, scared and determined little boy.

PART THREE
Take My Hand, Precious Lord

New York City

1968

Hey, Dolo

I don't have much time to write because Jack's back soon.

All is good with us here – it's neat being free and being away from them.

Thanks for letting me know my mom married him. If you see her, you can tell her that I'm doing fine. I don't want to see her again but I don't want her to worry.

I have a job in a poster store & they like my designs too. I drew the treasures on the shelf at home and then I tore strips out of it and stuck THE WORLD IS ON FIRE over it in newspaper type and they printed it, & it's sold 40 copies. I don't get any money for it but it is neat.

You asked if I was happy. I don't think happiness is something I feel any more. We're peaceful, me & Jack. You know I always thought he was the guy for me.

But there is love and people are free. The only thing is it's kind of a mess living here but it's a revolution and I don't think there's much time to sweep the floor in a revolution.

I miss you so much, Dolo. Write me and tell me how college is going and if you went on that date with that cute teacher.

Allie xxx

PS listen to Joni Mitchell 'Song to a Seagull'. I saw her at the Café Au Go-Go back in November. I know you'll say she's too flower child. She's a genius.

28

Spring 1968

He arrived in New York City in the middle of the night on a bus from John F. Kennedy airport. He had been dumped in Union Square – he knew this because the driver had taken pity on him and pointed at something, before throwing his kitbag out after him. 'You can stay there, kiddo,' he'd said.

Tom followed the direction of the driver's finger through the bus door to a blackened building showing fairly recent evidence of having been ablaze. Several of its windows were broken; the sign above the door was listing, rusting and sad. Tom squinted to try to make out its name. But he couldn't read it.

As the bus drove away Tom felt in his pockets and realized he'd left his glasses behind. He ran after it, managing to remain in the cloud of its fumes for almost a block, but it pulled away, heading out west across another bridge. Tom stayed in the middle of the road, yelling and waving his arms but it was no good. A yellow taxi driver wound down his window and swore at him to move the hell out of the way. Slowly, Tom trudged back to Union Square, blinking in the morning light. This, he told himself, was not an auspicious start.

After Jenny died, his headaches had got worse and worse, until he took the job working on the Westway and found that, in the evenings when he got back to Henry's, sometimes his head hurt so terribly that he couldn't see, like the bad old days. Eventually, realizing Celia was probably right, he went to an optician and was fitted with glasses, and found it a revelation. His right eye was doing all the work and shut down when it was too tired: he'd thought perhaps the blindness was coming back, that darkness was overtaking him again, like before. The first time he tried on the black framed spectacles in the optician's he had laughed with joy, recognizing the sensation of being happy in one moment like an old, forgotten flavour on the tongue.

'What's so funny, sir?' the optician had asked. 'Don't they fit?'

'They're perfect. Thank you so much. I like the frames too.'

'Hmm,' the optician, an older man, had said rather acidly, for Tom had rejected the sensible tortoiseshell or wire frames he'd laid out, plumping for thick black ones. 'You realize you look like some young Turk, don't you?'

'I beg your pardon?'

'Oh, some pop star, or politician, or artist. One of them. Someone in the news.'

Tom had laughed all the way home. And, when the optician's fluffy-haired blonde receptionist telephoned to say he was owed five bob and she'd give it back to him if he met her for a drink after work that evening, he'd found himself staring in the mirror. Were they . . . magic glasses? And then the following day, when he'd had a drink with Antoine, and Antoine had angrily told him he looked like Roger Vadim, Tom realized he was enormously fond of the glasses.

He had the glasses, and a taut, muscular frame from his building work on the Westway, and a kitbag, an army surplus jacket he'd bought the day before he flew; and when Tom caught sight of himself in the window at Heathrow

Airport before he went to check in he'd stared at his reflection, in astonishment, that this was who he was, this urbane, tall, lean . . . *man*. He hadn't recognized himself. And the first thing he'd done in NYC was to lose them.

Tom thought of that moment again, looking around wildly to get his bearings, as the bus disappeared into the horizon.

I am here, he told himself. I am in New York. Don't lose heart.

He slung his kitbag over his shoulder again, and walked. He did not know where he was going, only what Alice's voice had told him: head for St Marks, Tom. St Mark's.

After thirty minutes or so – during which time he talked to a pillar, punched someone in the stomach with his bag, stepped off a kerb, turning his ankle over in agony, and walked in a circle, ending up one block over from Union Square – Tom realized just how much he'd come to rely on the glasses and how unused he was to strange cities, new things. An all-night diner with glittery lettering was emitting an aroma of fried bacon so delicious he swerved towards it. Tom went in, and was seated in a red leather booth. He ordered some eggs over-easy, bacon and a cup of coffee, cradling the warm cup between his hands and gazing out of the window, marvelling at the feel of the city, coming alive, feeling like a citizen already. The coffee was warm. It did not taste like coffee he'd ever drunk before. It was delicious.

Am I from here? he found himself asking, as he left the diner. Did my mother walk on this street? Did she go into this park? This subway station?

Everything was different, but it was familiar too, like being in a film. A cop in a peaked cap walking in a straight line,

baton over his shoulder, stomach spilling over his dark trousers. Two girls, about his age, barefoot, tangled hair, strings
of beads, identically individual, aimlessly drifting towards
him and across Union Square, singing light, fairy-sounding
songs in broken little voices. A newspaper vendor, holding
out the *New York Times*, cap pitched low across his forehead.
Tom stopped to look. The print was different, close together
and elegant.

US JETS BOMB RAIL YARDS AND SUPPLIES

POLITICAL ACTIVISM, A NEW HIPPIE 'THING'

CROWDS CHEER IN HARLEM FOR RETURN OF

EXILED POWELL

A discarded copy lay on the ground, trampled and dirty.
The pages fluttered up and down. Words he didn't know –
Harlem, Rockefeller, President Thieu.

As he reached Union Square again someone was playing the Byrds' 'Turn! Turn! Turn!' out of a window at full
volume. Tom stood, swaying with tiredness, letting the old
words rush over him:

> A time to be born, a time to die
> A time to plant, a time to reap
> A time to kill, a time to heal
> A time to laugh, a time to weep

He turned. The sun was coming up, slotting its rays through
the east–west grid of streets, filling them will blazing light.
London was not like this. Nowhere was like this. Exhilaration surged through him.

The street numbers got lower – 13th, then 11th. He walked

down Broadway, past the Strand Book Store, past some young people gathered outside shouting at each other about Kennedy and Johnson and Nixon, past a curled-up figure – man or woman, he wasn't sure – sobbing in a corner. 'Can I help you?' Tom said, crouching down next to them, but they rapidly unfurled one hand and batted him away, slapping away his concern. 'Get off! He'll see! The Evil Eye will see! Leave me alone, you hear!'

Then he was at St Mark's Place, only it wasn't really a place, it was a long street, like all the other streets. Tom put his kitbag down by an ornate subway entrance and looked around. A man was sitting on some steps belonging to a redbrick building. Like a lot of buildings he'd noticed, it had iron stairs zigzagging across the front, all the way up to the top floor.

'Morning,' said Tom. 'Can you tell me if someone called Alice Jansen lives here?'

The man shrugged. 'What's she look like? Nobody around here has the same name they had at home, son.'

'I don't know,' said Tom. 'I think she's my age. She's from Orchard, New York. She came here five months ago. After Halloween.'

'Listen,' said the man, rubbing the frazzled hair on top of his head with his hand. 'You might as well look for a needle in a haystack, friend. Every last person here is a kid who's run away.'

'Is there somewhere they stay? Somewhere they gather?'

The man offered Tom his joint. Tom took a long toke. His companion nodded, as though he'd passed some test. He jerked his head. 'Go to Washington Square Park. That's a scene on the weekends, it's called a "Be-In". Alice and Merlin are usually there. Peace and love to you.'

*

Tom felt as though he had been in New York for four weeks, not four hours. The sun had risen, and a large clock in the window display of a department store told him it was 10 a.m.

He smelled the incense and the pot about a block away. As he approached he saw flowers strewn on the pavement, and two more young people passed out on some steps, and a girl – naked apart from a shawl, some flowers drawn around her collarbone and a dirty pair of ballerina flats – walking up to people, kissing them. She pressed herself against Tom, her nipples pushing on his chest. She smelled stale, of sweat and urine. Her dull brown hair had balls of tangles; a button was lost in one of the knots. Her smile was huge. 'Hey, brother,' she said. 'Hey.' She kissed him on the lips, smoothed back his hair. 'You're welcome here, brother. You're welcome.'

Someone offered him a drag on a joint; he took it, and another; someone else passed him some liquor in a paper bag; he drank it. A girl in a yellow pinafore handed him an antiwar leaflet – he promised earnestly to read it. One man was cutting another man's hair off, the discarded locks raining down on the ground, catching the morning sun. Several people were playing the guitar, different tunes, but it all seemed to meld together. He thought it did anyway. He wasn't sure.

He slept for a while on a bench, right there in the middle of everyone, and then joined some people singing songs in a circle – a few he recognized, like Bob Dylan, most he didn't. One girl sang her own songs, which people listened to solemnly, nodding along, until a guy kept trying to kiss her and she lost her sense of humour and stood up and walked away.

It was hot. Tom wasn't sure how long he'd been there. The early scene – the bus, the diner, the silent dark streets – seemed like something from a film from another era. This was life. This was now. Though his memory was hazy: why was he here? In the blossom-flecked square, as the incessant sound of the paddle on the drum pounded into his head, he screwed up his eyes to remember. Alice Jansen. He had to find her. She knew his mother. And then, exhausted, he fell asleep again.

29

When he awoke, it was late afternoon and the scene that greeted him was like a battlefield after the armies have left. Smoke rose into the air, a cloud of mist hanging above the park, men and women aimlessly wandering about, dragging stuff – rugs, bottles, bags, bits of wood – behind them. Lots more people were on the ground, as if they'd been knocked out. It was warm, too warm for March. He talked to a young girl and her best friend for a while, but they both kept miaowing like cats. On the bench next to him, a girl and a man were beginning to make it, she sitting on top of him, wiggling slowly around, he fumbling with his jeans. Tom didn't want to watch. Other people were watching, though.

He was so hungry he felt pretty weak. The sight in his good eye was blurred and scratchy and he could barely see anything. When he stood up, he stumbled slightly, and that's when he heard her.

'Let's go,' she was saying in that gentle, husky voice, and he knew it was her, instantly. 'I want us all to be turned on, sure, but first I want a meatball sub.'

Her hair was in her face, and besides he couldn't see much, and he didn't know what she looked like anyway. But he knew her voice. He sat up.

She was tall and slim, with golden hair that shook around her shoulders, and she wore wide torn jeans held up at the waist with something like a red tie. Her top half was a silk patterned wrap top with wide sleeves, red with coral and blue and green shapes, casually knotted at the midriff.

There was something about the style with which she carried herself that was utterly unlike most other girls. Like she knew something no one else knew. In spite of her height and slenderness, she walked with a long, slightly awkward stride, her hands stuffed deep into her pockets.

'You're strung out, Alice. You're not hip to what that whole Be-In was about,' the man with her said as they passed by.

'I was, promise,' she said, and he could hear the humour in her voice, and the gentle censure in his. 'But I want a meatball sub too.'

The man had his arm hooked round her neck, like she was a possession he had to carry, a barrel, or a box. He wore a sheepskin waistcoat and jeans and was bare-chested, with a collection of what looked like feathers and beads tied round his collarbone. His hair was long, like snakes, or waves, his beard stiff with dirt, sand, smoke, the city.

Tom stood up, his kitbag now a dead weight, and walked up towards them.

'Hey,' he said, his voice sounding ludicrously high. 'Are you Alice Jansen?'

She pushed a lock of hair out of the way and looked at him calmly. 'Who's asking?' She didn't stop walking, and he had to scurry alongside them. He wished he had his magic glasses, the ones that had made the optician's receptionist purr in her small suburban flat when he'd put them back on for her, the morning after he'd met her for that one drink.

Instead, he used his most English, charming voice. 'Might I have a minute of your time? Alone? It's quite important.'

She didn't look as impressed as he'd hoped. She raised her eyebrows. 'Oh?'

'I came to America to find you. You might remember me – my name's Tom. Tom Raven –'

'I don't know you, sorry.' But he was certain he heard a change in her voice. 'What do you want?'

'I spoke to you last year, before you left for the city.' He peered into her face, but the smoke, the haze, the sun shining in his eyes, his terrible vision meant he still couldn't see her properly. 'Don't you remember? My aunt, Jenny –'

'I said I don't know who you are, friend.' She started walking away, chewing at a piece of skin on her finger.

'What's the problem, brother?' said the man. 'We're all friends here.'

Alice moved closer to her companion, nestling against him and sliding one slim hand into the back pocket of his jeans. 'Anything you can say to me, you can say to Merlin. He's my guy.'

'But we spoke –'

'I said I don't remember you,' she replied, and he blinked, hearing the rage in her voice, and he knew straight away that she was afraid, of something or someone.

'Okay,' Tom said. 'I'm sorry. I wanted to ask you about Teddy.'

'Teddy?' the guy with her said. 'Who's Teddy?' He scratched his head. 'Allie, wasn't that weird –'

'Merlin, brother?' Someone came up to Alice's companion and clapped him on the back; he released his grip on Alice's shoulders and hugged him. They smiled at each other, nodding, as Merlin said, 'Alice and I were looking for some tabs. For later.'

The other guy pointed, slightly indistinctly. 'Gerry,' he said. 'Come here, I'll –'

They wandered off, and there was an awkward silence.

Alice tucked her hair behind her ears and smiled politely, arms folded, but her eyes were downcast, fixed on the cigarette butts on the ground.

'Some food sounds great,' said Tom hopefully. 'Could I buy you one of those meatball things? If you show me –'

'No, sorry. Look, I'd – I'd love to help you, but I – I can't. So good luck, okay?' She turned to leave.

'Alice – hi.' Tom caught her on the shoulder. 'Sorry. We did talk about Teddy, I'm sure. You know her, from home?'

'I don't know her, brother. You got the wrong person. Sorry.' And, just as Tom was about to protest this, Merlin reappeared and she said, 'So – let's go, shall we, honey?'

'Sure,' said Merlin brightly. 'Hey, good to meet you – friend.'

Tom's head swam, both from the events of the day and the feeling he'd hit a brick wall. He took a step back, into a guy in an army jacket decorated with peace symbols, and then sank down on to a bench.

'Hey,' Alice said instantly, and she crouched down next to him. 'You okay?'

'Just hungry. And tired. And stoned, really stoned,' he whispered, then added, even more quietly, 'Hey. I don't want to cause any trouble, but I flew from London, Alice. To find you. To see –' He closed his eyes. 'To see her.'

'Come back,' he heard her say after a pause. 'Just till you find your feet, you can rest, have something to eat, okay, Tom?' And she put her hand on his shoulder, the other hand chewing at the nail again.

'Are you sure?'

'I'm sure.'

'Thank you.'

*

'Here. Drink that,' Alice said flatly, when they were back at the apartment, and he had been shown down into a dark, dank basement, which appeared to be a kitchen that doubled as a bedroom. Merlin had vanished again. Alice slid a brown bottle of something over to Tom and pulled out a stool, gesturing for him to sit down. She lifted a bag of bagels she'd got from the bakery out of a string bag, then pushed them towards him. He stared at it – he knew what they were from a walk he and Gordon had taken over to Brick Lane years ago, when they'd sat on a packing crate in Petticoat Lane Market, eating them. That time, they'd been filled with salt beef and pickles. He took one, nodding thanks, his hands closing gratefully over it, and ate it almost frantically, the smooth exterior and chewy, yeasty bread perhaps one of the most delicious things he'd ever eaten. For the rest of his life Tom would remember that first New York bagel.

'Hungry, huh?' she said. He nodded, cramming the rest of the bagel into his mouth, so that he could not speak. His jaw worked up and down, but he couldn't swallow the large, hard bolus it formed in his mouth.

'Yes,' Tom tried to say, but he couldn't speak, and it came out as *Uechh*. He opened his mouth, and shut it, then swallowed frantically.

'Are you okay?' she said with concern. She turned on the tap and gave him a glass of water. He drank, but it wouldn't dislodge, so he carried on gurning and swallowing and chewing, and it was mortifying. As he did so, he saw her long, slender hands, the faint welts on her wrists from her leather bracelets and bangles. She tucked her hair behind her ear and turned away, and he liked her so much for that, for not watching him embarrass himself. He cleared his throat, but instead the last piece of bagel got stuck in his throat, and he started choking. A piece of slimy, half-chewed dense white bread shot from his mouth, ricocheting off the wall on to the floor.

Alice turned back in alarm, eyes widening. 'Christ, are you okay?' she said again.

Tom drank some more water, recovering, utterly embarrassed by now. He nodded, and rolled his eyes, and drank again, swallowing slowly. 'I apologize,' he said. 'Anyway. Ask me about something else. Anything.' He felt equilibrium return.

'Sure.' She folded her arms, head on one side and said, 'Okay, then. What's up with your eyes?'

'I had an accident when I was a kid. I lost most of the sight in one eye. I wear glasses, but I lost them this morning so the good eye' – he pointed to the left one – 'doesn't work terribly well when I'm tired.'

'Sure.' She nodded, considering what he said carefully. 'For what it's worth, I didn't notice until you walked into that tree on the way back.'

'Good to know.'

'Can I ask you something now?'

'Sure,' he said.

'How did you know it was me?'

'I recognized your voice,' he said simply.

'Oh,' she said. She kind of bowed her head. 'I recognized yours too.'

'You did?'

'Yes,' she said slowly. 'I – wasn't sure back there. You kinda surprised me.'

'But you knew it was me.' Tom didn't feel cross. He was intrigued as to why she'd lied. She wasn't a liar; he knew that. He cleared his throat, trying to work out what to say

316

next. 'When we spoke, back in November, you said you were coming here. You seemed to be having a bad time. I hope everything worked out all right.'

He didn't say that he'd spent five months saving up the money from his job to fly here, that he'd thought about her, wondering whether she was okay, every day since then.

'I'm sorry I had to go. Someone was coming back to the house. Someone I didn't want to see. But, anyway, that's in the past. I'm another person here and it's all good.' She sat down at the table, as the scant afternoon light came in through the basement window, diffusing round her face. 'Tom, I think you want me to help you find Teddy. But I can't.'

'I know where she is. But I don't want to go up there out of the blue. You know her, don't you?'

'Yes.'

'She knows you.'

'Of course.'

'Okay!' He clapped his hands, smiling. 'Alice, look. I wanted to ask you if you could telephone her, tell her about me, find out if she'd like me to go up there.'

'Why?' she said, her voice gentle. 'I don't understand why you have to go up there.'

In his pocket he felt for the ring. He had been carrying it since he left the UK, like Frodo Baggins. Where should he start? How?

Teddy is my mother. She met my father during the war. They had an affair. My father was married to someone else. He opened his mouth, then shut it. It wasn't the right time.

'I have to give her something. Something important. I'm the only person who can give it to her. Can you help me? Will you call her for me?'

She tore off a piece of bagel. 'I can't, sorry.'

'You can't?'

'She's away. She goes away every winter, to Miami, and she doesn't come back till – till May.'

He peered forwards, to try to see her expression, but he couldn't. 'Miami?'

'Yes, she's – got a – a house there. It's right on South Beach. The place upstate is shut up in winter. So I could call, but there wouldn't be anyone there. And, if you write, some-one else might open the letter and –'

'Oh,' said Tom, crestfallen. 'No, I wouldn't want them doing that. Oh.' He looked around the kitchen, not quite sure what to do next. 'That's fine. I might just hang on in New York until May – will you let me know, when she's back? From Miami?'

He could feel her eyes on his. 'Yes, sure,' she said. 'Sure. Listen – why don't you stay a couple weeks? Since you came all this way. You could explore the city. Hang out.'

'Where?'

'Here. You can stay here, okay? But just a couple of weeks or until you find a place. You can sleep in Ginger's room, or on the couch if Ginger's here.'

'Who's Ginger?'

'I met her at the poster shop I work in. She waits tables in a club on Bleecker too. Sometimes she's in Brooklyn but if her boyfriend's drunk she's here.' She looked him over again. 'She actually pays Jack rent, unlike the rest of us. She was here earlier – hey – that's her. Hey, Ginger.'

The kitchen door banged open and a flame-haired girl sloped into the room. She picked up a mug on the table and drank heavily from it, seemingly not caring what was in it, then wiped her mouth. 'Hey,' she said, and gave Alice a hug.

'Hey, brother,' she said, turning to Tom. She hugged him too. 'Good to see you.'

'This is Tom; he's from England,' said Alice.

'England!' said Ginger McKenzie in an exaggerated fashion. She had on false eyelashes and a load of thick eyeliner, but she gave him a friendly smile. 'Hey, baby.'

'He's cool,' Alice said. 'He'll stay in your room if you're not using it – is that okay?'

'Cool,' said Ginger. She leaned against the table. 'Hey, Alice honey. Merlin wants a beer.'

'Sure, sorry,' said Alice. 'I'll get it now.'

She turned and walked past Tom. His headache had stopped; he was no longer dizzy; the black spots in his vision had gone; and she was a few feet away, her hair out of her face, and he saw her properly for the first time.

For the rest of his life he remembered that first sight of her. He actually inhaled sharply, as though he'd been punched. She had one tiny dark mole below her left eye, almost heart-shaped. Her eyes were blue-green, fringed with thick dark brown lashes, and curiously far apart; her brows were dark. Her wide, rather flat face was serious, her expression almost blank, as though she were holding herself back, but when she smiled, as she did briefly as she passed him by, her beautiful eyes shone, apples appeared in her cheeks and a dimple formed on the left side of her face, and, oh, it was like the sun breaking through clouds after a storm. She was possibly the most beautiful girl he'd ever seen. He frowned, embarrassed, aware that he was blushing.

'So, hey, Tom,' Ginger said. 'You can have my room tonight. I'm working then I'm in Brooklyn. It's the first floor, at the back.'

'Can I pay you? I'm probably going to get a job and then I can –'

But she stopped him, shaking her head. 'It's cool. Make it right sometime. Don't worry, Tom. Peace, and love.' She gave him a kiss on the lips and left, trailing a scent of pot, cigarettes and sweat with her. Tom sank back into the chair. He stared up at the red plastic flowers draped around the fizzing, swaying light bulb. He could hear the sounds of Alice laughing with Merlin, someone coughing, police sirens.

'Well, I'm here now,' he said.

He told himself it was fine that he had no idea what came next. He hadn't known the other times either.

Hey Dolo

Thanks about the posters. I drew a new poster for a women's group that meets in the church on Astor Place. I got JOIN OUR FRIENDLY COVEN in newspaper print again and put it against a background of pine trees like witches' hats. I'll save you one.

Your date with the bartender sounds neat. I think a guy who one day could own a bar is a good person to know. Can you please write me and tell me how the next date goes. I didn't mean to be rude about him – I just think a guy who is at Beauty School training to be a beautician is maybe not a guy who likes girls that way. Yes, I think you look cute in jeans and I think flares would suit you. No, I don't think you should cut all your hair off – I don't think you are a Mia Farrow kinda gal. Yes, I love Lady Madonna, it is definitely in my top five of their songs.

Dolo, I wish I could talk to you. There's a guy who's turned up asking questions about Teddy. He's called Tom and he's from England. I spoke to him on the day I left – he called Valhalla, but thank God he didn't get through when they were there. He wants to meet Teddy, to talk to her. I don't know why he wants to meet her. No one goes to see Teddy.

Anyway, I lied to him, Dolo. I said she was in Miami for the winter and wouldn't be back for a while. It just came into my head. I have never lied before!!!!! I pray he doesn't know hurricane season starts there in a few weeks. I don't want him asking questions, but most of all I'm scared, Dolo. I'm afraid if I tell him about her and how to get there that something bad will happen to Teddy; most of all I'm scared my mom and Him will find out where I am and make me go back there, and I'll end up like her. Like I'll be trapped.

I'm free here. I won't go back, Dolo. <u>I will die rather than go back</u>. I've seen what they did to her. My dad explained it once. He was her only friend. I wonder how my dad could stand to stay there knowing what happened. But maybe it's what made it so hard for him?

So I'm putting him off, this guy Tom, I mean. I said he could stay a couple weeks and I'll work out what to do.

I can't believe I lied. He is a really nice guy, Dolo. He has something wrong with his eye. He has a nice face, dark eyes; his hair is really thick, and he's kind of broad-shouldered but not a beefcake, you know? He has a sort of Jim Morrison vibe but darker. Also, he is kind. Really kind. I hate lying to him. I have started biting my nails again (my mom would be so mad).

Two postcards – I will have to get an envelope. I'm going to dash to catch the mail. All my love, Dolo – come and see me in the city if you can? I miss you.

Allie xx

30

After the first days, Tom knew he was staying in New York for longer than two weeks. He would find a job, a place to live and wait for Teddy to reappear or for Alice to tell him where Teddy was. He was staying so he could go to meet his mother, give her Jenny's ring and complete the task he'd been set; but he wanted to stay for the summer, perhaps even into autumn. Something was happening, not just in the East Village, where something was always happening, whether it was a Be-in, a Sit-in, a Love-in, some new band of Warhol's at the Dom further along St Mark's Place, a fight on Astor Place or a fire in the Lithuanian deli down the way. There was something in the air, on the streets. It was electric, febrile, the heat already there even though it was only now just April. They were saying the scene was over in San Francisco, that the Haight-Ashbury dream was dead, that the war was never going to end, that society was going to burn. It was scary, but it was exciting. He wasn't just going to go back to England to live with Uncle Henry, stick his head in the sand again.

So he stayed, partly to work out what to do next, partly for the experience, but also, finally, he wanted to stay for Alice. He couldn't stop thinking about her.

The only trouble was he never saw her: she was at work, or out with Merlin or her friends. Sometimes he thought she was avoiding him, but Tom told himself not to be vain, or crazy – why would a girl like her want to avoid him?

*

One afternoon, lying on the sofa in the basement, as the sounds upstairs of someone, he thought Merlin and Alice, having sex grew louder and louder, Tom decided to go out for a walk. He'd get the latest *Village Voice* for the job ads, and visit Gem Spa, where he'd treat himself to an egg cream, his favourite New York drink.

He had a new pair of black, thick-framed glasses now, which had taken almost the last of his savings. On the busy pavement on Third Avenue, waiting for the lights to change, he was scanning the ads in the *Voice* when someone bumped into him.

'Oh!' he said in surprise. It was Alice. She wore a long orange-and-coral Victorian dress trimmed with lace and with a high collar. Lots of her clothes were old, and she wore them with cardigans and sturdy brown boots, not going barefoot like a lot of people in the Bowery and the East Village. Her hair was tied up in a knot. She was hugging a brown-paper bag to her chest, looking down at the ground, and as she looked up in apology his heart swelled as she smiled when she saw it was him.

'Hey!' she said, laughing. 'I'm so sorry. I was miles away. Where have you been?'

He showed her the newspaper and the drink and she nodded, and smiled, and the lights changed. WALK, WALK, WALK.

They crossed the road and stood on the corner of Third and St Mark's Place. It was a lovely afternoon, warm, fresh, with a light, scented breeze. For once, the manic activity on the streets had abated, the theatre of East Village life that was always open, whenever you went out. 'I was going for a walk,' said Tom. 'Will you come with me?'

'Ah,' said Alice. 'I promised Merlin I'd get him these.' She held up the brown bag. 'The Polish bakery over on Cooper Square sells broken cookies and stale bread. They're a good price too. If you eat it right away the bread's still pretty fresh. Merlin hasn't been out today; he's working on a plan for a new protest movement where we invade theatres and galleries holding signs and singing songs of peace. It's very powerful. He's writing it all down. I said I'd bring him some food.'

'It's such a lovely day. Just a few blocks,' said Tom.

She looked up at the warm, blue sky, and down at the paper bag. Oh, screw it,' she said. 'Merlin never brings me lunch when I'm working.'

'It's almost five,' Tom pointed out.

'You're so bourgeois, Tom,' she said, eyes twinkling. 'Who cares what time lunch is.'

'Where shall we go?' he said, unbelievably happy that he had her to himself, even if just for a short while.

They started walking down the wide avenue, right where Third merged with the Bowery. 'Let's go to Sara Roosevelt Park,' she said. 'It's long and thin and kinda crazy but there are kids there, paddling, and playing games. I walk there sometimes and sit and watch them all. The families, you know.'

'Does it make you miss home?' he said, but knew instantly that was the wrong thing to say.

'Me?' She walked a little faster. 'I don't ever miss home.'

'Oh, okay.' He nodded as though to indicate she didn't have to say any more, but she was striding ahead of him now. 'That's the one thing I tell myself when it's cold or we don't have any money for food or Merlin and I fight about whether to go to California. I say: Alice Jansen, you're okay. You're here. You're not back there.' She stopped abruptly, wrapping her arms round the bag of broken cookies and resting her chin on it. 'Anyway, let's not talk about me. You've been here nearly two weeks, Tom Raven, and I don't know the first thing about you, other than that you sure do need to wear glasses.'

He nodded. 'Go on, then, ask me what you want.'

'Okay,' she said, kicking a pile of syringes out of the way, and they carried on walking down the Bowery, in the sunshine. There was a man playing the bongos by the fire station, and a friendly dog on a string without any discernible owner that trotted alongside them for a while. Alice said hi to both of them. Both of them seemed to know her.

'Hey, Alice,' an old guy in a white coat and trousers said, raising his hand as they crossed another road. 'Come in later, I'll see what I can find for you!'

'Thanks, Morty,' Alice called. 'You're a doll.'

'Who's that?'

'Oh, a sweet guy. He works at the J&H – it's a Jewish deli, on East 4th and Second. He saves me lox; he knows I like it.'

'That's nice of him.'

'I know. Aren't people nice, though?' she said. 'So much more so than I realized they were. No one back home was . . . Anyway. It's delicious. When I've sold another poster, I'll take you there for lunch.'

'It's a date,' he said, watching as she held up the traffic, moving them across the road with a nod and a smile to the driver, who waved at her, almost in gratitude for holding him up. 'I'll buy a poster tomorrow.'

She laughed, and they walked on.

'So when did you move to London?'

'In 1955. I was nine.'

'Did you like London?'

'Not at first. I do now. It's – everything. Like here. Music, food, ideas, art. I really hadn't seen much of anything in that way before I moved there. We had nothing, my dad and I.' He was silent for a moment. 'I don't think about it very much. But really we had nothing.'

'So it was just you two? Where's your mom?'

He hesitated. 'She died when I was a baby.'

'Ah. I'm sorry that happened.'

'That's okay, thank you.'

'Haven't you been back? To Scotland?'

'Nope.'

'That must be kinda weird.'

'It is, I suppose. I missed it at first. I made up my mind not to think about it. Just to get on with it.'

'Is that why your American accent's so good?' she said. They were sitting on a bench in Sara D. Roosevelt, a long narrow park south of East Houston. Some kids were playing with an American football; some were hitting balls with a baseball bat into a net, and toddlers everywhere ran up and down the narrow paths and over the little rocky outcrops, screaming with delight.

'Why would that make my accent good?'

They had picked up take-out coffees. Alice was eating a broken cookie. She dunked it in her coffee, then dropped a few crumbs on the ground for an expectant sparrow, and said thoughtfully, 'Because you had a Scottish accent, didn't you? So you must have learned an English accent when you got to London, and I've heard you talking to people like you're an American too. You just get on with it, like you said.'

'Oh,' he said, floored by her insight. 'Maybe.'

She shrugged. 'It's useful.'

'Sure. But it also means I don't really know . . .' He

paused, because it sounded so dramatic. 'I don't really know who I am.'

'We shouldn't know yet, should we?' She took a drink of coffee. 'I don't know.'

'Do you mind? Does it bother you?'

She considered this. 'I think it does, yes. Yes. I think I went to sleep, when my –' She closed her eyes briefly. 'A few years ago. And I'm still asleep. And, lately, I'm thinking about waking up. You know, right before you open your eyes, you're aware it's coming.'

'Wow,' said Tom.

'Do you ever feel like that?'

'No,' said Tom. 'I feel like I'm removed from everything. That I'm on the sidelines, an observer. I'm not in the action. And I don't like that about myself.'

'Why do you think you're like that?'

He'd noticed before that she asked more questions than she answered. She was interested in everyone and everything. Ginger, Merlin, Merlin's sleazy friends, the boy down the road whose dad beat him, Morty from the deli, the hippies who slept in Cooper Square – she didn't try to tell anyone what to do, or give her opinion. She listened.

'My accident, with my eye, it changed lots of things,' said Tom. 'It brought my dad down to see me. It made me think about what I wanted. I want so much from life, don't you, Alice? Only I don't know how or when. And I feel . . . I feel, yes, on the sidelines, a lot of the time. Like I have to hold back, like I'm not sure who I am.' He took a deep breath. 'I think it's because of my parents,' he said eventually. 'That's why I'm here.'

'Oh,' she said, and she frowned. 'Your mom, dying, it must have been so hard. Do you remember her?'

He shifted a little on the bench so he was facing her. 'Alice, here's the thing about Teddy. Why I want to go and see her. She's –'

He could feel her tensing up, opening her mouth to speak. 'I can't help you –' she began, as he said:

'She's my mother.'

'What?'

'She's my mother.'

Alice leaned back as if he'd hit her. After a moment she said, 'But you just said your mother was dead.'

'She was my adoptive mother. Teddy and my dad had an affair. They met in the war.' Her eyes were huge, the horror in them palpable, but he ploughed on. 'Alice, I know you don't want to talk about it, but I'm going to go to see her. I made a promise that I would. My father and Irene – that's his wife – she adopted me, and they were going to bring me up but she died in a plane crash. I know Teddy came back here after the war. I know she promised to stay out of their way. But I thought it was enough time –'

Tom hesitated. He'd thought about this a lot since he'd been here. He knew enough about his own family to know that announcing he was Teddy's illegitimate son might cause problems for Teddy. Had Teddy told anyone? Where exactly was she and what life was she leading? If he turned up on the doorstep and she was married with kids, it would be dreadful. He didn't want to get her into trouble.

'I have to give her something,' he said eventually. 'A promise I made. And I know she's not back from Miami. But I have to see her, and I'd love it if you could come with me.'

There was silence, broken by the sounds of children's screams, and music floating out of a window on the street opposite.

'Tom –' Alice squinted, looking up at the blue sky. 'Tom – Teddy's different,' she said.

'How so?' Tom's heart was thudding in his chest.

'I can't really describe it. She's not like you or me.'

'Is she married?'

'No, nothing like that.' She sighed. 'She can't leave the house, okay? It wouldn't be safe.'

'It wouldn't be *safe*? Why not?'

Alice crossed and uncrossed her legs, then she brought up her knees under her chin, hugging herself. He turned on the bench and saw her face. She was really pale.

'Look,' she said. 'I don't think I explained properly before. I left for New York in November, after we spoke. My mom married Teddy's brother, around Christmas. My dad – Bob, Bob Jansen – he killed himself three years ago.'

'Oh, Alice.' He put out his hand, but she batted it away, scratched her neck, then chewed on a nail.

'It's – I don't want to talk about it right now. But my dad, okay, he was friends with Teddy. He used to look after the family estate. We lived there.'

'Right,' said Tom. Her eyes darted nervously about. Tom was suddenly reminded of the deer hunts that set off from Gatehouse into the hills. He had the strangest feeling he was hunting a deer, that she was the prey, a creature that might bolt at any time, and he didn't like it. 'Why did you leave?'

'Because Wilder Kynaston – that's Teddy's brother. He tried –' She cleared her throat. 'He's a writer. He's stolen my ideas, my words, for a book he's writing. He tried to rape me.'

Tom blinked, his mind racing to absorb the information she was giving him. He got snagged on the name. 'Wilder Kynaston. I've heard of him. He – what? Did he hurt you?'

'I got away. But he thinks I owe him a favour,' she said,

her voice dripping with contempt. 'He's got my mom acting like a servant. She's married him.' She swallowed. 'She married him so she could have a nice house and a nice life and so he has someone to do everything for him. He ruined Teddy's life; she's never leaving Valhalla now, and he took my mom too.' A couple of kids ran past, screaming, one of them holding a paper aeroplane. She smiled at them. 'I can't go back there. Ever. In case – he –' She shook her head, and her breathing became ragged, as if she were running, and she closed her eyes. 'In case they do it to me. What they did to Teddy.'

'Don't worry,' he said, and he rubbed her back gently, as she leaned forwards, hugging herself, like she couldn't stay upright any more. She was crying. 'Teddy . . .' she said once, softly. He kept on rubbing her back, saying, 'It's fine' and 'Don't worry.'

Eventually she said, 'It must be very strange for you.' She blew her nose on a handkerchief. 'I wish I could take you there. But I can't go back.' She was biting her lip and chewing her nail alternately, staring fixedly at nothing in the middle distance.

'I just want to see her,' he said after a while. 'I'll work out a way.'

'No. I want to help you,' Alice replied. He looked round, and saw she was shaking. She gritted her teeth. 'I'll call her. I'll call Teddy tonight. I'll work something out. Okay? Okay?'

'Are you sure?' It felt wrong to Tom, like he was forcing her into something.

'I'll call her tonight.' She breathed in, like she was relieved something had been decided. 'Tom, that must have been awful. I am sorry. Did you ever suspect they might have been lying to you? About who your parents were?'

'No,' he said. 'But . . . yes, really. I always had the strangest feeling, and I can't put my finger on it. That I was in the wrong life. Does that make sense?'

'It didn't used to, when I was little,' she said. 'It does now.'

'Have you ever been in love?' she asked him a little later. He nodded.

'With the girl with short black hair?'

'How the hell do you know that?'

'Because I've walked on the street with you three times and every time you pass a girl with short black hair you give a short little sharp sigh. Like someone's kicked you in the guts,' she said.

'Alice. Wow. That's far-out. How do you do that?'

'I'm a witch,' she said and shrugged, giving a small, weak smile.

'Can I ask you about Merlin?'

She stood up and threw the empty cookie-and-bread bag in the trash can. 'Sure.'

'Well? What's the situation there?'

'"The situation",' she said, in a terrible English accent, 'is that we're together.' She started walking on. 'Is it okay if we go back? I need to make sure Merlin doesn't need anything.'

'Is that – a forever thing?'

Alice stopped in the curving path, as a boy on a bike swept past them. 'I don't know. I love him. I've always loved him, really. He's good for me.' She saw the incredulity on Tom's face. 'We knew each other back in Orchard.'

'He's from Orchard?'

She nodded. 'He's a good person. He cares. He's lost people; so have I. I feel safe with him, all the time. And he's gentle, and doesn't shout. I hate people who shout. When

I came here, I ended up at St Mark's and so did he. We had a friend who died, and we've kind of held on to each other since then.'

'I see.'

'No, you don't. The only problem is the kind of guy he is means he's adored by everyone.' She stared out at the road. 'And really it's wild that a guy like him just carries on being adored even when society's breaking down.'

'What does that mean?'

'He was the king of our year, our school. Good family, blond, track team, all the clichés. And he drops out, leaves all that behind, and they still follow him like a cult leader. It's not what he needs,' she said earnestly. 'He's a good man, but he lets not so good people in, and it's a little, oh, I don't know. Tiresome.'

'He makes you do everything, from where I'm standing,' Tom said, and she instantly flared up.

'I'm not paying rent. I said I'd pay my way by cleaning and running errands; I like doing it. He's kind.' He wanted to put his arm round her, to tell her she was kind, truly kind for its own sake, not as part of some game.

But she stepped away, and the moment passed.

'What's your favourite film?'

'Oh!' Her brow furrowed, and she bit her nail. 'I . . . suppose it's . . . It's *The Sound of Music*.' She cleared her throat, whispering something to herself.

Tom said gently, 'Really?'

'No, not really,' she said very quietly. 'It was my dad's favourite. He used to watch it when he was feeling blue. He was blue a lot of the time. I hate it, actually. I fucking hate it.' She shook her head, and tears dropped on to her dress.

'Oh, Alice,' he said, and he did put his arm round her then, and she leaned against him in the street as she sobbed. 'I'm sorry. I'm really sorry.'

'It's been three years – it's stupid.'

'It's not stupid,' Tom said, stroking her soft hair, holding her callused, nail-bitten hand and squeezing it. 'There, there.' He didn't know what else to say, other than that; when he'd fallen as a child, his dad used to hold him and pat him and say, 'There, there.'

Miraculously, it worked, and she stayed leaning against him, her sobs lessening. A car horn sounded close by, and they jumped apart.

'Every year,' she said, 'for my birthday, he'd give me a treasure. I think I told you this. On the phone?' He nodded. 'A little ornament; I used to collect them.' She sniffed. 'Dogs, elephants, a brooch of my mom's, a Christmas ornament. Just silly little things. Beautiful. And the day he died, he told me . . . there were more. And he said I had to ask Teddy, and that it was something to do with – with Sevenstones. And they're the clues, and it's been nearly three years. And I've never found them.' She was crying again. 'I keep thinking if I just knew where they were . . . I could lay him to rest . . . Then I could probably say goodbye to him.'

He held her hand. 'Alice, Sevenstones is my family's house. It's in England.'

Her eyes flew open. 'It is?'

'Yes,' he said. 'It must be – do you think they're there?'

'But he never went to England. Oh!' she said. 'Did Teddy go there?'

'Yes, all the time, in the war,' he said. 'That's how they met.' His hands tightened on hers. 'Alice – she must have the final treasure somewhere. Maybe you can ask her, again.'

A frown puckered her forehead. 'Yes,' she said doubtfully. 'Yes, I could.' She released her fingers from his. 'Tom, that's amazing. I think I need a new favourite movie,' she said very quietly, and blew her nose on an embroidered handkerchief she took from her dress's sleeve. He loved her so much for that in that moment, the touching ingenuity of everything about her. *Alice Jansen, I love you.*

'I think you do. What about *One-Eyed Jacks*? That's a cracking film.'

She shook her head. 'Never seen it.'

'Or *Splendor in the Grass*?'

'I think it's just fine, but it's not exactly cheerful.'

'I used to go to the cinema every week while my dad was in the local town doing business. I've seen everything. Let me have a think.'

'*Pillow Talk*,' Alice said, blowing her nose again. '*Pillow Talk*'s a good movie.'

'Oh,' he said. 'Yes, it is.'

'I like you, Tom. Merlin said he wouldn't go see it with me.'

'I'll see *Pillow Talk* with you any time you want.'

'It's a deal.'

'Does he make you happy?' Tom said, circling back. 'Merlin, I mean.'

She considered the question carefully. 'I keep thinking about this. I don't think I'm someone who can be happy. I don't think it's in me any more.'

'Oh, Alice,' Tom said. He shook his head. 'You should be happy.'

'I'm happy enough.' She walked on. 'I don't ask for it. Hey, let's not talk about it any more.'

They crossed East Houston Street and went up Second

Avenue, walking in silence for a while. When they were five blocks from home, Alice said:

'Beatles or Stones?'

'Stones.'

She was walking backwards, facing him, her arms outstretched. 'Wrong! Beatles. Bob Dylan or Joan Baez?'

'Bob.'

'Also wrong. Whiskey or beer?'

'Whiskey.'

'Me too. Pot or LSD?'

'Never tried LSD, so I guess it has to be pot.'

'You should try it, Tom,' she said seriously. 'It's great. It makes everything go away.'

'I don't want everything to go away,' he said, wishing his heart didn't hurt when she spoke, wishing he could make everything better for her. He caught her wrist, just for a second, and she whipped it away from him. 'Sorry,' he said. 'I didn't mean to –'

'It's fine.' She stopped. 'Thank you, Tom.'

'What for?'

'For listening to me. For being – my friend.' She looked him in the eyes. 'If I can help you with Teddy, I will. I promise. I'll call her.'

He nodded. 'I don't want you to have to –'

'Let's see,' she said, but her face had that closed-off expression again.

They were back at St Mark's Place. She pushed open the front door of the building – it was never locked. From deeper inside the apartment they could hear moaning, the hushed sound of Merlin's voice.

'What the hell's going on?' Alice said. She caught Tom's eye and understood his hesitation, then turned away, running towards her bedroom. She was opening the door just as Tom caught up with her. A joss stick and a candle burned beside a purple-and-orange tie-dye wall hanging, which was flapping backwards and forwards. The candle was flickering, and something on the unmade fug of their bed was moving. It took several seconds before they could see what it was.

Merlin lay back, arms behind his head, and Ginger was crouched over him. Theatrically, he rose off the bed, his eyes linking with Alice's as he came.

'Alice –' Tom said, pulling at her sleeve, but she jerked away from him.

'What –' Merlin murmured, as Ginger, wiping her mouth, kneeled back on the bed for a moment, then whirled round, her eyes glazed.

'Hey, Allie!' she said. 'It's just rent. Are we cool, honey?'

Alice didn't move.

'Hey, Tom,' Merlin said. He smiled at Alice. 'You're back. Did you get the cookies, honey?'

'No, honey,' Alice said. 'No. I did not get the cookies.'

'Oh, that's okay. I'm going to sleep now anyway. See you, Ginger. Allie, if you go out again, will you –'

Alice turned around and walked out, leaving Ginger to get dressed. Tom stared at Merlin for a moment, but Merlin lay on his back and scratched his chest, and, giving a huge yawn, closed his eyes. Tom left, following Alice on to the front stoop.

'You said you like whiskey, right?' she said.

'I do.'

Alice lifted a bottle of Jim Beam out of a broken old plant pot.

'I keep it here in case I need something sometimes.' Alice put the open neck to her lips, gulping down two, three large mouthfuls, wiped the neck, then handed the bottle to Tom, who drank too, grateful for the fiery, fast rush of sensation it gave him.

Ginger passed them on the way out. 'I'll catch you later, Alice,' she said.

They were silent for a while, drinking, watching the evening sky. Alice reached into the plant pot and came up with a joint this time. She lit it. 'I keep a spare.' She exhaled. 'Jesus Christ.' She ran her finger up the bridge of her nose. 'Is she – is she really pretty?'

'Alice – don't be crazy. It's not about that.'

'I need to loosen up. Then I'd be happy.'

'Ginger's not happy,' said Tom. 'I'm not sure anyone really is, here.'

Alice drank a little more. 'I feel . . . wow, I feel weird. I think it's too much booze.' She pushed her long hair in front of her face, then started to laugh. 'Oh, Jesus, Tom. Thanks. I'm glad you're here.'

'You too.' He gave her a small nudge. 'And, not that it matters, but you are.'

'Are what?'

'Really pretty. Prettier than Ginger.'

She put down the bottle. 'Is this another line?'

'It is not a line,' Tom said.

She smiled at him, leaned against him. 'I like your glasses,' she said. 'Often with guys they're terrible, you know?'

Tom looked down into his drink. 'Magic glasses,' he said, and started to laugh.

'Magic glasses?' Alice said.

'It's stupid.'

'Tell me.'

'I can't,' he said. 'I really can't.'

'Try me.'

'My friend Antoine. He's jealous of the glasses. He says I get girls when I'm wearing them and that's the only reason I have them. So he calls them magic glasses.'

'I don't think that's the only reason,' Alice said, her head on one side.

Shouts came from down the street, about what Tom couldn't tell. He cleared his throat. The curious metallic scent of petrol fumes hit his nostrils. The shouting turned to screams. Alice, sitting on the top step, got up and swayed, and Tom stood up. 'Run!' someone yelled, and there was the sound of more shouting, and five young people ran past. One of them tripped, and the others stopped and dragged him up, then carried on running. 'They're coming!' someone screamed. 'He's got a gun!' someone else shouted. 'Police! *Police!*'

Tom grabbed Alice, his heart pounding. He pushed her back inside, into the hallway, and slammed the front door, turning the lock. He pressed her against the wall, covering her with his arm, peering through the empty triangle where some glass had once been. He could feel her panting against him.

'Tom, what the hell?' she said. 'Are you okay? It's just the guys down the street. It's always happening. Are you –'

Feet thudded past; there was the sound of glass breaking, swearing, thudding, falling sounds. Tom put his head in his hands, trying to block it out. Through the muffled sound, he heard a gun exploding, and it sounded like fireworks. Tom's head spun. He could hear only the fireworks sounds now, feel the prickling heat on his skin. He thought his brain would explode. He backed away against the wall, leaning hard into its mildewed, peeling paint as if trying to push it down.

'Hey!' Alice's voice changed. 'You okay?' she said. 'What's up?' She cradled his head between her hands. 'It's okay, Tom.'

'I – I don't like it,' he said, clearing his throat. 'Sorry. Bad stuff in the past.'

Crack – crack. Someone fired a gun again. Tom jumped. Outside, someone screamed. Tom thought he was going to be sick. He was flooded by panic, sticky, red liquid submerging him.

'Hey,' she said, her low voice soft. 'Hey, Tom. It's all right. It's really okay. It's outside. They're not coming in here. I promise. They're not.'

She raised her eyes to him. They were inches apart in the dingy hallway. As he stared at her, his vision cleared a little and he saw her face again. She reached up, and made as though to touch his cheek, but stopped. 'It's okay,' she said again, staring at him. They were silent in the dark hall.

Tom said quietly, 'Should we go to check everyone's all right?'

Alice patted his arm. 'No one's all right, Tom,' she said bleakly. 'No one is fucking all right.'

Her hands were gripping his upper arms. She slid them up, wrapped her arms round his neck, and her body rose up against his, to meet him, pushing him against the wall. She leaned against him, her hands cupping his head. She was watching him in the darkness. He could hear her breathing. She leaned towards him, and kissed him, and he moved forwards, meeting her body, his hands on her hips. Her cheeks were cold, smooth against his. Her tongue moved into his mouth and she sighed, her sweet, gentle Alice sigh.

She pulled him towards her, pressing her mouth against his so her teeth touched his lips. She tasted of cookies, and whiskey, and she was soft and hard at the same time, and, just as he was moving his hand up towards her chest, Merlin's voice called, 'Alice? Hey, Alice? I'm hungry, honey, got any food?'

Tom flinched, as Alice stepped back a little.

'You don't have to go.'

Her skin was flushed, luminous in the darkness of the hall. Behind her, the green and brown pre-war patterns on the wallpaper shone like woodland. She looked like a fairy queen. Yes, Tom thought to himself. I am too drunk for this. It's a mistake.

'I know I don't,' she said, with a catch in her voice.

'Okay,' he said.

'Thanks for today, Tom. Thanks. I – I'll –'

She blinked, and kissed him again, that scent of hers washing over him, and then she was gone, the police sirens still echoing in the background.

The sirens, the police, the breaking glass and shrieking, the people running through the streets, the chaos – it was not, it turned out, just another night in the East Village. Martin Luther King had been shot and killed in Memphis, Tennessee, walking through his hotel's parking lot.

The gospel singer Mahalia Jackson, who sang at Dr King's funeral, became one of Tom's favourite singers, but he only heard of her in the first place because of that time. For the rest of his life some sounds would be indelibly imprinted on his mind as connected to New York, '68. Mahalia Jackson singing 'Take My Hand, Precious Lord'. Sirens, whether from ambulances, police cars or fire engines, ululating wildly up and down Manhattan. Chanting marchers calling for nuclear disarmament, for an end to the war in Vietnam, singing songs, shouting in unison at the police, at the federal government, at the politicians. And footsteps: when Ginger needed the room and Tom slept downstairs, the sofa was right by the basement window and all night he was woken by people walking, running past, sitting on the stoop, fellow citizens of the world, up and down, back and forth, busy ants, only none of them following a pattern.

Spring turned into summer, a hot, still, heavy summer when the only release was violent thunderstorms that cleared the air for a matter of minutes before the tension started to build again. But that was what it was like, that summer:

everything felt like it was lurching out of control. And still Tom didn't leave.

He knew Alice wanted to help him find Teddy. He knew something was wrong. A week after their kiss, she had come to him, and said awkwardly, standing in the doorway of his and Ginger's room:

'Teddy's still away. She hasn't come back yet. She's not feeling well. I've told her a friend from England wants to see her. When she's back, she'll ask to see you. I'm sure.'

'Okay,' he'd said. He didn't know why she was lying, but he knew she was lying. What could he do, though? 'Thanks, Alice.'

'It's okay,' she said. 'Hey – Tom?'

'What?'

'Nothing.'

And so, he stayed.

About seven weeks after he'd arrived, early one May morning, Tom sat on his bed, the sofa by the window, looking out on to St Mark's Place, eating cereal, often the only food in the house. He was sketching the view, taking notes on different buildings – one of his favourite things was to walk round the city, drawing Manhattan fire stations, subway entrances, banks, churches, apartment blocks, all of which were utterly different from buildings put to the same uses in London. The light was clean and golden; there was hope in the air, the scent of pot momentarily cleared out in the fresh night breeze.

On the side table he had a little package for Alice. He had wrapped up Edward's little wooden house in tissue paper and he was going to give it to her. The final treasure, a link between his family and hers. He hoped in some way that, if she had it, it would – what? Make something better for her? Square the circle? He didn't know quite what it would do, only that he felt it was the right thing to do. He wasn't sure what he'd say to her.

Leave him, he's an idiot. Here's a present. Aggressive.

Hey, Alice! Shall we see Pillow Talk? *It's playing at the 8th Street Playhouse! By the way . . . I got you something!* Too eager.

Alice, can I smell your hair? Creepy.

Have this wooden house carved by my father to replace the present your father should have given you. I don't know why you won't telephone my mother for me, but that's fine, I think I'm falling for you. Any comments? Far too intense. Proposing-to-Celia levels of intense.

'Tom! Hey!'

Alice burst in through the open kitchen window, holding a large metal meat fork, sending the little package to the ground. Tom bent down, putting it by his side so she couldn't see it. 'Hey!' He held out his pencil absurdly.

She was giggling loudly. 'Shh!' She put her fingers up to her mouth, all of them, and slowly walked over to the alcove by the window, flattening herself inside. 'He's coming. Don't tell him, okay?' Her eyes were shining. 'It's a surprise.'

'Sure – who's coming?'

'Jack. Jack's coming.'

'Who's Jack?'

'He's a warlock,' she said seriously. 'He follows me around.' She licked her lips, shining eyes fixed on him.

'Alice,' said Tom. 'Have you taken . . . something?'

'It's the edge of the dimension,' Alice said. What was scary was she sounded completely normal. 'I can see you, and a thousand lights behind you. A thousand and one.' She pointed. 'You are on the river. You can walk. I can see her; she's with you. Lovely Tom.' She came towards him and ruffled his hair. 'Do you know you're the tidiest person I've ever met? Is your father dead?'

'No, he's not dead,' said Tom. He handed her his glass of water. 'You thirsty?'

'Mine's dead. I saw a deer before he died. I drank already, thank you. I drank at the Tree of Life.'

'Oh, God,' said Tom. Then he said, 'Of course you did.'

She peeked out of the window, staring up at the pavement. 'I don't see him. The warlock. Jack. He is the master.'

'Don't worry, he'll be here,' said Tom. He had seen people on acid before. There was nothing to be done to shake them out of it. If they were having a good trip, if they were digging it, who was he to interfere?

The door suddenly banged open behind him, making them both jump, and Merlin walked in.

'Hey,' he said, blinking hard. 'Hey, Allie. I didn't know you were back. When did you get in?'

'She came through the window,' said Tom. Merlin nodded, his blank eyes staring at Alice.

'You're a warlock,' she told him. 'The Cemetery Suppers, I saw you. I'd see Teddy, and now I'll see you. You're dead.'

'No, honey,' said Merlin patiently. He took her hand and patted it.

Tom said to Merlin, 'Has she taken a tab before?'

'It helps her sleep. It helps her think. She had a rough time before.' Merlin patted her hand again. 'We both did. But sometimes she's so far out I can't get to her. Allie, shall we go get some rest?'

'Elephants and black birds and cats and dogs and bears,' said Alice. 'All of 'em, on my shelf.'

Merlin nodded, disinterested, and flicked out a piece of dirt from one of his long nails. 'She and her dad were real close. She was there when he killed himself, you know. Flattened by a train. Day before her sixteenth birthday. She can't remember it. None of it. He was a nice guy, but he owed money everywhere. My father said he was a lost cause.'

Tom glanced at Alice, singing 'Happy Birthday' softly to herself. He put his head in his hands. His heart ached for her.

'He never gave her her last birthday present,' said Merlin, staring at his fleshy, exposed finger under the nail. 'She's still looking for it. When she's tripping, she's okay, you see. It makes it go away. Where we're from, it's too much about the dead. About the dead.'

Alice was nodding, tears running down her cheeks. She tried to climb out of the window. Merlin pulled her back gently. 'Hey,' he said. 'Hey, Alice, not that way. Let's go for a walk.'

'I want to stay here, Jack.' She was blinking, like something was getting through.

'Okay, Allie.'

She nodded. 'I don't like the world. I wish it was just us. Just us. Just us.'

'I know,' said Merlin, and he kissed her, and she whispered in his ear again, and Tom searched her face but it was as though she'd been taken over by someone else, like the terrifying horror comics he and Johnny used to get from the man with round glasses and a beard in military uniform on Portobello Road. 'Just us,' he said to her. Tom could not get over how empty Merlin was. His eyes were utterly vacant.

Tom watched them both, then, shifting a little, found the sharp corners of the little wooden house were digging into his thigh. He hid it in its wrapping in his pocket, very glad he hadn't given it to her.

*

Nevertheless it was with surprise that, a week later, right before the Memorial Day holiday, Tom found himself at City Hall as a witness to the wedding of Alice Mary Jansen and John Wilbur Maynard III, the Witch and the Warlock.

'It's legal, so we can start claiming welfare,' Merlin said, as a couple of his friends stood there, rigidly unamused at being pulled into a ceremony orchestrated by The Man. 'It's playing the system. It's cool.'

'It is,' said Alice, in a twenties lace tea dress. Tom could see how thrilled she was, how she clung on to her new husband like she couldn't believe it, staring at him with starry, starry eyes and flushed cheeks.

What on earth were you thinking, he wanted to say, and then he remembered her voice as she'd said, *I feel safe with him. All the time.*

As they kissed on the steps, Ginger, in a sari and silver thong sandals, threw flowers she'd picked from a square near City Hall, and assorted guys in kaftans and long hair stood around saying, 'Cool.'

'Hey, honey,' Ginger said to Tom. 'You coming with us, get something to eat?'

Tom shook his head. He raised his hand to the happy couple, and walked away. It hurt so much he could hardly breathe.

Bobby Kennedy, at the funeral of Martin Luther King Jr that April, had quoted Aeschylus:

Even in our sleep, pain which cannot forget falls drop by drop upon the heart, until, in our own despair, against our will, comes wisdom through the awful grace of God.

Hey Dolo

Dolo, everything is a little crazy and I don't know if it's because of the last tab I took. I don't sleep. I keep having dreams – you're not in them, but it would be neat if you were, because then I'd see you.

I married Jack. I'm sorry I didn't tell you, but until the day before I wasn't sure I was going to go through with it. I'm not sure why we did it. I know that I love him and it's what I've always wanted. But everything is messed up, Dolo. I thought going to the city would help and it doesn't, it doesn't.

I lied again to Tom, the guy who is looking for Teddy. I told him another huge lie and said I'd phone and get her to agree to see him when she's back from a long trip. I want to help him, but I want to help her. I don't want her to have to deal with anything; she needs to be kept safe. I don't want him to find out what's happened to her, because he – well, it's complicated, Dolo, it would hurt him a lot if he saw her. I said I would phone her. I haven't phoned her. That was weeks ago. I wake up every morning and the pot or the tabs or whatever aren't doing it any more – I can't get that vibe back. I want Teddy to be okay. I want Tom to be okay. I am the one in the way. I don't know what to do and I miss you so much.

Allie xxxxxxxxx

32

Laura Wilson worked at MacNair's Emporium, a bookstore on the Upper West Side. Tom started sleeping with her soon after he too began working at MacNair's. Laura was British; Scottish, in fact. She had short thick hair, a wild laugh, a fantastic figure and dancing, merry eyes. She put her hands on her hips and drank whiskey. She also liked Mahalia Jackson, and introduced him to other soul music: Aretha Franklin, Bessie Jackson and Billie Holiday. She'd gone to an all-girls' school in the north of England. She reminded him, a tiny bit, of Celia. She was nothing like Alice.

'In winter they put shots of rum in the beer,' she said, as they sat at a bar round the corner the evening after Tom's first shift. 'Bloody love rum.' She clinked glasses with him.

'Me too,' said Tom, wondering if he'd still be there in winter. 'I prefer whiskey, though.'

'I say, do you want to sleep together later?'

'Oh,' said Tom politely, taking a swallow and then downing the rest of his beer. 'Sure, why not?'

'Terrific,' said Laura. 'I'll be honest, I think I like girls. But I think I like you. I say, Cliff!' She raised two fingers together and gestured down the bar to their empty beer glasses. 'Two more please. Thanks awfully. Now, where were we?' She slammed her hand on the bar. 'Oh, yes. Winters are cold, and we're having sex later.'

'Great,' said Tom.

*

MacNair's was on the Upper West Side. It was a beautiful shop with huge windows on each floor and sliding ladders fixed to the long wooden shelves. It was owned by Amy MacNair, whose father, Ellery, was the sole survivor of a terrible whaling accident. His ship, *The Quoit*, had been attacked by a large blue and broken into bits. He had written a hugely successful memoir, *One Came Back*, about surviving on tins of whale blubber for two days while paddling about in the ocean, his companions floating dead around him in the water.

Ellery MacNair had found that no bookstores were willing to sell what he considered to be the requisite number of copies of *One Came Back*, so had opened one of his own. Tom loved this. It was what he liked about being in America, as he tried to get used to the idea of being half American: the sense here of going out and *doing* things. There was a photograph of Amy's father above the till as an old man, huge, walrus moustache, standing next to his little scull on Long Island Sound.

Tom had walked in to MacNair's Emporium the evening of Merlin and Alice's wedding. He'd gone drinking in a bar, then wandered a while and found himself on the Upper West Side. There was a notice in the window at MacNair's:

WANTED. PART-TIME BOOKSELLER, FULL-TIME BOOKWORM

'Another Brit as a bookseller? Hmm, I'm not sure we can have two of you,' Amy MacNair had said, arms folded.

'You won't employ me because I'm British?'

'It's that Laura's British. She speaks with that same accent you do,' Amy said, lifting a pile of John Cheevers out of a box and putting them in a cart. 'And when people come in I want them to think it's an American institution, not that they've stepped into a Noël Coward play about two uptight Brits. I'm sorry.'

Tom had not thought about going into the shop, had not planned on applying for a job, but, as he stood there, swaying slightly, the four whiskies he'd downed coursing through his system, he had started to see he had to get out of St Mark's Place, he had to earn some money – everyone else there seemed to exist on air and pot and love and peace. (And he was aware he needed to stop drinking whiskey to the degree he had been since his arrival in the States.)

'Well, gee, that sure is a shame, Miss MacNair,' he said slowly, in his best American accent. 'I'm a Yale man, you see, and I did my thesis on Faulkner, but I sure love Cheever.' He picked up a copy of said book and flicked through it. Amy's mouth dropped open. 'I'm a poor farm boy from the Midwest, but I worked my way through college selling ice creams. I can sell, Miss MacNair.'

'How do you do that?' Amy demanded. 'Are you an actor?'

'No,' Tom said. 'I'm used to putting on different accents. Can I have the job?'

'If you get a work permit, you can. And if you buy yourself a new shirt with your first pay cheque, sure, and brush your hair and lose a little of that hippie vibe. You look like something out of *The Little Rascals*.'

'Who?'

Amy looked satisfied. 'You'll have to learn some American cultural history if this is gonna work, Tom. Anyway. Congratulations. You got the job.'

Tom took to spending some nights at Laura's walk-up in Yorkville, across the park, and steering clear of Merlin and Alice when he could. She was married to Merlin now, and he had to accept that whole evening, the conversation, the walk, the cookies, the whiskey and the joint and the whole messy joyful painful arc of it climaxing in their kiss – it was simply a part of this disjointed, jagged summer, when you were never quite sure what would happen next.

'Hey, Tom,' Alice had said the morning after, and she'd put her hand on his shoulder, squeezing it, like a secret signal between the two of them. He had caught hold of her fingers, but Merlin had been in the kitchen with them, and she'd instantly jerked her hand away. He knew then she thought it had been a mistake, that they shouldn't have done it. And he knew too that she was damaged by what had happened to her. His heart ached for her, for the girl she had been who lost her father and indirectly her mother and her home and the woman she was. He knew he was probably falling in love with her. But she was married, and the last time he'd declared his love for someone it had been an unmitigated disaster. He kept quiet, and kept out of her way, and didn't ask about Teddy, and the summer went on.

But, if he was at St Mark's, Tom liked to sit on the stoop and smoke a joint, listening to the music floating out of windows, the people walking past, catching the faint evening breeze. He made things out of whatever he could: an aeroplane out of packing-crate wood, matchsticks and elastic bands; a bird from folded paper; a small tiger with a wire skeleton, brown packing tape wound round and round his limbs and torso, black stripes drawn on with a biro. He liked the sounds of the city going on all around him. In Scotland, in Montpelier Crescent, in his room at Pembroke, it had always been quiet.

One lunchtime, on a day off, he saw a letter addressed to him propped up against the skirting board. He sat outside to read it.

Dear Tom

How are you old thing? Thank you for your note telling me your address. We miss you very much. I'm getting on all right at the FO. Not much time for cricket, even less for jazz. I saw some of the old boys the other day. At Prendergast's wedding, to a Lady Cynthia something. Nice food, but very dry sort of affair, father a judge, lots of stuffed shirts there, and that drear Bampton, you remember, used to require one to massage his shoulders. Still as much of an oily oik as ever.

Antoine has been here, but has gone back to Paris. I miss you, old chap.

Blip blip – am enclosing a note from C. I know she feels rotten about it all, you understand, don't you? My mother and father asked me to pass their best on to you

– G

Celia's note was even shorter, in her large, looping handwriting, and catching sight of it again gave him a bolt of joy, like a pan-handler skimming for gold.

Tom darling

Heard you've gone to America. Take care, won't you. I hope you find what you're looking for. I heard there's a rumour put about by that cat Nita that I'm with Toby's brother – absolute rot, Tom. I barely know him. I just didn't want to get married, not then. I always loved you; it wasn't ever put on. Go well, darling, I do miss you dreadfully.

C

Reading this letter felt like stepping into Tutankhamun's tomb, a space and time from another era. Tom looked up; a neighbour was passing by.

'You okay Tolkien?'

'I am,' he said, smiling.

He stared at the notes, ran his fingertips over Celia's handwriting. Then he screwed up the letter, letting it roll to the ground, just as Alice appeared on her way back from work. 'Hey,' she said. 'You dropped that.' She picked up the letter.

'Thanks,' he said, taking it and shoving it in his pocket.

'How's your day?' she said, shifting her bag of groceries on to her hip.

'It was good, thanks,' he said. 'I'm having a beer. Want one?'

She smiled at him, tucking her hair behind her ear and, setting the bag down on the top step, she reached in and pulled out a bottle. 'Good idea.'

Settling down next to him, she clinked the neck of her bottle to his. 'Happy days, Mr Raven,' she said.

'Happy days, Mrs – Merlin?' he said awkwardly.

'Oh, no,' she said. 'No, no. I'm still Alice Jansen, you know.'

'Glad to hear it. How was your day?'

'Everyone's stoned on Lafayette Street. Two guys fell asleep on the floor of the store today. Someone's window got smashed.' She sighed. 'But I sold two of my posters, and I embroidered a tablecloth and some serviettes and they sold too.'

'Cheers to that, Alice.' They clinked bottles again. She scratched the side of her nose, and said, 'Hey, Tom.'

'Yes?'

'You should call me Allie,' she said. 'Most of my friends do.'

'Sure, Allie,' he said, wondering how strange it would be if he reached out and tucked back the stray lock of hair that curled on the outside of her ear like a question mark, wondering what would happen if he then kissed her neck, took her hand. But he didn't, and they sat in companionable silence.

'Is it okay?' he said. 'Being married?'

'It's fine,' she said. 'Just fine.'

'I'm glad.'

'Tom,' she said. 'I spoke to Teddy.'

'Oh, yeah?' he said.

'She's been sick,' she said. 'She can't have visitors. Not at the moment. In case she gets sick again. But in the autumn maybe. We could go up together. I could – we'll have to see. How she is. When she's better.'

'Okay,' he said. 'Thank you, Alice.'

She scratched her nose. 'That's okay. She is really sorry.'

'I'm sure. Don't worry about it.'

'Okay,' she said again; she took a long swig of the beer, giving him a quick sideways look.

They got into the habit of having a beer on the stoop most evenings. As the weeks passed and May gave way to June he realized that since the LSD tab she was – what? Different. It had taken her a long time to come back to herself; she'd said it was a bad trip, but she wouldn't say more, and he didn't ask. But out of that had sprung an unlikely closeness, helped along in part by Laura, who had met Alice with him in the Village at a Sit-in. They'd hit it off, and she and Alice had become close.

All his life Tom had wanted to be at the centre of something, not on the periphery, and here, in the small corner of the chaos of that year, he had accidentally stumbled on it.

33

On Midsummer's Day 1968, Tom sat on the stoop waiting for Laura and Alice. They were walking to Washington Square to hang out, maybe drop some acid, then to Bleecker, where a friend of Alice from the poster store was reading some of her feminist poetry at an afternoon event for which Alice had designed both the poster and the skirt Gemma was wearing to read the poems; then it was on to a club in SoHo where a band they liked was playing. The afternoon and evening stretched ahead of him, ripe with possibility.

He heard footsteps thudding doggedly along the pavement and looked up happily, as only Laura walked like that, as though she were furious with the pavement about something. She opened doors as if the knob had personally insulted her. She was on the verge of being fired from MacNair's several times a week for dropping books or slamming drawers or telling people not to buy a certain novel. ('Sure,' she'd told a young man the previous week. 'Buy Norman Mailer. If you're interested in being yet another guy who thinks he's dazzlingly original but who doesn't have a *single original thought in his brain*. But, if you're not, what about giving *Frankenstein* a whirl?')

'Good day, Raven,' Laura said happily. 'What a beautiful Midsummer's Day it is.' She inhaled, as if they were standing in a field in Wiltshire. 'Ah.'

'How was work?' said Tom, who'd had the day off.

She sat down next to him on the stoop and took a drag of his joint. 'Fairly exciting. You won't believe who came in.'

'Who?'

'Guess.'

'The queen.' A kid ran by bouncing a basketball, shouting for some other kids to follow him.

'No. Close, though.'

'Princess Margaret! That guy she's married to!'

'Lord Snowdon!' Alice had come outside and joined them on the stoop. She kissed Laura hello. 'The duke of Kent!'

'No, Alice, it wouldn't be exciting if the duke of Kent came into the shop.'

'I should say it would,' said Alice. The two Brits rolled their eyes at this. Alice, a hopeless Anglophile, was fascinated by the Royal Family and had, until now, had no British friends. She had read *The Little Princesses* by their old nanny, until it had fallen to pieces, and had once confessed to owning – as a child, she was at pains to make clear – a set of cut-out dress-up dolls of the queen and Princess Margaret. In turn, Alice found equally worthy of mockery Laura and Tom's lip service to republicanism intercut with a knowledge neither of them knew they had about obscure traditions and ancient members of the Royal Family. 'That's Princess Marina, widow of the previous duke of Kent,' Tom had remarked once, when Alice pointed at a picture of someone in a group photograph in *Life* that she'd found at work.

'How the hell do you know that?'

'I have no idea,' he'd said, as Alice started jabbing her forefinger at other people in the photograph. 'Lord Snowdon. Princess Alexandra. Dear God, this is embarrassing.'

It was one of the unexpected delights of knowing Alice, though, along with her head for alcohol; her talent at design – she had drawn a poster of the inhabitants of No. 5 St Mark's Place that hung in the dingy kitchen; her love of those little trinkets she called treasures and kept on the windowsill of her bedroom; and, as he had already seen, her hair-trigger temper, the anger that lurked just below everything, especially at perceived injustice.

Curtis, the delivery boy for the Riccardi's grocery store by Union Square, had been fired for eating a left-over cannoli. He lived further along St Mark's Place and Alice had found him sobbing his little heart out on the steps the previous week, having been beaten again by his father, who was a drunk. His eye was swollen shut and his lip was bleeding, blood clotting on his dark skin, thin frame trembling.

Alice had marched into the apartment building, dragging Curtis with her, and given his father, Mr Hutson, a piece of her mind, whereupon he had smacked her round the face, and she had punched him. She had broken a finger, and the nail had gone black and was likely going to fall off. But she was unrepentant.

'You don't treat your kid like that,' she'd yelled, as Tom, Merlin and Ginger, alerted to the drama taking place up the street by a neighbour, had burst in on this scene and pulled them apart. 'You have a kid, you look after the kid! I'm calling the cops on you!'

'I'm calling the cops on *you*, you dumb bitch,' Mr Hutson had hissed at her as Tom and Ginger held him back. 'You stupid fucking hippies, you think you understand. You don't understand.'

'Screw you,' Alice had said, and she had taken Curtis to Riccardi's to demand they give him his job back, which they instantly did. Then Curtis was installed in the box room Merlin had been using as a storage space for the magazine he'd written and had printed but couldn't sell. So now Curtis was staying with them, which meant someone else in the stinking hot apartment, a sixteen-year-old boy who ate twice what everyone else ate and jumped whenever there was a noise.

There was also a barefoot girl called Callie who sold love beads on the corner of St Mark's and Second Avenue. She had lank, grey-green hair and followed Alice from her job at the poster store back to St Mark's Place, sitting outside till Alice let her in. Alice gave her food too. Then, finally, there was the cat, Mrs Snow, that Alice had rescued from the half-demolished church around the corner, where she had been trapped in the empty nave window, frozen and refusing to move. Alice had climbed up with a sheet tied across her body and slung in the cat, wrapping it tightly so it couldn't escape. The cat, in as much as it liked anyone, being a cat, liked Alice. Tom was pretty sure Mrs Snow was a boy, but Alice took no notice of this. She saved scraps of food for it and it found her lap wherever she was – another dependant of St Mark's Place.

Callie and Curtis were making lunch for themselves when Tom, Alice and Laura went inside; like Tom, they were good at keeping things tidy, which was good, because Ginger and Merlin thought tidiness was unbelievably bourgeois.

Alice sat down next to Tom, and Tom said, 'Tell us who you saw, Laura.'

Laura lit a cigarette and ruffled her short hair with one hand.

'Now we're into Alice's list of everyone in the Royal Family and we'll be here till Midsummer is over.'

Midsummer. A year ago, he had proposed to Celia. A year ago, he had found Jenny. He thought of the rivers of ox-eyed daisies along the bank outside Sevenstones. The cool, cool dip of the stream, the strange lumpen upright stones erupting throughout the garden. Jenny's cold, plump hand, her blank eyes, her broken heart. Celia's body, arcing against the view of the hills, the white horse in the distance. His throat tightened. And he missed the place suddenly, with a raw longing that made him ache. A whole year. He shivered.

'You all right, Raven?' Alice said, her hand on his shoulder.

'Tom, don't glaze over,' said Laura. 'So one more guess. Who was in the shop today?'

'The Aga Khan!' Alice said.

'Nope,' said Laura, folding her arms and looking pleased. 'Jackie Kennedy!'

'No!' Tom and Alice said, in unison.

'I thought she was on some yacht in Greece!' Alice said. 'What was she like?'

'She was very thin,' said Laura. 'Wrists like matchsticks. But she spent ever so long over every book. And we had an author there, this rather WASPy writer who was in the shop waiting for Amy and he was trying to talk to her. He signed a copy of his new book for her and handed it to her and said, "Mrs Kennedy, I'm so sorry for your loss; your husband's service to this country was . . .", etc., etc.' Laura waved her hands. '"And now the loss of Senator Kennedy etc., etc.," and get this: she simply said, "I don't care to discuss it, Kynaston." Just like that. And then she clicked her fingers and the Secret Service chap leaped out from somewhere – he'd been reading *Valley of the Dolls*; I found it on the floor afterwards – and she walked out and left this Kynaston fellow, the writer, standing there holding his signed copy.' Laura's eyes were gleaming. 'Isn't that cold? I mean, don't you admire her for it? Alice – what's wrong?'

Alice had stood up, hands in her back pockets. 'Who did you say he was? Did you say his name was Kynaston?'

'Wilder Kynaston,' said Laura. 'I'd never heard of him, Alice, have you? He's from some posh upstate New York family. He knows Amy MacNair, anyway. He hasn't published for years, but now he's written some novel about American youth. How we're to blame for everything, yada, yada.' Laura was fond of an Americanism. She shook her head, not noticing Alice's expression.

But Tom had. He saw the colour actually draining from Alice's face, as if she were just skin and bone, as if she were melting. She put her hand to her chest.

'Why was he there?' Alice said. She began methodically piling up things like her sketch book and her volume of poetry that were scattered around the room. She took out a headscarf and tied it round her neck, then took her change purse, and her wallet. She hung the house key on the hook by the door. Tom watched her.

'The *New York Times* were interviewing him for his new novel in the shop. Actually,' Laura said, stubbing out her cigarette, 'I didn't like him much but I read an early copy of some of it and it is rather beautifully done. Amy says it's going to be a sensation. It's called *The Treasures*, or something like that —' Laura gave a sniff. 'It's about a young girl coming into adulthood, part prose, part poetry. There's an apple on the front cover, with a bite out of it . . . could be rather hackneyed but he does it in such a way —'

'He's at the bookstore? Right now?' Alice said, interrupting Laura. She was standing by the door.

Laura fanned her fingers through her short hair, which she did only when she was flustered. 'Yes. He was going to sign a whole heap of copies and then he's having dinner with

Amy and some old friends above the shop, I heard him say he's staying in the city tonight, but hey – Alice! Come back!' She turned to Tom, bewildered. 'What's wrong with her?' For Alice had simply run on to the street and turned west, hair streaming out behind her as she went faster and faster. Tom saw her then turn right, heading north. 'Dammit, Tom, what did I say?'

'I'll find out,' said Tom. 'Go on, Laura. We'll see you there. I won't be long.'

On the corner of St Mark's and Third, Tom stood panting, scanning the roads for any sign of her. MacNair's was on Broadway and West 77th, and he usually walked all the way there and back, but he thought Alice would probably take the subway. He leaped down into the Astor Place Station. A train had just drawn in; he jumped on it and the doors shut behind him with their usual aggressive wobbling *thwack*.

Tom stood still for a moment getting his breath back, wondering what he should do when he got to the bookstore. When they drew into 23rd Street, the crowds cleared and he spotted Alice at the other end of the carriage, her knees pulled up under her chin. He went towards her.

'Alice –'

She jumped; she hadn't seen him. 'Oh, Jesus, Tom. What are you doing?'

'I wanted to make sure you were okay. That author . . . Wilder something. Is he the reason you left? He's – he's the one, isn't he? He's Teddy's brother, isn't he?'

'I didn't mean for you to worry.' Her hands were clenched by her sides. 'I surprised myself, actually.'

He sat down next to her. 'Listen, don't go there and cause a scene, will you?'

Alice's eyes flashed. '*Cause a scene?*'

'I mean don't get upset –'

She laughed, a great, huge belly laugh, like she truly found this funny. 'Wow, that's good. Tom – I know you've had your troubles and all – but, really, man. Get your head outta your ass, as Ginger would say.'

'What?'

She turned to him, her eyes flashing. 'You're a piece of work, you know that? You drift in and demand things –'

'What things?'

'Everything! You've just taken everything since you've got here!' she said furiously, her face red, as if she were trying not to cry.

'Listen, if this is about our kissing – I know it was a mistake. I'm sorry –' he said, and she flinched, as though he'd slapped her.

'That's fine.'

'I just mean it wasn't the right thing to do –'

'No, it wasn't. I'm not a child, Tom, I knew what I was doing. Neither of us should have. But it's not a big deal. What is a big deal is you – demanding I give you Teddy just because you want to lay some ghost to rest.'

'It wasn't like that, Allie,' he said, cold fury taking him over. 'I didn't say that. I just don't want to go and find Teddy by myself when I don't know what the situation is. Because we're supposed to be friends, and you won't tell me the truth.'

'We are friends –' she said, her voice cracking.

'She's my mother, Allie. But you keep saying she's busy, or she's away, or she's ill. And I know she's not. I know you're lying to me, and I don't know why. I know you won't ever take me to her.'

363

'You could have gone to see her any time, Tom! Stop bringing me into this! Why are you still here?'

'I don't know!' he shouted. 'I don't fucking know!'

Because I'm in love with you, he wanted to say. *I am utterly one hundred per cent in love with you, Alice Jansen.*

'It's a theme park to you, a game. It's not to me. It's not to Merlin –'

'*Merlin* –' Tom said disdainfully. 'What the hell does that guy know about anything?' He pointed a finger at her. 'He's using you as a maid, for God's sake.'

'He's not using me! He understands, you – you – ah, you bastard!' She was incoherent with anger. 'You have no idea!'

Sudden, unexplained fury boiled over inside Tom. He turned to her, the plastic seat creaking. 'It's such hypocrisy, what you're doing. You told me about that teacher at your school who got you an interview at Barnard, said you could have a place there. The time she must have spent on that, the strings she pulled, and you laugh at her like *she's* an idiot. You talk about saving the world, about peace and love and the greater good. How is it the greater good for you to waste your life serving meals and fetching beers for a load of men sitting around talking about an equal society while a woman waits on them hand and foot? How about you get a law degree, fight the system like RFK did? Or open your own shop? Or take an art degree? How about you actually do something instead of – instead of alienating yourself?'

The doors opened and yet more passengers got on, surrounding them.

'Oh, screw you,' Alice said softly, her voice shaking. She put her hand to her face.

'What happens when the money runs out, Alice?' said Tom, and his voice was shaking too, but he was so angry he couldn't stop himself. 'Or if you have a kid? Who pays the mortgage and the bills then? He who pays the piper calls the tune —'

Alice slapped him, hard, once, twice, around the cheek.

'Oh,' said an older woman opposite with huge round glasses that dug into her large face. She peered at them. 'Well, now. That's not very nice.'

'No,' said Alice, tears pouring down her face as she stared at Tom, who was rubbing his face where she'd hit him. 'I know it's not.' She nodded to the woman. 'I'm so sorry.' She stood up, as the train doors opened again. 'I had to do it,' she said. 'I'm protecting you. And her. But you most of all. Just go home, okay?'

And she leaped off the train. Tom managed to follow her before the doors shut. 'Alice, let me finish,' he said. 'I wanted to explain —'

'Leave me alone,' she yelled back at him. 'Leave me the hell alone —'

Tom dropped back into the crowds; saw her turn and look for him; and his heart contracted at how alone she looked, how defenceless.

His cheek stung. He put his hand up, walking out of the station into Grand Central Station. He stood for a moment in the vast, beautiful aqua-green concourse, jostled by the commuters, looking up at the constellation frescoes on the ceiling, light falling in shifting shafts, the clouds outside causing the sun to flicker.

Now leaving from Gate 16, the 1.02 train to Poughkeepsie, stopping at . . .

He turned away, not sure what to do next.

Irvington, Orchard, Tarrytown . . . All aboard!

Orchard. Alice was from Orchard, he remembered. Teddy

was in Orchard. And, just like that, a miracle: the people ebbed and shifted, and a ray of Midsummer sunshine shone right down on her, or at least that's how he remembered it. He could see her, at any rate, striding towards the platform entrance. She wasn't going to the bookstore – of course she wasn't, she wasn't even on the right subway line for the Upper West Side. She was going back home to Orchard, because Wilder Kynaston *wasn't* there. She knew she'd be safe if she went back.

Tom smacked himself gently on the forehead, and ran to the ticket office. He'd missed the train he assumed she was on, but he caught the next one twenty minutes later. He sat watching the scenery flicker out of the window, the shimmering summer heat coming off the buildings, the sun sparkling on the river. His mouth felt dry. He was scared, but excited. It was happening. He was going back to where Alice came from, and he was going to find Teddy, his mother. He was going back to the past.

PART FOUR

To Everything There is a Season

34

Alice walked slowly up Main Street from the station, past the spot where it had happened. She stopped and listened. There was no noise other than the clinking of the cables overhead, tiny waves crashing on the shore of the distant river.

It was as though she had been here only the day before. She walked past Bygones, the antiques emporium where she and her dad used to eye up the china and glass trinkets, debating what to buy next. At Lana D's beauty parlour, she saw Dolores's mother finishing up a client's hair, laughing with her as both of them looked in the mirror: Alice shrank against the shadows on the sidewalk so Mrs Delaney didn't see her and then she caught sight of herself, a tall, slender shadow in the reflection of the bank windows, recoiling.

'Allie,' she said out loud. She felt him near, so close she could almost hear him saying it. 'It doesn't matter, honey. Doesn't matter!'

It was hot; she was hungry. She had run out without anything but her wallet, which contained a small roll of dollar bills that she had stolen from Jack. She had taken to stealing from her husband lately.

Her husband. She had married Jack Maynard.

Alice crossed over into the shade, walking up past the fire station, where Tony Pisano's dad, the fire chief, was polishing the front of the truck. He stared at Alice curiously, like he recognized her but couldn't place her. Alice smiled. 'Afternoon,' she said.

He touched his hand to his bare head. 'Afternoon, ma'am,' he said blankly. She remembered her reflection in the window. Perhaps she wasn't a girl any more.

And there, at the top of the street, was Mackie's. There was the pink marble counter with the sign behind showing the different ice cream flavours and combinations, and there was the booth by the window where she and her dad used to sit.

Alice walked to the window and pressed her face to the glass. Imagine, she thought to herself, imagine if this was all a bad trip. *All* of it. If he was just there, waiting for her, in his worn houndstooth jacket, having ordered his usual Rita Hayworth, his kind, round face smiling at her, waiting to hear about her day, to tell her some interesting fact or hum a line from a musical or laugh over some joke only the two of them found funny. His full, joyful laugh. There would never be anyone, anyone in the world, whose company she enjoyed as much as Bob Jansen's, or anyone who gave her so much pain throughout her life. Alice stood facing into the diner, her slim shoulders heaving as she forced her arms to her sides, trying not to sob.

Just one more day, she heard herself whisper. If she could have just one more day with him, to ask him what had gone wrong, how she could help, what he thought about the state of things, about RFK, about Nixon, about whether she was right to marry Jack, what she should do with her life, what he really thought of Wilder Kynaston, why he had borrowed from him. He had left her with so many questions. But, more than all of that, one more day so she could feel his arms around hers, his fingers squeezing her shoulder, rest her head against his chest, hear him tell her it was all okay, in his kind, cheerful voice. And then they would sing 'If I were a Rich

Man' or 'I Have Confidence' or 'When I Marry Mr Snow'. There was no one like her dad, no man as kind and silly and clever as him.

And suddenly she was back on that day, his final expression, the thousand-yard stare. How he had clutched her wrists and begged her to forgive him. The unreality of it, the sound of his death – how she had shut her eyes too late and seen too much, but also how she had done too little, not really believing that he would do it. The full force of the pain he must have been in that he hid from her, meaning she had let him down, and the pain of the loss of him both hit her at that moment, as though they were physical blows.

Alice stepped back, terrified. She could make out the shape of someone in the diner, staring at her, yanking the sleeve of another customer. 'Hey . . . isn't that . . .' she heard them say, but she couldn't see them: the sun was shining on the glass and her vision was blurred by tears.

All of it, dancing in front of her eyes in the midday sun. She crossed a side road, stumbling against a mailbox, cursed and wiped her eyes.

'Allie?'

She carried on walking, not wanting to stop.

'Hey! Allie? *Allie!*'

She turned around, tears streaming down her cheeks. A girl was hurrying up the hill. 'Alice Jansen? What the hell –'

'Dolores!'

'You – I knew it was you! I saw you through the parlour window! Oh, Allie! You're back!'

Dolores ran the last twenty yards toward her, into her arms. Alice flung her arms around her, smelling Dolores's old, familiar scent, cigarettes and perfume and hair spray, feeling the strength of her hug – she hugged furiously, did Dolores, like she did everything.

Laughing, they stepped back, and Alice kissed her friend's cheek, almost frantic with joy at seeing her. Dolores gripped her by her upper arms, staring at her, and Alice saw herself reflected in the horror and fascination in Dolores's eyes.

'That bad, huh?' Alice said.

'You look different, that's all,' said Dolores, and her expression was serious. 'You're a grown-up. You're – oh, Allie, I've missed you, honey.'

'You look different too,' said Alice, cupping her cheek. 'You look very cute, Dolo. What happened to the lipstick?'

'I moved with the times,' said Dolores. She was wearing less make-up, so Alice could see the freckles on her olive skin. She had on a dark shift dress, huge white daisies for pockets and daisies around the collar. Her black hair was no longer up, but in a sharp side parting, razor cut. Her kohl-lined eyes raked over Alice, her grip tightening.

'I did as well,' Alice said, looking down at her long, floral dress, which she had made, and the headscarf which kept her hair out of the way. She couldn't stop smiling at Dolores. 'We went our separate ways, fashion-wise.'

'Only fashion-wise, honey. You're still my best friend in the whole world, even if we're nineteen and too old for best friends. Here. Watch that car, the guy driving it is a maniac, even if he does have a super-cute brother.' Dolores waggled her fingers at a man in a Pontiac, who waved back, at the same time as moving Alice gently across the road, to the other side of Main Street, next to the path that led towards Valhalla and the gatehouse. 'He works at the deli. Allie, I swear, he gives me extra pastrami every time – honey, what are you crying for?' she said, when she turned back to Alice. 'What's happened?'

Alice shook her head. 'It's strange to be back. I guess I didn't want to think about home . . . you know.'

'I understand,' said Dolores. She squeezed her arm and they stood in silence for a moment. Alice gave a huge sniff. Dolores said, in a lighter tone, 'Hey, did you know Diane Hendricks is engaged to Frank Logan?'

'No way.'

'It's true. Their wedding registry is at Macy's. She wants eight bridesmaids in aquamarine.' Dolores's eyes were dancing. 'Keeps going around town saying Frank's going to stand for mayor when he's thirty. As if that makes them the new Kennedys.' She pushed her hair out of her eyes. 'Oh, Allie, everyone who's still here is real square. And, since Tag died, you can't say anything anti-war in this town. It's like even though everyone agrees we need to get out of Vietnam, just to say the truth makes you anti-American. It's nuts.'

'The world is pretty nuts.'

'You got that right. Hell, I miss you, Allie.'

'I miss you too, Dolo,' Alice said.

Dolores said, 'I want to go and cause trouble somewhere. Not get stuck here. I'm thinking of taking a trip to Europe. I had a schoolfriend in Chicago who lives in somewhere called Camden now. London, Allie! And Paris. And Venice. I'm going in the fall.' Her eyes snapped open. 'Hey! Come with me. Didn't you always want to go to England?'

Alice shook her head. 'I can't.'

'Yes, you can.'

'I'm married, Dolo. To Jack.'

'Of course,' said Dolores. 'Jack.' She opened her mouth, as if about to say something, then shut it again.

It was even stranger hearing the words here, back at home. She had a husband. She managed to forget it most of the time but it was true: tall, handsome, shy, beautiful Jack Maynard was her husband. Where had he gone, that boy she'd walked through the woods with? And what, really, had they ever had in common? What would they do for money, or jobs, or for any of it in the future? She hadn't the vaguest idea.

'Allie, you're so pale. Why don't you come home with me, have some lemonade or something? I don't have to be at college for half an hour,' Dolores was saying.

'No –' Alice began, her throat closing up. 'I have to get back there.'

'Get back where?'

'I'm going to Valhalla,' Alice said.

'Oh,' said Dolores. Her eyes were huge. She bit her lip. 'Are you sure?'

Alice nodded. 'I need to make sure Teddy is okay.'

'Do you think you'll ever come back here?'

Jack had asked her the same question when she'd first arrived in New York in November.

'Do you think you'd ever go back?' he'd said. 'If he wasn't there?'

'No,' she'd said. The two of them were huddled in bed together, and his hands were wrapped around hers, her head on his chest. They had just slept together for the first time, and he had cried, and she had wondered if that was it, because it didn't seem like something to make a big fuss about. But she'd told herself then, and in the months to come, that it didn't matter. She was here, with Jack, in the city. 'It doesn't seem real any more,' she'd said, nestling more closely against him. 'It seems fake. And I can't see myself there. I'm not that person any more. How about you?'

'My dad threw me in the lake to teach me to swim,' Jack had said, his long hair flopping in his eyes. 'He beat me when I flunked my senior year, took me down to the stables and beat me with the horse whip. He knocked up our nanny; she was twenty-one. I hate him,' he said, and he'd started to cry. 'I can't ever go back. They can't make me. I'll find something else to do, or I suppose I'll just die. I don't care much one way or the other.'

'I mean it, about going travelling, Allie,' Dolores was saying. 'I want you to think about it. Will you promise me?'

'Dolo, I – I really can't go.'

'You can.' Dolores was nodding. 'More than that. You listen to me, Allie. You won't speak to me after this maybe, but I gotta say it. You were so cool when I moved here. You'd lost your dad; you were always so stylish and hard-working and gentle; and you were so kind; you looked out for me, and –' Her voice thickened. 'You're so damn clever, Allie . . . You ask questions, you try to understand how the world works, and you're always making things. And I can't stand to think of you like that, in the city not doing anything, and I know your dad wouldn't like it either, and that's the only time I'm damn well going to say that to you, honey.' Her eyes were shining with tears. 'Come to Europe with me. Let's cause some more trouble. Let's work out what to do next.'

Alice rubbed her wet cheeks, then took Dolores's hands. 'I'll think about it.'

'Oh! Yay, Allie! Are you serious?'

Alice blinked, rubbing her eyes. She nodded. 'Let's do it. Let's go.'

But she was staring at something that had just caught her

eye. She took a step back, stumbling against a low picket fence, and Dolores's hand shot out to hold her up.

'Allie? What's wrong?'

Alice stood stock still, staring across the road. 'I –' she began.

'Allie?'

But Alice just shook her head, and continued to look straight ahead, at the figure directly in front of her.

It was her dad.

He was standing in the doorway of the diner. He dropped some change into his pocket, then lifted his hand and waved to her. She could see the gleam from the sun on his bald pate, just like that last day, and his grey, kind eyes. And she could hear the jangling of his keys, and the change. She could see the square outline of the book he'd been reading in the other pocket. *East of Eden*: she knew it; it was one of his favourite novels.

'Hey, Allie,' he said, and it was his voice, his kind, soft, amused voice that was sad, so, so sad. She'd never noticed before that the sadness was part of him, because she saw him only as her father, as the man who loved her and made everything magical.

'Dad –' she said, and it sounded so weird, to say it aloud. 'Dad? Is that you?'

But he didn't hear her. He stood on the sidewalk, looking at her.

'You couldn't have done anything,' he said. 'I had to go, Allie. I couldn't see anything any more. It was covering me, all the time. I wish I could have stayed, Allie. You – you understand, don't you?'

And he held out an apple, and there were trees all around him, as though he was walking through the orchards toward her.

Alice reached out to take the apple, her eyes swimming with tears. 'Yes, Dad,' she said, in a whisper.

He nodded, and bowed his head, and then jangled the loose change and looked up. 'I love ya, Allie,' he said. 'I always will. I hope you find the last treasure, honey. It's with Teddy. You know it's with Teddy.'

And he waved at her again, then walked down the street, into the setting sun, and as she watched him go he disappeared, as though vanishing into the trees.

'Allie? Allie!' Dolores was calling her loudly, and then shook her arm. 'Jesus, are you okay?'

'I'm fine,' said Alice, and she smiled at Dolores. 'Really, I am.' She took Dolores's hands. 'I was somewhere else.'

'I know you were.' Dolores gripped Alice's hands back. They stood facing each other on the street, smiling, and she felt warmth, love, years of knowledge, passing from her friend to her. 'I can't believe you're saying yes. Are you ready for it? We'd have to hitchhike and sleep in railroad stations and wait tables and go weeks without washing . . . are you sure you're ready for it?'

'Oh, I'm ready, Dolo,' Alice said, and she was laughing. She wiped away the tears, her body shaking with release. 'Believe me, it'll be a step up from how I'm living now. Give me till October. Then we go. Is that okay?'

'More than,' said Dolores.

'I love you, Dolo.'

'I love you, Allie.'

The gatehouse was empty, the windows shuttered. Someone had pulled down the ivy which had grown up since her father's death, leaving black triangular speckles over the rough, grimy render.

She walked past the orchards and up the winding driveway. Tiny green-grey apples budded on the endless trees. Her father's old ladder leaned against one. His ladder.

She remembered the time her mother had been in the city meeting a friend and Alice had gone looking for him one evening. It was a late September afternoon, a glorious, golden day, and when she eventually located him it was because she heard him snoring in the branches of the gnarled tree by the house, the oldest in the orchard. It had a wide-beamed main branch and, having climbed up using the ladder, he had fallen asleep. He looked like a Hobbit. He used to sleep all the time, Alice could remember that now.

'Don't disturb your father,' her mother would say. 'He needs his sleep.'

Sometimes he stayed in bed for days on end. Toward the end, he had been sleeping more and more. She remembered now how the house had gotten darker and messier, and how in the days before her birthday he had suddenly emerged, and everything was golden again, and he was making plans and was the life and soul of the house again, the glue, the heart, the grit in the oyster. All this, and she'd somehow forgotten it.

The porch was the same. The throw pillows on the benches. The bottle of rye whiskey still on Wilder's study windowsill, though not the same brand, a cheaper variety. Alice faced the front door. She wasn't afraid. She rang the doorbell.

Her mother answered the door almost immediately, an anxious expression on her face that froze when she saw her daughter.

'Allie – oh, Allie, honey! You're back!'

She flung herself at her daughter, clutching her tightly, as the noises from upstairs began.

'*Ravenoose! Ravenoose! Ravenoose!*' She could hear Teddy's chair creaking across the boards with the force of movement.

'Why are you here?' Her mother released her, gripping her shoulders. Alice stared at her. It was strange to really look at someone you know that well, to really see them through fresh eyes.

Betsy had lost weight. The thinness in her face was offset by short bouffant hair, apple cheeks, deep-set twinkling blue eyes that gave her a girlish look, but the thinness made her seem bird-like, like she was pecking for scraps.

'*Ravenoose! Ravenoose!*'

Alice said, 'I came to see Teddy.'

'Allie – come in and visit with me a little first,' her mother said. She clutched at Alice's shirt. 'Goodness, darling, you're so –'

'I know,' said Alice, half regretful. 'I didn't want to show up like this, but your husband, you remember, the one who tried to rape your daughter? He's in the city for the day so this is my only chance to be certain I won't see him. Can I go upstairs? Or can Teddy come down?'

'*Ravenoose! Ravenoose!*'

Her mother was flushed. 'Allie, I wish you could see it.' She lowered her voice. 'What I did for you.'

'What you did for me? You stood there and saw him on me, and you walked away, Mom. You walked away. You did more than that, in fact,' Alice said. She felt as though the anger was liquid and it was filling her up steadily, right to the top. 'You married him. You married Wilder Kynaston, Mom!' Alice placed her hands on the doorframe to steady herself. 'He stole everything. From me, from Dad, from me again. And nothing will ever happen to him.'

'I wanted you to leave. I wanted you gone.'

'It worked.'

'So you'd take up the place at Barnard. So you'd – be free,' Betsy said, her voice still low, fast, precise. 'So you'd have a chance. Listen to me, kiddo. Your dad couldn't do what he wanted all his life, and it killed him. I knew you had to get out – I knew if you didn't you'd end up like him, Allie –'

'I don't want to talk to you about Dad,' Alice said, furious at herself for the throbbing in her voice. 'I don't want to talk to you at all. I've come to see the house one last time and say bye to Dad, and I've come to see Teddy.'

'You have no idea,' her mother said with a thin smile. She folded her arms. 'So self-absorbed – even now you're all grown up.'

'I'm self-absorbed? That's rich, Mom,' said Alice, trying not to lose her temper. 'You abandoned me. Dad died and I needed you.' It was easier to say this in an angry way than to feel how much it hurt.

'You don't know what it was like, Allie, with him . . .' her mother said.

'I was there!' Alice shouted. 'Of course I know!'

'You were a child!' Her mother took a step forward, over the threshold on to the porch. 'You have no idea what it was *really* like, because I made sure you didn't! Do you know how many times he threatened to – to do it? How many things I've sold? Grandmother's diamond bracelet – the platters – the good silver – do you know how bad the man was with money, always chasing a dream without ever putting in the thought and the work you need to make a success of it?' Her voice was hoarse with base-note anger, her beady eyes round. 'Why do you think we moved out of the city, back to Orchard? Then out of the apartment into the gatehouse? He owed money all over the place, and most of the time he was so ill he couldn't see a way to pay it back. It was horrible, for years, and years.' She licked her lips, lowering her voice and slowing her words. 'Sometimes he'd be great for months at a time and I'd think, it's just me, overreacting. But, Allie, sometimes it was as though he'd been hit by a truck. He couldn't move. He shut himself away. He'd say he was going to the railroad, to the bridge, to the barn. I was terrified you'd find him one day, and then he –'

She wiped her mouth, her forehead, her neck.

'I didn't let you see how ill your daddy was 'cause you loved him so much and he loved you. So I did the worrying, honey; I was the Grinch. All I wanted – *all I wanted* – was to look after you both. For us to . . . have a little family. Do normal things. You know? No, you don't. Ah, I'm sorry.'

'Mom –'

'You couldn't see what it was like, because I didn't let you see, but that's okay.' And she waved her hand around, as if to say, *Surely this is reason enough for everything. Case closed.*

'You should have told me, Mom,' Alice said. 'You and Dad should have told me.'

'I couldn't.' Her mother put her hand on her shoulder. 'It wasn't for me to do that, Alice.'

'You should have tried, Mom.'

'I did the best I could, Allie. Sometimes that's all you can do. And your dad did too, but everything went to hell anyway. All those years I worried and then he went and did it and you were there. You had to see it. And I'm so angry at him still. I'm so damn angry.'

She winced, closing one eye, and they stood there, standing across from each other.

'I don't know what to say to that, Mom. You married Wilder Kynaston, even though you know what he did to me.'

'I'm sorry, honey.' There was silence. 'I don't know if it means anything to you, but I'm happy.'

'You're happy?' Alice laughed.

'After a fashion. With your father, I stopped knowing how to be really happy.'

Alice knew exactly what this was like. She felt nothing then except terribly, terribly sad for her mother. 'Didn't you love him?'

Her mother looked upstairs, then around, eyes darting everywhere. She said slowly, clearly, 'More than anyone, anything. But that's not enough. I tried my best, honey. I really did.'

'I – I know you did, Mom.'

'I'm sorry you can't –'

'Can't what?' And Alice realized it didn't matter. Nothing would be the same now; she was never going to sit round the table at Thanksgiving drawing turkey hands with Wilder Kynaston and her mom, and her kids would not one day run around the lawns of Valhalla. Once again, she just felt sad for her mom. And herself. And she was tired suddenly, like she knew it was over.

'Hey,' she said. She gave her mom a polite smile. 'I can't stay long, Mom. Can I see Teddy, please? Should I go upstairs?'

Betsy was suddenly brisk. 'I'll go get her. She's a lot worse lately, Alice. I think she misses you, and your dad. I'm no substitute, but then I never was, was I?' She said it without any rancour, and Alice didn't know what to say. And Betsy turned and went inside.

All Alice could think about was how much her father had suffered but also how much fun they'd had. She was sure that he'd want her to remember that. One time, he'd mended the very same ladder in the orchard that she'd just seen; it had broken again anyway and he'd fallen off, landed on the ground, feet up in the air like an overturned turtle. And now there was maybe no one who remembered him in the way he should be remembered. Just her.

In the end Teddy came downstairs, but it took a while to coax her out of her room, and by the time she was sitting on the porch the events of the day were catching up with Alice, as was the lack of food, and she felt quite faint.

'Teddy, hi,' she said. 'I missed you. How are you?'

Teddy sat on the bench, her huge eyes fixed on Alice. Alice leaned against one of the throw pillows, trying to make it like all the times before.

'How have you been?'

Teddy's arms were folded; her short shingled greying hair, which shook when she was angry or excited, perfectly still. Her face, unlined, unchanged; it was the most curious aspect of the whole affair, how young she still looked.

'I know you're annoyed with me for going away. But I had to leave. You'd have told me to go, if you understood why.'

A skein of geese, carping in the evening sunshine, threw a V shadow across the shimmering, placid river. Alice glanced over at it – thought she saw someone, standing by the bank. Was he still here, in another apple tree, in the boarded-up gatehouse? She blinked again – but he had gone. It was just her, now.

'Teddy, you know, I've been in New York. I met some

people who know you. A boy who knows you. And I wanted to ask you, about him coming to visit you sometime.'

Teddy's mouth opened in an O, her neat bobbed hair shaking. A howl like a seal's boomed around the porch, out into the woods. Betsy came running out.

'You mustn't get her all agitated, you hear?' She turned to Teddy and said kindly, 'You want your doll, honey?'

Teddy shook her head. '*Ravenoose!*' she said, pointing at Alice. '*Ravenoose!*'

'My friend, he's been to Sevenstones,' said Alice. 'He told me all about it.'

More noises. 'Do you want me to talk, like the old way?' Alice said, quietly.

'*Ravenoose! Ravenoose!*'

Her hands, waving around, as Alice watched the imaginary Teddy storm in, fling herself backwards on the bench and shove a throw pillow underneath her. Alice cleared her throat and said, in Teddy's voice:

Alice, my dear. You've caused quite a commotion, wouldn't you say? Why didn't you come back?

'You don't ask why I ran away in the first place.'

I know why you ran away, Alice. But to burn all your bridges. It's a little short-sighted, don't you think? If you run away because of one or two rotten apples, you risk giving up your whole life to them.

'Allie?'

Betsy Kynaston was in the doorway, an apron tied around her waist. 'What the hell are you talking about? Why are you waving your arms about like that? Standing up, performing amateur dramatics. Here, Teddy!' She wiped Teddy's mouth. 'She's upset – can't you see?'

'We always talk like this,' said Alice. She held Teddy's hand, as Teddy howled and banged her other hand on the chair.

'What's the point? She doesn't understand a word of it, Allie darling – not any of it.'

'That's crap, Mom.'

'Allie, she's a retard. Please don't upset her. And don't use language like that.'

As Betsy left, Alice turned to Teddy again. In her Teddy voice she said:

You should go. But the difference is that I have to stay here, don't I? I can never leave. And you're going again, aren't you? I want you to go, Alice, my dear. As soon as you can get out of me what you want.

'Teddy, I always knew about your life before the war,' Alice said evenly, her voice her own now. 'I knew about your school, about going to Vassar, to parties, how brave you were, how dashing, and how much trouble you caused!' She smiled at Teddy. 'My dad told me about how you cut your own hair and ate only green tomatoes. I heard about how you nearly died of meningitis. You should have died, and you didn't; you beat it back. I knew everything about you from everyone in the town, especially my dad. But I didn't understand what happened after you came back from the war, and it all stopped. He told me they did something to you, and that he was your friend, and that your old friends stayed in touch with you through him. But I never really *saw* you till he was dead, and then it was too late to ask the rest. I should have asked him, Teddy. I'm sorry.'

Teddy was rocking, hugging herself. Alice reached over and stroked her thin shoulder.

'And then this boy rang one day. He was asking about you. He said someone was looking for you, someone from the war. And Teddy, he didn't know anything. But he knew more than me. He's a nice boy. He's the son of someone you knew.'

'*RAVENOOSE! RAVENOOSE! RAVENOOSE!*'

'Shh,' Alice said. 'You have to let me finish.'

She looked around: on the lawn she could make out a figure some distance away, and she inhaled sharply, just as Teddy's cries grew louder and she slammed her hands on the arms of her chair. Alice turned to look at her, and found Teddy was pulling a thick envelope from under the throw pillow. She gave it to Alice.

'Ravens,' she said. 'Ravens. Sevenstones. Hidden. Found them.'

'Teddy, it's okay.' Alice leaned forward and patted her hand. The envelope was heavy. Inside were two letters and a package. She unfolded the letters and read them, her head spinning.

'Oh, Teddy,' she said, holding her friend's hand. 'Of course. *Of course.*' She stared into her huge, vacant eyes. 'I'm so sorry,' she said. 'But this is good. This is good, I promise, Teddy. It's going to be okay. Hey,' she said, turning her head and calling toward the trees. 'Come over here. We won't bite.'

She felt, rather than saw, the figure, approaching across the lawn. And so she said, 'Hey. Hey, Tom. We're waiting for you.'

Tom Raven stood at the bottom of the porch steps. He stepped forward and held out his hand to Teddy Kynaston. She did not move, merely stared at him.

'Allie,' said Tom, his eyes hollow. 'Please – I'm so sorry about this morning. About what I said. About following you here –' He was staring down at Teddy. 'Forgive me,' he said, in a quiet voice. 'What's your friend's name? She looks so familiar.'

'Oh, Tom,' said Alice gently. She wished she could make it easier for him. 'Tom, this is Teddy,' said Alice, and she saw his expression change. 'She's my friend.' She put the unopened package on the table, out of the way, and unfolded the two letters again. 'She's given me these letters to read. I'm going to read them out loud, if that's okay. I think you'll understand when you've heard them.'

Alice unfolded the first letter.

> Sevenstones
> Tallboys
> Wilts.

Dear Edward –

I've made the most enormous mistake; so have you. Yes it has been a lovely summer. Too lovely, as you've seen. I am having your child. I understand what a bind this puts you and Irene in. Irene is a trooper for saying all's fair in love and war – it's not true. I've hurt all the people I most care about, her, and you, and Jenny, of course. Poor Jenny.

When I was a child I caused my family enormous trouble. I had these fits, I think they were seizures, and my behaviour was what they called erratic. My brother had doctor after doctor come look me over, and they were all concerned that I had some kind of mental disorder. I'm sure that's the case, in that I always felt I was doing everything wrong – breaking things, causing trouble, not paying attention, not excelling in areas where I should, as a young lady, have been excelling.

The strangest part of it all is that when I joined up and became a driver all of that went away. I was good at my job, I liked the work – no, NO, Edward, I loved it. I loved the thrill and the camaraderie – heck, you know I'd have loved to have flown a Lysander or a Spitfire one time or more, but girls can't do . . . etc.

I wish my ma and pa could have seen me there, seen how happy I was. And those nights and days at Sevenstones. Those nights, Edward –

I love you, darling. I love you with all my heart and soul. I love you.

Tell Irene I am floored by her grace and generosity, by the offer she has made. I agree on one condition: that you raise the child as yours and never tell him who his real mother is. He must be a Caldicott and a Raven. He must never know. That is the only way I can agree.

My brother is coming to collect me after I've had the baby and will take me back to America. He sounds angry. But I'll get around him.

I love you.

I regret none of it, except not running away to find you sooner. I wish we had one more day at Sevenstones. One more night lying on the sarsen stone, gazing up at the moon. We are there, in the walls, in the air, in the dust, we are the past now. I will always be there.

I will love you and this child until my dying day.

Teddy

August 1946
Valhalla,
Orchard
NY

Dear Miss Caldicott

Thank you for returning my sister's books and other personal effects left behind at your house. I am sorry she was unable to remove them herself due to the nature of her departure, which was by necessity a surprise to her, and to those present, but it is agreed by all that sedation is essential for best medical practice and recovery. Lobotomy is a simple procedure & Teddy has responded well to the operation. She shows no signs of distress or of her former erratic mental retardation, which led to sexual incontinence and the birth of her illegitimate child, conceived with a married man, as I understand you are aware.

You hold some of the blame for your behavior with my sister and I hope that this episode, and her removal, causes you to reflect on your perverted tastes and to begin to amend them.

Teddy is back at home, in Valhalla, is well and happy, and leads a simple life. Her former wild behavior is, fortunately for her, a thing of the past. We are a loving family again. I ask that henceforth all correspondence between us cease.

Yours,
Wilder Kynaston

Alice's hands were shaking so violently as she finished reading that she could barely hold on to the letters. She felt a calm hand on hers, cool and soft, enclosing it. She looked up into Teddy Kynaston's blank eyes.

'Ravenoose,' Teddy said quietly. 'Ravenoose.'

Beside her, her son said softly to her, 'Yes. That's right. Raven house. There's a raven's nest behind the house, isn't there? I like the ravens. I like watching what they carry up to their nests, for their young.'

She was nodding, staring eagerly at him. 'Ravenoose.'

'I love it there. I think Alice would love it there too, don't you?'

And he sank to the ground and took a ring out of his pocket. He held it up to her, and she took it, staring at it, holding it very carefully between thumb and forefinger. After a few moments Teddy opened her mouth and said, very slowly:

'Who are you?' And she smiled at him.

'I'm Tom,' Tom said. 'And Jenny asked me to bring this back to you,' and he gently put his head in her lap, and she stroked his hair, smiling, the other hand still holding the ring as she stared out to the distant, wooded horizon.

35

Alice's father had visited Teddy every week; he'd known her all his life. Sometimes she gave him candy, or hair pins, sometimes apple pips she'd saved from her lunch. Sometimes she shuffled over to her bureau and gave him one of the ornaments that filled her bedroom – a cat, a dancing bear, a dog, a piece of sea-glass. She called them the treasures. To her, they were treasures. Bob Jansen took them, though he knew if his employer found out he'd get into trouble. He gave them to his daughter, who called them treasures, too.

In the apple cart, the year she turned fourteen and her father got the big loan from Mr Kynaston and took over the orchards, Alice, lying back among the apples, had once asked her dad what was wrong with the big girl who lived in Mr Kynaston's house. Her father had hesitated, then said:

'Teddy had an operation, in 1946, when she came back from Europe. The doctors performed a procedure on her. They wanted to help her.'

'Help her what?'

'Make her calmer, they said. They don't do it so much any more. They aren't sure it's a good idea. It wasn't a good idea.'

He'd climbed into the cart next to Alice, taken an apple and sat beside her in silence, eating away, and it was the closest he had ever come to criticizing his employer.

'I'm sorry I followed you here, Alice.'

'It's fine. I'm sorry for what I said.'

'Me too. The arrogance. It's none of my business what you do with your life. I just have one question. Where were the letters from?'

'She gave them to me.'

'What?'

'Teddy. She handed them to me, when I arrived. All this time, she's had them in her bureau, or someplace in her room. They were lost – maybe her brother found them and hid them. But she found them. She's been waiting all this time to give them to me. She knows what happened to her. She's been waiting,' she said again. 'She knew we'd come. She knew.'

'Oh, Alice.'

'Don't worry about me. I'm fine. It's you – I keep thinking about you, Tom –' He looked up at her. 'I had no idea this would happen today – you do know that, don't you? How do you feel?'

'Of course. How do I feel?' He put one hand over his right eye. 'I don't know what to feel. It's something to get used to. It's – mad. But I *know* her. The moment I saw her I knew it was her. And it helps, that she doesn't really know who I am. She was very sweet. She told me it's always nice to see family.'

'Oh, Tom.' Alice put her hand in his.

They were on the stuffy train, the steel girders of the bridge back into Manhattan flashing past them. It was still light. It was still the longest day.

'But, you know, it makes sense. There was always something so odd, so absent, about my childhood. My dear dad, he's lovely, but he wasn't up to it. How could he have been?' His eyes shone with unshed tears. 'God, Allie. He had to pretend my mother was his dead wife and she wasn't. And all this time he didn't know what had happened to Teddy either.

I think I know when he found out, too.' He shook his head. 'So he's mourning two women.'

'Did he ever go to see her?'

'I don't see how he could have done. I don't remember him leaving me, and he didn't have any money,' said Tom, considering it all. 'Oh, hell, it's complicated. The other idea I've been trying to get used to is that Irene wasn't my mother. And that means I was nothing to do with dear old Jenny and Henry. So God knows why they agreed to take me on.'

Alice looked out the window. 'I suppose they loved their sister.'

'Jenny loved Teddy so much she clearly thought she had to look after Teddy's child, for Teddy's sake, and for Irene's. But she couldn't tell anyone what had happened to Teddy – it was too awful and she felt partially responsible.'

'Why?'

'I'd imagine, given the tone of that letter from Wilder Kynaston, that Teddy's affair with a woman was one of the reasons they forced the lobotomy on her.' He put his hand under his chin. 'How, Alice? How on earth was it allowed?'

'It happened a lot,' said Alice. 'I know a girl in the city whose mother's in an institution, because she went crazy after having kids. Started drinking and having affairs. They wanted to calm her down.'

'I imagine that's how they justified it to Kynaston. And to Teddy. Poor Teddy.'

Alice was turning over everything she and Tom had worked out on the train back together. 'So my dad passed letters to your aunt through their friend Gordon – is that right?'

'I guess so. I can't find any of them. I'll ask Gordon if he has any. He knew all along. He kept trying to tell me.' He was staring out the window. 'But I guess they kept Jenny up to date with everything.'

'I think it's the one time Teddy was truly happy, the war,' Alice said. 'From what my father used to say about it.'

'I suppose the real hero is Irene Raven, and I never knew her either.'

'But it was convenient for her too. I think there were lots of heroes,' said Alice. 'Your dad . . . My dad. Your friend Gordon. Jenny, in a way. Irene wanted kids and they couldn't have them and there's her unfaithful husband presenting her with a kid she could raise as her own . . . What would have happened to you if she hadn't agreed to adopt you is anyone's guess.'

Tom was silent, watching the city flash past them, ochre-coloured light on one side of the skyscrapers, black flat shadows on the others. She put her hand on his again, unable to stop herself. Her warm skin rested lightly on his hands. She said, 'I always felt I knew you. From the first moment I heard your voice.'

He looked up, and something flashed across his eyes. 'I know,' he said. 'Me too.'

They sat in silence, hands clasped, until the train pulled into Grand Central.

It was dark when they got back to St Mark's Place. Alice was so tired by now that her head was aching. She could not remember when she'd last eaten. The lights were all off at No. 5. Alice fumbled around under the planter with the dead marigold plant and took out the key. 'Hey, Merlin,' she called.

There was no answer. She went downstairs, to the kitchen, and Tom's room. He followed her. There was a note on the dresser.

Missed you, Allie.

I might skip out of town for a few days, need to clear my head. I don't know when I'll be back. Go well, Allie. We can say we were here at this time of change. Peace and light.

J

Alice stood very still, holding the note in her hand.
'Everything okay?' said Tom.
'Yes,' she said.
Behind her, she sensed Tom's awkwardness. He said, 'I'm starving. I'm going out to the deli. Can I get you something? How about a meatball sandwich?'
'Oh.' Alice patted her pockets, embarrassed. The last of the roll of dollar bills had been spent on the train fare back. She had no idea where more money was. She was waiting to be paid for some posters she'd designed for a Love-in at the Astoria next month. Jack usually gave her money for food.
'I don't have any money,' she said quietly. 'I can owe you.'
'It's fine. I owe you. You got me a mother today.'
Alice smiled. 'Okay. I'd love a meatball sub. Yes, please. How do you know I like them?'
'I just remember hearing you say it once.' He smiled back at her. 'I'll be right back.'
'I'll get the place fixed up while you're out. Thanks, Tom.'
He nodded, his gaze holding hers just a second longer than usual. She was very aware of him, of the fact that no one else was there, of the heat, of the utter craziness of the day. She took a deep breath and turned back into the apartment, then set about tidying up the filthy kitchen, humming to herself

as she did so. Curtis, Callie and Ginger were all out, and the street was quiet.

Someone was playing an accordion; a dog was barking; someone else was chanting loudly, and there was the usual fight going on in the apartment opposite.

Alice stacked the bowls, put the beaded cloth over the butter, wiped the counters, swept the floor. She went back to the front stoop again and sat down: her empty stomach was making her head spin. She wondered when Jack would come back, if he meant her to find him. She wondered if he really preferred men, as Ginger had once told her she thought he did. She thought about her mother's glassy face, how all the grace and joy had gone out of it after too many long years were spent worrying about her father. Alice rubbed her eyes. She was so sick of it all, and there was nothing to do but keep going. She was nineteen and this was not the life her father would have wanted for her. Or her mother. She thought about her mother's face, telling her to go last fall, pushing her away, setting her free.

She thought about Teddy, how one night she had crept up to Valhalla in the summer after her dad died, when she felt really, really mad, simply walked in through the open door from the porch to see her in her room, how Teddy lay there, quietly, on her side, staring at nothing in her voluminous white flannel nightgown. Hello, Alice, she'd said, her words laboured but clear for once, maybe because she was on her side and speaking softly. Hello. Take me to the Raven House.

That was what she'd been saying, all these years. Take me to the Raven House. Teddy knew where she wanted to be.

A voice behind her said, 'Hey,' and she jumped. It was Tom, with the meatball sub. She was hungrier than she had ever been, and these last eight months she had been hungry all the time. She almost tore the sandwich off him, opening up the foil and shovelling in a huge bite.

'Sorry,' she said between mouthfuls. 'Dreadful manners.'

Tom shook his head, his mouth full. The chairs had vanished – furniture was often missing in St Mark's Place – so they stood across from each other, leaning against the rickety kitchen table and grinning over the sandwiches.

'Long day, huh,' he said, swallowing.

'In fact it's been the longest day,' said Alice, laughing almost hysterically, and then she found she couldn't stop laughing.

'Oh dear,' said Tom, almost to himself, as she bowed her head, still laughing.

'Sorry.' Alice wiped her mouth and took a swig from the whiskey bottle someone had left on the table. 'Listen.'

'I'm listening.'

'I never said something,' she said.

They had moved next to each other. Tom reached behind Alice and took a swig from the bottle. 'What?'

'I kind of . . . I was rude, when we first met. I didn't want you coming in and ruining everything. Trying to make me go back home.'

'Allie –' He put the bottle back down, the skin on his bare arm scraping her arm. 'Don't apologize.'

'And I was kind of a bitch.'

'You weren't,' he said.

'I was. The truth is, I was scared.'

'I know you were,' he said calmly. 'I know.'

Alice chewed the inside of her mouth, then gave a belch.

'Oh –' she said, but he just laughed, and belched as well.

'We're even. Aren't we? We always have been. I knew when we spoke, Alice, I knew you.' He took a deep breath, gave a shuddering sigh. 'I always have.'

Their hips were touching, their legs, their feet.

She put her hand on his arm, turning to face him, and their eyes met. Tom reached up and brushed her hair out of her eyes.

'Thank you,' he said quietly. 'For everything. And I'm sorry.'

'What are you sorry for?'

'For – coming over in the first place and being a prig today. For making you go back there. For our mothers. Both of them.'

'I had to go back there.'

'For taking up a bed here.'

'I'd have drowned if you weren't here.'

He took a swig of whiskey from the bottle and swallowed. She could hear something in his voice, a shaking. 'For kissing you too. I shouldn't have done it.'

'I kissed you, Tom. Don't worry about it.' She moved toward him a little more, and put the sandwich down on the table. 'Tom – I couldn't have stopped myself, even if I'd wanted to, or tried to. I couldn't.' She smoothed the hair away from his brow.

'That day in the park,' he said. 'With the broken cookies and the whiskey and when we talked. I knew it was right, I just felt it here –' He thumped his chest, and she saw his eyes were shining with tears. 'But I got it so wrong before, with that girl Celia I told you about. And I did again today, for what it's worth, but that night we were drunk and angry and you were freaked out about Merlin and when we kissed I thought this is how it should be, it's right, I know it's right, but it's the wrong time and I should have waited till it was. The right time. Because I'm falling in love with you, and you need someone – you need the right person.'

He put his hand on her cheek, his fingers stroking her skin so gently she could feel the whorls of his fingertips against her cheekbones.

'Have you finished?' Alice asked, smiling at him.

'I think so,' he said.

'It's the right time, Tom.'

They were very still, the motion of his fingers almost the only movement. She stared at him, and his large dark eyes, the good one and the bad together; his jaw was set, his full, wide mouth closed. And she reached up to touch his face, running her hands from his jaw to his cheek and through his thick, unruly dark hair, feeling her body respond as she did so, her nipples hardening under her shirt, a rushing sound filling her head.

'Anyway,' she said, her voice low. 'How do we know if we don't try?' She moved so she was against him, pushing against the table, their hips touching, their breathing ragged. He put his hands on her hip bones, smoothed them, moved his hands up, pulling her toward him.

Something, someone, thudded above them – Ginger shouting about something on her way out, a door slamming. Alice whispered into Tom's ear, 'Shall we go upstairs?'

'Yes,' he said, 'in a minute, just kiss me first –' and she did. He wrapped his arms around her, pushing her against the kitchen cabinet. He tasted of truffles, of woods, of fresh things, of the sky. He was delicious, heavy; she loved the smell and the bulk of him against her when he was so gentle in spirit. Alice said:

'To be clear I mean let's go to Ginger's room right away –'

'That's what I mean too,' he said, breathing in the scent of her and kissing her, his mouth hard on hers, his hand on her back, pulling her toward him.

36

Ginger's room had vast windows covered by thin net curtains, and looked out on to a tiny backyard where a kid played with a mitt and ball, throwing it at the wall over and over again, the thudding sound waking up Alice most mornings as Merlin snored next to her. *Thud-thud-thud.*

This is it, she thought, and she knew, as she unbuttoned her dress, as she tugged it over her head, as she knelt on the bed in front of Tom.

He held her hands, his face serious, and then he looked up at her with a smile of such sweetness, such dark, delicious happiness, that she felt the air had been sucked out of her and the room swam before her eyes. She wanted him so much, it was almost an ache.

He slid the shirt off her shoulders, smoothing his hands over her bare flesh. He stared at her for a moment, then took her hands gently in his and squeezed them. Then he moved his hands up to her breasts, his breathing laboured.

'Allie –' His mouth took her left breast, teasing the nipple, tonguing it back and forth, gently kissing her soft skin, her peaked, tight nipples, and with one hand he reached between her legs to touch her. Alice, closing her eyes, felt as though the sun was shining on her, warmth spreading over her tired, aching body. Somehow, he swiftly took his shirt off, then he came back to her, nudging her knees open. She knew, through the waves of tiredness from the longest day and the whiskey, she knew this was what it was supposed to be. She knelt up, easing herself on to him.

'Alice . . .' he said, his breath hot in her ear, his teeth on her skin. 'Oh, Alice . . . Finally. You'll tell me, won't you . . .'

'Tell you what?'

'If you change your mind – if you don't like it – tell me what you want,' he said, his voice husky. She shook her head and closed her eyes.

'I'm not going to change my mind . . .' She trailed off, drinking him in. She could barely speak, she wanted him so much. He kneed her legs apart and pulled her up so they were facing each other, entwined, like crabs, bodies locked together. His hand moved between her legs, and she could feel his hard cock pushing against her hand. Alice looked down into his face, kissing him, his hair, his neck, stroking his shoulders. They looked down to the space between them, and she edged on to him, so the tip of his penis was resting against her.

'Okay,' he whispered, kissing her ear, her jaw, her cheek, her lips, and as he did so he slowly thrust into her and she sank on to him, watching his dark, beautiful face, utterly in control, and then he started to move, and she rose and sank, moving against him too.

'Alice – you –' he said, and he smiled at her, and moved again. His shoulders, his ears – he tasted of salt, and smoke, and sweat, thrusting into her and touching her, pushing and licking her, and at one point he kissed her and reached up to look at her and her heart pounded, and she raised herself up to hold his head, to kiss him, kiss him, kiss him. They moved together like the waves of the shore, until she cried out, her voice husky with desire, and when she looked he was watching her. He thrust, hard, into her, and cried out, and she kissed him again, and again, his dear, darling face, his soft, sweet, hard body, the certainty, the strangeness of it all.

The following morning, she woke by degrees, the heat outside part of her, the sheets cool against her naked body, tired and sore and happy.

Tom was still asleep, his hair tousled, his face gentle, relaxed. She reached over and touched his cheek. He turned to her, enclosing her in his space, his arm flung over her, edging on his side toward her, then he moaned softly.

'Don't . . .' he said. 'It's the house in the trees. Don't go. Don't go.'

She stroked his face.

'Don't –' he said, and then, when she reached down to touch his hardening cock, he woke up, opened his eyes. 'Was I talking in my sleep?' he said.

'No,' she lied.

'That's good,' he said. He blinked, still half asleep. 'Good morning.'

She could not stop herself, did not want to. He leaned over and kissed her, the sheets soft against the warmth of their bodies. 'Forget it,' she said, letting the words slide out of her head as Tom slowly moved his hand down to between her legs, watching her, tracing patterns on her skin and deliberately making her come over and over again, his fingers touching her secret spot, telling her what she should do, what he was doing, how it should feel, asking her what she wanted, handling her alternately roughly and gently, and she realized that, as with her husband's name, everything about her marriage had been fake. They lay hooked together on their sides, and she could feel him growing hard again, so she rubbed him, lifting her leg over his, and he slid into her from behind, pushing into her, his hands on her hip and breast and Alice heard herself crying out, coming so loudly with pleasure, so viscerally, that it almost made her panic; and, for the first time since she had run away to be here, Alice understood what free love was really about, what sex was really for, how everyone should experience this, everyone deserved it, and how she hadn't known the truth about any of the words she was saying in those months with Merlin, not until yesterday.

She lay on her side, Tom's arm wrapped round her. She felt very calm. After a while he flung himself away on to his back. He reached for something in the air.

'Don't go,' he said again.

'It's okay,' she said, because she knew he was asleep again, and she smiled.

'Celia – come back. Darling – please, just come back. Don't go.'

Alice lay in bed, very still. He was quiet after that. She listened to the *thud-thud-thud* of the kid playing with the baseball, throwing it against the wall.

She slept again and woke an hour later. One of Ginger's drawings was on the wall, a sketch of Merlin, fist raised, his mouth open. Alice stared at it, trying to remember how she had come to be here. Then the events of the past twenty-four hours washed over her: the long day, the long night, the ending. She put her head on Tom's chest. He was warm, and comforting. He put his hand on her head, letting his fingers play gently but firmly in her hair.

'Do you have to go to work today?' she asked.

'Yes,' he said. 'But, if you want, I can stay here.'

'Oh! No, you don't have to.'

'Okay. Sure.'

'If you want, you definitely should,' said Alice, suddenly awkward.

She could feel his voice through his chest. 'I don't want to make things difficult with Merlin.'

She propped herself up on one elbow. 'His name's Jack, you know. He wasn't ever a Merlin. His family is very grand; they live along from Valhalla. He has a pool.'

'They always do,' said Tom.

'Tom –' Alice said. She looked down into his eyes. If it was going to be like this, it had to be like this now. 'We shouldn't have –'

He sat up. 'Oh. Perhaps we shouldn't.'

'I didn't mean it like that,' Alice said. 'But I have to tell Merlin. It's over.'

'It's over with him, you mean?'

She hesitated. 'Yes.'

Someone outside was chanting:

'HO HO HO CHI MINH / THE NLF IS GONNA WIN!'

'If that's what you want,' said Tom.

'I don't know what I want,' Alice said. She folded her arms under her breasts and stared at him. 'Everything is crazy right now, don't you think?'

Tom glanced at her breasts, then sat up and turned away, swinging his legs off the bed. He pulled on his jeans.

'It is crazy.' He swallowed, then he ran his hands through his hair and said shortly, 'Listen, Alice – thank you. For yesterday.'

'I'm really glad,' she said. She put her hand on his back. He swivelled round and kissed her, pushing her back on the bed, his skin on hers, the rough metal and denim of his jeans against her soft stomach. He held her face between his hands and kissed her again, hard. When they broke off, she said, 'I hope you think it was worth it.'

'What was worth it?' he said. His breath was soft, sour-sweet on her face. He sat up.

'The trip. Meeting Teddy – meeting your mother,' Alice said. 'What else?'

'Of course it was. I still can't quite believe any of it. I need to think,' he said.

'I know,' she said, and she pulled on a grimy T-shirt of Ginger's over her head. 'What are you going to do?'

'Now, or in general?'

'Whichever you want,' she said, and she ran her hands over his shoulders.

'We seem to be talking at cross purposes,' he said gently, but it made her want to cry. 'What are you going to do next? When the summer's over?'

'I don't know,' Alice said. She didn't want to mention her plans with Dolores. She wasn't sure why. 'I can't stay in New York. I need to get away from here,' she said, her fingers entwined with his.

'You're still only eighteen,' he said.

'I turned nineteen a few days ago.' She hated her birthday, because of what had happened. 'I don't celebrate it.'

'Okay. I mean you have so much time, Allie. So do I. You can do anything. You could still go to college. You *should* go travelling. Where would you go?'

'I was talking about it with Dolores, you know, my best friend back home.' She shrugged, feeling his fingers stroking her shoulder, her backbone, and his touch made it feel as though her skin was melting, as though the air between them was electric, magic, full of power. It was extraordinary, and it was awful.

Something made her say, 'Tom. Would it be crazy, do you think, if I went to Sevenstones? You mentioned it yesterday. I've always wanted to go to England – and my dad did too – I think he'd have loved for me to go there.'

He came toward her again, as if he couldn't help himself. 'Yes. You should go to Sevenstones.' He kissed her breast gently, licking and nibbling at it, then smoothed his hands over her stomach and waist. 'It's easy to get to. There's a bus to the nearest village now they've shut the station. You could walk from there. Across the fields, even.' He was kissing her neck, her shoulder, her lips. 'The house – it's in a stone circle. Right in the middle. They think it's older than Stonehenge. They don't know. But it's special. It's deep, deep time, the land there.'

Deep time.

He was standing up now and looking down at her with a strange expression; as if it was painful to see her, as if he didn't want to be there. Alice was sure, despite his lips on hers, despite his expression, his need for her, hers for him, that he was slipping away from her, that something was not right. She could not believe this was how it was, when only five minutes before they had been closer than a closed shell. She could smell him, smell her, smell the scent of sex in the room. Outside, the thudding of the ball and the mitt continued.

'You could go,' he said, and he hesitated. 'You should go.'

Alice sat up, her knees under her chin, the sheet over her legs. 'I want to go. For Teddy.' He watched her as he pulled his shirt over his head, and in the split-second his face was out of view she blinked, the heavy weight of grief making her eyelids feel like they were cast in lead. 'And – and I tried to tell her story, even if just to myself. So someone had heard her. I had this feeling she'd die without anyone remembering her as she was. And she seemed – she seems so remarkable to me.'

Tom covered his eyes briefly with his hands, and Alice realized what she'd said. 'I'm sorry,' Alice said. 'I keep forgetting. She's *your* mother.'

'But she wasn't, not really.'

The others, the ghosts in the room with them: Alice wanted them all to leave. She wanted to draw Tom toward her, climb on to him, sink down on to him, feel him inside her again. And these other people, they were all still there. He began looking around, making sure he'd left nothing behind. She watched him. 'What are you going to do?'

'I don't know what I can do. I'll try to go to see her again. I should go back home. Talk to my dad. I don't know if he knows.' He clasped his face in his hands and rubbed it, then stood up. 'You're right. I thought perhaps it'd be best like this.'

'Yes.' Alice was taken aback by the swiftness of the end of it, but she said, 'Hey. I don't think you should see her again. She doesn't really know who you are. She won't remember you. It'll hurt –'

'I wouldn't hurt her,' he said, almost angrily.

'You,' she said quietly. 'I meant you, Tom. I don't want anyone to hurt you.'

It was almost too hard to say. Her throat hurt.

'Yes,' he said, and his face was blank, his eyes fixed on her, haunted, heavy. 'When you go to England, let me know.' He stood up from the bed, wrote the address down on a scrap of paper and handed it to her. 'The key is under the stone to the right of the front door. You'll remember that, won't you?'

Alice nodded, fighting back tears. 'Of course.'

'Listen, Alice –'

'Call me Allie,' she said, 'I love it when you call me Allie.' She tried to sound jaunty, though her mouth was dry and she wanted to cry.

Celia – don't go, Celia –

'Allie,' he said, and it was like a breath of fresh wind in the airless room. 'Allie, I think I should find somewhere else to stay.'

'Sure,' she said, nodding.

'My job's the other side of the city. I thought I might see if there's somewhere I can rent uptown. Laura has space. I should just move in there.'

'You should,' she said, biting her lip, hating how fast this was, and yet nodding in agreement. 'Stay in touch, won't you?'

His eyes opened as if she'd slapped him, and then he caught her hand and pressed it against her heart. She felt it, warm, felt her heart beating underneath it, felt something pass between them.

'I don't want to cause you any trouble,' he said. 'You're married, Allie. I'll leave my new address at the bookstore, so you'll know where to find me.' He jangled his hands in his jeans. 'Oh –' He pulled something out of his pocket. 'Oh, no.'

'What's up?'

'Allie – she gave me something for you. I can't believe I forgot. I can't believe it. You left it behind, don't you remember? The package she gave you, with the letters.'

Alice looked at the small packet he was holding in his hand, brown paper, with string wound round and round it, and she thought of *The Sound of Music*, and smiled, a sweet, piercing sadness in her heart.

'Thank you,' she said. She felt hollowed out, but something shifted inside her, feeling hopeful too. The bulk of it sat in the palm of her hand. She raised it up and down. 'I'll open it later.'

'No problem,' he said. 'Do you –' He stopped. 'Do you want to go and get some breakfast, or a coffee? I have to go to work –'

'Oh, no,' she said. 'Thank you. I'm working at the store today. I'll grab some breakfast later.'

'Of course,' Tom said, buttoning up his shirt. 'That's – okay, then.' He stared at her as if he didn't recognize her. Then he paused at the door. 'Goodbye, Allie.'

'Oh. Sure. Bye, Tom. Thanks,' Alice said brightly, as if she'd just sold him a poster.

He left without saying another word. She heard him going down the stairs, the bang of the front door.

The moment he was gone, Alice pulled apart the string bow, tore open the paper. There was a letter, folded around something.

Dear Allie

I've been collecting these this past year to mark your sixteenth.

I've been saving. I borrowed from the bank to buy the orchards from Wilder, and it hasn't done so well, but these are my own savings, built up bit by bit since the day you were born, for you.

I don't know when you'll need this money. But one day, you might. And one day, I might not be here. Things are not good with me at the moment, and I don't know what the future holds. I wanted to tell you I trust you with this money. And the animals are to look after you. And Allie, finally, I wanted to tell you that you are beautiful, and perfect, and clever, and extraordinary, and you <u>must not</u> let life tell you otherwise. Carry on, carry on being wild and passionate and clever and impulsive. Move into the light, for it is where the best decisions are made and remember –

You didn't come this far just to come this far.

I am seeing you today, at Mackie's, for our sundae. I think it will be the end for me. I can't see a way. I will leave this with Teddy, and tell you to make friends with her. She has a strange way of telling me what I need to hear when I need to hear it. She needs friends. We all do.

Your loving father,
Bob Jansen

Inside was a thousand dollars, and several china animals. Two ponies, one grazing, one whinnying. Two dogs, a tiny sausage dog and a wolfhound, gambolling in different poses. Two red squirrels, chewing ears of corn. One otter, on its back, paws folded, face smiling in ecstasy. And another raven, its dark eyes shining. It stared at Allie.

Alice let her gaze slide over all of them, so still apart from her eyes moving that she realized after a while she was stiff. She picked up the roll of cash and stood up, pulling the T-shirt off again so she was naked, stretching up, reaching out, her body illuminated by the morning sun. The dollar bills fluttered slightly in the breeze from the window. She turned back to look at the bed again. Treasures.

I love you, she said to herself. *I love you. I love you. I love you.*

She thought about the treasures on her windowsill in the

room she shared with Jack. All lined up against the grimy glass, waiting for her to take them someplace else. Under the bed she kept the headscarves in which she'd wrapped the treasures when she left Orchard and a drawstring bag she'd made last winter. Inside the bag were little scraps of cloth she'd collected here and there, making dresses, alterations for friends. Curtis's gingham uniform, a discarded orange-and-red floral headscarf of Ginger's, one of Merlin's cheesecloth kaftans, a Liberty cotton handkerchief she'd stolen from Tom early on and, most recently, a pair of half-burned curtains after she and Callie set fire to them by accident one evening. Her mementoes of her time at St Mark's Place. Like Maria in *The Sound of Music*. She thought her dad would have enjoyed that, repurposing them to house her treasures.

Soon, she told herself, there'll be a place where I can unwrap them once and for all, putting them out where I'm going to stay. One day soon. But I have to get there first.

She lay down on the bed, surrounded by the treasures, looking out at the pale June New York morning.

Epilogue

The Seven Stones

I

17 October 1968

Dear Tom,

I am bidden to communicate with you in respect of your aunt's will and, learning from your father that you are working at MacNair & Co., a bookshop in New York City, I write to you care of that establishment, in the hope that this reaches you, and because all other attempts at contact have failed. Your father and I wish to let you know that Sevenstones is yours, according to the terms of my sister's will wherein whoever survives keeps the London house and whoever dies first has the gift of Sevenstones at their disposal. A certain amount of money was also left to you by her, which is placed in trust until you wish to use it, but the main point of discussion between your father and myself was the house itself.

Jenny and I agreed this before she died. It was her wish that your father should live there. It is closer to you, and his old RAF friends. It is a climate more suited to his rheumatism and she wanted to leave something behind

413

that one day might be yours too. Our family connection, as she termed it.

Your father is not well, Tom. He has been in hospital with recurrent chest infections. Living in such a remote place takes its toll. When he visited for tea a few years ago, he told me his cottage was in a state of disrepair; I didn't know until I spoke to him by telephone that he has been living in one room for eighteen months, as the roof has collapsed and he doesn't care to have it fixed or find the means to do so. The cottage has now been condemned and he is in effect shortly to be homeless. Therefore, I have asked him to stay at Sevenstones for the foreseeable future, feeling certain you will agree to this. My sister and I both came to feel we bear some responsibility for him.

We would appreciate some news of you and whether you plan to return before too long. In any event, the documents relating to the house need a signature from you. I hope that America delivers you to us safely.

Your father tells me that you have, via Jenny, discovered the truth about your parentage and its attendant facts. As you will perhaps have understood at the time you came to live with us, I did not wish for, nor take any part in, your removal from your own home and installation in Montpelier Crescent as a Caldicott.

However, time plays many roles in one's perspective. Therefore, I beg to remain your most affec. uncle,

Henry Caldicott

II

It was a bitterly cold December day when Tom landed at Heathrow Airport. In New York, the last traces of autumn's Indian summer still lingered in the city, and he had needed only a coat these last two weeks. In England the leaves on the fields and orchards visible to him as they began their descent were unswept, frozen on the ground, lemon-yellow and crab-pink-orange remnants of the great, calamitous summer of '68, when everything had been upended.

The great glass windows of the Arrivals hall were like a cathedral, shining wintry light on the passengers stumbling half asleep from the plane to waiting families or taxis.

'Tom! Over here, old boy!' Tom, struggling with his tattered kitbag, the strap of which had half worn away, looked up at the sound of his name and stopped dead in the hall.

'No!' he cried, and then clapped his hand to his mouth, a smile breaking across it. For his father was leaning on a barrier.

'Tom, my Tom!' Edward Raven exclaimed, shifting along the barrier to a gap where he embraced his son. 'My darling boy!' Unshed tears shone in his eyes as he gripped Tom's face. 'Darling boy!' he said again. 'Welcome! Welcome home.'

'What – why are you here?' said Tom, laughing. He pulled off his hat, dashing tears from his cheeks as he did. The sight of his father – it was lemon on a cut, and his heart hurt as he embraced him, knowing that it was pain because it was love.

'Why? Tom, I had to be here! Of course I did.' But he seemed to understand the meaning behind the question and hugged him tight without saying more.

Eventually Tom, drawing back, managed to ask, 'Are you all settled in the house?'

'Yes, my boy, very cosy. I cried my heart out, leaving the old cottage, but you know the roof had caved in during the last winter. Made it rather tricky.'

'Henry told me, in his letter.'

'It got the fireplace – huge hole right above so no heat. And the range, it rusted away, dreadful, really. By the end I was sleeping and living in the bedroom and the outhouse.' He rubbed his hand on his head. 'I can barely believe my luck, ending up at Sevenstones, dear boy. Your kindness is beyond anything.'

'I'm awfully glad, but, Dad, it's nothing to do with me. It's the Caldicotts, bless them both.' He paused for a moment, squeezing Edward's shoulder as the other passengers surged past him, the drivers in peaked caps picking up suitcases, a gaggle of air stewardesses adjusting their hair, a family of many generations crying and hugging in a group. Without being able to stop himself, he heard himself say, 'We had that marvellous time at Sevenstones, after my accident. And then you went away, and you didn't say goodbye, Dad.'

His father sucked in air between his closed teeth.

'Sorry,' Edward said. But he felt he couldn't get in the car, really go any further, until it was said. And they were so bad at this, at finding their way now when for years it had been just them, two halves inside the tight, cosy shell of the cottage. 'Dad – I do understand but –'

'Jenny wrote me a letter, Tom. At Sevenstones, that magical fortnight. She pushed it under my door, Tom, after we'd had words that afternoon. It was about what they'd done to Teddy, the lobotomy, how they'd dragged her away, how Jenny had had to watch.

'They tricked her,' he said. 'Told her that her brother was coming to visit her at Sevenstones. Teddy and Jenny were waiting there. Some clinic in Virginia, some doctor who'd done it all before, with male nurses stronger than Teddy or Jenny. Teddy tore one of her nails off, she fought them so hard. She ripped a piece of wood from the doorframe. Jenny tried to stop them. But it was no use: they simply sedated Teddy and bundled her into a car. Can you imagine it.' He put his hand over his eyes. 'I think the burden of carrying it with her had been too much for Jenny, all those years. She knew she was dying. But –' He swayed to one side, as a man in a suit and bowler hat swerved past them, racing towards Departures. 'I couldn't stay, after I knew. I'd found it so hard to give you up, but I'd told myself it was for the best. Then to hear that, that because of me, really, they'd cut her brain out, made her a zombie – Teddy! Ha! The girl with a mind like wildfire, racing everywhere.' He swallowed, his eyes bright. 'Tom, in the war, there were these trails of fire you saw when you hit one of their planes. You'd watch it hurtling to earth, streaking flames, plummeting into the sea. I kept thinking of that,' he said softly, his voice cracking. 'That's what they did to her. Because of me. And the shame of it – not knowing, not helping her, abandoning her to it – I hated myself for what I'd done to Irene, bringing this baby to her, the product of my affair with Teddy. Then Irene died, and look what they did to Teddy. The shame of it all – my boy, I was always the least important part of your story, your life. I thought to myself, I'll take myself back off to Scotland, clear out of it.'

Behind them came the roar of a plane taking off.

The hardest parts of it all were over. Nothing could hurt him now. He saw, through a haze, Teddy's hands in

417

Alice's, the long summer eve, the two women, thousands of miles away.

'But, Dad. That's utter madness,' said Tom, shaking his head. 'You must know that it was. You were my world.'

And he took out of his pocket the treasure he'd been holding on to since he'd got on the plane. The little wooden carved house. He put it in his father's outstretched hand and his father's raw, swollen fingers closed around it in a tight grip.

'You've kept it, my boy.'

'Of course.'

'All those years.'

'All those years, Dad.'

Their hands, touching.

'I met my mother, over there,' said Tom. 'I saw Teddy, Dad.'

'What?' his father whispered.

'Yes. Dad, she's – very different, I think, to how you'd remember her.'

'I'd forgotten. You're so like her, darling boy, you're *so like her* . . . God! How stupid I've been. I loved her, Tom. You'll never – no one will ever know love like it. There's the truth. That's what you came from. Love, my boy. Ah –' His face was beaded with perspiration. 'Teddy Kynaston. You saw her. Tell me. Tell me all about it.'

There was so much Tom wanted to say, so many words of hurt and pain and recrimination, but all he could think, standing there, was this: I still have him. He's here. He tried to do the correct thing.

He loosened his father's hands on him and slid the little wooden house back into his pocket, then picked up his case. 'I will. Let's go home.'

III

Six months earlier

'What the hell have you done?' Laura demanded, when Tom turned up on her doorstep the day after Midsummer's Day. 'Have you slept with Alice and broken her heart?'

'Me? No!' said Tom, wearily dumping his bags in the hallway. 'Well. I slept with her, yes.'

Laura stuck her foot in the way, preventing him from moving further along. 'You shouldn't have.'

'Oh, I don't know about that,' he said, and his tired, hazy mind filled again with images of Alice, naked, on top of him, underneath him, of the wild, animalistic way she cried out as he made her come for the first time, of the fury when she bit his hand, grinding against him, of the noises she made in her sleep, her lovely long body sprawled over most of the bed as he clung to the edge, helplessly trying not to fall off, not to wake her, watching her sleep, unable to believe that it had happened, and they'd both wanted it. But this morning . . . he didn't understand what had changed, only that something had. He had gone over and over everything in his mind, but couldn't understand what it was. He had been going to say: *I love you. Leave him. Let's go to England together. Start again. You can go to college. I can get a job. And we can be together. Because – it's obvious, isn't it?*

It *was* obvious, wasn't it? And then the cycle had started again, because he'd thought it was obvious before with Celia, and he'd got that utterly wrong.

'I saw her.'

'You saw her?'

419

'Sure. I went round this morning to see how you guys were, what had happened. And you'd gone. And she'd been crying.' Laura looked pretty furious, and when she was furious she sounded even more like a games mistress than ever. 'You bloody idiot, Tom. Alice is different. She acts tough but she's not.'

'I know that, Laura,' he said, annoyed with her but angry with himself, and before he could say any more she was lugging his bag up the stairs to her tiny Upper West Side apartment, flinging open the door with her foot. She nodded and pointed to the kitchen table. Tom sat down, Laura opposite him.

'The thing about Alice is she wants to change the world. But, also, she needs someone to take care of her. Normally,' said Laura, cautiously eyeing the Women's Lib banner she had unfurled the previous week at the Miss World convention that had got her arrested, lest it suddenly reprimand her, 'I think that stuff is absolute balderdash. But in her case, it's true and what's adorable with you two is that, Tom, you need someone to take care of you too.' Her expression softened. 'She told me about your mother, Tom. I hope that's okay.'

'Yep.' He put his hand on hers, feeling her kindness, her friendship.

'Sounds pretty damn hard.'

'It's just awfully strange. That's the situation at the moment. I came here to find her. I've found her. I gave her back her ring.' Laura reached round and took two beers from the ice box. Tom accepted the bottle she gave him gratefully and drank from it. He could see the Hudson River through one of the windows. It took him a moment to remember it led up to Orchard, to a woman in an old house, a woman who was a child, who was his mother. 'And now I've found her, what next? I suppose I go home. I had a postcard from my old pal Johnny; they're desperate for good labourers, so there's a job for me on the Westway if I still want it.'

'You're going back to England to be a builder?' Laura said, disbelieving.

He nodded. 'I'm serious. I want to be an architect. I think that's what I've always wanted to do. I grew up understanding how inside and outside work, how to make things. I read History, but the bit I always found jolly fascinating was the landscape part – where they lived, how they built, what space they made. I know, it's crackers, isn't it?' The little house was in his pocket, rescued when he'd hastily gathered up his things – too hastily, he knew now – and left St Mark's Place. 'I'm going to apply to study in a few places, in Cambridge and Manchester and London. And here – Yale. But first I need to learn how to build things. Do you understand?'

'Most architects don't learn by building things, as you put it,' said Laura, but her tone had grudging respect in it.

'They should,' said Tom, and, as he said it out loud, he realized that was what he wanted to do. He wanted to learn how to build, so no house of his would ever be shaken by rain or storms. He wanted to repair Sevenstones, make it someplace where Ravens could remain for decades, centuries, an honest, simple home living with its history. He raised his bottle to Laura.

'Thanks, Laura. For everything the past few months.'

'Yeesh,' said Laura. 'It's a lot.'

'Stop pretending to be from Brooklyn.'

'I'm bloody not.'

'You are.'

They were silent, looking out over Laura's tiny kitchen to the river.

'You're in love with her, aren't you?' she said.

Tom shrugged. 'Yes.'

'Tom!'

'Alas.' He tried to keep his voice light. 'I don't think she wants to know me, after last night. I think she got cold feet.'

'Maybe,' said Laura. 'Perhaps she didn't enjoy it.'

'Oh, God,' said Tom.

She saw he had gone pale and said, 'I'm teasing you, Tom darling.'

'But – what if it was dreadful? What if it was the worst sex she's ever had? I thought she was having an amazing time. I thought – oh, shit.'

'She's only ever slept with Merlin,' said Laura. 'And, believe me, she told me that was nothing to write home about.' She paused. 'I don't buy it,' said Laura. 'I don't want to sleep with men any more, but if I could have one more night with one man, it'd be with you, Tommy.' Her cheeks were slightly red; even Laura had her limits. 'Look, old thing, this is embarrassing, but I have to compliment you. You knew what you were doing. I got the impression Alice thought the same.'

Tom blushed too. 'Get off me, woman,' he said. 'Go and harass some other man, why don't you.'

'You all need harassing,' said Laura, draining her beer. 'So you know what it's like. I'm sorry, Tom. Perhaps it's just one of those things.'

Perhaps, Tom thought, as he drank with her. But he went back several times to St Mark's Place to talk to Alice, and she was never there. Callie had already vanished. Eventually

Curtis moved out, going to live in Harlem with his aunt; Ginger went to California; and Merlin had vanished off the face of the earth, a footnote in other people's stories and never at the centre of his own.

Tom wrote Alice letters, and a card, and telephoned, but the phone had never been connected when they lived there and he wasn't surprised when no one answered. He went to the poster store, and the owner said Alice wasn't working there any more, but Tom didn't think she was telling the truth.

After a while, even Laura stopped believing in his cause. Just a little.

'Tom, I get the impression she's not interested. Don't bother her if she's not interested, old thing.'

'I think she's avoiding me because she's afraid. Honestly, Laura.'

'Maybe.' It was the kindness in her voice which was the worst. She feels sorry for me, Tom realized. She knows it's over. She knows Alice has moved on.

The last time Tom walked past St Mark's Place, a few days before he flew back to England, a whole other gaggle of people had moved in. They sat on the stoop smoking pot, flirting; one of them had a guitar. Tom watched them from the other side of the road, smelled cooking, sweat, pot, heat, the end of summer. No trace of him, or Alice, Merlin, Ginger, Curtis and Callie, was left. Tom saw the cat, but Mrs Snow ignored him, as all good cats should.

He carried on walking. It was like they'd never been there at all, like the whole summer had just been a dream.

IV

Tom

I hope this letter finds you still at MacNair's. I followed your suggestion. I went to England. I have something to show you. Something that is rather a surprise but I hope you will like it.

Your father has written to me and we've spoken on the phone. He's been so kind. I'm going to Spain, then coming to London. So I wondered, if you are going to be in the UK anyway, whether you would meet me at Sevenstones.

Alice

The drive from the airport to Sevenstones was an hour and a half. Tom was quiet, staring out at the bare, grey countryside. Here and there, he caught sight of a tree with a lone rotten apple hanging from its bare branch, the wet black crops in the fields that hadn't been harvested, the dark and light contrasting again. He closed his eyes, his head hurting as it did when he was tired. He felt great calm, being here with his father, the words that they had spoken to each other.

After a while he said, 'The old house is looking after you, is it?'

'I love it there, Tom my boy. Absolutely love it. Very strange, being back, after all these years. But there's a proper bathroom, and the fire works, and it's cosy as anything, and I can walk to the shop. Might even have a new bath put in. The old one's almost rusted away.' He hesitated. 'Of course, that's up to you . . . when you've decided what you'll do.'

'I think a new bath is a marvellous idea.' Tom smiled, enjoying the reversal of their situations. 'Dad, whatever you think's best.'

'We'll be there soon,' said his father. 'I've got breakfast waiting for you. And a surprise!'

'What's the surprise?'

'You'll have to see, but you'll like it, I think,' his father said, looking in his wing mirror and overtaking at speed around a slow-moving car ahead – his father drove as if he were still in a Hurricane, to Tom's consternation. 'You know, we always said everyone came into the seven stones at some point or other during their lives ... Everyone. I met someone on Armistice Day last month in London who'd slept there the night before a mission. Known the chap for years, but no idea he'd bunked down there in the war.'

'Wonderful.'

'Dear old Gordon came down for the day, with his wife and children – did I tell you that?'

'Dad, no, you didn't, I'm so glad. How is he?'

'Rather plump, actually, although you have to remember it's been almost twenty-five years since we last saw each other. That fellow there – just popping around him.' Tom held on to the side of the car in alarm. 'Where was I? He's developed a taste for Italian food. Kept telling me I was making the sauce all wrong. I didn't have the heart to tell him I'd got it out of a can and was just stirring it in.' They both laughed. 'His little girl, Angela, she's a firecracker. Bright as a button, reading the Narnia books already. He'll come down again, now you're back. Wants to tell you what you should be doing next. Says Jenny asked him to keep an eye on you. Wonderful to see him again. Absolutely bloody wonderful.'

*

The roads grew narrower, and the sun rose higher, beaming white and grey light through the bare branches into the road. Eventually they turned past Tallboys and crawled up the final sloping lane towards Sevenstones.

Tom felt nervous, as he had every time he'd returned there since Jenny. His palms sweated; his face felt hot. 'Dad,' he said. 'What if –'

His father turned to him. 'Darling,' he said. 'You're quite white. Get out and walk the last bit. I'll park up. Let yourself in. It's quite all right, you know,' he added, patting Tom's hands. 'There are no ghosts.'

'Promise?'

'I absolutely promise. No ghosts, my boy. Just some porridge left over from breakfast, and a chisel with some shavings I should have cleared up.'

It was as though they were back in Scotland again. Tom got out of the car, unable to speak, and walked the last part of the way, marvelling at this place he knew so well but only in summer.

The garden in winter was bare, the lawn covered with dewy silver cobwebs glinting in the morning sun. He walked along the old lichen-covered wall and passed the pond. The water was frozen.

He could hear someone singing, and he stopped. The paving stones were not flecked with wild daisies and marjoram. The roses around the old stone porch had been cut back to grey-green sticks. Everything was different: ice frosting the grass so that it glimmered; the bare black zigzags of the branches against the sky; and the old, old house, and the stone next to it. He had the sense that, once again, he was back in the circle, surrounded by a protection that he could not understand but that he had always felt from the first time he had gone there.

The apple trees were bare, gnarled and twisted. In the hedgerow, a robin called loudly, and he saw its shining jet-black eyes watching him as he stood gazing around him, marvelling at how peaceful it was. He wondered about his father and mother, under the trees in the moonlight, about how much Teddy had wanted to come back here.

The sun was directly above. For the first time, there among the bare trees, Tom could see where the stone circle had been. He was standing in the middle of it. He could see the stone nearest the house, then another by the boundary, then another beyond that, and another . . . he turned round and round, marking each one in turn, until he counted to seven.

V

Dear Tom

Terrific news that you're coming back, old thing. It must have been quite a summer. Celia was in Paris, building barricades; she was arrested, and only released in August. She managed to throw something at Pompidou; our parents are furious, of course. She's back in England and says she's had enough revolution to last her a lifetime. I wonder if you feel the same way?

I'd love to see you, when you're settled. Tell me where, and I'll come to find you. Perhaps to that house Celia talks about so fondly. Dear Tom, welcome back & love.

Guy

VI

He had said the walk from the bus station was easy – but she thought perhaps he had never done it in winter. She had hobnailed boots on, a relic from her time in a police cell, for they had been left behind and she had tried them on and they fitted like they were made for her. So they had come on her travels with her, back to England, to Sevenstones, a place she had dreamed of as long as she had known of it.

The leaves under the ice in the puddles were acid yellow, raspberry pink. The bare trees stood starkly on the escarpment across the valley, black branches drawn like pen and ink against the white sky. Everything was glittering, and white. It was so cold, her throat seemed to freeze with each inhalation. She pushed the black metal gate into the churchyard and crossed over, down toward the other side of the village.

She had been waiting at Victoria for the first bus, sitting next to a garrulous grandmother off to see her daughter in Reading for Christmas. She'd listened politely, not at all sure what the woman was talking about but unwilling to spoil her fun, for she was trembling with excitement at the prospect of seeing her grandchildren again. 'Here,' she said, holding out her hand to her. 'I've made them these – aren't they something?'

Weren't people funny. She was a whittler and had carved the boy a cat and the girl a dog, the detailing exquisite. She watched as she replaced them carefully inside their pouch, thinking of her own treasures in her backpack.

The older woman had given her a Swiss bun and some of her tea from a Thermos, for which she was so grateful. Alice had come from Spain, where she'd flown in from India. A week ago she had been sitting in Jaipur in a pink palace eating mango, swatting away flies, cool water bubbling around her feet. Now she was here, in this glittering landscape of frost and ice.

Her shoulders ached, and her legs were weary, but she kept on going, because everywhere she turned was something new and delightful. The black earth, the bare hedges and trees, and the ruby-red rosehips, the fluffy white old-man's beard, the dark green holly, and yew, and ivy; and, for a little while flying and hopping alongside her as she walked, a chirping, talkative robin. She carefully shook out her pockets and threw it the last crumbs from the Swiss bun.

The land was ancient – well, all land was ancient. But, as she descended into the valley, past the church, she felt something, she was certain of it, crazy as it seemed. The first stone was at the edge of a wall, the boundary of the Sevenstones Estate.

I love you. I love you. Peering through a gap in the wall at the sloping circle, the smoke spiralling upwards, the clumps of waxy, cream winter roses in the wet soil against the ancient, long, low house, she inhaled and knew, simply, that she had come home.

VII

Tom stood looking at the house. His eagle eye saw the missing slates, the warped window frames, the bulging wall of the kitchen where the guttering had long vanished and rainwater trickled down the mossy green brick. It was his house, and his home now, and his responsibility. They had taken his mother from here, torn her away, ripped her from the place she loved best. He swallowed. He was here now.

'I am here,' he said, softly to himself.

Suddenly the front door opened and a girl came out. She was in a long skirt and knitted jumper, her hair tied up in a scarf. She carried a cup of coffee. He could smell it from here. Proper American coffee.

She started shaking out a sheet or a rug of some kind, all the while singing quietly, 'Yesterday', her voice lilting over the notes.

He walked towards her and she looked up at the sound of his approach. Her face broke into a smile.

'Tom darling,' she said. She smiled at him.

'My God!' was all Tom could find to say.

'I asked your father to keep it as a surprise.'

Her dark hair was long, tied back with a raspberry-red silk scarf, gold hoops in her ears. Her face was tanned, and thin.

'Celia,' Tom said, dropping his voice. 'What –'

'Tom,' she said. 'How beastly. You don't look at all surprised. I've practically escaped jail to come and find you, you know.'

She came towards him, and he saw how nervous she was. She caught his hands in hers, then swallowed, her eyes fixed on his, brushing her hair out of the way so that his hand could touch her face, in an echo of another time, another place, and it was deadening.

'Celia,' Tom said. He could not stop looking at her, in part because he did not know where else to look. 'My God – darling –'

'Are you surprised?' his father said, as if it were the most wonderful present. 'She arrived last night.'

'It's wonderful to be back here,' Celia said. Her arms

were wrapped around his waist, and she gazed up into his eyes. Her tanned face, her eyes that were liquid amber, her incredible, sparkling energy that had intoxicated him – he could feel it working its magic again. She tightened her hold on him.

'It's funny, being back here. With clothes on,' she said into his ear. 'God, I screwed it up, didn't I? Can you ever forgive me?' She stepped back. 'My father says that should be engraved on my headstone,' she said to Tom's father, who smiled indulgently at her.

'And how marvellous! You've made some coffee,' Edward said, rubbing his hands. 'Why don't we go inside? I must say, it's wonderful to – oh. Someone else is here, are they?'

They looked over to the path, where, framed by the blackened apple trees, a girl in a dark ochre cape was walking with a vast knapsack on her back, her hair tied into a knot on the top of her head, a thick knitted green scarf round her neck, her cheeks flushed in her pale face as she stared at the group.

'Hello! Who's this?' said Tom's father in a friendly way.

'I'm Alice,' the girl said, and she reached forwards to shake his hand. 'I know Tom, Mr Raven. How do you do? We spoke a couple of weeks ago –'

'My dear, of course,' Edward said, holding her hand in his. 'You're Tom's friend from New York. Heavens, I'd forgotten you were coming.'

'I wrote you to say it'd be today,' she said, swallowing and smiling. She slid her hands into her pockets. 'But I don't think the postcard arrived. My friend Dolores didn't hear from me either, and she's in London. I suppose postcards from Spain aren't the best way of communicating your arrival time. But I'm so glad to meet you, Edward. Thank you for having me.'

She turned to Tom and Celia. 'Hey, Tom,' she said. She

sounded so American, in this English place. He hoped she didn't notice; he hoped she was warm enough, and that her feet weren't wet. He could see how thin her face was, her skin tanned and clear. She looked free, in her cape and boots and knapsack. His heart, as always with Alice, seemed to ache at the sight of her.

'Alice,' he said, letting his arm drop from where it had been around Celia's waist. 'I didn't know –'

'Of course you didn't,' she said, and she smiled at him as though she couldn't believe he was there, and his heart dropped into his boots, then rose again, like a fairground ride. 'I've really screwed up with Dolores too, so if I may I'll leave a bag here, beg some lunch from you, then head back into London to meet up with her. I telephoned earlier; she's furious with me.'

'You must stay the night!' Edward cried, waving away this convoluted explanation. 'Ask your friend to stay!'

'I'll gladly have lunch, and possibly a nap after lunch, and then I'll go,' she said, turning to him with a smile. 'I just wanted to see the place. And I can see you have a lot of catching-up to do.'

They tried to persuade her, but she was adamant, and in the end she had lunch with them, a huge, warming stew that Celia had made, with apple crumble and cream afterwards, and Alice ate two portions of both, because, as she said, she hadn't had a square meal since September. She was so cold that she kept her handknitted jumper and scarf and cape on, and sat hugging herself under these clothes, eating heartily, chatting to Edward and charming him. Gracefully, once, she alluded to Teddy, and her father, and did it in such a way that Tom was reminded yet again of her grace and lack of gaucheness – he could never have pulled it off.

After lunch Tom showed her upstairs, and they were alone for a minute or so. She wanted to leave a bag of summer clothes behind, she said, which she wouldn't need in London.

'I can't believe you're here,' he said, wanting to say more, wanting to ask more. He sometimes thought the summer, the madness of it all, had been a dream. He wondered if it made him feel better about losing her, to think that it *was* all a dream.

Alice nodded. 'I made it here.' She smiled at him. 'Hug me, Tom. I missed you. I'm sorry it was such a messy ending. I'm sorry for all of it.'

'Oh,' he said. 'Don't be sorry, Allie.'

She was holding the bag in front of her, which got in the way of the hug. They smiled at each other.

'That's Celia,' she said, and he could see her looking round the tiny, low-ceilinged, warm room, her hands pressing on the render, the old oak beams. 'I'm happy for you, Tom.'

She put the clothes in Tom's bedroom, in the cupboard. He didn't know it then, but the treasures were hidden in the bag, at the bottom of it, and they never left the house again.

Edward was driving Alice to the station. As he started the car, Alice shook Celia's hand.

'It's lovely to meet you,' she said. 'I heard your name an awful lot this summer.'

'Really?' said Celia, turning to Tom with disarming frankness.

'We shared a house,' said Alice, getting into the car. She didn't look at Tom. 'He talks in his sleep.'

As she climbed in, and Tom watched her, the hands that had once held him whitening at the knuckles as she reached into the back of the car to put something on the seat, he saw her cape fall open. She deftly pulled it over her jumper again, but not before he also saw the rounded, neat bump.

He stared at her. She looked down, grasped what he'd seen and opened the car door.

'It's not yours,' she said. She smiled at him. 'I'm with someone new. I met him after Merlin left. You don't have to worry, Tom.' She glanced at all of them. 'It was quite a summer.'

'Oh,' Tom said. He felt like Bugs Bunny in the cartoon, when the rabbit stands on a rake and it hits him in the face. 'Congratulations, Alice. Where is he?'

'He's meeting me in London,' she said. 'We'll go back together.'

'How are you feeling?'

'I'm fine,' she said. 'I'm a little tired, but hey.' They held each other's eyes a moment more.

'I love babies, how exciting,' said Celia. 'Have you got any names lined up?'

'Robert, if it's a boy,' she said. 'And I like Emma, if it's a girl.'

'Emma,' said Celia. 'That's perfect. Oh, Alice, I do hope all goes well.'

'Thank you,' Alice said, and she smiled happily.

'We'd better be off, I'm afraid, if you're really catching that train,' said Edward, as though he hoped she wouldn't catch the train. Alice pulled the door shut and waved through the window at them both. Tom waved back, thinking for the first time that waving was idiotically strange – waggling the bones in your hands from your wrists. Why? Why do it? His whole body seemed to be alternately water and fire.

They drove away, and he carried on waving.

Celia, standing behind him, slid her arms round his waist,

and together they watched the car disappear into the rosy glimmer of sunset.

He could smell her lovely hair, feel her wiry, fine body against his. He rested against her, not sure how to say what he had to say.

'You slept with her, didn't you?' she said. 'It's fine, really, it is.'

'I did,' said Tom.

Celia made a murmuring sound of assent, then said, 'She's lovely.'

'She is,' he said.

He was still staring after the car.

'Is that baby yours?' Celia said.

'I'm pretty sure it is,' Tom said. He turned towards her. 'In fact, I'm absolutely sure it is.'

Celia stroked his arms again, pinched his face, messed up his glasses. 'Dammit, Tom darling.' She kissed him. 'Well, then. You'd better go after her, hadn't you? Isn't there a bike in the shed? Can you ride it?'

'Yes!' He was nodding and running at the same time. 'Yes,' he shouted again, slithering down the path and into the house, where the treasures were, running to fetch his coat, and wallet, and bike pump, and whatever else he'd need to chase after Alice and bring her back, back here, back home.

Acknowledgements

I have wanted to write a sequence of novels about a family and a house spanning several decades for a long time and finally having the chance to do so is incredibly special. It is down to one person who has told me not to thank her so often, so I hope she won't cross this out, and that is my editor /namesake, Harriet Bourton. She is not only an extraordinarily imaginative, thorough, dedicated editor, responsible in large part for the nature of the book you hold in your hands now; she is also a positive and kind collaborator, and a dazzlingly effective strategist. I feel unbelievably lucky she is on my side. Thank you, HB.

Many years ago, in my editorial days, I was a Penguin and, as all ex-Penguins know, the pull of the mothership is eternal. Being published by Viking Penguin has been a dreamy experience. I know how hard it is to get books in people's hands so:

Thank you hugely to the calm and talented Rosey Battle; marketing dynamo Georgia Taylor; Richard Bravery and Emma Ewbank for a cover that from the off has defined this book in a way I couldn't, a stunning piece of design and pitching; Annie Underwood for production mastery; Emma Brown in editorial management for her patience; Anna Ridley for making me feel I deserved to be there; wonderful Sam Fanaken and her warm heart and vision, and all of the ace sales team; Jessica Adams and the international sales team; Brónagh Grace and Penguin Audio; and of course thanks to Preena Gadher, a brilliant leader and thinker. And; finally, to my girls Olivia Mead and Juliet Dudley for their campaign of chats but also strategy and cooperative working and a generous, boots-on-the-ground, old-fashioned approach to bookselling that has been so exciting to be a part of.

ACKNOWLEDGEMENTS

A solo mention must go to Donna Poppy, copyeditor extraordinaire and another piece of good fortune for me in that she was able to work on this book. It is without a doubt a fact that it would not be something I am as proud of now without her tireless, detailed and inspired edits. In a time when facts seem so unimportant to so many people, it was deeply heartening to get the chance to make *The Treasures* so much better. Thank you, Donna, I am so grateful.

I would like to thank my American friends and family for their help and advice on matters NYC / Hudson Valley / in general: my aunt over the ocean, Martha Bashore, Jan Houghton, Lance Fitzgerald, Dolores McMullan and Reagan Arthur; and to dear Dave and Lisa McNair for my favourite / favorite day of 2023.

I would like to thank my daughter Martha for saying 'Oh biscuits!' all the time, as I stole it and used it for my heroine; and my mum, Linda, for her advice on sixties music, which is weird as she is only thirty-two.

My final thanks go to everyone at Curtis Brown: Leah Valaydon, Maggie Dickinson, Grace Robinson (late of this parish), Emma Jamison, Sam Loader and Hannah Young, my girl Ligeia Marsh and most of all my agent, Stephanie Thwaites. Being an author is not a one-shot event; it is a career and many, many authors don't get the career they want or deserve. Thanks to you, Steph: I have more than I could have dreamt of. You are calm and forceful, thoughtful and wise, as well as dynamic and effective. You gave me that compass two years ago and everything you said then has come true. You're the best.

This book is for my darling mother-in-law, Susie, with my very great love and thanks for all she has given us over the years. She is one of the most remarkable people I know and the warmth of her love, if you are lucky enough to have felt it, is enough for all the years ahead.

The Treasures is about Alice, Tom and Sevenstones, about one family and the home they build over the decades. The epic story of the Raven family continues in the next enthralling instalment of the Sevenstones trilogy . . .

THE THREADS

Coming soon . . .

Follow Harriet on Instagram @harrietevansauthor or sign up for her newsletter on Substack: theladynovelist.substack.com for news about release dates and events

HUDSON

RIVERS.

Highway

Express

Ave

West End

Ave

W 72 St

Amsterdam

W 86 St

Columbus

Hayden Planetarium and Natural History Museum

New York Historical Society

Ave

W 57 St

W 59 St

Central

Park

Metropolitan Museum

CENTRAL

Central Park South

Frick Collection

Museum of Modern Art

Rockefeller Center

Chrysler Bldg.

Fifth Ave

E 72 St

E 86 St

Museum

57

60

Park Ave

Lexington

Third

Second

First

St. Vincent Ferrer

Ave

Ave

Ave

Ave

York Ave

Grd Central St.

United Nations

Roosevelt

CARL SHURZ Park

Mansion

Queensboro Bridge

WELFARE ISLAND

QUEENS